Following the Path

Steven F. Deslippe

Edited By: Edit This One, LLC., Fairfax, IA.
www.editthisone.com

Published By: Edit This One, LLC d/b/a Wordy Gerty Publishing

ISBN 978-0-9981046-4-5

Acknowledgements

*** A special thanks to Tina Rosekrans (www.editthisone.com, LLC) for taking the time to proofread, make suggestions and edit this novel.   Without her help, this novel more than likely would never see the light of day and it would probably just stay on my computer for no one else to read. ***

*** I would also like to acknowledge those authors whose work I not only thoroughly enjoy reading, but have inspired me to work hard at this craft and put forth the best possible story I could — Steve Perry, Stephanie (S.D.) Perry, Nyx Smith, Diane Carey, William Shatner, Stieg Larsson, Sherrilyn Kenyon, Laura K. Hamilton, Kevin J. Anderson, Kristine Kathryn Rusch, David R. George III, Dayton Ward, Michael A. Martin, David Alan Mack, Una McCormack, Keith R.A. DeCandido, Jana Oliver, Kristen Beyer & Christopher L. Bennett.

***** This book is dedicated to the memory of my first cousin whose life was senselessly cut way too short. ***

R.I.P.

Ryan Barron
February 13, 1986 to April 17, 2016

~ *"Make today count. You only have today once."* ~

Prologue

Life could not be any better for Antonio. His biggest headache; the reason he had spent a good majority of his life in prison, was no more. The enemy had officially been eliminated. Yes, he could have done this a long time ago, but making a man suffer through an emotional pain was more satisfying than relieving his burden by simply killing him.

In the end, it had been worth it. Maxwell Banks had all but walked right up to his doorstep and asked him to do the deed; begged to have his pain end. And of course, Antonio was more than willing to oblige his enemy's request. It was a rewarding moment that he could not have foreseen, but relished nonetheless.

Now, it was time for his organization to move on; move forward with his plan to conquer all of Detroit. He could have thrown a party to celebrate his achievements, but that was not what he wanted to do. He instead, wanted to enjoy his good fortune with just one person, a woman who had been the only one to warm his sheets — and then his heart. A deep emotional connection had never developed for her, but he admittedly would always care.

A ray of light found its way through the side of Antonio's bedroom curtain; it was enough to accentuate the company in his arms. Lenora Lexington had one arm draped across his uncovered chest, her face was tucked partially into the crook between his neck and shoulders, and her bare breasts pressed up against the side of his body. It was a bit constricting, but Antonio wasn't about to complain. Every time he bedded this ex-cop, she rocked his world and kept him feeling young.

He was in his late fifties; she, for some reason, hadn't aged a day. Why that was, Antonio did not know — but he wasn't about to complain. If he had his way, he would stay right where he was and enjoy every inch of Lenora for the rest of the day — but Antonio had responsibilities. And now that the last meddling cop was out of the way, it was time to take his vision to the next level.

He gently extricated himself from Lenora's blanketing and then slipped out of his bed. After throwing on his robe, he looked back at her; she was as appetizing as ever. This reoccurrence, though slightly different each time he experienced it, always helped Antonio during stressful times — the world around him after all, was one that he just did not wish to conform to. Whenever things seemed to be going wrong, Antonio could always count on his subconscious to take him back to a time where everything was perfect — and Lenora Lexington had been the icing on his cake.

He wished that she hadn't died. To him, she was that lost puppy who had finally found a home. She gave up her career as a police officer and had committed herself to Antonio's cause. Leni would have undoubtedly become a key player in the growth of the D.U.O., but the enemy was once again responsible for not allowing that to happen. If it was at all possible to kill someone, bring them back to life, and then kill them again, Antonio would do that to Maxwell Banks — several of his repeated deaths would then be committed in retribution for Lenora Lexington's.

He left his bedroom and headed toward his kitchen. Once there, he opened up the fridge; his intent was to get himself a glass of orange juice.

'She deserved to die.'

Antonio stood frozen. Yes, this was a dream, but never before had he ever heard a voice other than Lenora's. This one, though hushed and somewhat inaudible, belonged to a man — and it sounded all too familiar.

With a chill now residing in his spine, he quickly tried to restructure his reoccurring dream. Usually in this section of it, he would leave the bedroom and go get a glass of orange juice, drink it, then go back to his bed. There, he would slide back under the covers and begin to again, explore every inch of Lenora's near perfect body.

Deciding against a glass of orange juice this time, Antonio shut the refrigerator door and headed back to his bedroom; stopping once he got to the threshold. Lenora was not in his bed like she had always been — she was gone.

'She was a traitor! You are a criminal!'

"Who's there?" No one answered Antonio's question.

'Lenora got what she deserved! And you're next!'

"What the..?" Antonio woke up from his unsettling dream; his bed and pajamas were both soaked in sweat. He, like everyone else, would have an occasional nightmare, but never before had he had a dream that rattled his nerves like that. This reoccurring dream of Lenora, Antonio would have at least twice a month, but never had it changed that much — and never before had an unknown voice, an unseen presence, been there. Antonio did not believe in premonitions or visions, but this unsettling experience was something that he simply could not dismiss as being an aberration.

He got up out of his bed, stripped himself of his soaked pajamas, and headed straight to his bathroom. He then jumped into the shower and took the hottest one that he could tolerate. When that was done, he dried off, wrapped the towel around himself, and stepped in front of the steamed covered mirror. He nearly fell over; it wasn't his own reflection that he saw behind the haze, it belonged to Maxwell Banks.

Hastily, Antonio took a hand towel and wiped away the steam — Maxwell's image promptly disappeared. He knew that he wasn't going crazy, but he also knew what he had seen. His enemy, a currently dead enemy, had apparently decided not to leave him alone. The dead man had used his dream and his bathroom mirror as conduits to send him a warning. The war that Antonio erroneously thought was over, he now feared, wasn't.

The look that he got at the graveyard from the governor should have been his first clue. Christopher White's eyes had been one of determination and assurance. Antonio should not have blatantly dismissed it as being anything more than just a man venting his anger. He should have understood that the demise of his organization's enemy was not going to prevent another from stepping into their shoes — but at the time, Antonio simply did not feel threatened.

Now he did. Though he had no proof that someone else was going to be coming after him and his organization, he could not dismiss the possibility of it actually happening. He had to protect his assets — and himself. Yes, he was letting an unexplained, disturbing experience influence his decision, but if Antonio had learned anything over the years, it was when to pull back and allow the fire that he started to burn itself out before he even thought about igniting another one.

If he were to tell his subordinates about what he had just experienced, he was certain that they would just dismiss it as being nothing but a hallucination that had been manifested by his overworked mind — and maybe that was actually the case. But Antonio felt that he had to do something unconventional to ensure that the Detroit Underworld Organization's existence continued. He didn't care what Louie and Sal thought, and he didn't care if they did not understand why he was going to do this. He was the boss and he was going to do what he believed was necessary, and he was going to do what he felt was in the best interest of everyone associated with his organization. They just had to find a way to deal with it.

1

Just over two weeks had passed since Salvadore Batiste contacted Major Terrance Burelli. It hadn't been that easy, but he was able to exile the conversation he had with the man to the deepest parts of his mind. That small piece of his life was ancient history, and he felt relatively confident that he would be able to continue on in a normal existence without any more ghosts making an unwanted appearance.

The unit that Terrance was in command of, the S.N.A.F.U., had just wrapped up an intense two-week training session at Alert, in Nunavut — the northernmost permanently inhabited place in the world. Upon the unit's return to their base in Houston, they all were granted a much needed; much earned fourteen-day leave as a reward for their extra hard work and dedication to their nation.

Using this opportunity to leave his recent, unexpected stress behind, Terrance decided that he was going to take his son, who was also a member of the same military unit, home to visit his mother in Columbus, Ohio. His son, Terrance S. Burelli Jr., or T.J., as he had always been called, had only seen his grandmother a handful of times over the past seven years — mostly due to the fact that much of his young adult life had been spent in the service.

"I'm really glad that the both of you decided to just stay here at home during your leave and not go anywhere," Mrs. Edith Burelli said.

"I couldn't have thought of anything better to do with our time off, Mom. Ever since I got my promotion, we almost never get to see each other anymore."

"Honestly, Grandma, I was gonna go to Vegas with a bunch of the guys from our platoon. But once again, dad used his famous guilt-trip-torture-technique on me and forced me into saying no."

T.J.'s grandmother looked over at her son and saw a rather genuinely perturbed look on Terrance's face; it caused her to laugh inside, knowing her grandson was only kidding about Vegas and just said what he did to see if he could get a reaction of some kind from his father.

After kicking off his shoes at the front door, T.J. walked over to his grandmother, gave her a kiss, and then a warm embrace. "Well then, after the hellish two weeks of training that I've just been put through, I'm sure you won't mind if I take a rain check with the obligatory catching up tonight. I'd really like to just relax in front of the television and have some quality time to myself."

"Come on now, T.J. You've barely seen your grandmother since you left high school and joined the military. You could at least..."

"Do you know how long it's been, Dad, since I've had a chance to chill in front of a television and watch anything? Besides, I want to watch the baseball game. I'm tired of just reading the results on the net, days later. The Dodgers are playing the Reds... and there is actually a chance that they might even make the playoffs this year after what... ten years?"

"Go right ahead, T.J.," Edith said. "We'll have a lot of time to catch up on things."

"See, Dad, I knew that Grandma wouldn't mind." Terrance Jr. gave his grandmother another big hug and kiss — he then turned and headed down the stairs.

With a contented smile on her face and joy in her heart, Mrs. Burelli walked over to the fridge and proceeded to pour herself a glass of sim-milk. Too her, all was good in the world — but apparently, that was not the case in her home. As she was taking her first sip, she saw her son standing just off to her left; he was lightly tapping his foot on the kitchen floor —apparently, he was not too happy that his authority had been overridden.

"What?"

"I wish you wouldn't contradict me when it comes to my son, Ma. He is a much disciplined young man when he is wearing the Union uniform and I want him to stay that way when he is off base."

"Well... I run this base, and I'm telling you to let my grandson enjoy some peace and quiet away from the everyday bullshit that you put him through." Not wanting to ruin the good mood she was in,

2

Edith took her glass of juice and headed for her bedroom, leaving her son behind to stew in his emotions.

The moment Terrance Jr. set foot in his grandmother's basement he saw the brand new state of the art, ion particle imaging, 3D projection television set up near the far wall. If you were one of those who were behind in the times, then you would not have noticed the TV at all. From a distance, it just looked like an ordinary antique armoire. However, the long, narrow piece of decorative looking glass that was set into the top section of the bottom half of the cabinet was the actual TV projector — the component itself was no bigger than a box of chocolates and was designed to be retrofitted into almost any piece of furniture, or custom made unit. *'Oh... way cool!'* he thought.

Since the game wasn't scheduled to start for another hour, Terrance Jr. decided to fire up his grandmother's computer and go to his favorite website so that he could catch up on the latest news and information. While he waited for the computer to finish booting up, he thought to himself, *'Hum... my grandmother just bought the latest technologically advanced television set, yet she still refuses to update this old piece of junk that she tries to pass off as a modern day computer. I bet you any money that she is still running WINDOWS 10. All that she has to do is jump on the net, go to the right website, and download the hack for the latest Windows TW–PE (Trans Warp – Pro Edition) — which is so simple to do, and then she'll be set till she dies.'*

Once the computer was ready to use, Terrance Jr. went to the site and chose to download a two-week summary of news and entertainment — he then transferred the articles from the computer onto his own palm-top (he would have normally searched individually for the articles that he wanted to look at using that device, but he had burned through his monthly data allotment a few days earlier while he was still up north).

A few minutes later, Terrance Jr. had roughly eighty pages loaded — half of which he was sure he'd have no interest at all in reading. *'All right, this ought to get me somewhat up to date on everything our mainstream media deems to be newsworthy. So I'll just plop my over-drilled and still half-frozen ass on the couch over here and turn the ball game on.'*

3

T.J. quickly scanned through the articles, deleted what he was already aware of, as well as the ones that he classified as frivolous junk, and then organized the rest of them into separate folders. He then spent just under an hour reading the collected sports news in order of sequence, while mostly listening to the baseball pregame show in the background; occasionally glancing up to watch bits of it. After he finished with the sports, he deleted them and accessed the other folder that contained the remainder of the articles.

Just as he clicked on the first news segment in the folder, from the top of the stairs, T.J.'s grandmother yelled down to him. "Yes.., what's up?"

"I was just wondering if you were getting either hungry or thirsty."

"No, I'm not really that hungry. But I would be forever in your debt if you could please bring me down a cup of green sim-tea with a touch of lemon."

"Ok. I'll be down with it in a few minutes."

"Thanks a lot, Grandma. Love ya."

Instead of directing his attention to the news article he had just opened up, Terrance Jr. focused it instead on the television. *"Finally, the Reds have a decent team this year.., but their bullpen..? They've certainly earned their nickname, 'The Cardiac Kids'. It's a damn good thing that I don't bet any money on them. Especially tonight since the Dodgers have that pitcher throwing with the A.I. left arm* (Artificial Implants — People whom have mechanical limbs or artificial organs replacing or enhancing the ones that they have or had) *— there should be a rule against that!'* After watching the first few batters of the game and getting annoyed with the Dodger's pitcher, he turned his attention back to his palm-top and continued to read the articles.

The first few articles he scanned over looked somewhat interesting, but far from intriguing. So he deleted them and opened up the next one. Immediately, the bold title at the top of the screen snagged his attention. It read —

4

Hit-sville, A.C.U.

'*I wonder what this is all about,*' he thought. No sooner had Terrance Jr. began to read the article, his curiosity became engulfed.

> "*Organized crime in the city of Detroit has once again reared its ugly head. Maxwell Banks, a onetime highly regarded police detective, was found brutally murdered yesterday. Twenty-five years ago, Mr. Banks lead a police task force that successfully apprehended the Detroit Underworld Organization's boss, Antonio Marcone. Shortly after the man's conviction, Mr. Banks and three other police detectives from that same task force were victims of a warehouse explosion; an explosion which only Mr. Banks was lucky enough to have survived. On that same night, his wife, Sylvia, was found murdered, and his newborn son, Sabastian, had gone missing.*
>
> *Late last week, due to some expert maneuvering and interpretation of the law, Mr. Marcone's lawyer, Howard Swindle, was able to convince the courts that an injustice had occurred which directly resulted in the unlawful conviction of his client. Because of this, he was able to procure Antonio Marcone's early parole.*
>
> *Once this happened, speculation soon followed that Mr. Banks may have felt that our justice system had failed him and that Mr. Marcone's premature release needed to be addressed, personally.*
>
> *According to the police department's official report, Mr. Banks was found sunken in the Detroit River. He had been brutally beaten, bound, gagged, and shackled. His body had been wrapped up in a tarp, placed into a steel coffin-like box, and encased in concrete. And although it had yet to be verified, the police estimated that Mr. Banks' body had been in the river for just over a week before it was found.*"

Terrance Jr. set his palm-top down onto the coffee table and tried to imagine what the life of Maxwell Banks had been like. Without actually being in his shoes, it was hard for him to speculate, but the one thing that T.J. was fairly certain of, was that an attempt at revenge for what had happened to those he knew and also loved, had to have been the reason why the man was now dead. '*That is way too much shit for one person to have to deal with, especially having those horrible memories of the deaths of three of his fellow officers forever haunting him. Not to mention, the murder of his wife and the disappearance of his son. That had to have been way too much pain for one man to have to live with for that long of a period. It's no wonder he cracked and went out for blood.'*

T.J. picked his palm-top back up and stared aimlessly at the article again — a feeling of sympathetic pain for the troubled man enveloped him. *'I wonder what ever happened to his son.'* After a few moments of thought, Terrance Jr. turned his attention back to the article so that he could finish reading it.

"According to those who knew Mr. Banks, he had spent his entire life trying to determine whether or not his missing son was dead or alive. Unfortunately for him, he was never able to get an answer to that question."

Through his seven years of military service, T.J. had experienced his fair share of pain. During his first full year of service, his platoon had been sent in a peacekeeping role to several war torn countries, including Somalia during its most volatile period of unrest. Several times he experienced death first hand as members of his platoon were gun down just a few feet away from him — and it truly bothered him when he was placed in a position on occasion to fight an enemy whose army was made up of young children that had been taken from their homes and forced into being soldiers. But the thing that troubled him the most, memories that he never wished he'd experienced, was the horror of seeing entire families murdered in the shanty they had called home. It just turned his stomach. So T.J. could kind of understand why someone like Maxwell Banks would throw away the remainder of his life and pursue a futile vendetta. There were times when someone would be placed in a situation in which they felt they had nothing else to lose because everything they had that meant something to them had already been taken away.

"Here's your sim-tea with lemon," Edith said as she was walking down the stairs. You best be careful with it though, as it's really hot."

"Thanks a lot, Grandma," T.J. said, as he placed his palm-top down on the coffee table. "Hey… do you happen to remember hearing about that cop from Detroit who was gruesomely beat up, murdered, and then sunken into the river?"

"Yeah, I remember it. It was a big story… and all over the national news. Personally, I try not to watch or read too much awful stuff like that if I can help it."

"That is kind of awful, isn't it? I hope I never get put into a situation like that where I feel I have no other choice but to do what that cop did."

"It's an insane world we live in, T.J. I don't think that I ever need to worry though about you doing something like that. You're smart enough not to attract any trouble… unlike your father."

"Dad? Get into trouble?" Terrance Jr. said, with unambiguous sarcasm.

"Yes… your father was a real shit disturber when he was younger. Thank God the military straightened his ass out and he actually made his own father proud." Edith turned and headed back toward the stairs. Stopping at the foot of them, she turned, and then wished her grandson a good night.

Upon replying with those same meaningful words to his grandmother, Terrance Jr. took a cautious sip of his fresh sim-tea and picked up his palm-top to re-read the article on Maxwell Banks one last time. Unlike the first time though, he did spend a few moments looking at the picture of the dead ex-cop that accompanied the article — the one thing T.J. noticed, was that the picture definitely showed what the passing years of stress and inner turmoil had done to the man.

Fifteen minutes later and his sim-tea finished, Terrance Jr. shut off his palm-top, shut off the television, as his Reds were already getting their asses handed to them, and headed up the stairs to get himself a good night's sleep.

Admittedly, Antonio's organization had suffered because of his unavailability. The stress from not being there every day to properly run the D.U.O. had taken a strong willed, driven individual, and morphed him into a bitter, vengeful, old man. He knew that his wanted retribution would one day come — and it was that belief which allowed him to not only stay patient, but it helped to prevent him from giving into his everyday surroundings and succumbing to the influence that was a byproduct of being around so many others that were as well, incarcerated.

Now that what he had waited twenty-five years for, had occurred, Antonio was adamant that he was not going to waste another day and fully enjoy what time he had left on earth — starting with, trying his damndest to regain a somewhat normal existence. It should have been easy for him to relax, as there was not one foreseeable obstacle in his way — but for some unknown reason, he just couldn't. His recent disturbing dream was not the mechanism behind his inability — it was because there had recently been several rumors of which he simply could not dismiss. Supposedly, the city's police department had finally admitted that his organization was a real threat and subsequently had placed it right at the top of their priority list. In a twisted sort of way, their doing this had given Antonio what he had always wanted — recognition. Officially, he had now become someone that they deemed significant.

No longer could he fly under the radar and do whatever it was that he wanted. He not only had to be more careful than ever before, but an adjustment needed to be made in the way he did business. Therefore, to assure that the D.U.O. continued to exist for many more generations, Antonio made a very radical business decision — he had to temporarily cease local operations. Admittedly, he had ruffled way too many feathers over the years. That, and with the known guilt pertaining to the brutal execution of Maxwell Banks now added to his résumé, Antonio felt that it was time to take a step back and let things cool off for a while. He knew that what he wanted to do was going to come with plenty of opposition, but he didn't care. The D.U.O. was his baby, and he was going to make the decisions that to him, made sense — he and he alone was responsible for the continued existence of the organization.

The first thing that he did was to send all of the non-essential personnel to various semi-isolated locations throughout the Union, with orders for all of them to simply lay low. Following that, he was going to take Sal and Louie with him someplace overseas where no one would think to look. Yes, they could simply just stay in Detroit and out of everyone's hair, or go anywhere else in the Union where they were not yet known, but Antonio knew that it would only take one stupid mistake from either him or his two associates to give law enforcement that one key piece of evidence they longed to acquire to arrest them all and shut down the D.U.O. for good.

As illogical as it sounded, it made perfect sense to him that the three of them needed to get as far away from Detroit as they could — and fast. Antonio didn't need to be 'in the office' to continue his operations, as he had proven that during his time locked away. He had a lot of connections around the world of which he could ask a favor of — and he also knew that wherever he chose to go, it wouldn't take him too long to establish a temporary satellite base of operations in order to keep things running. Only when the time was right would they return. At that point, he would continue on with his long-term plan for gaining complete control of the Motor City and maybe even one day, obtaining nationwide domination.

"I don't get why you want to do this, Antonio? I mean, now that Maxwell has finally been eliminated, we basically have free rein. Even the police are afraid."

"They're not afraid of us, Louie. We've essentially been laughing in their faces for decades and now they've had enough. I fear that it will only be a matter of time before they break down our door."

"Then we will just have to take them all out one by one."

"That wouldn't be the smartest thing for us to do, Sal."

"But we can't just stop what we've been doing for the last twenty-seven years. We are very close to owning this town. And once we do, the law will be in our back pockets."

"That is our ultimate goal, Louie. But as it stands right now, the law is just as close to shutting us down as we are to signing their paychecks. I know that it looks like we are taking two steps back instead of moving forward, but my reason for us leaving town right now makes perfect sense to me."

Louie didn't agree; neither did Sal. But both sat patiently in their chairs across from their boss's desk and listened to him as he explained why he wanted to do this. Antonio acknowledged that they had no other choice but to eliminate Maxwell Banks, because he would have continued to be a thorn in their side until the day that he died.

Just the constant threat he posed, and his reputation for showing up unexpected, was enough to prevent the expected growth of the organization from occurring. And although Antonio was willing to allow the majority of the blame for all of this to fall on his shoulders, his associates' personal contempt for Maxwell had also contributed to this mess. They had gone way overboard — instead of simply eliminating the enemy; they each had to have their fun. Now, as a result of everyone's egos, they ended up drawing an immense amount of unwanted attention to themselves.

"Way to go, Sal. This was all your idea. I always knew that you were nothing but a fuck up."

Sal promptly turned and shot Louie a look that could not be misinterpreted; a look that clearly stated if he had been only a few feet closer, he would not have hesitated to shank him. "It wasn't my idea, you brain dead idiot. It was yours."

"Shut up! I don't want to hear it. We are all guilty." A moment of unnerving silence followed as Antonio slightly shook his head and thought. *I can't believe that I am actually regretting having my lawyer fight for my early release. Things were so much easier when the only thing I really had to worry about was my Alzheimer-suffering, eighty-year-old bunkmate. Now that the three of us have to go into hiding together, I doubt very much that I will be able to put up with Louie and Sal's constant bickering. I swear that they were both unhappily married to each other in a past life.'*

"I'm sorry, boss," Sal apologized. "I accept full responsibility for my part in this." Curiously then, he asked Antonio whether or not he already knew where he was going to take them. Selfishly, he was hoping that they would be going someplace warm and tropical, because he just really wanted to be lazy, look at as many nearly naked women as he could, and work on his tan.

"I have chosen five possible destinations for us. However, I have yet to decide which one it will be… and before any of you decide to throw in your two cents worth, the place will be determined by me alone." Antonio then made it known to both of his associates that their ultimate destination will be made based upon the business connections he has with certain people who could easily hide them, as well as the ease of accessibility to the Union — the last thing Antonio needed was to have to jump through hoops in order to run his organization from overseas.

"Well… it can't hurt to hope that you'd be taking us to some place like Turks and Caicos, or Jamaica, Rio de Janeiro, or Cancun. Hell… I'd even go to Cuba."

Louie just slouched back in his chair, mumbling to himself. "You're going to go to Hell anyway, Sal. Why not just go there now."

Unlike certain parts of Antonio's body that were slowly starting to break down due to his getting older, his hearing was still really good. And yes, he had clearly heard Louie mumble that comment about Sal. However, he decided not to reprimand his number one for that remark, for he actually thought it to be somewhat humorous.

Again, Sal was struggling to hold back his displeasure toward Louie; he was getting tired of the man's habitual wisecracks. Today though, Sal recognized that it was not a good day to force Louie into investing in a new set of dentures, so he just bit his tongue and mentally added this instance to his ever-growing list of reasons to one day remove him from the picture.

Before the obvious tension in the room between his associates got to a point where one would actually kill the other, Antonio said, "Now… both of you listen to me very carefully. I am only going to say this once, so pay close attention. You either stop antagonizing each other or I won't hesitate to downsize. There are after all, still plenty of empty plots available where Banks is buried."

Louie sat there amused. He knew that Antonio hated it when he and Sal chose to indulge themselves with petty name games or childish behavior. However, he just couldn't resist taking one more jab at his associate, "If you eliminate our subordinate now, I will be more than willing to pitch in half of what the cost of his final resting place will be."

That infuriated Sal. He gripped the arms on his chair tightly, knowing just how close he now was to doing something that, although satisfying, would probably cost him everything that he had worked so hard for. One day, whether he was still alive or not when it happened, he knew that karma would come back and bite Louie real hard in the ass.

"Just because you are my right hand man," Antonio looked sternly at Louie when he was speaking, "don't assume that you are indispensable." He then sat back in his chair, wondering how it was that he was able to easily survive twenty-five years of incarceration, only to come back here and be subjected to a different kind of prison; one where the inmates refused to grow up. "You know, I've never understood why, nor do I want to know why you both insist on personally attacking each other." Antonio got up from his chair and walked over to his library wall. He then removed a half a dozen books to reveal a miniature safe that had been hidden behind it. "Better yet, maybe I'll save myself some money and just leave you two behind. That way, the police could snatch you both up and take the heat off of me. Then, I'll go find me some small island in the Mediterranean Sea and retire a happy, sane man."

"No, that's quite all right," Louie, responded. "Wherever you want to go, I'm sure that it will be fine with the both of us."

"Speak for your..." Sal promptly felt a swift kicked on his shin, preventing him from finishing off what he was about to say — Louie did this because he knew that their boss would have no problem following through with what he had just threatened to do.

"All right boys, here are the possibilities." Antonio pulled out a map and some booklets from his safe. He opened up the map and laid it across his desk; on it were five different places that he had already circled in red: Stockholm, London, Paris, Frankfurt and Tokyo.

Sal just sat still with a stoic look on his face; he most certainly did not want to go to any of the destinations that Antonio had chosen." Are you sure about these places, boss? Not one of them has enough sun or sand for me.

'It's not the sun or the sand, it's because the age of consent for those countries isn't sixteen or less,' Louie thought to himself. "To be honest, I really don't care where we go."

"Well I'm glad that you don't care where we are going, Louie, because I'm not telling you or Sal. The last thing I need is for our pending location to be learned by those who we are intending to get away from. Therefore, I will let you both know where we will be going when you return here in three hours time — our flight leaves at eleven p.m."

"Tonight?" Sal said a bit surprised. "Um... Well, I don't have an up to date passport."

"You don't have to worry about your passport, Sal." Still in Antonio's left hand was the small stack of booklets that he had also taken out of the safe. He put them down on his desk, clearly showing his men that their passports had been taken care of. "You just have to worry about getting your asses here by nine p.m. sharp, or I won't hesitate to leave either of you behind. Is that clear?"

"Yes, boss," Sal and Louie, both said in unison. "We'll be here on time."

That evening, Terrance Jr. kept tossing and turning. He didn't understand why he couldn't sleep, as never before in his life had he ever had a bout with insomnia. All that he knew was that he couldn't get the article about Maxwell Banks out of his head. Something about it had stuck in the back of his mind and was bothering him for some unexplained reason. When he did manage to finally get to sleep, his subconscious took him there.

He was sitting in a beautiful, inner city home — and although he could not see himself, he could plainly see that Maxwell Banks was sitting across from him. His dream felt so real. It was scary, yet it was familiar and comforting — almost as if he belonged there.

Maxwell smiled at him, got up from his seated position, and walked away; T.J. stayed where he was and observed the man as he made his way over to a beautiful young woman who was holding a baby in her arms. It was easy to see that this was everything that Maxwell Banks had ever wanted in the world: a family, love, and happiness.

Unexpectedly, his dream altered. No longer was T.J. sitting in a beautiful home, as he was now in a much smaller apartment. It wasn't at all a depressing place, but the warmth and inviting nature just wasn't there — it felt stale and cold.

A few minutes later, Maxwell walked into the room and then stopped about ten feet away from where T.J. was standing. It was easy to see that the man had changed. No longer did he look happy. He had all but transformed into a desperate looking, wounded, and lost old man — a shell of his former self.

After a few unsure moments, Maxwell extended his hand. At first, T.J. thought that the man was asking him for help, but then he realized that he was actually inviting him to come closer. He wasn't scared, but T.J. wasn't just sure if accepting this man's invite was the logical thing to do.

Though his dream had been far from a nightmare, Terrance Jr. woke up in utter bewilderment. *'Whoa,'* he thought. *'That was just so weird dreaming about that dead cop. I have absolutely no idea who this man even is, yet for some reason, I strangely feel drawn to him.'*

After T.J. had his morning shower, with his palm-top in hand, he went straight down to the basement. After plopping his ass onto the old leather sofa, he turned on his device and re-read the news article about Maxwell Banks — his hope was that by doing so, he'd find an answer as to why his all too real and chilling dream had occurred.

Feeling this odd connection to a stranger, didn't make any sense at all too him. Nevertheless, his curiosity was urging him to learn why, so he decided to use his grandmother's ancient computer again and do some research on the dead cop — Terrance Jr. had hoped that by finding some more information about the man and his life, he might be able to come up with a logical explanation as to why the article had such a profound effect on him.

After about an hour surfing the web, T.J. was only able to gather a little bit more information about Maxwell Banks. He was able to find out that the man had moved to San Antonio, Texas, shortly after his wife's murder and son's unexplained disappearance, that he had a brother named Sydney, who also lived in San Antonio, and that he had started working as a private investigator right after his relocation there.

He closed his eyes and again Terrance tried to figure out what it was about this man that just wouldn't leave him. But of course, he found no explanation — he continued to draw a blank. *'There has to be something?'* he thought. *'I don't understand why this is bugging me like it is?'* He re-opened his eyes and looked back at the computer screen. He then ran an image search, looking for more pictures of

Maxwell Banks, hoping that they would help him assemble a better idea as to who this man had been.

After only a minute or so, he found a thumbnail image of the man as an RCMP cadet. When clicked on it to make the photo larger, the word 'impossible' promptly popped into his head. He stared at it in disbelief — this simply had to be a coincidence. Had this man been his doppelganger? T.J. didn't know what to think. Nevertheless, he saved a copy of the photo, found a few more uncanny images, and then saved them as well.

Once he had collected a dozen photos, he transferred them to his palm-top, and then printed out the one of Maxwell as a cadet. Uncertainty and curiosity continued to consume him — he just could not stop staring at the picture. *'Man, does he ever look like me. Almost like he should be my... No... No way would that be possible.'*

Terrance Jr. leaned back in the computer chair and looked up, staring briefly at the ceiling. His mind began constructing multiple scenarios — all of which, he felt, had no plausibility to them. Desperate to find an answer, he hastily snatched up his palm-top off the computer desk, and re-read the article.

Everything that had been going through his mind up until then just seemed to be so far-fetched — that was until he came to that one specific segment in the article that his eyes refused to move beyond. *"...he had spent his entire life trying to determine whether or not his missing son was dead or alive. Unfortunately for him, he was never able to get an answer to that question."*

'Missing son? Could that be me?' he thought. *'No, that couldn't be me. My father told me when I was ten that my mother had died from cancer when I was real young, and that he had made a promise to my mother that even though he was not my biological father, he would adopt me and raise me as his own.'*

Terrance Jr. was now confused more than ever — only because he had never really been given any information pertaining to his birthfather, other than the sickening event that led to his mother's pregnancy. All of what T.J. knew, and all of what he had read, was now forcing him to irrationally second-guess his own existence. *'Is it possible that my father may have actually lied to me? Could that dead cop be my real birthfather? There's no disputing how much this man's pictures looks like me. This is so bizarre. I need to get some answers... I deserve the truth.'* After hastily shutting down his grandmother's computer, Terrance Jr. took his palm-top and went upstairs in search of some clarification. "Dad!"

"Christ, T.J. Keep it down, will ya. Your grandma is still sleeping."

"I need to show you something."

"Can it not wait till I'm finished my breakfast?"

"No. I want to show you it, now." Terrance Jr. literally shoved his palm-top into his father's face. "Here, read this."

"Don't be so damn rude. Please take that away from in front of me and I'll look at it after I'm done eating my breakfast."

Terrance Jr. didn't want to wait until then, so he grabbed his father's plate of bacon and eggs slid them off to the side. "I don't care if you think I'm being rude. Please... just look at this. It is very, very important to me."

"Why is this thing so damn important that it can't wait ten minutes until I'm done eating my damn breakfast?"

"Just humor me, will ya?" He then shoved his palm-top back in front of his father. "There was this ex-cop who was killed in Detroit a few weeks ago. It says here in this article that..." T.J. pointed to the spot he was referencing "...twenty-five years ago, someone had killed that ex-cop's wife and his newborn son ended up disappearing without a trace."

"It sounds like a very interesting story, T.J., of which I really don't care to hear all of the details. Now give me back my breakfast before it gets too cold."

Terrance Jr. reluctantly took back his palm-top and handed his father back his breakfast. He then walked over to the refrigerator to get a glass of orange juice, because he needed something to drink while he tried to think of a different way of presenting his case. *'The direct approach, I guess? That's as good of a way as any. He'll either tell me the truth or think that I'm totally crazy.'* Terrance Jr. went back over to the kitchen table, juice in hand, and sat down directly across from his father so that he could look him straight into his eyes when he asked his question. "Do you know my birthfather's name?"

"No. Why would I know that?"

16

"The circumstances surrounding my conception were not swept under the rug."

"True… but I was never told the man's name."

"Why not?"

"Your mother was already going through enough pain during her final few days. The last thing I wanted was to make her relive any part of what she went through."

That was a declaration that T.J. could honestly accept. It was entirely possibly that his father had no idea what his birthfather's name was. However, something inside of T.J. was yearning for clarification. He knew the story, but now he no longer seemed to unconditionally accept it. "Did you really adopt me?"

"Say what?" Terrance Sr. answered, as he tried not to choke on the bacon in his mouth. You're kidding, right?"

"No, I'm not kidding." T.J. crossed his arms, put his elbows on the kitchen table, and stared at his father. "Did my mother really die from cancer?"

"Of course she did. That's the stupidest question you've ever asked me. Is this really necessary for you to be asking me these questions that you already know the answers to?"

"Yes. For me, this is necessary. And I'm questioning the facts as I currently know them to be." Terrance Jr. stood his palm-top on end and faced the screen toward his father. "Do you see these pictures?" He then swiped through the images one at a time, pausing long enough for his father to get a good look at them. "Do you not think that there is an uncanny resemblance between these pictures and myself?"

Terrance Sr. took only a brief glance at each of the pictures. "Yeah… sort of, I guess. So what are you getting at here, T.J.?"

Terrance Jr. shut off his palm-top and then bluntly asked, "Do you think that man could be my birthfather?"

"Anything is possible."

Anything was possible. Maxwell Banks could very well be his father. And if he was, then the story T.J. was told was an outright lie. He needed to find out whether or not that was the case. "Am I really adopted?"

"Yes! You are, and will always be, my son."

17

"I'm not too impressed that you two buttheads woke me up!" In her bathrobe, Edith Burelli entered the kitchen — and it was easy for both T.J. and his father to see how displeased she was that their verbal jousting had woken her prematurely. "I've had just about enough of you, my grandson, giving your father the third degree. Whatever it is that is bothering you, save it until after breakfast is finished."

"I'm sorry, Grandma, but I believe that he is intentionally withholding an answer to a question that will clarify the uncertainty that I now have."

"You are grasping at straws, T.J. I fail to understand why you seek answers to something that does not need any further explanation."

He honestly felt that his father was full of shit. And quite frankly, the inability of a given straight answer was exactly what Terrance Jr. had expected to get. In fact, his father's deliberate refusal to even humor him only added more doubt to his speculation. T.J. admittedly, was searching for something that by all accounts, probably wasn't there — but his heart was telling him otherwise. That feeling deep down inside of him had convinced him that the lack of hard evidence was all he needed to have doubt. He simply believed what he believed. "I need to get away from here for awhile." T.J. slammed back his full glass of juice, put his empty glass down on the table, and headed for the front door.

"Where in the hell do you think you are going?"

"Out! I need to clear my head." Terrance Jr. intentionally grabbed his father's car keys off the small antique table that sat next to the front door of the house, opened up the door, and then left.

"Where in the hell do you think you are going with my car? Get your ass back here now!"

A few moments later, Terrence Jr. jumped into his father's mustang and sped away. He had no idea where exactly he was headed, but he just needed to get out onto the open road and drive somewhere — and he hoped that whatever direction fate had pointed him in, took him to a place where his questions might at least start to get answered.

Once T.J had left, Terrance took a moment and reviewed in his mind the photos that his son had shown him. The man was a stranger to him, but it was also easy for him to put two and two together. Those

18

images, plus the incident that had occurred, just two weeks ago in which Sal had unexpectedly called him, was what had allowed him to figure out who the individual was. His past had suddenly reared its ugly head. He should have humored the Sicilian that day and listened to what he had to say. Had he done so, Terrance would have undoubtedly been prepared to deal with this bump in the road. Now, his near perfect world was more than likely going to have a cataclysmic ending — and there was nothing that Terrance Burelli could do to stop it from happening.

2

Perplexity, isolation, inner turmoil, and deceit — so many unconfirmed variables had continued to confuse him. It had become nearly impossible for Terrance Jr. to completely separate what he had always known from what was pure speculation, formed by all of the self-charged static that was now shorting out his brain. A lot of information had been transmitted via unfamiliar signals and codes, which then caused what few facts he had to become scrambled and polluted, leaving him with nothing but a flooded emotional cesspool to wade through.

After driving east on Interstate 70 for almost an hour, Terrance Jr. pulled his father's car into a countryside gas station and filled it up. He wasn't planning on adding more debt to his credit card, but the situation that he put himself in left him with no other choice. It was either pay for the gas or start walking home — fifty miles was just too far away to be doing that.

During his stroll back to the car after paying for his gas, he looked eastward down the road and saw a billboard advertising a restaurant called 'Kellin's Family Grill'. In that moment, T.J. was brought back in time. When he was a teenager, there were two local locations. Then, the place quickly became popular, all but forcing the successful business to rapidly expand and eventually, it was franchised out. However, it was that very first location where almost every day after school, T.J. and his best friend, Baylor Wilson, use to hang out. With his father away from home because of his obligations to his country, and his grandmother, who at the time worked at the Mount Carmel St. Ann's Hospital as a nurse until six almost every evening, T.J. found that the restaurant was as good a place as any to hang out with his friend and other classmates until she got off of work.

It was that momentary blast from the past that gave T.J. the direction that he was looking for. He decided right then and there to look up his old buddy, as there wasn't another person, while growing up in Columbus that T.J. had trusted more than Baylor. In fact, his friend had become the closest thing to a biological brother that he would ever have.

Once he had returned to the city limits, it had only taken him fifteen minutes to track down his old friend. And the moment that Terrance Jr. had laid eyes on him, a small weight felt like it had been lifted off his shoulders — just enough to make him start to relax some.

After exchanging the obligatory man-hug, they both went up to Baylor's apartment and cracked open a beer. By the time their first ones had been finished, T.J. had been filled in on everything that had happened in his friend's life since they had last seen each other, four years ago.

It wasn't nearly as easy for Terrance Jr. to open up, as he just wasn't sure how Baylor would react to his wild hypothesis. In fact, it had taken the consumption of half of his second beer before he finally found the courage to tell him why he had come for a visit. He didn't know why he was finding it difficult to come clean — his old friend after all, wasn't someone who would openly laugh in your face at something that appeared to be too outrageous or impossible. He instead, always kept an open mind.

Knowing that he could not procrastinate any longer, T.J. finally spilled his guts and told Baylor what it was that he speculated — he then showed him the limited 'evidence' he had compiled about Maxwell Banks. By the time he was finished doing that, his third beer was gone — he normally wasn't that big of a drinker, but under the circumstances, T.J. felt that he needed it while he made, what he believed, was a fool of himself.

In all of the years that he had known Terrence Jr., Baylor had never before been given a reason to doubt his friend's word — and today was no different. So after a few awkward moments and a few more sips of his third beer, he moved over to the other side of the bed and sat next to T.J. "Ok… You just laid some serious shit on me. The question is… what do we do now to find out whether or not what you suspect is actually true?"

"I don't know? That is why I came here to see you. Things were just fine before I let my curiosity knock on the door. My life; my family was perfect… or so I thought. My career in the military was moving along quite nicely. Hell I, not too long ago, was promoted to Second Lieutenant."

"I'm sure that there was a little influence there from your father."

"Hey!" Terrance Jr. turned and shoved his friend, harder than he had actually intended. "I got my promotion without that lying asshole's help."

"Hold on there, bud! Before you criticize your father any further, you should at least give him the benefit of the doubt until your suspicions are proven. I mean, you have no idea whether or not he is lying to you."

"You're right, I don't." Terrance Jr. needed to find a way to clear his thoughts, so he lied down on the bed and stretched out. He stared aimlessly at the ceiling as if he were searching for a clue that had been cleverly hidden within the seams of the one-foot square tiles. After a few moments of quiet thought, he said, "Are you still heavily into computer hacking, Baylor?"

"No! Not anymore. Why do you ask? What hare-brained scheme are you cooking up in that 'not-currently-making-sense, alcohol-influenced' cranium of yours?"

"I'm not sure?" Terrance Jr. continued staring at the ceiling above. He knew that the clues he was in search of weren't going to be found by looking where he was, but it seemed to act as a focal point for his thoughts; it strangely was allowing them to slowly sort itself out. "All right, this is what I need you to do for me. First, I need for you to do whatever it is that you do and see if you can access the information archives for San Antonio, Texas. Then, I need for you to try to access the records office for the State of Michigan."

"Oh no! It's been over three years since I hacked into any governmental computer network. And they, for the record, are heavily guarded and extremely secure? The last time I tried to gain access to one, I got busted."

"You did?" T.J. replied, very surprised.

Although he was ashamed at what he had done, T.J. was his best friend, and Baylor didn't really have a problem with telling him what had happened. So he went on to explain to him that the U.B.I. (Union Bureau of Investigation — once the Union was formed, the

United States' FBI, and Canada's RCMP, were merged into one mega-bureau) had caught him trying to hack into the White House computers. At the time, Baylor had a rather obsessive crush on the president's daughter and only wanted to leave her a harmless, personal vid-mail message.

After his confession was done, he then made it clear to T.J. that he had just over a year of probation left to go from that incident and that he'd rather not have to go through that humiliation all over again — nor did he want to risk going to jail."

"Baylor... Baylor... Baylor..," Terrance Jr. said, with a bit of a smirk on his face. "I see that you haven't changed. You still think with your other head, first."

He stared right at his friend with an unimpressed look on his face that could not be mistaken. He usually was able to ignore the comments that others would make pertaining to his alleged lack of sexual activity and the method he would implore to compensate for it, but it utterly annoyed Baylor whenever his best friend would jump on the bandwagon.

"I'm sure you've learned from your mistake and I won't pressure you into doing anything you don't want to. I would though, really appreciate it if you would at least go to the information archives for San Antonio and try and find me a listing for Maxwell Banks, as well as retrieve any relevant personal information that you can about him."

"You really want to find out if you are that man's missing son, don't you?"

"Honestly... I don't know? "Terrance Jr. only had to show Baylor one of the pictures he had of Maxwell Banks and remind him about the man's son's disappearance, in order to solidify his reasons for coming to see his best friend.

"Under normal circumstances, I'd have said that you've truly lost your mind, bud, but I think your suspicions may truly be warranted. Give me five minutes, and I should be in the San Antonio information archives."

"Cool. And when you're done with that, I need for you to search high and low until you find your balls, as I would really like for you to try and gain access to the server that has all the governmental records for the State of Michigan?"

"I know where my balls are; nice and safe and still intact. Sorry, but the San Antonio archives are as far as I go."

While Baylor was busy searching for the San Antonio information archives, Terrance Jr. had gone over to the mini fridge that Baylor had always kept well stocked. He removed two more ice-cold beers and cracked them open. Though this was now T.J.'s fourth, his adrenalin must have been really pumping for he had very little, if no visible buzz at all — and considering everything that had happened to him so far in the day, it really wasn't surprising.

He stepped out through the balcony doors that were directly beside Baylor's mini fridge, and sat down on a partially broken lawn chair. Staring out at the buildings that surrounded the apartment, he tried to relax by absorbing as much of the early afternoon's pure air as he possibly could. *'Because I let my imagination get the best of me, I just may have ruined my life and destroyed my family.'* T.J. just sat there in deep thought, occasionally second guessing his decision to chase a 'what if'. *'If I had not known I was adopted, more than likely I would have just dismissed my likeness to that dead ex-cop as being nothing but a coincidence.'* In retrospect, he could have just turned around and gone straight back home, but something deep down inside his soul was telling him that he had made the right decision. Whether or not he was the long lost son of Maxwell Banks, he needed to know, as it was the only way that he felt he could move forward with his life.

Three minutes was all that was needed before Baylor had successfully obtained some information for his friend. However, he was certain that T.J. was going to be disappointed. Nevertheless, what he had was basically what his friend had asked him for. "I found some information, but nothing that is going to put your uncertainty to rest."

"That's fine, bud. I have to start somewhere."

Baylor took out a pen and wrote down the address for Maxwell Banks, private investigator. He then walked out to his balcony and handed it to his friend.

"Damn! I knew that was what he did. I could have gotten that same information from using the phone directory app on my vid-cell."

Remembering then that he had another beer with him for Baylor, Terrance Jr. handed it over.

"So what are you going to do now?" All that you have so far is this address." For what little time it had been outside, the sun had started to warm up Baylor's beer. Nonetheless, it would be considered a sin to dump it out, simply because it was just not cold enough to drink. So he cracked it open, took a healthy sip, and just patiently sat there and waited for his friend to make a decision.

T.J. hummed and hawed for a few brief moments, trying to figure out what he was going to do next. The only thing he knew for sure was that he wanted to see this through. For him to find the answers that he was looking for, he knew that he could not drag his butt and hope that they'd find him. No matter how scary that first step might seem to be, he had to find the strength to take it. So he turned, looked at his friend, put his hands in his pockets, pulled out his car keys, and then freely displayed them. "By chance, would you happen to be up for a little road trip?"

"How did I know that you were going to ask me that?" Baylor replied. "You do know that I just can't drop everything and..."

"Oh... come on now, bud. It's not like you have a job to go to right now. Remember? You told me when I first got here that you recently lost your job... Ain't that right?"

"Yeah... and your point is?"

Terrance Jr. stepped forward and placed his hand upon his friend's shoulder. "My point is that your life, as we all know it, consists only of getting your daily thrills via many Internet porn sites. Admit it. You're a sim-sex junkie and you have no real life."

"What's wrong with enjoying the finer things that the world-wide web has to offer?" Baylor asked.

"Nothing is wrong with it, but there is more to life than grabbing your dick and double clicking. I swear that you are physically attached to that damn computer of yours. Come on now, Baylor. I'm offering you the chance to live dangerously for once: nothing simulated, holographic, or virtual — just your first real life adventure."

Baylor slugged back his beer, crushed the can, and threw it through the open balcony door toward the recycle bin at the other side of his room — he missed badly. He then stood up, swayed a bit, stepped back inside his apartment, and expelled a weak sounding belch. After shutting off his computer via a voice command, he then said, "Ah, what the hell, I do need a vacation. But don't ask me to drive."

They spent the next five minutes gathering up some essentials for their trip as well as taking a moment to relieve their bladders. After that, the two of them piled into T.J.'s father's car and headed out on the road to Texas. This trip, Terrance Jr. hoped, would help to finally put his mind at ease. But there was also a chance that this trip could end up with him opening up some doors that should stay closed. And if that were to happen, T.J. was uncertain that he had the ability to shut them again.

Sadness continued to encompass both Sydney and Savanna. It had been just over two weeks since Maxwell's death and neither one of them was even close to accepting that he was actually gone. However, the world wasn't going to stop until they were ready to deal with their loss. They somehow had to find a way to either deal with all of their emotional pain, or find the strength to put the necessary time needed for healing on the back burner so that they could do what needed to be done.

In order for Maxwell's brilliant legacy to officially come to a close, all of his personal belongings first had to be sorted through and packed up. It was a daunting task, and one that Sydney wasn't relishing having to take on. Nevertheless, it had to be done, so the first thing he did when he arrived at the agency this day was to make his way into his brother's office. "Come on, Savanna, I need your help." He knew that it wasn't going to be easy for her, as his brother's unexpected death had hit her harder than he initially assumed it would.

Clearing out his brother's office was an undertaking that he could actually do all by himself, but the sooner it got finished, the sooner the rest of what needed to be tended to, could be. "Please... I really could use your help with this."

"I can't do it, Sydney."

Savanna's emotions were wreaking havoc on her worse than what a 5F tornado would leave behind. She had spoken few words the entire trip back home to San Antonio after Maxwell's funeral, and had spent nearly a week after that secluded in her own apartment. Today was her first full day back at the agency. It was strange; the place felt cold and empty — almost like she didn't belong there anymore. Her thoughts were baseless, but it felt like she was violating Maxwell's memory by just being where she was. For some reason, she just couldn't gather up the strength that she knew she needed to do what had to be done. To her, walking into Maxwell's office and packing up his personal belongings, was essentially the same as purposely forgetting that he had even existed.

"You know very well that my brother would not want us to cry the melancholy blues over him. He would only want us to honor and admire his legacy for what it was."

"I know, Sydney." Savanna could not help but continue to feel sorrow. The more she thought about her boss, the more she had to wipe away the tears that would freely trickle from her eyes and down her cheeks. "I loved Max so much. You know he was like a father to me; the father that I never really had. I still can't believe that he is gone." She paused for a moment and tried to regain her composure, but it was extremely difficult for her to do so. Her mind took her away from the present and caused her memory to flash chaotically; it suddenly travelled unwillingly down a torn up road to the past that led right to the most painful parts of her early life.

Savanna never knew her biological father. Her mother, at seventeen years of age, had been five months pregnant with her when she had received a phone call with the news that the father of her unborn child had been killed in a car accident; his life taken by a drunk driver. As devastating as it was, her mother, Eleanor Rivard, was able to gather up the strength she needed to continue on alone and raise her daughter. When Savanna was three, her mother found love again and married her stepfather, twenty-five year old Robert Wisdom III.

Almost from the moment that her mother began her relationship with her stepfather, Savanna had felt uncomfortable around him. She was too young to know why, but even at that young age, she knew she didn't really like him. When Savanna was eleven

*years old, she began to feel unsafe and afraid of her stepfather. And it
was then that she finally understood why she had always felt the way
she did around him.*

*There were many times when he would do little things around
her when her mother wasn't home; like 'accidentally' walk into the
bathroom while she was bathing, brush up against her developing
womanhood, or speak to her in a manner in which only adults would
speak.*

*Shortly before her twelfth birthday, her mother had
unexpectedly passed away due to a sudden and unexplained illness.
Then, right after Savanna and her stepfather had returned home from
her mother's funeral — it happened. Her stepfather crawled into bed
with her, telling her that he was there to help comfort her with the loss
of her mother. But instead, he used her vulnerability to his advantage
and had done the unthinkable. From that day forward, Robert Wisdom
started to sexually abuse her; raping her almost on a nightly basis.*

*Only a few months after all that had begun, her stepfather had
lost his job of fifteen years due to a sudden plant closure. His
unemployment insurance didn't last long and he quickly began to run
out of money, so Robert Wisdom decided that he was going to use the
only asset he had left in order to make money and survive. Savanna
didn't share one ounce of his DNA, so he felt as if she was his inherent
property and he could do whatever he wanted with her. And since, in
his mind, she had never fully accepted him as being her stepfather, no
regret would be there with what it was that he wanted to do — force
her to begin to work as a child prostitute.*

*First, he pimped her out to a few of his fellow laid off workers.
Then, he offered her to strangers whom he had met at the local bars.
After about a month of that, he believed that he would be able to make
even more money by forcing Savanna to work the streets.*

*Six months to the day that he began to pimp out his
stepdaughter, he recognized that it was time to off load his property
before she became the cause of his possible future arrest — he needed
to get rid of Savanna and disappear, so he had made an arrangement
to sell her to a well know local pimp named Stitch.*

*It was during the official 'signing over' of Savanna that she
had first met Maxwell Banks. Fortunately, Savanna's stepfather did*

not know what Stitch looked like and he ended up inadvertently attempting to sell her to Maxwell. At the time, Maxwell had been working on a separate case to rescue another young girl who had been kidnapped by Stitch. His police career had been over for three years by this time, but he still had the ability and permission of the local authorities to make an arrest if the situation he found himself in, warranted it. And that was exactly what he had done that day to Savanna's scumbag of a stepfather.

Maxwell had never intended to let his heart be touched, let alone by a victim as young as Savanna was. At that point in his life, he had yet to heal from the wounds of his past. But almost instantly, he felt a bond forming between him and Savanna; a bond that quickly strengthened and ultimately, they were able to help each other's devastating scars begin to heal.

The temperature in the city on this early April day was unseasonably high — certainly, no one who ventured out outside would complain. At the same time, the city of Detroit looked somewhat neglected and unkempt. On the ground, lay small mounds of dirt, tiny rocks, and the odd remnants of crystallized snow cakes; an involuntarily collection courtesy of the accumulated piles of snow having been pushed up there during the past winter.

Sydney had only been to Detroit once before — and that was because he had flown there to meet up with his brother so that they could both fly home to Ottawa together to attend their father's funeral. This time, he was here at the insistence of his sister-in-law, Sylvia, as she had wanted him to be there for the birth of hers and Maxwell's first child; Sydney's first nephew.

Children were never a planned part of his life. And when the time finally came for him to hold baby Sabastian for the first time, he was hesitant. The child was so tiny; Sydney was afraid that he was either going to drop or crush him. He was content to just look at the newborn from afar, but once Sylvia dumped him in his arms and walked away, Sydney knew that he was stuck.

Sabastian had only been in his arms for a few minutes and he was ready to return him to his mother. But Sylvia insisted that he

spend some quality time with his nephew; knowing full well that
Sydney wasn't going to be around often enough to bond with him.

Slowly, the need to hand off this unwanted responsibility began
to fade and Sydney began to change his perspective on children —
even the thought of having one of his own someday had briefly crossed
his mind. Now, suddenly enamored at the precious bundle in his arms,
he just sat there staring at his sleeping nephew and feeling the warmth
that his tiny little body exuded against his T-shirt. Never had Sydney
imagined that he would feel something like this — in his arms and in
his heart.

By the time Sylvia had decided that it was time to retrieve her
son so that she could feed him, that family bond had been created and
Sydney's life had changed — even Maxwell could see it.

There had been very few unforgettable moments in Sydney's
life — that had been one of them. Little did he know at the time that
moment would be the only one he would ever have with his nephew.
Sometimes — no, quite often, life just turns out to be unfair.

Sydney knew that if Savanna were to find anything she
deemed to be sentimental while they were packing up Maxwell's
office, all of the uncontrolled emotions that still ran inside of her
would immediately surface and cause her to become upset even more
than what she already was. So he made the decision right then and
there to tackle his brother's office alone — at another time. It made
sense to him that he should just call it a day and take Savanna home. It
was easy for him to see that she still wasn't quite ready to walk back
into the agency and do what needed to be done. It was best that she
just stay away for a bit longer until she was fully ready to help him —
he just hoped that it wasn't going to be months from now when that
finally happened, as there simply was no reason to keep paying the rent
for a place of business that was no longer operational.

As the both of them were about to leave the agency, a
demonic-like chill suddenly crawled up Sydney's back; it caused him
to pause just long enough to be confronted by a wraithlike image that
stared directly back at both he and Savanna.

"Hello. Um... I hope that I have the right place? Is this the detective agency of Maxwell Banks?"

Savanna wanted to scream at the top of her lungs. Instead, she just covered her mouth and face with both of her hands and uncontrollably, started to shake. Sydney just stood there, aghast, as he didn't know what to say. Instantly, he was brought back in time to when he and his brother were both young. "What the..?" he whispered to himself, as he glanced over at Savanna and noticed that she was as white as a hospital bed sheet and appeared as if she were about to faint. "Are you all right, Savanna?"

She didn't answer his question. She instead, just stood there petrified — Sydney was at a loss. His first instinct was to go to her side and help, but his own body didn't want to move — the stranger that stood at the threshold of the agency dominated his curiosity.

Without removing his eyes from the young man at the front door, Sydney forced himself to back up a few steps until he was able to place his arm behind Savanna's back — he did this to ensure that she wouldn't suddenly fall over.

"I'm sorry," Terrence Jr. said, with honest regret in his voice. "It wasn't my intention to upset anyone." T.J. never expected to get the kind of reaction he did, but what had just happened only helped to increase his own suspicions.

"My name is Sydney Banks. I'm Maxwell's younger brother. Could you just wait right there for a moment, please?" Sydney then led Savanna by the arm and guided her back over to her desk chair. "Let me get you a glass of water, and you just sit here and relax. I'll see what this man wants, ok?"

Savanna looked up at Sydney; the look of shock on her face was apparent. She then took a few deep breaths and said. "I'll... I'll be fine in a minute."

After getting her some water, Sydney invited the mysterious stranger inside. "I'm sorry, it's just... Well, you see... my brother Maxwell has recently passed away and... you really look a lot like him."

"I apologize again if I have spooked anyone, Mr. Banks. My name is Terrance Burelli Jr., and this is my best friend, Baylor Wilson."

31

"It's a pleasure to meet the two of you." Sydney then reached out his hand and greeted both T.J. and Baylor. The moment his hand touched T.J.'s, that same chill returned in his back; with a little more intensity this time — it was a sensation that only confused him more. He was unsure at that moment if this feeling that he was having was the first signs of a cold coming on, or if it was some strange forewarning that something unforeseen was about to take place.

Sydney glanced behind him to quickly check on the condition of Savanna. After seeing that she was starting to relax, he moved himself over to her desk and carefully leaned back against the corner of it. He couldn't help but be mesmerized by the uncanny likeness of this stranger's appearance to his late brother. Again, he was brought back in time to when both he and Maxwell were young. "I'm sorry for staring. It's just that I can't believe how much you resemble my brother. So... what can I do for you, Mr. Burelli?"

Terrance Jr. removed his palm-top from the small satchel that he had brought with him. He then showed it to Sydney; the article about Maxwell's death was already on the screen. "When I read this, there was something about it that really stuck in my mind. I wasn't quite sure what it was at first, but it refused to leave my thoughts all that night and caused me to have a strange, all too real dream. The next day, I decided to do some research on your brother in order to try and find a reason as to why I had been affected like I was. Then, when I saw a picture of him when he was a young cadet, it hit me." T.J. minimized the article on his palm-top screen and then pulled up that photo he was referring to. "Can you imagine what it felt like to me when I saw my own mirror image staring right back at me? Well... then again, I guess you can. My showing up here basically had the same effect on you, didn't it?"

"Yes it did, Mr. Burelli. We both thought for a moment that we had seen a ghost. You really do look a lot like a younger version of my brother."

So far, the conversation had gone smoother than what T.J. had thought it would. But that didn't mean that he could be presumptuous — he still needed to tread lightly, as there were two very hurt individuals here who didn't need to be led astray. "The article about your brother stated that he had a son that disappeared twenty-five years ago. Was he ever found?"

"No, he wasn't. My brother had spent his entire life trying to find him, but was unsuccessful. Why do you ask?"

"May I ask what his son's name was?"

"His name was Sabastian. What do you want to know that for?"

That was something that T.J. never expected; he now had one more bit of information that again helped to validate his suspicions. "You see, Mr. Banks, this is what I know." T.J. then proceeded to tell Sydney his own personal story. He first began by explaining that his adopted father had told him, when his mother was only sixteen years old, her high school gym teacher had raped her and she ended up getting pregnant. When what had happened became public knowledge, T.J.'s apparent biological father couldn't deal with what he had done and chose to commit suicide instead of facing up to the statutory rape charges that had been laid against him.

T.J.'s biological mother was apparently a deeply devoted Christian — and being that meant neither she, nor the rest of her family, believed in abortion. For that reason, his mother chose not to terminate the pregnancy. However, only a few weeks after his birth, she suddenly developed some severe, migraine-like headaches; headaches that turned out to be an inoperable brain tumor. She unfortunately died three months later.

T.J. had also been told that his adopted father had lost both his wife and son during childbirth. His birth mother's mother and adopted father instantly befriended each other when they met at the same hospital that Terrance's wife had just passed away in and where T.J.'s mother was being treated for her tumor. They spent hours that day talking and consoling each other, and by the end of their conversation, Terrance had offered to adopt the woman's grandson, since she felt that she was simply too old to be a mother to a new born child and raise him if her daughter didn't survive the radical treatments that the doctors were using — which she unfortunately, didn't.

As soon as T.J. had finished with his incredible story, something grabbed his curiosity; he turned his attention away from Sydney and the others in the lobby as his eyes located a separate, private office with the door wide open. Something inside of him urged him to go to that room and see what was in there. When he walked inside, he spotted a family picture on the desk. Curiously, he picked up the cracked framed photo and looked at it — it was a picture of Maxwell Banks, his wife, and newborn son.

By now, Savanna's shattered nerves had returned to an almost normal state — and she didn't like the fact that a complete stranger had just walked into Maxwell's office, uninvited. "Mr. Burelli. I would appreciate it if you would please come out of there. I'm not sure what it is that you are looking for, but whatever it is, I'm sure that it is not in there."

Terrance Jr. didn't even hear Savanna talking to him. He just stared at the picture in his hand; a picture that he knew he had never seen before, yet the people in the photo felt all too familiar to him.

With the cracked frame in his hand, he walked out of the office, stopping in front of Sydney. "Mr. Banks, my full name is Terrance Sabastian Burelli. I'm twenty-five years old and I was born on June fifteenth, two thousand and ten. At least, that's the day that I was told I had been born."

"Wait a minute!" Savanna said, as her mind immediately created a hypothesis. "Are you trying to say what I think you are?"

Sydney was still somewhat confused, though he had a pretty good idea as to where this was all headed. But there was only one way to find out what this stranger was after, so he figured that he might as well come straight out and take a wild stab at what he had thought this man wanted to know. "You think that you may be my brother's long lost son, don't you?"

"Yes… well, I'm… really not sure?" Terrance Jr. said while he continued to stare at the picture in his hand. After a few moments of thought, he handed it to Sydney. "I don't think I've ever really accepted the explanation of my adoption. Although up until a few days ago, I really didn't care, as I liked the life I have been living. But once I saw that picture of your brother, Mr. Banks, all the tiny doubts that I had ever had, began to surface and grow. I don't know for sure, but all I can say is that I think there may be a slight chance I could be him."

In that moment, Baylor moved over to his friend and tapped him on his shoulder — he wasn't sure why, but he felt that he should interject. "T.J. I, um… I think that maybe we should just leave."

After a few awkward moments of silence, Terrence Jr. decided that his friend was right — he had given two people hope, when he had no proof to submit to them. "I am really sorry for scaring you earlier. And I think that it was a big mistake for me to come here. Please accept my apology for wasting your time."

"Hang on there a minute!" Savanna rose out of her chair and grabbed Terrance Jr. by the wrist before he took that first step toward the exit. She wasn't sure why she had done that, but her gut was telling her not to let this stranger leave. It was a long shot, but there was a reason as to why this man had taken a leap of faith and came to the agency this day in hopes of putting to rest a wild hypothesis that he felt strongly about; a feeling that Savanna now also had — and she wasn't about to let this man leave until she too got some answers.

After insisting that both T.J. and Baylor stay and take a seat, Savanna walked to the back kitchen nook and poured two cups of sim-caf for their guests. She returned a few moments later with the beverages, gave it to them, and then motioned for Sydney to follow her into Maxwell's office. After closing the door to ensure their privacy, Savanna said, "Sydney, we can't dismiss this man's beliefs. For Maxwell's sake, we have to find out for sure whether or not he is Sabastian — no matter how slim the odds may be."

Though Sydney wasn't one for believing in premonitions, he now understood why he had gotten that chill down his spine, and he knew that he'd be stupid to just dismiss this improbability that now sat in the agency's lobby. "I agree." Sydney left Maxwell's office and walked over to the kitchen nook; Savanna walked straight back over to her desk and sat down. Sydney poured two more cups of sim-caf and then brought them over to Savanna. After giving one to her, he said, "I have a feeling that we're going to be here for quite a while until we figure out whether or not you are my brother's missing son."

Terrance Jr. thanked both Savanna and Sydney for the fresh cup of sim-caf and for agreeing that his suspicions just might be warranted. "I really appreciate you doing this."

After a short conversation took place, the four of them decided what their best course of action was going to be. Sydney would be responsible for tearing apart Maxwell's office, as his task was to try and locate any bit of information that his brother had about his son. Savanna volunteered to go through all of Maxwell's files and try to find anything that may be of relevance. Terrance Jr. was asked to search through Maxwell's desk and steamer trunks, and Baylor was asked to try and retrieve any important files Maxwell may have or once had on his computer.

"I don't know why you want your friend to access Maxwell's computer," Sydney said. "We looked thoroughly through it when my brother was still presumed alive. I don't recall ever seeing any files on there about his son. My brother must have kept all the information that he had about Sabastian on an external storage disk or back-up stick and then hid it. His missing son was a sensitive subject that he rarely would talk about, so I'm thinking that he probably kept all of the information he had on him in a safe place that only he knew about. Or, knowing my brother as I do, he probably took it all with him when he left for Detroit."

"Baylor's a self-taught techno-geek. Even if your brother erased all of the information he had on his computer pertaining to his son, some of it might still be retrievable."

"Or he could have hidden the information on a virtual drive or sent it off into Cy-space," Baylor pointed out.

"Cy-space?"

"It's a place, similar to the old Microsoft Cloud, where you can store information. Unlike it however, Cy-space allows you to split a file into millions of pieces, like stars in the galaxy, and then strategically store them all around the net. But unless you have the proper net coordinates for all of those pieces and the sequential code to reassemble them, they are just useless pieces of data junk. It is by far, the most secure way of protecting any sensitive or personal information that you have."

"I doubt if my brother would go out of his way to use that kind of available technology to hide information about his son."

"I agree," Savanna stated. "Maxwell didn't like to use any form of modern technology unless it was necessary to complete a job. He was an old-school trained cop who did things the old-school way."

T.J. looked at his friend and smiled; Baylor knew immediately that his friend wanted him to do something that he knew he shouldn't. "Once you've confirmed that the hard drive is completely empty and there are no pertinent files on it that can be retrieved, and since Savanna has told us that Maxwell's personal computer has direct access capability to the Michigan State Capitol Building, I would like for you to use that secure network as a hub to then hack into the Detroit Police Department's main computer. Once you've done that, I want you to try to get me all of the files that you can about Mr. Bank's police career. And then... Who was it again that your brother was after the day he was murdered?"

"Antonio Marcone," Sydney replied.

"And see if you can find us whatever information is available on him. Ok, bud?"

"Wait! Let me get this straight. You want me to infiltrate, what will end up being multiple government servers, and then gather a whole bunch of information for you; information that I would be willing to bet is classified?"

"You only need to look at it and then document what would be important. Think of it as being the same thing as when you would look over my shoulder in biology class in order to see what answers I had given on our bi-weekly test."

"What you're asking me to do is nowhere near close to that. So um... No!"

"Why not?"

"You must have a short memory T.J., as I seem to recall telling you just before we left my place to come here that I don't go hacking into secured governmental networks anymore. Remember? I got caught. I would rather not have to deal with those fuckin' Feds again. And I definitely don't want to get thrown into jail for computer hacking. Do you have any idea what would happen to me if I were to get thrown in jail? My tight little white virgin ass would look rather inviting to some three-hundred pound hairy biker dude."

"Your wild imagination is making you panic for no real reason. Just because you got caught once, doesn't mean that you'll get caught again. I'm sure you'll remember not to make the same stupid mistakes that got you caught the last time. Besides, I'm not asking you to hack into the White House computers. I'm only asking you to hack into the computer system for the Detroit Police Department."

"The route I would have to take to get there would not be straightforward. Homeland Security will undoubtedly be notified that someone, namely me, is trying to backdoor into a government network."

Savanna walked over to Terrance Jr. and handed him two rather large boxes that were filled with files (after she had spent the time refilling everything that had been scattered all over most of Maxwell's office, she was able to condense them into two boxes). She then let it be known that she didn't think it would be necessary for Baylor to hack into the Detroit Police Department's computers because all of Maxwell's police and personal files on Antonio Marcone were inside these boxes.

Terrance Jr. accepted the boxes from Savanna and quickly scanned through the first file folder he removed from the top box. After being satisfied with what little he had just read, he handed the boxes over to Baylor and then asked him to kindly cross-reference all of the information that was in them with what he was going to learn once he was able to hack into the Detroit Police Department's network. "I'm sorry, but I don't want to take a chance on you possibly missing anything that may be of importance."

"Fine!" Baylor reluctantly agreed. "But if I get caught, I will be draggin' your ass down with me. And when Bruno gets horny, you better be willing to take one for the team!"

Everyone was working hard at the task that they were assigned. After disappointingly realizing that Maxwell's computer had no significant files that were worth looking at, Baylor reluctantly began his task of hacking into the Detroit Police Department's system.

T.J. didn't have much luck either when it came to Maxwell's desk and steamer trunks — both had electronic security locks on them. This frustrated him. If the locks had been the old-style pad lock, then

he felt that this kind of obstacle would not be much of a problem —
but he just didn't have the knowledge he needed to pick, bypass, or
short out this kind of electronic locking technology.

Sydney also wasn't having much luck searching through his
brother's office, so he decided that he would concentrate his efforts on
the large closet in the back corner. As soon as he had opened the door,
his mouth dropped. The closet had been stuffed neat and tight with
boxes — it looked like an enormous corrugated puzzle box. Sydney's
first thought was that it would take him weeks, maybe even months to
go through. But he didn't have that kind of time, so Sydney hastily
grabbed the first box that was directly in front of him and yanked it
out. Of course, it had to have been the wrong one for nearly the entire
closet emptied down on top of him.

For a good thirty seconds, the laughter in the room seemed to
overtake the urgency that had consumed everyone up until then.
Personally, Sydney was one of those individuals who hated a laugh
coming at his expense. However, under the circumstances, he let
everyone enjoy what was in all actuality, a harmless moment of joy
before they returned to the mission at hand.

The only thing that had mattered when this undertaking had
started was to find that one bit of evidence; that one clue that could
prove T.J. was Maxwell's long lost son. Unlike everyone in the
agency, Savanna's laughing had only lasted a few seconds — but that
was only because she had noticed something unusual about the bottom
drawer of the partially empty filing cabinet that she had been going
through. As strange as what she was looking at, seemed, she was even
more baffled with her own apparent lack of astute observation, as she
had opened that particular filing cabinet drawer an estimated five
thousand times or more over the years and had never once noticed
what had now grabbed her curiosity.

She removed the remainder of the files from the drawer and by
using a letter opener, carefully removed the false bottom of it to expose
what had been hidden underneath; a rather old looking file folder.
"Hey, everyone! I think that I might have found something here." She
removed the file that had been long ago hidden and looked at it — it
was marked '**CONFIDENTIAL**' on the outside. Carefully, she
opened it up and began to scan through the contents. She immediately

realized that she was looking at a photocopy of some medical records from Henry Ford Hospital; records that were dated June and July, two thousand and ten."

"Hey! I think that I've found something also!" Sydney held in his hand a firebox that had been hidden behind a small false panel at the back bottom corner of the closet. He was so excited with anticipation that without thinking, he hurriedly stood up and severely whacked his head on the top shelf of the closet. His sudden pain caused him to forget what else was around him; he stumbled backwards and unknowingly stepped onto one of the fallen boxes that were left scattered all over the floor behind him — he would have face planted himself onto the floor if it wasn't for his ability to reach for, and grab the edge of the desk with his right hand.

The urge to laugh at Sydney's expense once again was immediately there, but Savanna refrained from doing so. And as humorous as it was with what had just happened, there were more important things than fully enjoying the result of someone's misfortune. "Um… what do you have there, Sydney?"

Because the office was what would now be considered a disaster area, as it was littered with boxes, papers, and a lot of junk, he took what was in his possession and carried it out to the lobby area for everyone to see. When he got to Savanna's desk, he then plopped the firebox, and himself, down — he wasn't having a good day so sitting seemed like the most logical move for him to make because he just did not want to risk embarrassing himself any further.

He then proceeded to open up the box, fully expecting it to be locked. But to his surprise, it opened right up. *'How convenient?'* Sydney thought. *'I'm surprised that Maxwell chose not to lock this.'* He dumped the entire contents of the firebox onto Savanna's desk. "Let's see what we have here." Lying on the desktop were several photos of Maxwell and Sylvia before they were married, a couple of old wedding photos, his brother's wedding ring, an award of merit that Maxwell had received in high school, and two small sealed brown envelopes.

Savanna grabbed both envelopes from the top of her desk before Sydney could get his hands on them. Both of the envelopes had a date written on the front; one envelope said June, two thousand and ten, and the other one said June, two thousand and thirty-five.

"I think you should open the envelope that say's June two thousand and ten, first," Terrance Jr. said. "My guess is that what we could be looking for will most likely be in that one."

"Yes. I think you may be right," Sydney concurred.

Savanna undid the butterfly clip at the top of the manila envelope and removed the contents from inside. She quickly scanned over the papers and exhaled a slight bit of victory. "I believe that what we have here is exactly what we have been looking for." Savanna gently held in her left hand a copy of Sabastian's birth certificate and in her right hand, she held a copy of baby Sabastian's fingerprints.

"May I please see those documents?" Terrance Jr. set down the other file onto Savanna's desk that he had been holding in his hand, reached out, and gingerly took the two pieces of paper from Savanna — he then briefly glanced over them.

"So what exactly is in that hospital file that I handed you earlier, Mr. Burelli?"

"I really didn't get a chance yet to see what was in it." Terrance Jr. then gently re-inserted both the fingerprints and the birth certificate back into the envelope from which they came, clipped it shut, and handed it back over to Savanna. He then picked back up the file folder marked '**CONFIDENTIAL**', and read its contents out loud. "It says here that on June fifteenth, two thousand and ten, Sabastian Banks was born to the parents of Maxwell and Sylvia Banks. It also says how long the baby boy was and how much he weighed at birth, what his blood type is, and even his DNA profile." Terrance Jr. then lowered the file down to his side and looked over at Sydney, as an unlikely realization suddenly enveloped him. "This is all the information that we need to find out for sure whether or not I am your brother's long lost son."

Hearing the conversation that was going on in the lobby area, Baylor let his curiosity take him away from his task inside of Maxwell's office and he walked over to the threshold of the door. "Hey, T.J.? Is the military not required to keep a record of each officer's fingerprints and DNA profile?"

"That's correct bud... just in case something was to happen and they need to identify someone's..." T.J. stopped in mid-sentence, as he just clued in to what his friend's train of thought was. He realized at that moment that all he had to do was turn on his vid-cell, call the clerical office at the Military Base in Houston, Texas, and request access to his military personal file — then he'd have all the information that he needed to figure out his true identity. But then another thought came to him; one that had a distinct possibility of being true if the suspected lies were indeed being lived. "You know Baylor, I could do that, but I don't think that I should trust my official records. I know that it may come across as being incredulous, but if my suspicions are correct, then my 'father' quite possibly used his military credentials to access, and then falsify my official records... just in case I one day doubted who I really was."

"I agree with you, T.J. We should error on the side of caution and get the necessary tests done ourselves." Sydney then turned his attention over to Savanna and said, "Hand me the other envelope so that I can take a peek at what's inside."

Savanna's look was an obvious one of selfishness — though probably unintentional. Not giving anyone else a chance to object, she opened up the envelope and began to scan its contents herself. As she was doing this, Terrance Jr. walked over to the sim-caf machine and poured himself the last of what was in the pot. "So I guess all that is left to do is to get some fingerprints taken of myself and compare them with the ones that we just found."

"Whoa!" Savanna said. "You would not believe what this is that I've got in my hand?"

"I really don't give a shit what it is!" Sydney was quite upset that his brother's secretary had chosen not to give him the opportunity to look at the envelope's contents. Not so much because of her childlike behavior, but because it was he who had not only found the firebox, but had to suffer through pain and humiliation to get it. In his opinion, Savanna was just trying to be a glory hound. He no longer cared what was in that last envelope. All that he wanted to do at that very moment was to get Terrance Jr. to the police station so that he could get a digital scan taken of his fingerprints.

"Don't you think that maybe what I have here could be just as important as finding out whether or not T.J. could be Maxwell's son?"

"Fine!" Sydney stated. "Please tell us all about this goddamn important information that you have now found. I'm sure we all can't wait to hear it!"

"Stop!" Terrence Jr. demanded. "If whatever it is in Savanna's hands wasn't important, then I'm sure she wouldn't have insisted that we know."

After a moment of awkward silence, both Savanna and Sydney turned toward each other and somewhat, sort of, quietly made a truce.

Once he believed the tension that had been there was gone, Terrance Jr. asked that Savanna share with everyone what was inside the last envelope.

"Well... what I have here is not only Maxwell's last will and testament, but a rather lengthy letter addressed to his son." Forgetting that no confirmation had yet to be established that Terrance Jr. was indeed Maxwell's long lost son, she placed the will and letter back in the envelope and then handed it over to him.

Immediately, his curiosity enveloped him. He accepted the envelope from Savanna and was about to look at its contents, but remembered one important detail — no proof was yet there that he was who everyone in the agency hoped he might be.

He allowed his conscience to take over. Without hesitation, he promptly returned the envelope back to Savanna. "Please put this back in the firebox. I should not look at Mr. Bank's will and personal letter to his son unless I... I do turn out to be him." Terrance Jr. took a seat in the chair that was next to Savanna's desk and leaned back — he then covered his face with his hands so that he could gather his thoughts.

After a few moments of unnerving silence passed, Sydney suggested, "I think, Savanna, you should make a call to the San Antonio Police Department and ask for Captain Lutherage. I believe that he still owes Maxwell a few favors."

"That's a good idea. Hey listen... I'm really sorry for the way I acted."

"Apology accepted. I too am really sorry for being a jerk."

"Good. Now that you've both kissed and made up, can we go get the answers that we are looking for?"

Baylor's voice resonated from Maxwell's office, grabbing their attention all at once. "Hey... I'm going to be at least another forty-five minutes to an hour longer than I thought. Hacking into the Detroit Police Department's main server is turning out to be a hell of a lot tougher than I thought it would be. Especially since I discovered that they are linked into a C-4 network. I've had to waste a lot of time re-routing everything that I've done so far through multiple servers from all around the world. I've never attempted to hack into a security system like this one before. And if I'm not careful here, I'm liable to set off one of the many security traps throughout this rather complex data infrastructure."

"That's all right, Baylor," T.J. said. "The three of us have to leave for a while anyway. So take all the time you need... and don't get caught."

Upon their arrival at the San Antonio Police Department, the reaction of those in the building when T.J. first appeared was almost identical to that of the reaction he had gotten only a few hours earlier from Sydney and Savanna. It was apparent by the amount of shock throughout the place that Maxwell Banks had made a lot of friends and had left a hole in the lives of those who had known him — especially Captain Lutherage, as was quickly established by his near choking experience upon his first glance at T.J.

Savanna, who also knew the captain fairly well, walked over to him and encouraged him to take a seat. After pulling a chair up to the front of his desk, she went on to explain everything they knew so far. It seemed impossible to believe what he was being told — Captain Lutherage was admittedly, at a loss for words. But the more he looked at T.J., the more he started to buy into the hypothesis presented to him. Yes, it was a possibility that seemed remote, but it was also one that he knew he could not readily dismiss.

Immediately, the captain issued a request to have a digital scan taken of T.J.'s fingerprints. He was well aware that he still owed Maxwell more than a few favors — and even though the hard evidence that Savanna had submitted to him was what they needed to help put to rest any doubt that may be there, a disheartened Captain Lutherage knew that this had all come just a bit too late. He understood that

Maxwell's death was what had launched the chain of events that has now led to this moment, but if things could have only happened differently, maybe a good man would still be alive. Nevertheless, if it does turn out that T.J. Burelli is indeed Sabastian Banks, then not only could the healing process begin, but one of the debts that he had incurred to Maxwell will have been paid off, posthumously.

Terrance Jr., Savanna, and Sydney, had hoped that this was going to be as simple and quick as getting the results from an x-ray. But the forensics labs quickly made it clear that the two fingerprint comparisons would take quite some time to complete. The reason for this was that the twenty-five year old prints of baby Sabastian had begun to deteriorate and they first needed to be digitally reconstructed before a match could be determined.

With time now to kill, the three of them left the San Antonio Police station and headed for the UT Health Science Center at the University of Texas Hospital. They had planned on going there anyway, but had hoped to at least have the results of the fingerprints in hand by then. It wasn't that they needed to get a blood and DNA test taken if the fingerprint results confirmed what they had hoped, but everyone wanted to be one hundred percent sure before any kind of celebration took place.

Now, came the hard part — waiting for the results that not only could change T.J.'s life forever, but the lives of two strangers who would then immediately become an important piece to his existence.

Once they had finished up at the hospital, the three of them returned to the agency. Not knowing if he was or wasn't, suddenly seemed to be more nerve-racking for T.J. than what he could have ever predicted. But he couldn't even begin to imagine what it was doing to Savanna and Sydney — they had after all, recently lost a key part of their own existence. However, he was also aware that a missing part of it returning to them would do a lot to help ease the burden they each now shouldered.

You couldn't have asked for a better day; there wasn't even a cloud in the sky. Only a minimal breeze was blowing; just enough to keep the summer air from becoming unbearable. It was the perfect day to do something radical or maybe even dangerous. T.J.'s father was

off on a short military assignment down in Panama, and his grandmother had gone out on her weekly bingo binge.

Both Baylor and T.J. had begun to get really, really bored sitting around the house doing pretty much nothing, so they decided that they would borrow T.J.'s father's car and go for a drive — of course, both of them were only fifteen at the time and unlicensed. Neither of them really knew how to drive a car, but that didn't matter, for they thought that it couldn't be any harder than it was driving a car in their favorite video game, Grand Theft Auto XV.

Terrence Burelli's mint condition, fully restored, vintage burnt orange Barracuda Fastback, had been kept in storage inside his mother's garage for almost two years. He really didn't have any time to drive it because his military career was just beginning to take off. He was a motivated man with an ambition to rise up through the ranks of the military as fast as he possibly could. It was why he would be the first one to volunteer or accept any and all available assignments that came his way — and it was that kind of dedication and commitment; a willing sacrifice that would unfortunately take Terrance Burelli away from his family more than he would have liked.

The odds looked pretty good that T.J.'s father would never find out that they were going to take his vintage car for a short cruise, but that didn't mean that they could be careless either — Terrance Burelli knew every nuance of his restored vehicle and surely he would notice anything, no matter how small it was, that happened to his pride and joy.

Once they removed the tarp that protected it, T.J. and Baylor got into the car and drove off to an area of the city known amongst the youth as 'easy street'. It was common knowledge amongst the teenage boys in the area that any good looking guy could easily meet and score themselves an equally good looking young girl in this part of town. And sure enough, it had only taken them a few minutes for their internal hormonal radar to lock onto two girls who didn't hesitate for a minute to go for a ride with them.

This was the greatest feeling in the world to the both of them — the awesome classic car that they were driving, instantly looked even better with the two prizes that now sat inside with them, nestled in their arms.

After about fifteen minutes of cruising down the street, they all agreed to head on down to the lake. Once they got there, they parked the car at the end of a secluded, old abandoned wooden pier to enjoy the view — but enjoying the view wasn't exactly what the boys had in mind. What they really wanted was to get past first base for the first time in their lives and this seemed like the perfect spot to do just that.

Success had been much easier to attain then what either had expected. The two girls who they picked up were either in the same boat as they were, virgins, and wanted to take that next step as well, or they were sluts that were looking to take another cherry and add to their reputations. Whatever the reason was that they chose to get into the car, T.J., nor Baylor, cared — all that mattered to them was to experience something other than an innocent kiss.

Things were moving along quite nicely. In fact, both of them were just about to advance to third base when a strange sound suddenly encompassed the area of the car. Perplexity enveloped them, as they instantly became aware of the odd noise. After a few seconds of not being able to figure out what it was that they had just heard, both T.J. and Baylor passed it off as a freak occurrence and returned to their education at hand. That was a big mistake, because only moments later, the pier started to give way — and the car began to roll forward. Panic erupted; the two girls screamed as they both clung tightly to the boys.

Being the novice driver that he was, T.J. had absolutely no idea what to do. However, before either he or Baylor were able to come up with a way to stop what was now happening, (not the girls from essentially blanketing themselves on top of them), the entire pier gave way and the car plunged nose first into the cool waters of Lake Erie, taking all four of them for an unplanned, early-spring swim.

Neither one of them ended up hitting that home run, but easily, they had been caught stealing by T.J.'s grandmother. Edith was furious with her grandson for taking his father's priceless car and for giving it a bath in the lake. That though, was nothing compared to what wrath T.J. assumed was in store for him when his father found out.

He prepared himself for the worst when his grandmother called his father that evening at the military base in Panama. But all *that his father had to say was that he and his son would have a 'man to man' discussion when he got home. Two weeks later when his father had finally returned, they had that chat. Terrance let it be known that he was very disappointed in his son with the choice that he had made and that the day would come when he would have to 'make things right' for his bad decision.*

To say that T.J. was both shocked and relieved that he wasn't going to get the beating of a lifetime was an understatement. However, he never in a million years would have thought that the way he would have to 'make things right' would be when he had turned eighteen that he would all but be forced into enlisting in the military?

Years later, in hindsight, that had turned out to be the best thing that could have ever happened to him. It hadn't taken T.J. long, once he had started his military career, before he had thanked his father for putting him on the right path; a path that was going to allow him an opportunity to grow and become a driven, well respected, and honorable man.

Baylor walked over to Terrance Jr. and tapped him on the top of his head with a pen. "Earth to T.J., are you still with us? What planet are you on there, bud?"

"Um… Did you say something?"

"You're staring aimlessly off into space and you're fidgeting with that wireless computer mouse on Savanna's desk."

"Yeah… I just can't seem to concentrate too well right now." Terrance Jr. let go of the mouse. "I'm sure that if you were in my shoes, you would probably be acting the same way that I am."

Baylor couldn't deny that. However, he felt that his friend's feelings had to be put aside for the moment because he had some information that he wanted to present; information that he was able to attain while everyone was out. Once he had garnered the room's attention, he couldn't wait to pat himself on the back. "Not only was I able to stealthily maneuver right on through the C-4 network, I was able to successfully infiltrate the police department's servers; severs that surprisingly were protected by some pretty advanced security measures. Also… and here is the part that everyone should be thankful for, I was able to make what I did, look like D.U.O. was the one who did the hacking."

"I'm glad you were able to succeed, Baylor... but just hold onto the information that you were able to obtain for now, as I'm not even sure if or when we will need it."

"Wait! You mean to tell me, T.J., that for the last two hours, I've risked losing my anal virginity for you... and you're not even sure yet if you're even going to need the information I found?"

"I'm sure we will need it," Savanna said, "but I think that your friend just wants to wait and see what the test results will be first."

A moment of a well-timed disruption of the unwanted tension in the room was all that it took for T.J. to jump up out of his chair — the beeping of an incoming vid-call had startled him. Time instantly froze. T.J. was all but sure that this call was for him, yet he wasn't even certain that he wanted to answer it.

"Would you like me to answer it, or do you want to?" Sydney asked.

"I... Ahhh..." T.J. sunk down into his chair, making it almost appear as if he were molded into it. He looked over at Sydney, then back over to Savanna with an odd stare, trying to get one of them to clue in to the fact that he was incapable at that moment of handling the news; whether it was good or bad.

Sydney could see what Terrance Jr. wanted of him — and he could understand the young man's reluctance to want to hear the results first hand, so he took the liberty and answered the call for him. It was Captain Lutherage on the other end, calling with the results from T.J.'s fingerprint comparisons.

The captain proceeded to inform Sydney that unfortunately, only a portion of two of the fingerprints from baby Sabastian were in good enough shape for the lab to restore and compare — and the results were inconclusive. Even though part of the prints did match, it just wasn't enough to confirm without a shadow of a doubt that T.J. was indeed, Maxwell's long lost son.

After a few moments of apologetic silence, Captain Lutherage let his opinion be known, stating that he now believed what they all hoped — but cautioned them as well to hold off on the celebrating until they got the test results back from the lab at the hospital.

After thanking the captain, Sydney disconnected the vid-phone, leaned back in his chair, and sat there quietly — an obviously disappointed look was on his face. After a moment, he turned his attention to Terrance Jr., and apologetically spoke, "I'm sorry there, T.J. Um... I really was hoping that we would have received the answer that you are looking for with just the fingerprint results. I guess we have no other choice now but to wait for your blood and DNA test results to come in to be sure."

Clearly, everyone could see that Terrance Jr. was extremely distraught. Savanna briefly thought about going over to console him, but decided against it. It was not her place to do that. They were, after all, strangers who were each searching for an answer. And until they had a definitive one, Savanna knew that T.J. had to deal with his emotions all on his own.

"More waiting isn't really what I want to do right now. Christ... the longer I keep sitting around here without knowing whether or not I am Sabastian Banks, the faster I will go grey. That's one thing that I never wanted to be was visibly grey before I turn twenty-six."

"That would be kinda cool, actually. You most certainly could use a more distinctive look," Baylor said; a little sarcasm and frankness were both intended with his words.

Terrance Jr. certainly wasn't in the right frame of mind to catch his friend's double meaning. Because of this, his immediate reaction was to send his best friend a look that he could not misinterpret. No maliciousness was there, but the message was loud and clear — now was not a good time to bust someone's balls.

"Oh, lighten up, will you?" Baylor demanded. "The more you worry about what might or might not be, the tougher this is going to be on you. You just have to be a little patient... no pun intended."

Terrance Jr. got up from his chair, went over to the sim-caf machine, and poured himself a fresh cup. For a moment like this though, he wished that there was the old kind of regular ground coffee in the agency or some Red Bull 2.0. He really needed a major caffeine pick-me-up at that moment to help him settle his nerves and to keep himself coherent.

With his freshly poured cup of sim-caf in hand, T.J. proceeded to return to where he had been sitting. Two steps from the machine, another vid-call came through, yet again jolting his nerves and causing him to spill nearly half of his fresh sim-caf. "SON-OF-A… DAMN!"

For safety reasons this time, Savanna answered the call. "Hello. Yes, he is here. Could you hold on one moment please?" She motioned for T.J. to take a seat at her desk and take the call — but he didn't budge; it was more than obvious to everyone that he wasn't up to answering this vid-call either. But Baylor refused to let his best friend chicken out this time, so he decided that he would sneak up behind him and do his best to nudge his ass over to the vid-phone so that he could answer the call.

There didn't seem to be too much resistance in his friend at that moment — that certainly surprised Baylor, considering that T.J. was a strapping young military man who could have easily hip tossed him to the ground. When they arrived at Savanna's desk, he pointed to the chair and stood adamantly right behind his friend — T.J. got the hint and took up a seat in front of the vid-screen.

As much as he could before he received the news that could potentially change his and everyone else's lives forever, Terrance Jr. gather his jumbled thoughts and then answered his call. Like a little schoolboy who was in trouble with his principle, he just sat there attentively and listened to what the hospital lab had to say. Once his call had been completed, he immediately covered his face with his hands — even though he knew that it was a useless attempt at locking himself in a bubble. But he didn't know what else to do. He just needed to forget that the world existed for a few moments in order to comprehend the enormity of the news he had just received.

No longer was T.J. teetering on the edge of uncertainty — he now had an answer to his question. Through no fault of his own, he had been living in a well-thought out lie. The path that he had been born to walk had been diverted by an individual, he now suspected, who had been motivated by utter selfishness. It was now up to him to find his way back onto the correct path. But for him to do this, he first had to take control of his unbridled emotions, search deep within his own essence, and find the strength he would need to right all that had been wrongfully done to him — and his family.

51

What was it that had caused the doubt in his mind to surface? He didn't know, but he had been right to question who he really was. The results from both the blood and DNA tests had come back positive — ninety-nine point eight percent positive. Terrance Jr. was not the person whom he always thought he was. He was without a doubt, the long lost son of Maxwell Banks.

T.J.'s face had stayed buried in his hands for an uncertain amount of time. Nobody else in the room even attempted to speak to him; they just stayed quiet and allowed him all the time that he needed to deal with this news in his own way.

After about five minutes, he finally removed his hands from his face. He then looked at each of the anxious individuals in the room, as he rubbed his tear-laden eyes dry, and tried to find the right words to say. To his surprise, the entire room respectfully stood still. No one approached him nor did they even know what to say. They only knew that, out of respect, they had to keep to themselves and wait for T.J., the young man born as Sabastian Banks, to speak. "My whole entire life has been nothing but a lie. I mean… the man who raised me, purposely lied to me. And on top of that, a malicious man is responsible for fuckin' up my whole entire life. So… what do I do now?"

Sydney and Savanna had hoped that Terrance Jr. would turn out to be Maxwell's long lost son. Yet for some reason, the revelation that he was still seemed very shocking to them both. "Um..," Sydney struggled to find the right words. "I can't imagine what you are going through right now. But both Savanna and I are more than willing to help you in any way we can."

T.J. got up from his chair and faced his 'uncle', nodding his head in agreement. "Yes… I am going to need everyone's help… especially you, Uncle Sydney. I mean, I guess that you're the only real family I have now." He then went back over to the sim-caf machine and poured himself another cup. With his back turned to everyone else in the room, he took a couple of sips. After a few uneasy moments had passed, he was able to calm himself down enough where he could function somewhat normally.

After taking another small sip of his drink, he turned so that he was facing everyone else in the room, and then said, "I was born

Sabastian Banks. From now on, that is what I want to be known as…
Ok?" He then walked over to Savanna's desk and sat on the corner of
it, looked directly at both her and his uncle, and said, "I would like for
the both of you to do me a big favor. Could you both please get this
agency straightened back up and in working order?"

"Why?" Sydney asked, curiously.

Without answering his question, Sabastian left his leaning
post, walked straight into his father's office, and he picked up that
family photo he looked at earlier in the day. He stared at it once again;
this time what he felt inside was much different. He couldn't help but
feel lost seeing that picture of himself as a baby being held by both of
his birth parents.

He stepped over to the office window, with the picture in his
hand, and stared out at the park directly adjacent to the building. "First
things first, I have to leave and go tie up a few loose ends." He turned
around and faced his uncle, who had made his way to the threshold of
Maxwell's old office. "And then when I get back, I'm going to finish
what my father had started… my real father. The black cloud that
hangs over our family has to disappear… forever!"

"What exactly are you getting at here, T.J...? Um…
Sabastian?"

"I'm going to make the people responsible for everything, pay
dearly for what they have done. They will not have the last laugh. I
can promise you that."

"If you're intending on going after Antonio Marcone and his
whole organization, then you're as crazy as your… my damn brother
was. Look what the hell happened to him. The same thing will happen
to you if you go through with this stupid idea of yours. You just came
back to our family. For God's sake, please just leave everything alone
and forget about it."

"You don't need to worry about me. I'll be careful not to
make the same mistakes my father did. I can take care of myself. I've
had seven years of military training; five in special ops. I am highly
capable of handling any situation that may occur." Sabastian then
exited his father's office and walked back through the main lobby area,
stopping at Savanna's desk. There, he placed his hand on her shoulder
and asked her for one more favor. "I'll be back in a few days. Could

you please gather all the information that my father has on Antonio Marcone? I don't even care how trivial it is. I need to familiarize myself with what this man is all about."

"You really are going after him, aren't you?" Sydney asked.

"Yes I am," Sabastian replied, firmly. "And I could surely use your support and your help."

At that moment, Sydney was brought back to just a short time ago when his brother had asked of him the exact same thing — and he refused. But knowing that he could not change the past, he decided at that moment not to make the same mistake again. This time, he would support his nephew with everything he decided to do, no matter what the risk. "Ok, I'll do whatever I can to help you." Sydney then walked over to Sabastian and hugged him tight. Never, did he honestly expect that he was ever going to have another opportunity to hold his nephew. And now that it had happened, he was going to do what his brother never had the opportunity to — he was going to be there for Sabastian and love him like any family member should. Yes, that moment was odd for the both of them, but it quickly became one of meaning.

After that family embrace was over, Sydney picked up the brown envelope that Sabastian had earlier refused to look at; the same envelope that contained his father's last will and personal letter — he then attempted to hand it to him. "Do you wish to take this with you? I mean.., now that you know who you really are."

"Not right now, Uncle Sydney. I'll look at it if I have time when I get back." Sabastian then turned and faced his longtime friend, Baylor. "I would like for you to stay behind and give Savanna and Sydney a hand."

Without hesitation, Baylor agreed. Sabastian then walked over to his best friend and placed his arm around his shoulders. "And we are going to need that information that you hacked for us after all."

"So what if I don't wish to give you that information now?" Baylor asked.

"Yeah right, bud. You'll give it to me. You always do for me what I ask of you, because I am your only true friend."

"Once again, you're right," Baylor acknowledged, sarcastically. "What would my trivial life be like if I didn't do everything that you ever ask of me?"

"Your life would be as insignificant as one single star in the entire universe is."

"So then… you're saying that the odds are only one hundred billion to one that I might actually be relevant?"

After a short laugh shared between the two of them, Sabastian said his goodbyes. He then walked out of the agency, heading out in search of some more answers; this time, it was answers to the other questions he had that all of sudden, became even more important now that he knew who he really was.

3

The past forty-eight hours had been nothing but chaos and confusion ever since T.J. had stormed out of the house. Edith had been affected the most by her grandson's hasty departure, as she had spent the majority of his young life raising him because her own son, Terrance, was always gone away on one of his many military assignments.

She was a strong-willed woman — that was because there had been numerous times over the last seven years that both of her boys were sent half way around the world by the military to some remote, dangerous, and volatile country. The not knowing anymore than what was absolutely necessary had forced Edith to become an overly patient individual with a strong resolve. This was what had ultimately helped her to stay assured that those whom she loved would always return home safely.

It was that same inner strength which now helped her to believe that her grandson was all right — but that didn't mean that she still wasn't worried sick about him. She had spent the majority of the past couple of days in her own little world, sitting on the front porch in an antique rocker, and knitting — she knitted so much that she had almost accumulated enough items to be able to set up a booth at the local flea market.

Terrance knew how strong of a person his mother was — but he also believed that what she was focusing her attention on to keep from worrying about her grandson was not at all healthy. So he decided to head out to the front porch; his intention was to speak with her about what she was doing, because he wanted her to stop what he believed was a senseless obsession with knitting, and come back inside the house where it was a little cooler and more comfortable. "Please, Mom. I really wish that you would put down those knitting needles and come back inside the house. It's not good for you to be out here all day in the blistering heat. I'm sure T.J. will be home soon."

"Maybe so, but I'd feel better if you would turn on the computer in the basement and use that satellite tracking program you have installed on it and try to locate your car. At least then, I'd have an idea as to where my grandson is."

"I've already thought of that, but I think that it is best that we just let T.J. figure out all on his own whatever it is that has gotten him so confused. If I attempted to track him down like that, he'd immediately become aware that the G.P.S. in the car had been remotely activated. That would only help to convince him even more that I am trying to stop him from confirming this wild hypothesis of his. Remember... he is still a young man trying to find his way. This is just one of those instances where an inquisitive young mind has allowed unfounded thoughts to form and cause confusion. I did, after all, basically force him into joining the military, and now, he is finally rebelling against me for that." Terrance maneuvered himself so that he was facing his mother, then placed his hand on her shoulder and said, "You need not worry. T.J. will be just fine. He is a highly trained military specialist and he can take care of himself. Once his emotions have cooled down he'll become his rational self again and he'll come back home."

Edith nonchalantly reached down, tempted momentarily to stick one of her knitting needles into her son's foot — but instead, she placed all of her knitting stuff back into the canvas bag that had been lying on the porch beside her rocker. She then got up and faced her son, staring at him with a very displeased look on her face. "My grandson would not have taken off like that had you not done something to make him so mad. What did you do to him?"

"I didn't do anything. I have absolutely no idea why he is so pissed off right now."

"Don't you go and lie to me, Terrance Mathew Burelli! Your father knew never lie to me, and you know very well that I can always tell when you do it."

As Terrance was trying to think of the right words needed to convince his mother of his innocence, a sound in the distance caught his attention — he turned away from her wrath and looked down the long gravel driveway. Under normal circumstances, he would have been happy with what he was seeing, but his gut was telling him that the moment his approaching cherry red, Ford Mustang GT III got to the house, the shit was going to hit the fan.

Three-quarters of the way down the driveway, Sabastian stopped the car. Inside it, he just sat there, waited and watched as the sun began to disappear behind the house; a coincidental metaphor that represented the pending showdown that was about to take place.

Through the early evening ambiance, the car's headlights locked in on the front of the porch and held Terrance and Edith in place like a pair of statues in an odd-looking nativity scene. After a few moments of uncertainty, Terrance finally took the initiative and broke away from his illuminated suspension. For his mother's sake, he was glad that his son had returned home. However, he was all but certain that open arms were not awaiting him. Why exactly his son had inexplicitly left, he could only guess — but that really didn't matter, as Terrance had already accepted that his past had returned to haunt him. The only thing that he could do now was try his best to limit the damage from the pending storm, knowing that when it was finally over, the family he loved and cherished was going to have a lot of rebuilding to do — if any remnants of the damage done could even be salvaged at all.

As he headed directly toward the car, a purpose in his step was there that could not be misinterpreted. However, he had only gotten a few yards away from the front porch before the car's engine roared back to life. Slowly, the vehicle then started to back away; it forced Terrance to halt his forward progress.

"Come on now, T.J. Why don't you shut the engine off and step out of the car so that we can talk?"

The car stopped backing up and then it pulled forward, turning a few degrees to the right. The driver's window then slowly inched down, fully exposing Sabastian behind the wheel. "You fucking lied to me, you bastard! My whole existence has been nothing but an elaborate, well thought out charade!"

"I never did, my son. Please shut the car off and…"

"I'm not your goddamn son, you fucking asshole!" Sabastian revved the engine, jockeyed the shifter back and forth, and rocked the car. This was his message to the man, who Sabastian had nothing but contempt for, to stay away.

Terrance was completely taken back by the way his son was acting; he had never been this defiant before. This was not good. What he feared now seemed as if it had indeed come to fruition. What small thread of hope he had held onto had just fell from his fingers. No other option was there now for Terrance to explore — he simply had to walk across a very large patch of eggshells as delicately as he could. "I'm sorry that I didn't listen to you the other day. Please T.J., just shut the car off and come on inside the house so that we can talk about whatever is…"

"You just stay the hell right where you are or I'll throw this car back in gear and leave. Oh, and just for the record, I've disabled the G.P.S." Sabastian revved the car's engine, again rocking it back and forth. "So tell me, my so-called grandmother. Have you been living the same lie as he?"

"I don't understand what you are talking about, T.J?" Not only was Edith Burelli beginning to get upset, she was also confused about the nature of the conversation that was taking place. The only thing she understood was that her grandson was convinced that her son had lied to him.

"My name is not T.J. or Terrance Jr. My real name, my birth name is Sabastian Banks. You remember that article and photos I shoved in front of your face at breakfast about that ex-cop who was murdered in Detroit? You remember how I said that I had thought that his picture looked a lot like me? You weren't interested at all with what I had to say. You just brushed me off. Well guess what? I went and did my own investigation and I found out that the murdered cop is indeed my biological father."

There it was. No other road was there for him to take that would allow him to avoid his past. Terrance had prayed that this day would never come — yet deep down inside, he knew that it would. *'Now what should I do?'* he thought. *'Should I come completely clean or should I continue to fashion more lies and try to make these wounds not seem so deep?'* "Would you please just stop this, T.J.? You are beginning to really upset your grandmother."

"You can just shut the hell up for a moment and let me finish saying what I came here to say! I went to San Antonio, Texas, where I met that murdered cop's brother. He had in his possession an existing fingerprint, blood type, and DNA record of Maxwell Bank's missing son. I took the necessary tests needed to verify my own suspicions, and the tests proved without any doubt that I am his missing son."

Edith could not believe what she was hearing. Her one and only grandson, really wasn't even her biological grandson at all. She turned to her son, now as pissed as Sabastian was, and demanded some answers. "You lied to me also, Terrance. How in the hell could you lie to your own damn mother? I want the whole truth right now!"

Terrance did not know what to say. He just stood there graceless and dumbfounded. He wondered how much his 'son' really knew. Did he know the whole story or just bits and pieces of it? Terrance lowered his head; the realization of where he now stood in his family's eyes was easy to see — there was no chance whatsoever of escaping the hole that he had dug. All that he could do was try to preserve what little dignity he still had.

With his decision now made, he trudged shamefully over to where there were cords of wood piled up — there, he leaned up against them. Knowing that he would probably go to hell for what he had done, and accepting the probability that he was never going to get his 'son' back, Terrance proceeded to lie some more. "You're right, um… T.J., I have not been straight with you. That story I told you about your mother being raped when she was a teenager by her gym teacher isn't true." Terrance paused, determining in that moment that he could probably get away with stretching the truth instead of concocting another bold-faced lie.

His performance continued, first by his wiping away a few well-timed fake tears that flowed down his cheeks. He then followed that by saying, "Even your grandmother doesn't know all of this, but while I was stationed overseas in Italy, I met this woman and instantly fell in love with her. We had only been together for a few weeks when she told me that she was pregnant with our child. Feeling that I had to do the right thing, I quickly married her. Seven months later, my wife and I were in a terrible car accident. I wasn't hurt that bad, but my wife and unborn child had sustained severe injuries. The doctors at the hospital told me that the only way my wife and the baby would even have a chance to live would be for her to have an emergency C-section. Unfortunately, my wife died on the operating table while giving birth to my son. A few days later, my son began to experience complications that were directly attributed to the car accident. The doctors did their best, but they were not able to save his life either. Ironically, he had died on the same day that your birth mother had been murdered." Again Terrance paused for a moment to wipe away some more fake tears. "I just wanted to have a son so bad. I know that it was selfish, but..." Terrance left the log pile and sauntered back over to the house. After sitting down on the top step of the porch, and again pausing to wipe away some more fake tears, he continued, "I felt like I had to do something, no matter how drastic it was, so the moment I returned home, I decided to go through the black market and contacted a man who said that he could find me a young infant boy. What I didn't know at the time, but discovered a few months later, was that the man whom I had made that deal with was the one who had actually killed your mother." One more time, Terrence paused; this time, he looked in the direction of his own mother and then continued to pile on the fake tears. "Don't blame your grandmother, as she only knew that I had lost my wife in the car accident. She never knew that I had lost my newborn a son as well. I just could not bear to tell her that her first and only grandson had died. She had no idea I had done what I did. I hope you can look beyond my transgressions and forgive me.., my son."

"I'm not your damn son," Sabastian reiterated, "nor will I ever forgive you. My real father was still alive when my mother was murdered. He never gave me up for adoption. If you knew of the murder, you should have been a man, gone to the police, and owned up to your involvement."

The truth that he was looking for, he now knew was not going to be had this day. In fact, he was pretty sure that he was never going to learn it from the man who raised him. For that reason, there was no need for him to stick around any longer. However, Sabastian's heart was allowing one person to deserved his compassion — his love, so he gestured for his 'grandmother' to come over to the car. "The only thing I believe that your son just said to me is that you knew nothing of this." Sabastian then motioned in the direction of his 'father' with his eyes. "I don't hold you responsible for any of that man's lies and deceptions. And even though you are not my biological grandmother, you will always be that to me. I love you very much. However, I've heard more than enough bullshit from your son today, so I am going to leave. Could you please pack up my stuff and ship it to San Antonio for me?" He then handed his grandmother a piece of paper with an address on it. "Please don't tell that lying asshole where I will be, as I don't ever want him to know."

"Can't we all just sit down here on the porch and work this out like civilized adults?" Terrance asked.

"There's nothing civilized about you," Sabastian declared. "Stay the hell out of my life!"

"What about your military career?" Edith asked. "You are supposed to go back soon. You just can't go AWOL!"

"Yeah, I know that," Sabastian replied. "Since I already have seven years completed, I can apply to have my status changed from active to reserve. Then in three years, I can officially leave the military when my tenure is over. He then leaned out the car window and kissed his grandmother goodbye on the cheek. When she was about halfway back to the house, Sabastian floored the Mustang and impetuously sped away, dispensing a large billow of dust and stones in the direction of his ex-father.

Before he returned to his grandmother's place, Sabastian had decided that he was going to abandon his ex-father's car once he had done what he had come to do. There were several reasons for his decision; the first one being that he just wasn't sure if Terrance would call the police and report it stolen. The second reason being, he remembered that he could use his A.C.U. military credentials to take a last minute 'bereavement' flight, paid for by the government. He didn't care in that moment that he was going to be taking advantage of the privileges that came with his enlistment and take a non-essential flight out of Ohio; he just wanted to get far away from the man who had lied to him and get back to his real family as soon as possible.

Five minutes or so after he had left the home he had grown up in, Sabastian pulled the mustang into a convenience store parking lot; this was where he had decided to abandon the car. However, before he walked away from it, a thought came to him that he would normally never consider. He knew that his ex-father had a tendency to leave his wallet and other valuables inside the vehicle; a bonehead, lazy, foolish thing that he did of which Sabastian had no qualms about claiming. He was in no way a thief, but taking what was there was in essence, an aptly parting F.U. to Terrance Burelli.

Sure enough, he hit the jackpot, as his now ex-father had left inside the car's center console a brown banking envelope that contained three hundred dollars. After using some of that money to buy some goodies for his trip, Sabastian determined it would be best that he not take a cab from the convenience store to the airport — his reasons for doing this had no justification, but he wanted to ensure that no clear trail was there to be followed, as the last thing that he wanted was for his ex-father to track where he was going.

Ninety minutes after he had started to hitchhike, he was waiting comfortably inside the terminal at John Glenn Columbus International Airport for his ride home. Ideally, a direct flight to San Antonio was what Sabastian would have preferred to take, but once again he felt that it was necessary to error on the side of caution — it was why he decided instead, to take a red-eye flight to Albuquerque, New Mexico, and from there, rent a car in order to drive the rest of the way to San Antonio.

All throughout his flight, Sabastian kept going over and over in his mind everything that Terrance Burelli had told him. A small portion of truth, he believed may have been camouflaged within his words — but he knew for sure that the majority of it was nothing but a pile of horseshit. Not only that, but his gut was telling him that the man had many skeletons in his closet — some of which he suspected his ex-father would do everything in his power to take with him to his grave. *'Whatever it may be that he is hiding from me, has to be something that if I were to ever find out, would probably destroy what little dignity he has left.'*

The drive from Albuquerque to San Antonio was just as mentally confusing as his flight had been. But it wasn't the unknowns that continued to flood his thoughts — it instead, was his memory. All of his growth, his experiences, his sorrow, every accomplishment and proud moment, which had helped to shape his life, had been tarnished — all thanks to a man who had successfully impersonated his father.

One day, Sabastian would get another chance to confront Terrance Burelli — and when that happened, if he didn't get the whole truth from him, he'd more than likely sever whatever ties there might still be. Admittedly, the temptation was there for him to just slam the door closed on his ex-father forever. However, after some soul searching, Sabastian decided to leave it open a tiny crack — it was all up to Terrance on whether or not that door was permanently shut. But until that decision was made, the answers Sabastian sought would have to wait as he had other matters of importance that took priority — the first of which called for him to take that initial step into what will surely be unchartered waters.

Sabastian was more than willing to accept the baton that was being passed on to him. And without any hint of reservation whatsoever, he embraced the huge responsibility that came with it. Like when he would serve his country, restoring his true family's honor was his born duty. And even though that entailed his having to go up against a man with absolutely no morals, he wholeheartedly believed that the path he was about to walk was one that he was destined to walk all along.

"Hey, T.J! Ah… I mean, Sabastian. It took you a long time to do whatever it was that you had to do. You were gone for almost three days. Where the hell did you go?"

"I went back to Ohio, Baylor. I wanted to confront that lying bastard. And as I suspected, he didn't give me the answers that I had been looking for. Instead, he just fabricated another elaborate story… which I know for a fact had more holes in it than a target at a firing range."

"Who exactly are you talking about, Sabastian?" Sydney asked.

"I'm talking about Terrance Burelli Sr.; the man whom I thought was my father. I wanted to find out why he had lied to me for all of these years."

"So what exactly was his reason for doing that?"

"He didn't give me a reason. I mean, what he had said to me may have had a grain of truth to it to some degree, but what part of it was the truth, I just do not know for sure."

64

"So enlighten us here," Baylor requested. "We'd all like to know what happened when you confronted him."

Over the next half hour, Sabastian let everyone know what had taken place when he got back 'home'. After his story was completed, he excused himself, walked into his father's office, sat at the desk, and looked at the framed cracked photograph of himself, his biological father, and his mother. "As of now, Terrance Burelli is the least of my worries," Sabastian said out loud, but to no one in particular. "I have a more important issue that needs to be addressed before anything else. I have to make right what has wronged the Banks family for the past quarter-century."

Sydney, who had followed his nephew into his brother's old office, partially closed the door after he entered. "As much as I can understand your desire to do that, I selfishly would wish that you would reconsider.

"I've already told you that you don't have to worry about me, Uncle Sydney. Antonio Marcone is going to pay for messing with our family. And you can cash that promise at any bank you wish."

Savanna slowly opened up the office door and joined both Sabastian and Sydney in their conversation, bringing along with her a bit of good news. "Oh by the way, while you were gone, we put together as much information as we possibly could for you about Antonio Marcone. Baylor was able to work some incredible magic on the computer and compiled some really good information."

Sabastian thanked her for her hard work. He then got up from behind the desk, maneuvered past Savanna and Sydney, and exited his father's old office — they followed him out. From there, he made his way over toward his best friend and gave him a rather stiff whack on the back in appreciation for the good work he had done — that unexpected 'love-tap' caused Baylor to spill a bit of his sim-caf. "I'm going to go out for a couple of hours. If you need me for anything, you can find me down the street at the Ironworks Gym."

"Why?" Sydney inquired, curiously.

"It's been more than five days since I have done any sort of physical training. I want to be sure that I'll be in tip-top shape before I go after Antonio Marcone. Besides, I have a lot of negative aggression that I still need to get rid of and a good workout will do just that.

When I get back, I'll want to go over all the info that everyone has gathered for me."

"Then what are you going to do?" Sydney asked.

"After studying all the data, I'm going to go to Detroit and try my best to find the man."

"Then what?" Sydney said.

Sabastian didn't answer his uncle. He instead, went over to the small fridge in the back kitchen nook and grabbed himself a rather large bottle of water to take with him to the gym. Right behind him, Sydney followed. "Then what?" he reiterated.

"I don't know. I'm just going to have to figure this out as I go."

He had already committed himself to supporting his nephew. Still, he didn't think that it would hurt to try to dissuade him one more time. "So… if I got down on these old creaky knees of mine and beg you to reconsider your plans, would you?"

"Listen, Uncle Sydney. I've made up my mind… and I'm sorry that you don't really approve. But I am going to do this… I have to."

"We really didn't need a DNA test to prove to anyone that you are my brother's son? You're just as crazy as he was to want to take on an insane madman like Antonio Marcone."

"Like the old saying goes… the apple doesn't fall far from the tree." Sabastian then placed his right hand on Sydney's shoulder in an 'everything's going to be all right' gesture. With an assured smile on his face, he then headed out the door to go and work out.

After spending two long days studying every single file that his biological father had accumulated, and reviewing the information that Baylor had obtained, Sabastian boarded an airplane and headed for Detroit. This time, he did not have to use his A.C.U. military credentials to buy the ticket, as Savanna had given him the agencies credit card to use, along with a small slush fund; money that Maxwell had always kept around the office for emergencies.

Just before his arrival in Detroit, Sabastian remembered that a former military friend of his was from there. Jerrelle Dakota Robinson was a woman of a mixed ethnic heritage; her mother was Native

American and her father was African American. Her lineage also included an interesting fact that she proudly would tell those who asked, as the ancestral tree on her maternal grandmother's side could be traced back to the late sixteenth century indigenous Brazilian tribe, Terena.

Unfortunately, Sabastian's relationship with Jerrelle ended nowhere near amicably. In his eyes, she had been solely responsible for the situation that led to her being dishonorably discharged. Admittedly, she had a temper that she just could not find a way to control; a temper that had gotten her into trouble one too many times throughout her life. It was partly why she joined the military, and it was the catalyst behind her getting the boot — all because Sabastian's father, Major Terrance Burelli, had lit her fuse. What had happened was —

Unexpectedly, Jerrelle had been invited to participate in one of the on-base military residences' gaming nights. Although these places were generally off limits to everyone except for senior officers, she knew that a once in a lifetime opportunity to gamble with her superiors was one that she just could not turn down.

It had been commonly known throughout the base that Jerrelle loved to play cards; either poker or black jack — and was good at both. She was so good at cards, that none of her fellow soldiers were willing to lose any more of their hard earned money to her.

The senior officers were always up for a new challenge. And that particular night, they knew that they were going to be short a player for their monthly game, so they openly invited Jerrelle to join them for a night of Texas Hold-em, just to see if she was as good at cards as what the rumors claimed. Unbeknownst to all of Jerrelle's military brethren, she had developed a knack for counting cards; a self-taught talent that she had acquired as a youth on the streets of Detroit. And it was that ability which had also allowed her to recognize when someone else was cheating.

That night, she had decided to play fair — she didn't think that it would be a wise move on her part to take advantage of her senior officers. But never in a million years did she think that her friend's father would do what he did — and he didn't hide it well either. Had it been once or twice that night, Jerrelle would have just ignored it, but his blatant cheating had taken place every single hand. Counting cards was one thing, but going under the table and deliberately switching out your cards with a stashed deck was a reckless maneuver — only an utter moron would be that sloppy when trying to deceive someone.

After an hour of watching Major Burelli switch out his cards, she threw down her hand and declared that she was done. She wasn't going to say anything; she was just going to leave. But those who were in the room all objected, stating that they had made a special exception in order to allow her to play cards with them.

In that moment, she drew an unfounded conclusion — the whole entire evening had been planned in order to see how she'd react. Her known anger issues were still very prevalent, even though the disciplined world of the military had admittedly started to help her gain some control. In her mind, all of these senior officers were intentionally trying to get her to blow a gasket because they either wanted to simply enjoy a laugh at her expense or they were trying their damndest to get her ass dishonorably discharged. Whatever the reason was, Jerrelle was not going to play their game.

In hindsight, she should have just walked away at that moment — but that was something she had never done before in her life. Instead, she felt that she had to stand her ground — without stepping to hard on the wrong toes. So she simply sent an accusatory glance over at Terrance Burelli; staring just long enough in order to imagine herself ripping of his head — that brief amount of time was also long enough for everyone in the room to understand just how unimpressed she was with the major.

Although no words had been exchanged, Terrance Burelli felt the need to plead his innocence; his fellow brethren each supported his claimed affirmation. This show of injudicious solidarity caused Jerrelle's short fuse to get lit — and it quickly reached a point where she was seriously thinking about taking a swing at her friend's father. Her doing that though, would only accomplish what she was convinced they wanted from her.

Several of the senior officers looked like they were anxiously waiting for her to explode, but Jerrelle wasn't about to appease them — not because the angel on her shoulder had somehow been able to stay there long enough to convince her not to, but because she knew that if she stayed around any longer, what she wanted to avoid, would become a reality, as the last thing she wanted was to return to her old life and an awaiting sentence that she would be obliged to complete.

After surprisingly making it through the evening without an incident, Jerrelle was surprisingly called in to see her commanding officer the following morning. She was then promptly notified by him that she had been put on report for inappropriate conduct and warned that another such report would be cause for some disciplinary action to be taken against her.

Again, her anger started to boil, as she had done nothing wrong to warrant this verbal reprimand. In fact, she was stunned that what had taken place in the officers' residence had been reported to her commanding officer — the card games themselves, though technically not illegal because they took place on base, were known to be frowned upon by the upper brass of the military. However, they had continually chosen to turn a blind eye to them because not once had the gatherings ever gotten out of hand.

Needless to say, this unnecessary warning she had received, fueled Jerrelle's contempt for her friend's father. In fact, she became so incensed at the preposterousness of it all that without taking a moment and thinking of what the consequences might be, she stormed over to the military conference building and barged inside, where she then promptly disrupted the in progress symposium.

As soon as she entered the building, she took a direct route to where Major Burelli was sitting. She stopped right in front of his table and immediately made it known to those who were sitting around him that he was a liar, a cheat, and an asshole. It wasn't just her intent to center out Terrance Burelli in front of everyone for the fucking bastard that he was, the vindictive part of her personality wanted to ruin his reputation. So she jumped up on top of the table and made sure that the entire room full of delegates, dignitaries, and military officials, could clearly hear her when she openly accused the man of being a crooked piece of scum who had ripped her off the previous night.

Out of the corner of her eye, she could see that the M.P.'s were making their way over to her from the rear exits of the room. She knew that if she left, escorted by them without incident, then she would probably just end up with another proverbial slap on the wrist — but she just didn't care at that moment. Whatever form of disciple that was to come as a result of what she now felt she had to do, she was willing to accept. The perfect opportunity was there, and she wanted to make sure that her point was taken seriously.

Right before the M.P.'s had arrived, she jumped off the table and in one unexpected move, hauled off and decked the seated major. Needless to say, Jerrelle had gotten lucky when it came to the consequences of her actions. By the time the results from her hearing had been handed down, the provisions that went along with her decision to initially join the military had expired. And even though she had disgraced the uniform of her country and been kicked to the curb, she really had nothing to complain about, as she no longer was bound to the system.

— At the time of the incident, Sabastian had defended his father, not knowing that those statements Jerrelle had made about him may actually have been true. He wasn't sure if his ex-father was a cheater, but he now knew for sure that he was definitely a liar. Some big-time sucking up on his part would definitely be required before his old friend would even contemplate helping him out.

Not knowing exactly where in Detroit he should start to look for Jerrelle, Sabastian decided to first try his luck in the New Woodward district of the city; also recently dubbed by those who frequented the area as 'The Hub' in the 'D'. Sabastian recalled her telling him several times before that this was the area of the city where she used to always hang out — and it was also a place where she more often than not, got into some kind of trouble. The last occurrence, although it oddly hadn't taken place there, her record and reputation was all the ammunition that the courts needed to force her into an ultimatum — either risk doing three years of jail time or enlist into the Ameri-Can Union's Military. Not wanting to go to jail, she reluctantly chose the military. At the time, she truly doubted that anything good would come from this unwanted option. And although no significant changes in her had taken place during or after her dishonorable discharge, she did feel like a different person — she just didn't really know what that difference was.

Thankfully, Jerrelle had made it just past three years of military service. Had she been thrown out before that time, she would have then had to serve whatever remaining time she would have been short of the three year period in jail — plus another year on top of that for not completing the mandatory requirement set out by the judge.

'Let's see here… If I were a delirious, malicious, egotistical female, which one of these so-called high class second-rate establishments would I frequent?' Unsure of where to begin his search, Sabastian chose to just walk about 'The Hub' until he came across a place that he felt might be the kind of establishment where Jerrelle would hang out. Lucky for him, he didn't have to walk the entire twenty-block area, as he just happened to be stopped in front of the right place at the right time.

Sabastian must have been having a good day without even being aware of it, because approximately thirty feet in front of him, two rather tall and robustly built A.I.'s exited out of the 'Hole'n D'Wall Nightclub' — not of their own freewill, mind you, but it clearly appeared as if somebody really didn't like them too much.

Satisfactorily, Sabastian smiled as he looked over toward the front entrance of the bar. Right there, walking out of it, was who he came looking for — and she was angry as hell.

"Get up you assholes!" Jerrelle ordered. "Get up and fight like the sorry excuses for the artificial idiots that you are."

Believe it or not, that stern command came from a damn good-looking woman. At a glance, her appearance generally did not intimidate anyone. She stood approximately five-foot seven and weighed just shy of one hundred and twenty pounds. Her hair was straight, deep reddish-brown, and somewhat long. And although her face didn't have any distinctive features, her brown-green eyes and dark complexion seemed strangely to help enhance her evilness whenever she got angry.

Today, like most days, the clothes she wore would be considered mundane: her denim jeans were not too tight and her dark-grey, half-cut T-shirt contained no ads or sayings — it also barely concealed her slightly above average endowment. "Get up you low-life useless pieces of trash! You both need to be taught a serious lesson.., one that your mama obviously forgot to teach you once you finally got off the tit. You see, we women… We're not put on this earth for Cro-Magnon men like yourselves to use and abuse or jump on and ride like a surfboard whenever or wherever you feel like hanging 'ten'. That of course, I'm sure is an exaggeration. Maybe the next add-on you get, should be one that would compensate for the 'six' I would be willing to bet you both were born with."

Sabastian just stood there and enjoyed the verbal assault, quietly laughing under his breath as his old friend was on a roll. And although the two A.I.'s probably deserved the ass-chewing they were getting, Sabastian was certain a lesson was all that they needed and not the ass whooping he feared was going to come next.

So that did not occur, Sabastian strategically made his way closer to Jerrelle, while at the same time, making sure that he stayed back behind her line of sight, as he didn't want to spook her and receive an unexpected spin kick to the head. "Well… I see that you haven't changed one little bit. That short fuse of yours still lights as easy as ever."

Immediately, Jerrelle pivoted and saw her old military buddy standing there with a wry smile on his face. "T.J.! What the fuck are you doing in my city?"

"It's real good to see you too."

"You know that I have nothing to say to you. You have until I'm finished pulverizing the snot out of these two assholes to leave Detroit. I don't ever wish to see you or that crooked son-of-a-bitch you have for an old man ever again. For your own safety, just go back to the military and stay there."

Sabastian looked over at both of the A.I.s that Jerrelle had bounced out of the bar and of whom she wanted to rip limb from limb — he could actually see a bit of indecisiveness on their faces. All that he really wanted to do was speak with his old friend, but until the prey that was on her radar was gone, that would not be possible.

Like so many times in the past, it was up to Sabastian to look out for the best interest of his old military friend. Yes, she might end up hating him even more then what she already did, but he needed her to stay out of jail. So he took a purposeful step forward and addressed the A.I.s. "Trust me when I say, she may look harmless, but if you half-breeds don't wish to add anymore artificial parts to your bodies, then you best high tail it the hell out of here real fast before she does what she obviously intends to do to you."

Needless to say, those two A.I.'s took Sabastian's advice and split — not because they were afraid of her, but they were smart enough to see that she was one of those psycho type chicks who could actually do some serious damage to them. "What the fuck did you do that for? They deserved what I was planning on doing to them."

"You do remember, Jerrelle, I used to always watch your back. I did my best to try to keep you out of trouble."

"You're full of shit!" After taking a few seconds, she redirected her obvious disappointment toward her old friend and said with the utmost of intent, "You know what? Since you shooed away my fun, I ought to go ahead and do to you what I was about to do to those two."

There clearly was a savage look in Jerrelle's eyes — it was one though, that Sabastian believed he could sooth. "Have you forgotten that we are evenly matched? There is no need to be wasting your time or mine.

"I have lots of time to waste."

"Come on, now. We used to be good friends... or have you forgotten that as well?" Sabastian then extended his hand, hoping for the gesture to be returned.

"At one time... yeah, we were," Jerrelle acknowledged, blatantly refusing to accept Sabastian's attempted handshake at the same time, "but we're not anymore." After a few seconds of tension shared between them, she said, "Just get lost. I don't ever want to see you again."

"Well... I'm not leaving, as I came specifically to straighten a few things out." Sabastian then took a few steps toward his old friend only to be halted by her raised hand.

"We have nothing to straighten out." Jerrelle was starting to get annoyed with her one-time friend and his petty talk, so she turned her back to him. She then headed back toward the front entrance of the bar from which she had earlier exited. Just as she was about to cross the threshold of the front entrance, she suddenly stopped, turned back around, looked sternly at Sabastian, and said, "I can understand your willingness to stand by your old man's side and support him, but you failed to look beyond the trees and just accepted what you could only see in front of you. At that point, it became crystal clear to me just how much of a friend you really were. I don't need people like you in my already fucked up life. Goodbye forever, T.J.!"

Jerrelle pivoted around and went back inside the establishment; she purposely left her past standing out on the sidewalk and hoped he would get the hint that she wanted nothing to do with him. But Sabastian wasn't about to be abandoned. He had come a long way to speak with her and he wasn't leaving until she heard what he had come to say.

After first letting two somewhat inebriated couples walk in ahead of him, Sabastian entered the establishment. Once inside, he couldn't even find his own feet for it was extremely dark and full of smoke, the music was loud and distorted, and the place stunk of beer, drugs, and even reeked somewhat of urine. Why Jerrelle would frequent a place like this, he had no clue?

Carefully, he made his way to the bar, maneuvered himself onto the cleanest seat that was available, and then scanned the room as best as he could — he did not find Jerrelle anywhere amongst the patrons inside the better-than-half-full club. Eventually, his old friend was going to have to come to the bar and get herself another drink. Therefore, Sabastian decided that it would be best that he stayed right where he was, observe the place, and wait. However, he hadn't been seated for more than a half a minute when he felt this strange, hot and sweaty, callused hand, fondle the back of his neck — right along with some stagnant breathing which repulsively penetrated his ear. Underneath this nauseous exhalation then came a masculine toned, vulgar, and unacceptable offer, which in turn made Sabastian want to smash the individual in their face.

Not wanting to cause a scene, he promptly vacated his seat and headed toward the back exit of the bar. Again, luck couldn't have been a more important advantage for him, for over by the alleyway exit he saw Jerrelle standing nose to nose with one of the club's bouncers. As Sabastian began to maneuver toward his ex-friend, another bouncer came out from around the corner and headed straight for her waving a shock stick. It didn't stay in his hand for long though, as Sabastian stepped up behind him and promptly extricated it. After tossing it off to the side, he placed the man in one of the many sleeper-types of holds he had learned from his S.N.A.F.U. training, a hold that quickly caused the bouncer to lose consciousness.

As soon as Sabastian had disposed of the oversized gnat, he looked over at Jerrelle and could not help but smile. She had also efficiently disposed of her own opponent. "Before you even open your mouth, Jerrelle, you're going to listen to what I came here to say."

"Then you best make it damn quick, T.J."

"Not here though. As soon as someone figures out that two of their doormen have been decommissioned, this place is going to get crazier than a circus sideshow freak farting fire."

After leaving out the back exit, Sabastian motioned for Jerrelle to follow him. A couple of alleys, a church parking lot, and two blocks later, they stopped. It was here that Sabastian believed they had ventured far enough away from the club that any chance of them being pursued, seemed rather slim.

At a bus stop bench was where they continued with their conversation. "Ok, with it now appearing as if we've cleared all foreseeable danger, I'm giving you one minute T.J. to say to me what it is that you risked your health to say."

After a moment spent catching his breath, Sabastian said, "What I want to tell you is that the sorry excuse for a father I have has also gone and stabbed me in the back."

Bewilderment instantly stunned Jerrelle — yet at the same time, she found what Sabastian had just told her somewhat difficult to believe.

"I just found out a few days ago that for the past twenty-five years, the bastard has been living a big lie… and the big lie was me."

"What the hell are you talking about, T.J.?"

"Major Terrance Burelli, my dear old dad is far from that. My name… My name is not Terrance Burelli Jr. My real birth name is Sabastian Banks."

"Sabastian?" Jerrelle repeated as she let out a slight chuckle. "Yeah right.., whatever you say." In all honesty, she could care less what her old military friend had to say to her. However, she was curious as to how this anecdote was going to end, so she decided to humor him for a bit longer — although, she had no intent on letting him think that she was actually buying into any of it. "I wasn't born yesterday. So if I were you, I'd get to the point before I knock you out for actually thinking that I am gullible enough to believe what surely is going to end up being a very poor, composed of fiction."

"I swear to you, Jerrelle, that what I've said is the honest truth. Do you remember hearing in the news a few weeks back about that former Detroit cop who had been murdered?"

"I'm assuming that you are referring to the one that they found encased in concrete and sunk in the Detroit River. So what's this got to do with you?"

"A lot."

Jerrelle doubted it, but she could not deny what she was seeing; that same seriousness in her ex-friend's eyes that she had seen many times before. For that reason alone, she no longer felt an urge to blatantly dispute what he said, just because it seemed to be a bit too farfetched. "Ok. I'm all ears."

"Twenty-five years ago, that cop's wife was murdered and his young son had disappeared."

While shaking her head in acknowledgement at Sabastian's statement, Jerrelle removed a package of gum from her front pants pocket. After extracting and unwrapping a stick, she placed it into her mouth and then let the foil wrap fall from her hand onto the ground. "Let me guess... You think that you could be his long lost son? Please... That's absurd."

"I don't think I am. I'm one hundred percent positive that I am. I'm the spitting image of him." Sabastian then showed Jerrelle the photo he had on his palm-top of Maxwell Banks as an RCMP cadet.

"Just because you think that you look like the man, doesn't automatically make you his kid. Where's your proof, T.J.?"

This conversation was now heading in the direction that Sabastian had hoped it would. He now had Jerrelle's attention. However, he knew the time that she was giving him was soon going to disappear if he couldn't find a way to take her skepticism and turn it into an unquestionable belief. "I went to San Antonio the other day and found his younger brother, Sydney. He had an existing record of his missing nephew's fingerprints, blood type, and DNA profile. After a few medical tests, the results came back positive. I matched them all perfectly."

Jerrelle deliberately chomped away at her gum. "Ya, right! You know, I've got better things to do than to listen to a desperate man stoop to such a pitiful level in order to try and repair what can't be. Take this as a friendly warning; one that will never happen again. Leave my city and go back to being a good little soldier under your father's command. Otherwise, the retribution that I one day intend to get against your father, will be achieved by proxy. I hope you have a good insurance plan." Jerrelle then turned her back and started to walk away from Sabastian.

"Just you hold on there a minute!" Without even thinking that he may have just made the biggest mistake of his life, Sabastian reached out and firmly grabbed Jerrelle by the arm. He then stood nose-to-nose with her and stared coldly into her eyes. "I'm not fuckin' joking! Will you discard you cynicism and just listen to me?" Sabastian was lucky, for if it had been anyone else that had grabbed her arm as hard as he had, Jerrelle would have sent that person straight to the hospital. However, that always fearless person whom she had once known, never before had backed down when he knew that he was in the right. And with the way he was now looking at her, she no longer could deny what was transpiring right in front of her.

Jerrelle yanked her arm away from Sabastian and stood there motionless for a brief moment. She thought back to all the years of trust and respect that she once had for her him. Her back had always been protected and never before, had he lied to her. The remembrance of that fact must have been why the usually short fuse she had, never got lit. Had that happened, she undoubtedly would have done something to Sabastian that she was now certain, she would regret.

"All right T.J., I'm listening."

"When I tried to confront my so-called father, he made up this elaborate story. He tried to convince me that he had purchased me when I was a baby via the black market." Sabastian then went on to explain to Jerrelle in detail the entire tale that his ex-father had told him. Once he was done, and after a few moments of awkward silence, he extended his hand apologetically to Jerrelle, hoping that this time she might find some room in that stone heart of hers to accept his genuine offering. "I don't know if this is too late or not, but I'm real sorry for not believing you back then. I should have realized that my so-called-father, that bastard, was a two-faced lying, anal retentive asshole."

Hearing her old friend's sincere apology was something that she never thought she'd ever hear. She had built up so much animosity toward him, not once had she ever contemplated giving him an opportunity to do what he just had — nor did she think that she'd consider accepting his admission. It was in moment when she decided that she was ready to bury the hatchet and re-connect with her old friend. This had never happened to her before, but for once in her life, she truly believed that she might have completely misjudged someone. "You really are serious, aren't you?"

"For as long as you've known me, Jerrelle, have I ever not been completely honest with you?"

Jerrelle removed the gum from her mouth and stuck it on the back of the bus stop bench. She then looked her old friend in the eyes and did something else she never thought would happen — she returned the apology. "I too am sorry. I should not have been so closed-minded. It's my fault that I let our friendship be destroyed over something that had absolutely nothing to do with you."

"I can understand why you did what you did. I probably would have done something similar if I had been in the same situation that you were in."

Jerrelle rose up off of the bus stop bench and re-sealed the bond that had been broken by extending her hand. After a few quiet moments of a renewed understanding, she smiled. "I don't know where to even begin, I mean… I don't even know what I should even call you?"

"You can start, Jerrelle, by calling me your friend again."

The handshake then turned into a long 'I'm sorry, my friend' embrace; an embrace that became a bit awkward when the city bus stopped in front of them, as it naturally had assumed that they had been waiting for it. Ignoring the stopped bus, they both felt at ease now that they had renewed a friendship that never should have gone sour.

Not knowing what they should do next, they just started walking, side-by-side, down Woodward Avenue in the direction of the river. "Oh and... what the hell was going on with you and those two doormen back inside the bar?" Sabastian asked.

"They were just a little upset at me for tossing out those two A.I.'s. Apparently, those jackasses were the boyfriends of the two doormen."

After a brief chortle and a roll of the eyes at what Jerrelle had just confessed, Sabastian started the task of explaining to her in detail everything that he had learned about his real father, Maxwell Banks, and his nemesis, Antonio Marcone. By the time he had finished, they had walked eight blocks to the riverfront to an area that at one time had been a train yard.

They both climbed up onto an old loading platform and sat quietly staring across the river at the city on the other side, Windsor, Ontario, Canada. The few moments of unsure silence between the two of them was soon broken when Sabastian took the initiative and opened up his soul to his old friend by letting his emotions enlighten his already amazing story. By the time he had finished elaborating on everything he had been through during the past few days, the normally unyielding Jerrelle had a brief show of emotion herself — a small tear, which she nonchalantly wiped away.

Out of respect for her old friend, Jerrelle just sat there quiet. She had a feeling that Sabastian hadn't just come to Detroit to apologize; that he actually wanted her help with something. And sure enough, when he finally revealed what that was, Jerrelle placed her hand on her friend's leg and looked straight into his eyes. She didn't have to answer him, as the relief that consumed him was easy for her to see.

This was the moment that a small part of her had always held out hope for, but honestly never thought would occur. And now that the rift in her friendship with Sabastian had been repaired, an opportunity just might one day present itself for her to get what she so desperately wanted — revenge against Major Terrance Burelli.

With Sabastian now on her side, she knew that the chances of what she yearned for, had increased tenfold — all that needed to happen now were for the planets and the stars to align, and then the asshole Major would promptly regret the day he had decided to screw with Jerrelle Dakota Robinson.

4

Savanna had briefly mentioned that the day before Sabastian's
father had been murdered, he had received an unexpected vid-call from
a past acquaintance of his named Chevy; his old reliable snitch.
Sabastian had to start somewhere, so it made sense to him that the
informant was first person that he needed to have a talk with. But, this
wasn't his city, so he asked Jerrelle to use whatever connections she
had in an attempt to find out exactly who this Chevy person was and
where he was located. Once she had gathered all of the information
that she could about him, they would then get back together and figure
out what their next logical step would be.

The next morning, with Jerrelle out and about looking for
information, Sabastian had decided to use his free time to do two
things: head out to the Holy Cross Cemetery and pay a visit to his
parent's gravesite, and then make an unannounced appearance at the
State Capitol Building where his father's ex-boss was. His arrival
there, Sabastian was certain, was going to shock a few more people.

He had walked the grounds for about five minutes before he
finally found what he was looking for. Minus the few blades of new
grass that were beginning to poke through the bare earth that had been
laid atop of his father's burial site, finding where his parents were laid
to rest was surprisingly easy. As he approached, a flood of emotions,
some that he had never experienced before, began to surface. He oddly
felt out of place; like he didn't belong — like a stranger who
disrespectfully was disturbing their peace. He thought about turning
away and leaving, but he just could not move, as a weird feeling
consumed him and held him there in place.

Opting to disregard what was overwhelming him; Sabastian
took a few steps toward the head of his mother's grave, knelt down,
and then placed the flowers he had brought with him inside the copper
vase that was there. Again, an unexpected sensation ran through his
veins. This time, it was a feeling of pain — of loss. Unbeknownst to

himself, he began to weep; not for the loss of his parents, but because of the love he knew they had for him of which he would never know or feel.

He knelt there for — he didn't know how long, but knew that as much as he didn't want to say goodbye, the time had come for him to take the first step down the path that he had been born to walk. "I promise you both that I will not rest until our family's honor is restored."

After making his declaration, Sabastian left the cemetery and headed for the State Capitol Building. As he was ascending up the front steps of it, an uncertain thought popped into his head. This was a governmental office building and he wasn't sure if he would be allowed to see Christopher White unannounced — but he had to. So after a few moments spent looking around the front lobby area, and then determining where the governor's office was located, Sabastian decided that he would try the same method that Savanna had told him she and Sydney had successfully used. *'Here goes nothing,'* he said to himself.

Relief washed over him when he made it to his destination unimpeded. But just because he was where he wanted to be, didn't mean that he was going to get what he came for. Nevertheless, Sabastian confidently entered the anteroom, walked up to the reception desk, and said, "Good afternoon, miss. By chance would the governor be available? I wish to see him if that is at all possible."

Sylvia had been filing paperwork at the rear of her rather large cubical area, so her back had been facing her desk and the main lobby area of the office. The governor had no appointments booked this day, so she immediately knew that once again, someone had slipped past their security. This was happening all too frequently and Sylvia was beginning to get just a little bit perturbed.

In response to her unwanted visitor, she slammed closed the filing cabinet drawer; her actions caused Sabastian to slightly flinch and instantly feel uneasy. *'It must be that time of the month,'* he could only assume.

With a series of unkind words ready to be spoken, Sylvia turned to face this individual; her intent was to give them a piece of her mind for their unauthorized arrival and then call security to have them escorted off the premises. However, it was the unexpected surprise that froze her in place. No longer was she pissed off — she instead, was totally stunned. She didn't mean to, but she just could not help but stare at this young man; this rather ghostly, unreserved image that was standing only a few feet away from her. Sylvia didn't know who this man was, yet she thought that she must, for this stranger seemed dauntingly all too familiar to her.

"Um… Are you all right, miss?" Sabastian asked.

After a few uneasy moments, Sylvia collected herself and apologized for her needless staring. "I'm sorry, it's just… you look so much like a younger version of someone that I met not too long ago."

"I didn't mean to spook you like that. I've come here to see the governor, if that is at all possible? I wish to talk to him about an old friend of his."

Sylvia's mind was still a bit out of sync, but she was able to notice that Sabastian was wearing a State Capitol tour badge that read 'Bill'. *'I need to have a little talk with whoever 'Bill' is about his missing tour badges,'* she thought. "Um… and who might that friend of his be?"

"Maxwell Banks. I'm his son, Sabastian."

A slight chill raced up Sylvia's spine. This strange encounter had just taken an unexpected turn and was beginning to get just a little bit too surreal for her. However, before she could even fully assemble and ask one of the many questions that was still formulating in her mind, it instantly brought forth the day she had met Maxwell, and fused it with the exact moment when she first saw this stranger. She felt as if she was living in a moment of déjà-vu — only this was way too real to be possible. *'Could this actually be Maxwell's missing son?'* she thought. *'Or am I just an unwilling participant in a bad episode of the twilight zone?'*

Choosing in that moment not to search for the answers, Sylvia decided instead to just place this mystery in the lap of the governor and let him figure it out. But there was one problem with doing that — how she was going to approach her boss with this little problem and not come across as being completely off her rocker?

After a few moments spent gathering her thoughts, she turned on her vid-phone and created an excuse that she hoped would get the governor to come out of his office. She told him that she had accidentally spilled her sim-caf onto the health care budget documents that he had asked her earlier in the day to file — Sylvia just hoped that he wasn't sharp enough today to remember that she never drank sim-caf.

Less than a minute later, the governor came out of his office. On his way toward Sylvia's desk, he said, "What do you mean you spilled sim-caf on those documents? Since when did you start drinking..?" Disbelief surrounded the governor, for he stood there staring at Sabastian like Medusa had just frozen him. Immediately, his memories took him back twenty-five years. "JESUS-FUCKING-CHRIST!" he said under his breath.

It took more than a few moments for the shock to wear off, but eventually the governor was able to gather himself. However, he certainly didn't want to jump to any conclusions, so he invited Sabastian to take a seat in the lobby area. Sylvia promptly took up a seat against the front edge of her desk; the governor and Sabastian each claimed one of the unoccupied chairs that were lined up against the wall and directly across from her.

It was a good thing that Christopher's schedule this day was wide open, because his unexpected meeting with Sabastian had lasted more than an hour — and at the conclusion of it, he realized that yet again, his life had changed. Maxwell's death had affected him more than he ever thought it could. Now, with the man's long lost son suddenly appearing at his front door, a second chance was being given of which he never thought would come his way. No longer was Christopher going to follow the rules — and he didn't care what the outcome might be. He was going to listen to his heart from this moment forward and do whatever was necessary to help make things right.

After Sabastian had finished explaining his unbelievable story and what his intentions were, he sat there quiet for a moment and allowed the governor and his secretary to absorb it all. He fully expected that a vehement protest would be given pertaining to what he was planning on doing — and that was all right, as he honestly never came here to receive the blessing of his father's friend. He only wanted his help with one thing.

Christopher had admittedly made many mistakes in his life. The largest of them all was not turning a blind eye to his responsibilities and helping his longtime friend with his crusade. Maybe it was the succession of past mistakes back when he was a police captain, or maybe it was the fear of the repercussions that would follow if he were to buck the system and do what he knew in his heart, just had to be done. Whatever it was, that no longer seemed to matter. In some capacity, Christopher White had represented the people of Detroit and the State of Michigan for a combined thirty-five years, and he knew that his ongoing servitude wasn't going to last forever. The end of his career was just around the corner, so if he was ever going to step up to the plate and help to make things right, now was the time — and whatever backlash was to come from this, he was content to accept it.

Without an ounce of hesitation, the governor agreed to help Sabastian in any capacity that he was able to, starting with his asking Sylvia to copy all of the digital and hard copy files that he had personally accumulated over the years on Antonio Marcone. Then, he took a few moments and informed Maxwell's son about all of the currently known D.U.O. activities in and around the State of Michigan. Lastly, Christopher let Sabastian know where the organization's new headquarters was located — on the top floor of the recently renovated, New Book Cadillac Hotel and Casino.

"I really do appreciate all of your help, Governor. However, I don't mean to be rude, but I must be going. I've been here much longer than I anticipated and I'm running way behind schedule. I have to meet up with an old friend of mine very shortly."

"Hold on a minute!" The governor promptly left the lobby area and went back to his office, returning a few moments later with a small box in hand. He placed the box on top of Sylvia's desk and removed the contents, placing them into Sabastian's hand. "This was your father's police revolver and badge. I always kept it as a personal homage to the best damn cop that ever worked for me. I think that you should have these, so that you have something of your father's to remember him by. Besides... your father's gun may one day come in handy." The governor then paused for a moment, staring at Sabastian and briefly reflecting on his own past. "It's just a damn shame that your father never had the chance to find you before he died."

"I too wish that I had the chance to find my father before then, but unfortunately, it took his death for me to search out who I really was, or I probably would have never known."

After shaking the governor's hand and saying goodbye to his secretary, Sabastian left. What awaited him, he could only speculate. However, with what he had just learned and with now having a small piece of his father with him, he felt more confident than he had before that he was going to finish what should have ended a long time ago.

They had previously made arrangements to meet at the River Rat Restaurant at two p.m. for a late lunch. That had come and gone; Jerrelle was the only one there on time. Even though they both had vid-cells, they had unthinkingly forgotten to exchange numbers. Therefore, waiting for Sabastian was the only thing that she could do.

To pass the time, Jerrelle took up a seat at the bar side of the restaurant and ordered herself a beer. She loved beer, but hated being in places like these; places where she felt like a fish out of water — which was confirmed by the looks that she was receiving from some of the stylishly dresses patrons having either a business luncheon or an informal date. *'With a name like 'River Rat', you'd think this place would be more of a dive,'* she thought.

By the time she had finished off half of her Stroh's Bohemian Pilsner, Sabastian had finally joined her at the bar. "I'm sorry that I'm late, Jerrelle. I didn't realize how far of a drive it was to the State Capitol Building. Plus, I was longer than I thought I'd be at my parents' gravesite." Sabastian flagged down the bartender, ordered himself a pint of Budweiser, and asked for a menu — with everything that Sabastian had been through over the past few days, he barely had time to eat and his body was beginning to feel the lack of proper nutrition.

"I kind of figured that you would visit your parents' graves, T.J... I mean, Sabastian. That must have been hard on you?"

"Yes, it was." Sabastian kind of chuckled to himself, for he knew that it would take some time for Jerrelle to get used to calling him by his birth name. After all, it was still weird for him to accept that he was actually someone other than who he always thought he was.

During his little laugh, the bartender had returned with his beer and to take his order. Jerrelle was really not that hungry, but Sabastian had encouraged her to get something to eat, not knowing what the rest of the day would bring.

"So… what happened at the governor's office?"

"Well, I certainly shocked the hell out of everyone there, especially the governor. I look so much like my real father that he almost swore he saw a ghost."

"I really don't care if he swore that he had a visit from God himself," Jerrelle said mockingly. "Did you learn anything that could help us?"

"Maybe? The governor did give me a copy of some files he had on the D.U.O…, but I have yet to look at them. However, he did inform me of something that I did not already know. Apparently, Antonio Marcone and his organization's operations are now based out of the New Book Cadillac Hotel and Casino. So what information did you get from your sources?"

"It was nearly impossible for me to find out any sort of information on that 'Chevy' person. I was forced to let some past skeletons out of the closet; skeletons that I had wanted to keep dead and buried for good. These people all owed me small favors that I had intentionally forgotten about. I really never ever wanted to see their butt-ugly faces again, but..." Jerrelle took a healthy sip of her beer; enough to finish most of it. "…rumor has it that Chevy lives in an old seedy apartment above an abandoned service garage on Cadieux Avenue." Jerrelle handed Sabastian a small piece of paper with his address on it.

"That's awesome. So then, I guess that we should go and pay this man a visit?" Sabastian took a healthy swig of his beer, emptying almost half of the pint.

"Of course… but not until you reimburse me five hundred bucks," Jerrelle declared.

"Five hundred bucks?" A surprised Sabastian repeated. "What for?"

"Because I had to pay for the information, so you owe me."

"I thought you just said that those friends of yours owed you some favors?"

"They did," Jerrelle reiterated. "But the information that you wanted was worth much more than the favors that I had been owed. Those only got them to willingly look for Chevy. The five hundred is what got me his address."

"Fine, just add it to my tab, will ya, Jerrelle?"

"Tab? What tab? You haven't earned the right to start a tab with me yet."

Sabastian knew that was a cheap shot, meant only to remind him that even though they had just buried the hatchet, a small part of Jerrelle might still hold a bit of a grudge toward him, so there was no reason to argue her point. Sabastian felt that it was just best to let her words end there, finish off their beers, lunch, and then head out the door before Chevy got wind of the fact that someone was looking for him.

While on their way to visit Maxwell Banks' old snitch, it was decided that Jerrelle would be the one to not only check and see if Chevy was home, but to scope out the place and memorize its layout — it wasn't that Sabastian didn't have the ability to do that, but if the man they sought saw him and figured out who he was, what they had planned would be for not.

Ten minutes after Jerrelle had left her parked car to conduct the recon, she returned — their target was nowhere to be found. They knew that they had the right place, so they just had to be patient and wait. Sabastian was; she wasn't — yet, no other choice was there for them but to hang around until Chevy came home.

Like the previous night, Jerrelle's mindset was the same as it had been when she wanted to all but kill those two A.I. assholes. Unlike last night though, she hoped that Sabastian would at least let her have some fun because she was in the mood to hurt someone — and that certain someone was an individual whose believed betrayal deserved an ass-whooping, if it indeed turned out to be true.

"So where in the hell did you get this car, Jerrelle?"

"I inherited it from my father after he passed away. Why do you ask? Don't you like it?"

"On the contrary, this car is definitely cool. But you have to admit that this is the kind of classic car that will draw a lot of attention."

Jerrelle's car was a mint conditioned, fully restored, deep wine colored, custom 69 Chevrolet Camero SS that had the classic double eight inch metallic grey stripe down the center of the entire car. The interior and the exterior were all original, but the mechanical components were not — everything had been brought up to date. The car's original V8 engine had been replaced with a modern one that ran on hybrid fuel. The manual 6-speed transmission was changed out for a high performance 7-speed and the entire chassis and suspension was upgraded — it was a beautiful piece of machinery. Jerrelle's father, Trévon Robinson, had customized the car himself by using the knowledge and experience he had gained throughout his twenties while working in the pits for several different NASCAR racing teams.

"What's wrong with a little attention? I like people to feel my presence. That way, when my prey sees me, a sense of fear instantly invades their already uneasy minds." Jerrelle abruptly stopped the conversation she was having with Sabastian because she had noticed that a man was coming out from the side alley of the building they had been watching, and walking in the direction of the front door of the garage. "It appears that luck is on our side today, Sab. I guess that we don't have to be here all night after all."

"Sab? What did you call me that for?"

"Because you went ahead and changed your damn name on me," Jerrelle reminded him. "Now I have to call you something and Sabastian just isn't working for me. It took me a while to decide between calling you either Sab or Sabby... I even contemplated calling you Sabrina. And even though you do on occasion display some female tendencies, I'll be nice and just call you Sab from now on. You're just gonna have to get used to it."

"Call me whatever you want, Jerrelle, as I really don't care at this moment. Our objective right now is to put the squeeze on this guy. You do remember what you're supposed to do, right?"

"I may be a little out of practice, but I haven't forgotten how to execute a proper infiltration. You just be ready for your cue... Sab."

They both vacated the car and headed out toward their positions; Sabastian would wait at the back of the apartment until it was time for his presence to become known and Jerrelle would enter through the front. And if everything went according to plan, they would both have a lot of fun messing with Chevy — especially Jerrelle, for she needed to act completely opposite of what her actual personality was.

He had made himself quite a bit of money working for those who needed something done or passed along, and he had no problem selling out those who had trusted him — if the price was right. He did whatever he felt he had to do to survive.

Chevy no longer needed to live in a lower class district of the city, but he had grown up in these types of surroundings and this was the area of the city where he felt most at home. But just because he chose to live where he did, didn't mean the interior of his place looked like it hadn't been touched since it was first built some fifty years ago. In fact, his entire place had recently been renovated and updated — a personal reward to himself for all of the hard work he had to do throughout his life. Unfortunately, some good people had to be thrown under the bus over the years — and the semi-luxurious lifestyle he was now living in was a direct result of his willingness to do just that.

Although Chevy was in great physical condition and still a few years away from turning fifty, the stresses from his chosen life, combined with the many injuries that he had suffered throughout it, had caused him to appear much older than he was — even his voice had slightly changed; it was much rougher sounding than it once had been. "I'm so glad that I ran into you, René," Chevy said to an empty room. "It's been way too long since you left me and ran off with that harlot, Tilly. And I'm extremely glad that you chose to move back home where you belong. There is so much that has happened that I want to tell you about, but I'm not too sure where I should start. Oh, I know. I should start by telling you about Maxwell Banks. You remember that damn annoying cop who would always harass me and take advantage of my kindness. Well.., you would not believe what happened to that cheap bastard."

While the conversation with his invisible friend continued, Chevy made his way toward the kitchen. As he was pouring himself a glass of water an unexpected knock on his front door startled him. "Shit! Someone is here. I think you should go and hide in the bedroom, René. I'll see if I can get rid of whoever it is." Chevy walked over to his front door, slightly pulled back the curtains, and took a quick glance through the window. He then opened up his apartment door a small crack; just wide enough for him to speak with the stranger who was standing on the other side. "Um… what can I do for you, miss?"

"Hello, my name is Jeri." Jerrelle stood there wearing a dirty blonde wig while smiling overtly at Chevy; her intent was to give off the impression that she was a not too bright first year college student. "Um… I'm canvassing door-to-door for the Intentional Disea… No, I mean International Disease Foundation. Would it be possible for you to help this worthy cause with a small donation?"

"Sorry, but I just gave away the last of my paycheck to the Society for Washed-up Politicians. With all due respect, I am getting sick and tired of your kind of people constantly bugging me for money. Besides, you should be soliciting in more respectable and safer neighborhoods than this one."

One look inside Chevy's apartment, and Jerrelle could see that he was full of shit. The man had money, but he was just being difficult. Before she even started her presentation, she had suspected that this task of hers wasn't going to be an easy one. This guy, after all, was a street snitch, and her past experiences when it came to dealing with these kinds of people told her that none of them were completely trustworthy — or commonsensical. Therefore, in order for her to accomplish her goal, Jerrelle knew that she had to push the man's buttons a little harder and hope for a reaction that she could then manipulate. So she began to cry disappointingly; her tears were hard to dismiss — even for an individual who more than likely, was a bit unstable. "You're a mean old fart!"

Jerrelle had never thought about pursuing a career as an actress. But with the way she had easily made her face look flustered and let the heavy, fake tears flow, it was now an option that she might just consider exploring one day if she were to ever get her own life straightened out. "Is it like your number one mission in life to purposely ruin the day for someone else?"

Opening up the front door all the way, Chevy stood at the threshold, looking face to face at this distraught young woman — he was beginning to buy her act. "I didn't mean to make you cry, miss. I'm sorry, it's just… I've had a really bad couple weeks and I just wish to be left alone."

"But I don't want much from you, sir," Jerrelle replied. "Just one minute of your time is all that I need."

Now feeling completely like a jerk for upsetting this young woman, Chevy apologized for the way he had treated her and invited her inside.

"Thank you, Mr..? I'm sorry. I don't know your name?"

"My name is Roy Chevalier... but my friends call me Chevy."

Jerrelle stepped inside the apartment and walked over to the coffee table that was positioned in the center of the living room. "Mr. Chevalier, sir. I have some pamphlets here for you to look over that fully explain what the International Disease Foundation is all about." Jerrelle reached into the leather satchel that she was carrying and pretended to sift through it, trying to find the non-existent pamphlets. "These pamphlets I have here describe in detail everything that we are currently involved with. The one disease that we really need funding for right now is the mutated AIDS A2 virus."

While Jerrelle was feeding Chevy all the bullshit she could, Chevy peered nonchalantly over his shoulder to the bedroom and urged René to go back inside and hide. "I promise you, miss, that I will look over your pamphlets and send your organization a donation. Unfortunately though… I mean, I don't wish to be rude or anything, but I don't have time to discuss this with you because I do have an appointment that I have to get to very soon."

"Ok… sure," Jerrelle acknowledged. "I'll leave, but only after you promise me that you'll also show my pamphlets to your friend?" Jerrelle continued to shuffle through her satchel, making it look as if she was determined, yet at the same time, frustrated that she couldn't find the correct pamphlets.

"My friend?" Chevy was now confused. *'It could not be possible for this young woman to actually see René, could it?'* he thought. "Um..? There is no one in this apartment but the two of us, miss."

"Sure there is. Just because I am blonde and an insensitive joke is generally delivered behind my back, doesn't mean that I am also blind. Is that not a friend of yours standing right directly behind you?" Jerrelle removed her right hand from inside of her satchel and she pointed directly behind Chevy.

Chevy turned to look and instantly froze. "Who in the..? Get the hell out of my apartment whoever you are, or I'm gonna call the police!"

"Go ahead and call the police," Sabastian encouraged. "But that wouldn't be a wise choice of yours considering that there is now a .357 magnum pointed at the back of your head. Ain't that right.., Jeri?"

Chevy pivoted back around and looked directly down the barrel of Jerrelle's gun; the satchel she had with her was now lying on the floor. At that moment, it became obvious to Chevy that it had been used to hide her gun and had contained no pamphlets in it whatsoever. It had also become clear to him that this young woman was no dumb blonde either, for her wig was also on the floor next to the empty satchel. "Oh please let me blow him away, Sab. I haven't killed anybody in quite a while. Though, I do promise to not get as much blood on you as I did the last time."

"Door-to-door canvassing?" Chevy said, cynically. "That was good. I'm impressed." He glanced back over his shoulder at Sabastian; a slight smirk could easily be seen on his face. He then turned about face and slowly raised his hands above his head. "Whatever it is that you people want, I don't have it. So you're just wasting your time. If it is money that you're after, I wasn't kidding earlier when I told you that I gave away the last of my paycheck."

Before they had entered the apartment, Sabastian had already assumed that Chevy wasn't going to willingly give them the information that they had come looking for. And even though it may be deemed as being ethically and morally wrong, just like when he was on one of his military assignments, if the situation called for it, he was prepared to do what he felt was necessary to accomplish his goal.

Sabastian calmly walked right up to his father's old snitch and gave him a backhand across the mouth. He then followed that up with a boot to the kidneys, which sent him directly into the white synth-leather couch that was near where Jerrelle was standing. "I think you know why we are here, Chevy, so don't screw us around!"

While Sabastian was trying to persuade Chevy into talking, Jerrelle picked up her wing and satchel and began to nonchalantly snoop around the apartment. She had all the faith in the world that her old friend would be able to get the information they needed, but finding something incriminating that they could use against him would all but assure that Chevy would not end up with any life-long scars after they left. Then again, Jerrelle had a feeling that if they didn't get what they had come for, Sabastian just might cross the line in retaliation to what had happened to his father. It was then that she realized the irony in her thought — she, actually having to be the one to prevent her old friend from going to far.

"Both of you are fucking crazy!" Chevy said, as he wiped a trickle of blood from his mouth with his left sleeve. "I don't know who you are or what the hell you want?"

"That there is my Oscar winning actress, Jerrelle, and I am her agent, Sabastian... Sabastian Banks. I'm sure you remember my father, Maxwell, don't you?"

Chevy sat there stunned, now realizing why he had briefly frozen when he had first seen this young man — he was also pissed off at himself for not seeing the clear resemblance between Maxwell and his resurfaced offspring.

While still on the edge of his couch, Chevy again wiped off a small trickle of blood that was dripping out of the corner of his mouth. He then said, "I figured that you would make an appearance one of these days, but I didn't think that it would be so damn soon. And I should have realized who you were after you hit me. You hit as hard as your father did." Chevy reached up with the back of his right hand this time and wiped off some more of his blood. "I am very, very sorry for what happened to your father. I honestly didn't know the information that I had supplied to him was bad. Believe it or not, I do miss him very much."

Jerrelle fired a shot from the threshold of the living room that barely missed Chevy's left arm — the bullet shattered a ceramic vase that sat on top of the table that was right next to the entrance to the apartment. "Bullshit you're sorry! Tell me something, Chevy. How come you have a room key to an Executive Suite at the New Book Cadillac Hotel?"

"Ok fine, I lied. I do have some money. I am actually somewhat financially secure, as you can tell by the décor in my apartment. But I don't like to flaunt my wealth around when I'm out in public. That's why I live in this part of town. I have the suite reserved for when I want to have a good time and impress the higher-class ladies. There is nothing wrong with doing that once in awhile, is there?"

"Don't get smart with us, asshole!" Jerrelle walked over to Chevy and showed him what she had in her right hand. "And I am assuming that this A.I.M. Enterprises V.I.P. membership card that I also found belongs to you?"

"It does."

"And how does someone as unscrupulous as you end up with a privileged card like this?"

"To those who gave me the card, they see me as being a very important person."

"And who might 'they' be?"

"I'm not answering any more questions from a selfish, twisted bitch like you. You can go and fuck yourself, for all I care."

Chevy's demeaning words was all that it took for the anger that had been there from the previous night to return. In Jerrelle's mind, the man had now raised himself up to the same level as those two A.I. assholes from the bar. No longer was she simply here to help her friend get the information he sought, she just wanted this snitch to experience her wrath, so she sent a swift hard kick to the side of Chevy's head — it caused him to fly over the edge of the couch and onto the floor. "It would be wise of you to truthfully answer my questions."

"And why is that, Cruella?"

Before Jerrelle had a chance to respond in-kind to being essentially referred to as a dog killer, Sabastian held up his hand — she reluctantly backed off. "You know, it's really stupid to play Russian roulette with someone who is just as deadly as an actual gun." He then took a few steps toward Chevy and said, "So, it would be in your best interest to co-operate with us, as it would be a damn shame to let someone other than you enjoy this rather fine apartment that I can only assume you worked so hard to create."

While giving Chevy a few moments to digest just how serious his declaration was, Sabastian requested that Jerrelle hand the V.I.P. card over to him. After glancing over it, he realized that it was no ordinary card. And although he did not know the reason why his father's old snitch possessed such an item, it was easy for him to assume. "Why is it that you have a V.I.P. card that is associated with the D.U.O.?"

Chevy refused to humor Sabastian. Instead, as he was finally getting back up to his feet, he just blankly looked at him. Jerrelle, on the other hand, wasn't about to let him plead the fifth, so she gave Chevy another swift kick. This time, she made direct contact with his right kneecap; his face promptly made contact with the hardwood floor.

"We can do this all day, you know," Sabastian said, as he stood over Chevy. "The sooner you tell us what we want to know, the better chance there is that you will not need a ride in an ambulance."

"You and your rabid two-bit whore can go to hell!" Chevy stated as he, with the aid of the sofa's arm, pulled himself back up onto his feet.

Any derogatory comment directed toward Jerrelle would be the same as someone stupidly pouring gasoline onto an already raging fire — it fueled the explosive nature that continually smoldered within her. She had been called a lot of things over the years, but whore was one of those key words that instantly lit her fuse.

With the obvious fire that now burned in her eyes, Sabastian knew that any chance of getting the information they had come for without any causalities being the result, was lost as the Tasmanian devil that lived within his friend, was about to be unleashed.

Without any sort of hesitation, Jerrelle struck Chevy with a solid two-handed thrust. He was subsequently launched three feet in the air and he landed hard up against the front window — the force of the impact was powerful enough to shatter the double thick glass pane and rendering Chevy firmly planted inside the window encasement. If it were not for the security bars on the outside of the window, Chevy more than likely would have gone completely through it.

For his own safety, Sabastian wisely stepped completely out of his friend's way and allowed her some space. Rarely, had there ever been a time in which Jerrelle did not succeed in getting her point across — especially when someone had called her one of the words on her list that she hated the most. No matter how suppressed a mind was, she almost never failed to successfully retrieve any forgotten memory. "Were you involved with the death of Sabastian's father? Answer me you spoiled heap of ground beef!"

Chevy was in a daze; he could hardly lift up his head. Blood not only poured out of his mouth, but a good portion of his body was now covered in an abstract-like crimson blanket due to the massive amount of gashes that he had sustained from crashing through the window.

After spitting out some blood onto the hardwood floor and taking a few moments to organize his thoughts, Chevy extracted himself from the window. It was then that he finally decided to give in — although his words began with a sarcastically toned idiom, "As a blind man once said while he pissed in the wind, I do believe that it's all coming back to me now."

Chevy struggled to stay upright. With a great deal of effort, he was able to prop his battered body up against the wall next to the broken window. He then looked at Sabastian and said, "I was offered a very lucrative sum of money from Louie Mazotti; an offer that no man in his right mind could refuse. It was enough money for me to buy a small island if I wanted to. All that I had to do was to help him with the elimination of your father. You know... your father once saved my life when I was a young man. He was, at times, a good friend to me. But he was also a very gullible man, as he didn't look out for his own best interests. I did."

Finally, Sabastian had gotten the verification he sought. Did it bother him that Jerrelle had resorted to violence to get the information? No. His father had been literally beaten to death, so in his eyes, it was a bit of poetic justice. However, he was unprepared for the fact that a man, who was supposed to have been his father's friend, had betrayed him for money. "You were one of those few people who my father trusted. How could you do this to him? How could you live with yourself for all these years, knowing that you betrayed his trust?"

"It was tough at first. You know the old saying... time heals all wounds." Chevy finally started to regain a bit more of his strength; he was now able to stand up without the aid of the wall. He then turned his body slightly and leaned his forearm up against the edge of an old antique roll-top desk. "Why don't you go back to Ohio and ask the man who raised you about betraying someone's trust? He did... and that is why you are still alive."

"What the hell are you talking about?" Sabastian instantly replayed that last statement of Chevy's in his head. He didn't quite understand what he meant, but he was certain that those words were a clue to something that would again change his world. Then, a puzzling thought surfaced in his head. "If you know who Terrance Burelli is, then you knew all along where I was. Why didn't you say anything to my father?"

"I have my reasons." Chevy slowly opened up the roll top desk and took out the cigar box that Antonio Marcone had recently given to him. He opened it up and motioned toward Sabastian with the contents that he had just removed.

"Watch out, Sab! He's got a gun!" Jerrelle instinctively raised hers.

"Don't even think about it, bitch! If you don't want anyone to get killed here, then you will put away your gun." Chevy turned his attention back to Sabastian and erratically waved his weapon. "Your father was a decent man, but an extremely obsessed one at that. Whether you believe me or not, I really did like him." Chevy paused for a moment to cough up some of the blood that had been trickling down inside his throat.

"Put the gun down, Chevy. Nobody here needs to die." Hoping that Chevy didn't pay too close attention to what he was about to do, Sabastian slowly reached around behind his back, trying to locate his father's gun. He did, but...

Chevy didn't seem to care at all in that moment about what it was that Sabastian was doing. He knew what he was about to do, and he was content that this was the way things just had to be. "I'm sure you don't believe me, but I am very, very sorry. Oh, and one more thing. Goodbye, René... my old friend."

"Please, Chevy, I beg of you not to..."

Slowly, a crack of light had begun to shine through, slightly opening up the long and dark enigmatic corridor of the tunnel. When Sabastian and Jerrelle first entered it, they assumed that they would be able to begin to assemble all the necessary clues they needed to eventually accomplish their goal. They knew that they would come across a fork in the road eventually — even a dead end or two. However, because of a burning desire to get some answers, an incident had unfortunately happened that probably could have been avoided, all because of their overzealousness. The result of their actions was now something that they each would be forced to live with for the rest of their lives.

Trying to make some sense out of this meaningless tragedy was something that neither of them at that very moment was able to do. Their forcing that path open too wide, too fast, had resulted in a heavy price being paid. It wasn't supposed to happen like this. Chevy was not supposed to die. They could only hope that his choice to end his own life was somehow his way of making restitution for his decision to turn against Sabastian's father. Then again, the man probably knew too much damaging information and decided that it was best to protect what he knew and prevent it from ever coming to light. Then, there was that statement, which Chevy had made just before he decided to end it all. *"Ask the man who raised you about betraying someone's trust. He did... and that's why you are still alive."* That had totally caught Sabastian off guard; it was a statement that he never expected to hear — and it had really struck a chord with him. His curiosity was craving to understand it, but he soon recognized that its clarity wasn't what was important. Until he had done what he had set out to do, it would have to be put aside for another day.

What bothered him more than the rest of the unknowns was how badly they had handled the situation. Their first attempt at gathering information had resulted in someone's self-termination. Both Sabastian and Jerrelle immediately recognized that they needed to adjust their current strategy. They were not conducting a military mission; this was real life. The techniques they possessed for extracting needed information had to be re-evaluated, as the last thing they wanted was another unnecessary death blooding their hands.

As soon as they got back into Jerrelle's car, Sabastian just sat there staring straight out the windshield, unsure of what to do next. He had seen someone die right in front of him before, but this was different — and Jerrelle could easily see that what had just happened was really bothering her friend. But she also knew that for them to complete their objective, Sabastian had to quickly regain his focus and forget about what they had just been a witness to; what they had unintentionally contributed to.

Jerrelle took the initiative and suggested that their next move should be for the both of them to head straight to the New Book Cadillac Hotel and Casino and use the direct approach. But as easy as that sounded, Sabastian didn't think it would be wise to try and go for the throat of the enemy without first having it be exposed. They needed to be cautious and calculating, as it was too early in the game for the Detroit Underworld Organization to become aware of the fact that someone else was gunning for them. What Sabastian wanted to do instead, was temporarily retreat. In his mind, he thought that it would be best for him to go back to San Antonio and reconvene with Baylor, Savanna, and Sydney. Not only did he welcome their opinion, but being far away from the Motor City would also make it much easier for him to get his thoughts organized. And once he was ready to resume his mission, if he and Jerrelle happened to come across a situation similar to what they had just experienced, then the chances of the same result occurring would be less likely.

With his mind made up, Sabastian asked Jerrelle to use whatever resources she had while he was away, without adding to his tab, to gather whatever pertinent information she could. Then, in a few days time, the two of them would reestablish contact with each other and determine what their next best course of action would be.

———————————————— ꙮꙮ ————————————————

Sabastian was adamantly against going directly to the root of the problem; Jerrelle completely disagreed with his sentiment, as her inner fire was coaxing her into taking the direct approach and face her friend's enemy without the obligatory net. But out of respect for his wishes, she chose instead to try and acquire some information in a completely different way. She had mad gambling skills, so it only made sense to her to use them at the New Book Cadillac Casino and purposely draw a little attention to herself.

To set up her convincing alibi, since she didn't have already it to start with, she first had to win more than twenty thousand dollars at the public black jack tables before she would be allowed to play at the high rollers table in the Elite Game Room — she just had to remember to pay attention to what she was doing and be careful at the art of counting cards so that she would not get caught.

Upon successfully winning the necessary amount of money she needed, she inquired about moving into the Elite Game Room. Her request was granted, and the on duty floor manager escorted her there. Upon her arrival, Jerrelle was told that she'd have to wait for a bit until a seat became available for her at the table. That annoyed her, but the complimentary double shot of Jim Bean on the rocks certainly made up for the inconvenience.

Thankfully, her wait hadn't been too long — thirty minutes was all that had passed before a seat finally opened up. Immediately, she felt out of place — and not just because almost everyone in the room was wearing the latest in fashion trends. She usually didn't care that she didn't fit in, but she preferred not to stick out like a sore thumb either. Getting noticed for her wardrobe was one thing — getting noticed for her gambling skills was what she soon needed to happen.

Jerrelle's plan was to spend the first five minutes or so establishing an inaccurate portrayal of who she was and her playing abilities amongst the other gamblers in the room. Intentionally, she lost the first two hands she had played, making stupid decisions that a rank amateur would make. She won the next one, and then lost two more before she won another.

She now felt like she had everyone in the room convinced that she was just one of those many gamblers who would occasionally get lucky, but really didn't know what the hell they were doing. Now, it was time for the next phase of her plan, so with that assumed opinion of her now established within the room, she began. "Excuse me, miss. How many hands am I allowed to play at one time?"

The female A.I. black jack dealer was in the middle of collecting the loser's chips from the previous hand when Jerrelle had asked her that question. "You are only allowed one hand per deal, miss."

"Only one?" Jerrelle made sure that she had an obvious disappointing tone in her voice. "What do you mean, only one hand? Can't you see that I'm not doing too well at the moment? I need to maximize what little luck I may have left while I still can."

"Sorry, miss," the dealer apologized. "But one hand is all that you are allowed to play in this room. Those are the house rules."

"Well, that really sucks." Jerrelle leaned back in her seat and again, she put her acting skills to work by pasting a rather large pout on her face. She didn't need to do anything else after that to establish her disappointment; everyone in the room could clearly see it.

With the attention she wanted now on her, Jerrelle just sat quietly and played her next hand. This time, as if by a stroke of luck, her hand came up twenty-one. From that hand onward, Jerrelle continued to win.

The opinion of Jerrelle's gambling ability from the majority of those in the exclusive game room had quickly changed; the other few just assumed that luck had simply fallen into her lap.

So as to not draw any possible suspicions to her cheating ways, Jerrelle occasionally folded one, sometimes two hands in a row — even though the cards that she had folded had the potential to become great hands.

The longer she played, and the more hands she won, the atmosphere in the room evolved — there was now intrigue and excitement within it. Everyone now had no choice but to pay attention to Jerrelle and concede to the fact that she was on an incredible roll. Even a few of the gamblers who had been there for a while, chose to vacate their own seats and take a break in order to watch up close a rare occurrence of incredible luck take place right in front of them.

Jerrelle knew just how good her abilities were at counting cards. However, she couldn't dismiss the fact that she was in the middle of an amazing winning streak. Never before had she been on this kind of roll while playing Black Jack — and she doubted that it would ever happen again.

About forty-five minutes after her streak had started; Jerrelle had begun to sense that someone, not presently in the Elite Game Room, was carefully watching her. And sure enough, her suspicions were confirmed just a few hands later.

Across the way, she saw a man enter the room that she immediately pegged as a man in a position of importance — and she was right. He was the casino's general manager and she knew the very moment her eyes locked onto his that she had worn out her welcome. At that point, Jerrelle decided to begin the final phase of her plan — slowly begin to get under the dealer's skin. "You know, there could be a nice sized tip slipped your way if you were to bend the rules just a bit for me. All that I want is to play more than one hand at a time."

"Sorry, miss," said the dealer while collecting the chips from the previous losing hands, "I'm not allowed to do such a thing. And I can't make any exceptions. I have to follow the rules."

"Fine!" Jerrelle received her next hand and immediately split the pair of aces she had. She then reached over to her pile of chips and placed an equal amount on each hand, making her bet a total of a hundred-thousand per hand."

The dealer stepped back for a moment, completely shocked at what Jerrelle had just done. "Are you sure you want to do that, miss?"

"Jesus!" Jerrelle said emphatically, as she raised her hands up and off to the side. "Don't tell me that there is a limit on how much I'm allowed to bet?"

"No, miss," the dealer, replied. "This table has no betting limit."

"Good! Then I've changed my mind. I want to double down on both cards." Jerrelle took two hundred thousand dollars more in chips and split them between both her cards. "You may deal the cards now." *This is too easy;* Jerrelle thought as she smiled inside and watched the cards miraculously fall into their proper places. "Hit me. Hit me again."

"Blackjack and Twenty-one," the dealer called.

As everyone in the room let out a loud cheer in celebration of Jerrelle's amazing win, a rather rough hand gently made contact with her shoulder. "It seems that you've maxed out the table," the casino's manager said, as he stood behind Jerrelle. "I'm sorry, miss, but I'm gonna have to end your night right now."

"But I'm not done playing yet," she declared.

"I'm sorry, but as general manager of this casino, I have the authority to cut people off from playing. Would you please follow me up to my office so that the casino can pay you the amount that it owes you?"

Acting very pissed off, Jerrelle crossed her arms and briefly refused to leave the table. She then slowly stood up and sent a very unnerving gaze toward the A.I. black jack dealer. "I'm really not at all impressed with being cut off." She then left the table and followed the casino's manager out of the Elite Game Room to the main casino elevators. As she rode them up to the man's office, she reflected on how easy it had been for her to complete the first part of her plan. She had even been mildly impressed with herself because she had never before cheated with this much ease, nor had anyone even slightly suspected her of it. But now came the tough part for Jerrelle — finding out just how connected the casino's manager was to Antonio Marcone and the Detroit Underworld Organization.

The elevator stopped at the fortieth floor and Jerrelle expected to get out right there, but the casino manager told her to stay put. He then removed his ring of keys from his belt clip and inserted a specially made, odd-looking one into the elevator's control panel — he then turned the key and entered a four digit personal access code into the number pad on the panel. The already opened elevator doors, closed, and they ascended up one more flight to the secured, private top floor of the hotel. From the elevator, Jerrelle followed the manager down the hall a short distance until they reached his office. Upon entry, she was encouraged to take a seat in the chair across from the desk and was then told to wait — the manager excused himself and left his office.

Once she was alone, Jerrelle scanned the room with her eyes; absorbing what personal information she could about the casino's manager. There wasn't much there: a few pieces of art, a degree in business administration from Michigan State University, a framed Michigan State college football jersey (which Jerrelle assumed was the manager's since the name on the back of it matched the nameplate on his desk), and two separately framed pictures of a woman and pre-teen girl beside the vid-phone on his desk — they undoubtedly were the manager's loved ones.

Her mind promptly formulated a scenario, and if what she speculated came to fruition, then Jerrelle was certain that she had some leverage. Although she really didn't want to use such tactics, she tucked that supposition into the back of her mind, just in case her initial plan did not work and she was forced to tug at the man's heartstrings in order to get what she came for.

Five minutes later, the manager returned with a small black satchel. "There is one point two million dollars in cash in this satchel... the entire amount that you have won tonight. Under normal circumstances, we'd give our winners a certified check. However, I am certain that you would rather not have to pay taxes on what you have won, nor do we want to have to convince the gaming commission that we did not purposely allow you to win all of this money. However, from this moment forward, you are banned from ever gambling at this casino again. Either you are a very talented card player who should only be playing in Vegas tournaments or, as I suspect, are unequivocally skilled at cheating."

Jerrelle had been contentedly leaning back in her synth-leather chair; her feet were resting on the corner of the manager's desk. Her posture could not be misconstrued as anything other than haughty — it was done so on purpose, knowing that the general manager's opinion of her winning ways would undoubtedly include an accusation.

There was no reason for any sort of rebuttal to come from her — he was right, after all, so after being handed the satchel full of money, Jerrelle removed her feet from the corner of the desk and placed it onto her lap. She then opened it up and spent a few moments in thought, staring at what would be more than enough money for her to live out the remainder of her life comfortably. It had always been a dream of Jerrelle's to one day live a completely different life than what she'd always known — now that was possible. But that dream was not what she came here to achieve. And even though it felt great to take the casino for what she did, she had a plan for this money — bribery.

She removed four of the twenty-four wads of hundred dollar bills that had been inside the satchel, fanned out one them in front of her face, and quickly verified with her eyes that all fifty thousand of it was real. She then placed the two hundred grand into her pouch. "I am very insulted that you would even accuse me of cheating. The next time I am in the mood to gamble, I'm gonna go across the river to Canada and play. At least my winnings there will be paid to me by a legitimate casino." Jerrelle closed the flap on the satchel that still had the remainder of her winnings in it, and placed it on top of the desk. She then looked directly into the casino manager's eyes and said, "Being that you are in a position of power here, I can only assume that you are fully aware of everything and everyone associated with this hotel and casino. In fact, I am willing to bet that you could supply me with the rather delicate information that I am eager to learn."

The manager reacted to Jerrelle's words with a slight bit of perplexity as she placed her left hand on top of the satchel and opened it back up, freely displaying its contents for the manager to see. She then enticingly proceeded to slide it forward, showing the one million dollars that was still inside to the casino's general manager — she didn't care that she was bribing the man with the majority of her winnings, because she knew that it was dirty money to begin with. "You can have what is left inside this satchel if you tell me what I want to know."

The manager sunk back in his chair, looking at Jerrelle as he inaudibly chuckled to himself — her gesture had all but confirmed that she had indeed cheated at blackjack. He should have been pissed off that this had been allowed to happen; yet he wasn't. There was a small part of him that hated the idea of working at this casino, and he almost felt obliged to bow down to her impudently, well executed plan. "I must say that you have a rather large set of cojones, lady."

The manager had worked for this casino, and the one it used to be in its previous incarnation before the takeover, for a total of twenty years — he was also one of the few who were brought over to Book Cadillac Hotel when it became what it was today. At the time, he felt lucky to have been asked to stay on, but once he had discovered who his employer really was, regret quickly consumed him

He should have quit right then and there, but the big picture was staring him in the face — his wife, and at the time, his newborn daughter, deserved the best and he simply could not throw away a good paying job based upon a principle. These days though, he was finding it more and more difficult to ignore his conscience.

The money this woman was enticing him with; he just couldn't take his eyes off of it. In fact, it was giving him a reason to remember all of the bullshit that he had to endure throughout the years. *'Oh, the things I could do with that money. No more worries. No more headaches. No more guilt.'*

As much as he disliked the idea of working for the Detroit Mob, he had worked his ass off to gain the position he had and knew that he had earned it. However, an unexpected out clause was suddenly being offered — one that he knew would probably never come around again. The only drawback to it though, was the potential consequences that he may one day have to face should he accept it. He needed to take a moment and figure out if throwing it all away would be worth the gamble.

Jerrelle was fully aware of the difficult position that she had just put this man in. Nevertheless, she wasn't about to leave without getting what she came for, so she removed her hand from the satchel and left it alone on top of the manager's desk. An unguarded temptation always helped to entice someone into making a hasty decision — especially when they were contemplating whether or not to take that leap.

Giving the man the necessary time that he clearly needed to think, Jerrelle leaned back in her chair and watched the hands on the clock on the wall behind the general manager's desk, tick. If he were able to resolutely refuse her offer within the next two minutes, then she knew there would be no chance whatsoever of her walking out of there with the information she sought. If he was still undecided after that, then she felt confident she would be able to complete the last phase of her plan.

It may seem impetuous, but the manager knew that Jerrelle's offer was just too good for him to blatantly dismiss. He was ready to retire — but he was only going to take that big step if what she wanted, didn't put him in a position where he would be slicing his own throat.

He needed to know what her angle was before he committed to anything. "Ok. You can ask me what you want to know and then I'll decide whether or not to answer your question."

Jerrelle looked directly at the manager and informed him that all she wanted was to learn everything that he knew about Antonio Marcone, Louie Mazotti, Salvadore Batiste, and the rest of the Detroit Underworld Organization?

He should have been stunned at this woman's inquiry, but he wasn't. For some reason, a suspicion had been there that this was the road she was going to go down. The obligatory knife had just been placed in his hand, and it prompted him to quickly regret his willingness to cut his own throat in exchange for financial security. As much as he would be all right with leaving Michigan and spending the rest of his life on some tropical beach, selling out the D.U.O. really wasn't the smartest thing to do — he knew them all too well and knew what they had done in the past in order to put themselves into a position to grow into the conglomerate that they are now.

After a few moments spent organizing his thoughts, the manager said, "You must have a death wish there, lady. Forget it!" The casino's manager slid his chair closer to his desk, and then pointed with his right hand toward his office door. "Just take all your damn money and get the hell out of here."

"One million dollars! I can see it in your eyes just how much you what it." Jerrelle picked up the manager's nameplate off of his desk and read it out loud. "Mr. Jason Hernandez. This 'tax-free' money is all yours if you are only willing to give me what I want." Although she had hoped that she didn't have to go there, the leverage she had, needed to be used. The man was still balancing on top of that proverbial wall — and he needed a little coaxing to jump on down to the other side in order to gain his freedom.

First, she enticed Jason by pushing the satchel on an angle, stopping it right next to the two pictures sitting on the edge of his desk. She then said, "Just think of the stability that beautiful family of yours would have if you would only humor me with my one simple request." Jerrelle motioned with her eyes toward the two framed pictures; the manager acknowledged her hint. She could tell in that moment he was now thinking with his heart and not his head — this was a good sign.

Jason Hernandez immediately became confused. His instincts were telling him to pick up his phone and call for security, but what was most important in his life was what was causing him to pause — his family. The money in the open satchel continued to entice him. He could not stop thinking of the possible future that his family could have. His precious young daughter, the apple of his eye, the little jewel of his very existence, could have anything that she ever wanted, and more — and all that he had to do was to be willing to appease this woman's ballsy request.

For the past ten years, he had been praying that the perfect opportunity would one day present itself and allow him to leave this casino and cut his ties with the Detroit Underworld Organization — little did he expect that it was going to come with such a high risk attached to it.

If Antonio and his associates weren't already in hiding half way around the world, then he would not have thought twice about having security escort this stupid woman directly over to Antonio's office so that he could deal with her — but Jason could sense the devil on his shoulder encouraging him to take the offer that no man in his right mind could honestly refuse.

Although he was still battling internally with making the right decision, he got up from behind his desk and moved over to the wall directly to his right. He stopped in front of a painting of the city of Detroit, touched the middle of the top frame, and the painting lowered to reveal a hidden wall safe. Once it was open, Jason knew that he could not change his mind. This was the toughest decision he ever had to make — and as much as he knew that he should not, he just could not help but think that the one million dollars would all but secure his daughter's future.

After reaching the conclusion that he was willing to accept whatever consequences may come as a result of accepting this woman's bribe, Jason opened up the safe and removed a small hardcover black book and a computer memory stick. "For as long as I have worked here, I tried not to get myself too heavily involved with anything that was connected to my employer unless I felt that it could be of benefit to me one day. Right now, I don't know exactly where Antonio Marcone, his close associates, or the rest of the members of his organization are. The only thing I know for sure is that everyone involved with the D.U.O. has temporarily dispersed and that Antonio is somewhere overseas. Here is a duplicate log of all of his reliable connections throughout the world. And here is a stick containing enough damaging information, both past and present, concerning crimes that he is either guilty of or connected to."

Jerrelle quickly flipped through the pages of the black book and determined that this item was definitely a crucial piece of information that she could not pass up. The information that was on the memory stick though, was something that she'd have to trust was actually there, for she really didn't think that the general manager of this casino would let her use his computer to thoroughly look it over. Nevertheless, she was content with what she had acquired, so she shook Jason Hernandez's hand and sealed the deal. She then got up from her seat; her intent was to leave through the front door, but the manager stopped her.

"Without a key, you won't be able to use the elevator. I would have to escort you down to the next floor before you could leave on your own, and I would prefer not to take the risk of having anyone else seeing us together... even for just the few brief seconds that it would be." Jason walked over to the beautiful antique grandfather clock that was positioned next to the hidden safe. On the front of it, there was this elaborate gold emblem. Just like the painting, Jason Hernandez reached up and touched it; the clock quietly slide open to the side, revealing a dedicated hidden staircase that went all the way down all forty-two flights to the private underground parking garage. "You can discreetly leave my office by using these private stairs. Oh, and a... this meeting never took place."

Jerrelle acknowledged what the manager had just stated and thanked him again for his help — she then headed down the secret staircase; black book and memory stick in hand.

As soon as the grandfather clock returned to its unsuspecting original position, Jason Hernandez quietly spoke to himself, thanking Jerrelle for giving him the perfect opportunity he had been looking for to wash his hands of any association to the Detroit Underworld Organization.

After returning to his desk and retrieving the open satchel from on top, he sunk back into his office chair and reflected. There was no turning back; the deed had been done. He just prayed that his decision to sell out his boss would not end up becoming the worst mistake he had ever made.

———————————— ○○ ————————————

Throughout the flight back to San Antonio, Sabastian was unable to keep his head clear — he knew that he could not allow the unknown to cloud his judgment. Still, what Chevy had said to him just before he took his own life did nothing but increase the animosity he already had toward his ex-father — it also assured the belief he had that Terrance Burelli had been lying to him his whole life. But what made it worse than finding out what he had, was that someone out there had actually known about the truth of his disappearance and chose to keep quite. *'I just don't understand why Chevy would do that,'* Sabastian thought. *'I mean… it's obvious that the man had a few stability issues, but he was supposed to be my father's friend.'* Sabastian just stayed lost in thought, unable to find an acceptable answer to his questions no matter how hard he searched for them.

It seemed like a longer than usual flight back to Texas, but upon his return to his father's agency, Sabastian felt better; more invigorated than he had in almost a week. "I'm back," he said as he entered the office. "Is everything ok?"

"Yes, everything is fine, I guess," Sydney answered.

"Don't lie to your nephew," Savanna said, as she too entered the office, bringing lunch with her for everyone. "What your uncle means is, individually we're all right. But as far as finding out any new information about Antonio Marcone… well, forget it. We've run into nothing but roadblock after roadblock."

After listening to Savanna's full report, Sabastian felt somewhat disappointed. Yet, he suspected even before he had left for Detroit that when he had returned, there would be no new information waiting for him. He never assumed that finding Antonio Marcone and completing his father's mission would be easy. If it had been, then Maxwell Banks would have surely accomplished his goal and he would still be alive today. "So.., have you found anything new, Baylor?"

"Not anything significant to want to do back flips over." He stayed focused the entire time on his computer screen and continued on with his work. "Sorry, bud."

About thirty minutes later, right as everyone was finishing their lunches, Savanna's vid-phone buzzed. She answered it and was surprised at the caller's unexpected request. "Someone named Jerrelle Robinson wants to talk to you."

Sabastian went into his father's office for a bit of privacy and booted Baylor out of the chair. However, instead of leaving the room, he just stepped off to the side and allowed Sabastian to sit down and take his call.

His conversation with Jerrelle had only been for a few moments when the unexpected words that she had said to him, suddenly allowed his uncertainty to disappear. And although he was curious, there really was no need for him to inquire how she was able to acquire this new information for him. The only thing that mattered now was to try and figure out exactly where it was overseas that Antonio Marcone and his associates were.

What he was going to do once he had located the enemy, he had not a clue? To him, this was going to be like an unstable bridge that he would first have to test, then take his time and maneuver across it slowly so that he made it all the way over to the other side. The end was something that he knew he could not rush toward — it could end up being fatal if he did.

While listening to his friend's phone conversation, inspiration had hit Baylor. So he left the room and headed over toward Savanna's desk — he then helped himself to her computer and began to work his magic. This time, without being asked, Baylor proceeded to hack into the Metropolitan Detroit International Airport's main server. As soon as he was able to gain access to it, he began the process of eliminating flights overseas. Three minutes later, he had achieved success. "Bingo!"

"Hang on there a second, Jerrelle." He had no idea why Baylor had suddenly left to go into the lobby. Nevertheless, Sabastian placed his friend on hold, and then inquired through the open doorway, "Did you find something, bud?"

"After hearing that Antonio had left for somewhere overseas, an idea popped into my head." Baylor then took a moment and studied the information on his computer screen. After he found what he was looking for, he printed out a copy of it and brought it to his friend.

Sabastian briefly looked it over, but was unsure as to what use this information would be to him. "So… what does this have to do with where Antonio Marcone might be?"

"Well, according to the information that is in your hand, it is my expert opinion that if someone were hastily to leave the country for someplace across the pond, I believe that he would choose either one of these three places: London, England, Tokyo, Japan, or Paris, France."

Sabastian looked back over the printout, trying to see how Baylor had come to his conclusion. "So what makes you so sure that those are the possible places that he may have fled to?"

"According to this, these three cities have the most frequent overseas flights out of Detroit. Which would make the availability to get a flight at the last minute, that much easier." Baylor was just about to further explain his theory to Sabastian, when Savanna had told him from within the lobby that something else had just popped up onto her computer screen.

Without any hesitation, Baylor left the office again and returned to where he had been working. After printing out the new information, he went back to where his friend was — but before he handed it over to Sabastian, Baylor took a moment and studied it. "I also ran a search for a complete list of people that had recently flown overseas from Detroit within the last five days whom had purchased last minute tickets. If you look at the second printout that I just handed to you, not counting the four women on that list, you'll see that there were four tickets purchased for London by a man named André Martin, three tickets purchased for Tokyo by a man named Tony Ignatius, and three tickets purchased for Paris by a man named Anton Marciano."

After scanning over the printouts a second time, the wheels in Sabastian head finally began to spin. Within a few seconds, he came up with his own theory as to where Antonio Marcone could have gone. However, he first wanted to confirm his suspicions, so he asked Baylor where he thought the enemy might be. "I think that there is a very good chance that he has fled to Paris.

"I don't agree," Savanna said as she entered Maxwell's old office. "First off, Antonio's middle name is Ignatius, so I'd bet you that he took that flight to Tokyo under the alias Tony Ignatius. The second reason is… if you had actually studied your father's files, Antonio Marcone has plenty of illegal business interests over there. With all of his connections in Japan, it would be relatively easy for him to access and then continue on with his operations from over there."

In that moment, Sabastian was thrilled that Savanna was there to help. This theory of hers had all but squashed his suspicions. Now, he understood why she had been an invaluable asset to his father. He certainly was looking forward to putting everything behind him, spend some quality time getting to know her and his uncle on a more personal level, and then try to figure out what direction he wanted his life to go in.

Sabastian was about to ask her to book him on the next flight to Japan when he suddenly remembered that he had left his old friend on hold, so he turned his attention back to his vid-phone screen. Before he could say anything, Jerrelle instantly became her fiery self and raked him over the coals for putting her on hold for as long as he did — he also knew that it would be futile of him to try in any way to stop her from ranting. The only thing he could do was to just let her blow off her steam and then try and smooth things over with her afterward.

When Jerrelle was finally done with her diatribe, Sabastian cautiously let her know what Baylor had discovered and where they now suspected Antonio Marcone and his merry men had gone.

It hadn't been as difficult as he had suspected when it came to getting his friend to understand and accept his explanation, but once he realized that Jerrelle had, she was adamant that she accompany him overseas. And as luck would have it, she apparently had a trusted ally of her own that lived in Tokyo. Therefore, it was decided that she would fly over there by herself and establish contact with that person. Once she had, she would then meet up with Sabastian at their hotel and figure out what their next course of action would be.

5

Japan — this perfect archetype metropolis of urban distinctiveness, with its state of the art high-tech wizardry, multitude of delicious cuisines, and enriched history, is what most modern societies strive to achieve, yet seldom do. They see in this template, what they think they can only dream of. Yet in reality, this haven of modern creation, steeped in tradition, does its best not to show its true colors. What easily can be seen is appetizingly sugarcoated to make everyone think that they, as a country, are more than a few steps ahead in every aspect of life. The thrill, the excitement, the wonders, the fantasy, the beauty, and the history — it is what attracts people to come. However, what can't be so easily seen is what exists in a furtive world where a learned secret could be the only reason needed for an unsuspecting life to be erased from existence. Nevertheless, there are those with an extensive résumé of criminal activity that are drawn to it like a magnet because of the belief that they can easily live and prosper within that underground world, safe from ever being found, and free to continue on with their corrupt lives.

Immediately after arriving in Tokyo, Jerrelle flagged down a taxi and proceeded to try and track down her older half-sister, Bai Lin Nori Melee. Both have the same father, Trévon Robinson, but her mother, Yūko, was pure Japanese. She stood slightly shorter in stature than Jerrelle did and she had the capability of being just as ruthless. Her straight jet-black hair, with sporadically blended copper color highlights, usually hung neatly braided all the way down to the middle of her back. Her light-brown eyes, perfectly accented her light-brown skin tone. But what stood out more than her near flawless physical features was the tattoo of a two-headed dragon that lay right across her entire back. The beautiful piece of detailed artwork appeared almost real — and Bai Lin wasn't afraid to freely display it so that those among the masses who recognized its significance will understand that she is not one to be messed with.

Centered perfectly in the middle of her back is the dragon's body. Its tail lay right across her left ass-cheek and then it continued on down, wrapping around the leg a few times, where it then ended in the middle of her calf. Each one of its hind legs wrapped around her hips and then ended at her pelvic region, and the dragon's forearms follow Bai Lin's own arms and blend in with them. Its wings wrapped around each side of her torso and then partially folded over each other as they lay across her stomach. The dragon's necks each draped over both of her shoulders and its two heads rested facing each other on her upper chest area, with its tongues dangling on down between the middle of her breasts.

The reason for Bai Lin having such an elaborate piece of body art is because she is a chartered member of Japan's most feared underground organization — the Extremist Clandestine Liberation (E.C.L.). And because of her association with this group, Jerrelle simply couldn't just pick up her vid-cell and call her sister whenever she wanted to. It sucked, because it meant that she had to go about finding Bai Lin the hard way — and if she just happened to knock on the wrong door while she looked, she would more than likely become chum for a school of sharks to feast upon.

In retrospect, Jerrelle should not have let it be known that she had a Japanese contact, but she had volunteered to be a part of Sabastian's mission, which meant that she had agreed to tread some dangerous waters. If Bai Lin's lifestyle didn't require her to stay anonymous to the outside world, and secluded from her family, then what Jerrelle said she would do, would easily be accomplished in a matter of only a few short minutes.

The Marunouchi business area in the Chiyoda District of the city was a place that Jerrelle remembered her half-sister telling her would be the place for her to go if there was ever an emergency and she needed to get a message to her — although she wasn't told where in the district to look.

Just a few blocks behind Tokyo Station, sits one of the more recently revitalized and re-configured sections of the district; that being the Chiyoda Niwa outdoor plaza. This four-block area consisted of traditional and modern restaurants, tea huts, and unique gift shops, all cleverly arranged throughout a beautifully landscaped garden and sculptured park. But as beautiful an area of the city as this was, Jerrelle could feel it in her bones that she was going to regret doing what she was about to. *'Hello? I'm a stupid Union citizen who only wants to learn the whereabouts of one of the members of the Extremist Clandestine Liberation,'* she said to herself, cynically.

Cautiously, she walked up and down the entire plaza, astutely studying all of the businesses and trying to determine which one of the establishments would be her best bet — and safest to try her luck at first. *'Well... this restaurant looks as good as any to walk inside and kick over the hornet's nest.'*

She entered the establishment and was greeted almost immediately by the maitre d'; a man elderly in stature, exceedingly well groomed, and very distinguished looking. And although he looked harmless and trustworthy, Jerrelle knew that she had to use extreme caution and assume that what she could see on the surface was probably not this man's true nature. "Excuse me, sir. By any chance do you happen to speak any English?"

"Yes a I do, miss," answered the maitre d'. "Please a follow me and I'll a escort you to your table."

"I'm sorry, but I'm not here for lunch today. Instead, I was hoping that maybe you could help me. If you don't mind, I have a question that I wish to ask you."

"Ok. I'll try my best to a answer your question. But I'm a sure that you a know what they say... Just because you a don't see a price tag, does not a mean that it is a free." The maitre d' then greedily held out his right hand. "You a know that this is a very good day when you see an old man like a me smile wider than the backside of a sumo wrestler."

That was an image that Jerrelle didn't need to visualize. She was here to get some information, so she opened up her pouch and pulled out a money clip. "I sincerely hope that this will keep you smiling for a long time after I have gone." Jerrelle then slipped the man twenty thousand yen. Satisfied that he had been compensated enough, the maitre d' encouraged Jerrelle to proceed with her question.

She thought for a moment, trying to recall what her half-sister had once told her was the proper phrase to use if she was ever in Tokyo and needed to contact her. *'I pray to the God everyone here*

116

believes in, that what I am about to say to this old man doesn't get my half-black ass killed.' Jerrelle took a deep breath and then said, "Do you happen to know if an eclipse radiates brighter here in the Far East?"

His smile immediately disappeared as he contemplated Jerrelle's question, while at the same time, curiously studying her. After a moment of awkward silence, the maitre d' politely excused himself, turned, and walked away — he went straight through a beaded doorway that was only a few feet behind where he had been standing. As soon as he had disappeared, Jerrelle thought the worst; her mind immediately became convinced that what she had feared before she walked into this restaurant was actually going to happen.

She should have bolted right for the front door in that moment, but for some unexplained reason, she didn't. *'This is a bad idea — I should leave while I still have a working set of legs.'* If she didn't let this play out, she'd never know if her uncertainty was warranted. Besides, she was not a coward — even though her gut was telling her to get the hell out of town.

Jerrelle took a quick survey of the restaurant to see what her options would be if a last second escape was needed. However, her reservations quickly dissipated when the maitre d' returned a few moments later — alone, with a brown envelope in his left hand.

"The a answer to your puzzling question is a… yes. Though you a know that an eclipse can be blinding, you feel compelled to a look at it anyway. Only after a short period of discomfort, will it a then become clear… but you a must be willing to suffer through some pain in order to obtain what a you seek." After answering Jerrelle's question, the maitre d' handed her the envelope — he then disappeared back through the same beaded doorway.

She wasn't quite sure what his words had meant — and she hated riddles. However, she took his message as a friendly warning and mentally prepared herself for the unknown. Something, she felt, was going to happen to her between now and when, or if, she saw her sister, because she was pretty sure that her search for Bai Lin was no longer going to go unnoticed.

Jerrelle turned around and cautiously left the restaurant. The moment she had stepped outside, she quickly surveyed the surrounding area and determined that there was no imminent dangers nearby, so she hailed herself a taxi — luckily, one just happened to be conveniently pulling up to the restaurant that had an elderly couple inside.

Once the passengers exited the taxi, Jerrelle stepped inside the vehicle and immediately opened up the envelope; not paying any attention to the fact that the cab driver was speaking to her (as if she could understand Japanese anyway). She was surprised to find that the envelope contained a one-way train ticket from Chiyoda to the far western district of Hachiōji. The ticket also came with a note that said, *"Kōun, imōto (Good luck, little sister)."* She didn't want to read too much into what was in her hand, but she felt a bit more relaxed than she did before, as it now appeared that she had actually chosen the right place to begin her search for Bai Lin. Now the question was — were there going to be any surprises waiting for her in Hachiōji?

She almost got out of the cab at that moment, realizing that the train station was actually only a few blocks away from where she was — but then she remembered that she was supposed to meet up with Sabastian at their hotel at one o'clock in the afternoon. She looked at the time on her vid-cell and determined that she still had time to do that before her train departed. However, her meeting with him was going to have to be a very short one, because the last thing that she wanted was to miss her ride to Hachiōji and then be forced to again knock on more doors in order to try and locate her half-sister.

Sabastian strolled up to the front desk at the Hilton Hotel in the Shinagawa District, carrying only a slightly oversized duffel bag. Behind the desk was an A.I. male desk clerk who was clearly outfitted in the latest Japanese A.I. hardware; hardware that had him connected directly to the hotel's computer system. He never touched a keyboard — everything that he wanted to do, was completed via a wireless link between his artificial intelligence and the half-inch thick, opaque, glass-like vertical computer screen that was positioned in front of him.

"Hello, there. My name is Sabastian Banks. I do believe that I have a reservation here for two."

"Yes you do, Mr. Banks," the desk clerk said — his voice as well, had an ever so slight mechanical tone to it. "May I ask where your wife is?"

"She couldn't wait to do some shopping," Sabastian lied, "so I dropped her off down the street at the outdoor mall. She should be arriving here shortly."

"I see, Mr. Banks. Unfortunately…" The desk clerk then apologized to Sabastian, claiming that due to unforeseen circumstances beyond the hotel's control, his room was not quite ready to be occupied. So the clerk suggested that he just leave his bag at the front desk and head into the hotel's lounge to relax and have a drink. The clerk then assured him that his luggage would be taken care of and then sent up to his room when it was ready. Also, since Sabastian was being inconvenienced by having to wait, he was informed that his drink would be compliments of the hotel. The clerk even recommended that he try their very popular specialty drink; the one called a 'Japanese Delight'.

Bed rest was what Sabastian had really been looking forward to, as he hadn't gotten much quality sleep since his life had become so damn complicated. He knew that he wasn't supposed to meet Jerrelle until later in the day, so he had planned on getting to the hotel as early as was possibly in order to get some much needed rest. That idea though, had long ago been ruined, because his flight had ended up arriving more than an hour late, so the inconvenience of his room not yet being ready, wasn't as big of a deal as it should have been — his want wasn't going to take place anyway. All that Sabastian could do now was just go with the flow. He thought about going outside for a bit and allowing the fresh air of this beautiful day to envelope him, but a stiff drink was surprisingly, calling his name. After everything that had happened to him, alcohol, more than a heavy dose of fresh air, is what he believed was going to help him to relax.

Inside the hotel's lounge, instead of accepting the complimentary specialty drink, he went and ordered himself a double scotch on the rocks. When the time finally came for him to go up to his room, he figured that the scotch would help to put him to sleep much easier than the Japanese Delight would. However, no sooner had he ordered his drink, he was approached from behind by a well tanned, stunning blonde woman.

In Sabastian's mind, she looked to be in her late twenties — but he was terrible at guessing someone's age. She stood just over six feet tall (that was only because of the five inch stilettos she had on), and definitely looked like the model type. This stranger was exquisite and beautiful beyond all imagination — and she surprisingly, wasn't Japanese.

'Hum... I know that Japan is a very welcoming country, but I doubt very much that this woman is actually the Japanese Delight that the desk clerk was referring to?'

The woman placed her right hand on Sabastian's shoulder, leaned in close to his ear, and spoke softly, yet with confidence, "I believe that you are the man I am looking for."

Many impure thoughts promptly raced through Sabastian's mind; the sound of her voice, and the warm air that she expelled against his skin when she had spoken, was all that he needed to give in to whatever it was that she wanted. However, Sabastian quickly reminded himself that he wasn't on vacation and a one-night stand wasn't one of the reasons why he had flown halfway around the world. Nevertheless, with the idea that it could now actual occur, what kind of a man would he be if he were to refuse what would surely help to take away all of the stresses that had consumed him since his life had done a three-sixty.

Sabastian received his drink from the bartender and as a gentleman should, he invited the young lady to join him at a table. As he pulled out the chair for her to sit, more thoughts ran through his head — this time they were thoughts of intrigue. He sat himself directly across from her and took a healthy sip of his scotch. It was hard for Sabastian not to drool over this stranger's immense beauty — but before he even had a chance to speak, his company leaned forward, giving Sabastian the perfect, unobstructed view of her hypnotic eyes, her amazing smile, and what resided down the front of her top — that was all it had taken for Sabastian's mind to slip seamlessly into the gutter. Admittedly, he was a prototypical male, and it had been a long time since those natural urges had been sated — it was just so unfair that a woman had the ability to put a spell on a man, simply by teasing him with what she had been born with.

"It's not safe for me to stay here too long," she said, softly. "Here... This is for you." She then removed a sealed legal sized white envelope from inside of her purse and slid it across the table.

This was not what he had expected — her room key, maybe, but not what she had just handed to him.

"Your name is Sabastian Banks, correct? My name is Sharice Cortland."

Perplexity now enveloped him, as he never expected that anyone would recognize him — he wasn't even used to who he really was yet. However, this now made him that much more curious as to whom this woman could be. The collection of impure thoughts that had been there, then promptly disappeared. The only thing that he was now still interested in, was what it was that this stranger actually wanted from him.

"I'm sure that you are wondering who the hell I am?"

Sabastian looked curiously at the woman and simply nodded his head.

"Well, you see... it's like this. My mother was an agent for the B.I.A. (British Investigation Agency), and she would occasionally help your father on his cases. Over the years, my mother kept detailed records that she had gathered for him of all the D.U.O. operations that were linked to many of the countries on this side of the globe."

Sabastian's interest grew — not how he initially thought it would, though. It was simply because she was apparently aware of the existence of the Detroit Underworld Organization.

Sharice paused for a moment as she accepted her dry martini from the waitress. She took a sip of it and then continued on with her explanation, letting it be known that she had always been interested in her mother's line of work and that she had followed in her footsteps and became a B.I.A. agent when she had turned twenty years old. Unfortunately, five years ago, her mother had passed away from a brain aneurysm — and from that moment forward, she had assumed the role her mother had undertaken when it came to assisting Maxwell Banks with whatever she could. Sharice then concluded her story with an unbelievable bit of information; something that he would have never in a million years speculated upon. "You see, Sabastian, my mother was your aunt... your mother's older sister, Sonya."

As if a light switch had just turned on in his head, this previously known information promptly returned to Sabastian. When researching his father's history, he discovered that his mother's sister's married name was Cortland, and that she worked as an agent for the British Government. However, before this conversation had even started, he, for some reason, had already completely forgotten about it.

Unlike he had initially thought, Sydney Banks wasn't his only living blood relative — this woman was as well. She was his first cousin, and he was disappointed in himself for not immediately recognizing who his family was. It was a mental error that could be blamed on his being tired, but he'd rather blame his faux pas on his hormones. Consequently, he felt as if he should find an appropriate method of kicking his own ass for even going where his mind should have never wandered.

Sabastian took a healthy sip of his double scotch and tried to let sink in all that he had just been told. "So then… we are cousins?"

"Yup! I see that the detective in you is already starting to surface. Anyway, my mother told me that the day would come when your father would need what is in this envelope. However, since he has recently passed on, I thought that you might need it instead." Sharice got up from her seat and walked over to Sabastian, bent over, and gave him a real big hug. "Like my mother was for your father, I will do whatever I can and I will be there whenever you need me. But I must leave now. Goodbye, Sabastian. It's great after all these years to finally meet my cousin."

Sabastian must have had a sudden brain cramp. Although she was apparently his family, it must not have yet fully sunken in, as he leaned back in his chair and watched her leave the lounge in a whole new, weird sort of way. Some would have probably misconstrued the way he watched her leave the lounge as being creepy, but he couldn't help but admire just how beautiful she was. *'Yeah, you can certainly tell that we're related. The good looks are definitely there.'*

After his cousin walked out the hotel's lounge, Sabastian sat back up straight and retracted his implicit tongue. He then thought, *'That would have been totally messed up if we did end up in my hotel room and not knowing that we were related.'* Then something else hit him, something much more significant than a near incestuous escapade. Sharice had not told him how she knew who he was and how she knew where to find him. So he hastily got up from his chair and sprung toward the exit. "Sharice! Sharice!" He looked around for his apparent cousin, but she had disappeared faster than a hundred dollar bill lying on the sidewalk.

Realizing that he had made yet another amateurish mistake; one that could end up costing him quite a bit somewhere on down the road, Sabastian went back into the lounge and reclaimed his chair. He was beyond angry with himself for taking Sharice at face value and for not asking her to explain in greater detail everything that she knew and how exactly she knew it. *'I have to get better at this investigative thing and be smarter than I have been or I'll probably end up like my father,'* he thought.

After another sip of his double scotch, Sabastian determined that there was simply no need for him to rack his brain over the stupid mistake that he had just made. From this moment forward, he needed to focus on his objective. When he and Sharice crossed paths next, he would then take the opportunity to have her verify her claim before he officially accepted her as being his actual blood relative.

Sabastian finished off his drink, took out an ice cube from the empty glass, and put it in his mouth. He sank back down in his chair, sucked on the ice, and tried to relax — but he found that hard to do, as his mind kept on wondering whether or not the woman claiming to be Sharice Cortland, was actually she.

When Sabastian just happened to glance at his vid-cell to see what time it was, he immediately realized that Jerrelle was late for their scheduled rendezvous. That, which he would normally make it a point of mentioning, was irrelevant at the moment. He really couldn't think straight and needed the extra time to organize and settle his thoughts. Besides, he owed Jerrelle one for being late himself the other day when they had their first meeting.

While he patiently waited for his friend, Sabastian ordered himself another double scotch. Right after the waitress had left his table, in walked his old friend. "Before you say anything... Don't! I'm only one handful of minutes late. Besides, I got sidetracked. As I was getting out of my cab, this gorgeous, tanned, tall blonde woman was standing just outside of the hotel... and I couldn't help but admire her beauty. Too my surprise, she wanted the same cab that I had just come here in. So I held it there for her. And being the friendly, personable individual that you know I am, I stuck around and held open the door for her. Man, I wouldn't mind losing my lesbian virginity to someone like her."

"Say what?" Sabastian was stunned at what had just exited from the mouth of his old friend.

Jerrelle got the exact reaction that she had hoped for — but what she didn't expect to see was just how low Sabastian's jaw had dropped. "I never said that I was completely straight, Sab. There is a certain type of women that I am attracted to."

"Yeah, well… you just forget about that one," he insisted.

"Why?" Jerrelle asked, inquisitively.

"Because… I said so. Just forget about her. Right now, just fill me in on what you've been able to find out so far."

Jerrelle pulled up a chair directly across from Sabastian and was about to explain to him what had happened to her, but stopped. She then took a moment and surveyed the entire lounge, as she wanted to make sure that no one was within earshot. Once she was satisfied that what she was about to tell Sabastian would not be overheard, she continued.

In an almost whisper like tone, she let her friend know that she believed she had made the connection that she needed in order to find her sister — but she also made him aware of the fact that she still was going to have to tread very lightly and hope that she did not go somewhere where she was not welcomed.

Not having any idea as to who the E.C.L. were, but assuming nonetheless that they were a faction of some kind that were not to be taken lightly, Sabastian asked, "So.., how long do you think it will be before you are able to make contact with your half-sister?"

"I'm not sure." Jerrelle just sat there at bit irritated; she was very thirsty and the only apparent waitress in the place was engaged in a conversation with the lounge's bartender. Not wanting to draw any attention to the two of them, she chose to refrain from calling out to the waitress and instead, decided to exude some rare patients. "Hopefully, I'll see her very soon. So what's in that white envelope that you have sitting on the table in front of you, Sab?"

"I don't know. I haven't had a chance to open it up yet. You know that blonde woman that you held up the cab for? The one you have the hots for? Well, she is the one who gave this to me."

Jerrelle slouched back in her chair; her peripheral vision caught sight of the waitress approaching their table with Sabastian's second double scotch — she fervently eyed it. "So that is why you want me to stay away from her. You have the hots for her too."

"No, I don't!" As he was accepting his drink and paying for it, Sabastian openly explained to Jerrelle who the supposed identity of that woman was.

Jerrelle was just about to order herself a beer from the waitress, when she glanced at her vid-cell and realized that if she didn't leave within the next ten minutes, she'd probably miss her train. For that reason, she did not order anything — she'd just have to get something at the station before she got on the train.

After taking a sip of his fresh scotch, Sabastian curiously opened up the envelope, removed its contents, and read the file that was inside to Jerrelle. The file was a copy of a document that all but confirmed what his father had believed, but had no proof of — Antonio Marcone had been shipping all kinds of weapons to Serbia. The document also established the fact that the head of the C.R.A.P. (**C**ommunist **R**evolutionary **A**ssembly **P**arty), Vladi Chemzot, had been Antonio Marcone's main client. Also with the file was a small envelope that had been paper-clipped to the backside. Sabastian took it, opened it up, and then scanned its contents — it was a copy of a letter that had been sent to Sabastian's father, five years ago, by a man named Ken Fu Sung; a Criminology Professor at the University of Tokyo.

"Wish I could stay, Sab, have a drink, and talk more about you hot cousin, but I have to catch a cab and take it to Chiyoda. I have a train that I cannot miss." She didn't have to, but she showed Sabastian her ticket as proof that Hachiōji was where she was supposed to go. "So while I'm off searching for my half-sister, maybe you should use your free time and go and talk to that Professor Sung?"

"I might as well since I don't have any other leads right now."

Jerrelle got up from the table and without any sort of hesitation, picked up Sabastian's second double scotch, and slammed it back.

"Hey!" Sabastian yelled, unimpressed. "Are you gonna pay for that?"

"I don't think so. Just take it off the five hundred you owe me for that information I got for you about Chevy. Besides, there is no sense in letting good booze get watered down by melting ice… and with what I fear lies ahead for me, I need all the liquid courage I can get." Jerrelle then turned around and began to leave the lounge, but not before telling the waitress to bring Sabastian another double scotch.

"…And don't you even think of going near my cousin!" Sabastian demanded.

"Don't worry, Sab. It's not like I would really want a serious relationship or anything. But I am curious to find out if she is a natural blonde."

Jerrelle arrived at the station a little later than she had planned on. Luckily, she hadn't missed her train; it was running behind schedule due to some minor mechanical issues. So with some unexpected time on her hands, she decided to go and grab something for the trip from the restaurant that was inside the station. To her surprise, the place looked like a typical late twentieth-century, small town, Northern American greasy spoon — complete with what looked to be a few less-than-desirable looking regulars. Standing behind the restaurant's service counter was a middle-aged, heavy set, Asian woman. Her hair was evenly streaked in grey, it was long, and had been haphazardly twirled up into a bun.

To Jerrelle, the woman didn't appear too clean either, as her clothes were extremely stained, along with being soaked in sweat. The t-shirt she had on was also filled with holes and she wore a pair of worn out baggy sweat pants that were mostly covered by a kitchen apron — it, she assumed, was more than likely soiled with a bit of everything that was on the menu. "Um… excuse me, miss. Could I please get a large cup of sim-caf... and can I also get a couple of those delicious looking, caramel flavored rice cakes to go?"

"Uh, ok. Just a… one second." The lady behind the counter promptly turned and started to yell in Japanese through the small service window at the young man doing the cooking in the back kitchen. "Ah… sorry, miss. You say you want a medium Chai tea?"

"No.., I said that I would like a large sim-caf and two caramel flavored rice cakes."

"A large sim-caf and a two rice cakes. Right away." Instead of taking care of her order, the Asian lady turned her back to her in order to again chastise the young cook; Jerrelle could easily see the irritation that was beginning to show on the middle-aged woman's face, as the man refused just to stop his verbal assault.

The exchange between the two seemed to be more than just a disagreement. In fact, it soon became apparent to Jerrelle that the middle-aged woman was getting very close to blowing a gasket — the young cook after all, just wouldn't stop his tirade and go back to manning the kitchen.

Finally, the Asian woman had enough of the young cook and his blatant disrespect. She stopped engaging him, took a second to compose herself, and then turned to address Jerrelle. "Excuse me... I be just a one moment. I be not too long." She left her post behind the counter and, with purpose in her stride, headed straight into the kitchen.

"But, miss... I'm going to miss my train."

From the moment the Asian woman walked into the kitchen, the arguing progressively grew to a full-blown shouting match. To Jerrelle, it just didn't seem like an amicable end to this disagreement was going to happen anytime soon. In fact, her mind was trying to coax her into just forgetting about her sim-caf and snack, but her curiosity held her in place.

Within less than a minute after she had made the decision not to leave, a loud crash resonated from within the kitchen — an uncertain silence followed that almost immediately. Jerrelle's first instinct was to run into the kitchen and see what the hell had just happened. But this wasn't Detroit and she didn't want to get into any trouble here in Japan, so she stayed where she was. But when nothing but silence continued, and the Asian woman had not returned as she had promised, Jerrelle could only assume that someone, or both, had gotten hurt.

Again, her better judgment was trying to get her to leave well enough alone, but she honestly didn't think that a quick peek into the kitchen would be that big of a deal. Besides, if the two of them were indeed hurt, someone had to help. "Hello? Is everyone all right in there? Hello?"

The most logical place for Sabastian to look for Professor Ken Fu Sung was the university. Upon his arrival there, he instantly became a bit overwhelmed, as he never expected the university campus to be as large as it was. His initial idea was to first find the administrative building and then inquire about the professor, but he soon realized that every sign on the campus ground was written strictly in Japanese — so much for finding his own way around.

It took him almost fifteen minutes to find someone that spoke English well enough that could direct him to where he wanted to go — the Law Faculty Building. Once Sabastian found it, it again took him a bit of time to find someone else who could help. When he finally did, luck must have been on his side, as that person just happened to have been the Dean of Law, Professor Yu Har Phat.

After a brief introduction, and some time taken to convince the Dean that his intentions toward Professor Ken Fu Sung were genuine, Sabastian was able to find out that the man had actually retired three years earlier. He had also been told that the former professor still lived at the same place he had, ever since he was a young man — in Minato, at the Tenpi Keikoku Pier, on his large-sized catamaran.

"School must have been in because there were tens of thousands of fish swimming curiously around us. Flocks of seagulls also flew precisely over our heads; careful enough to not get too close for us to touch them, but still close enough to be admired. I was thrilled that Mother Nature allowed us to share this near perfect day with her out here in the middle of the Gulf of Mexico while we boundlessly sailed free from the daily norm. It felt so unreal; so wonderful.

My father had decided that he was going to take me on an adventure, far away from any sign of civilization so that I could experience what just wasn't possible back home in Ohio. I had never been this happy before in my life — but I was also sad, as this was the last day of an entire week spent with my father out there on the ocean.

Unbeknownst to me at the time, that week would turn out to be the last one that I would ever get to spend any quality time with him. My father knew that his life was gonna change once our week was over. Yet, his reasons for choosing to do what he was going to do just didn't make any sense to me.

From the end of that week on, in my mind, he had decided to blatantly ignore his family and skip out on his fatherly obligations. At twelve years of age, like most adolescents, I needed my father — especially since my mother had never been around. It just did not make any sense to me why he had made that choice. For many years, I didn't understand it and I believed that I must have done something wrong for him to not want to be home and not be there for me.

It wasn't until I was older and had enlisted in the military before I fully understood the sacrifice that my father had made — that was also when I first remembered feeling pride in him for choosing to dedicate his life in servitude to his country."

"Hey, buddy! The cab driver startled Sabastian and brought him out of his flashback. "You a here now… but this is as far as I can a go. The pier is all the way a down there." The cab driver pointed the way toward the longboat docks.

"Thanks for the ride." Sabastian paid the cab driver and he began the long walk; first down a rather long and steep flight of concrete stairs, then all the way almost to the end of the wooden docks. As he approached the slip to where the professor's boat was tied, he had noticed that a ponderous individual was leaning up against a weathered pillar. Sabastian made his way directly over to that person, hoping that maybe he would be able to confirm that the professor was living here. "Pardon me. I am looking for…"

"I know a who you are looking for," the ponderous man said. "He's a no here, so I think that you betta just go away!"

"How do you know who I am looking for?" Sabastian was beginning to think that there were no secrets here in Tokyo, for everyone seemed to know whom he was and what it was that he wanted.

"Fo da good of your health, I give you a thirty seconds to a turn around and a go back to a where you come from, as you not a welcome here." The ponderous man righted himself, took a step away from the weathered pillar he had been leaning on, and then cracked his knuckles in plain view of Sabastian.

To any other person, this man was surely intimidating and even frightening. Sabastian was certainly no small man, but he was somewhat undersized compared to this individual. And although Sabastian's military training was more than enough for him to feel confident in his ability to handle the threat that this man posed, he had no desire to get into a fight — but it looked like that was what he was about to do.

The ponderous man began to roll up his long sleeves. While he did this, he stepped forward intently, ready and willing to defend his territory. However, before he had a chance to get close enough to strike, an elderly looking man, who appeared to be in his early seventies, emerged — he had been inside the boat that was secured to the same weathered pillar the intimidating man had been leaning on.

"That's enough!" The old man said, as he walked up and placed his hand on the ponderous man's shoulder. "I'm the one you seek. Professor Yu Har Phat called and warned me that a very assured young man had been to the university in search of me. I don't know who in the hell you are, and I don't know what in the hell you want, but what I do think is that you should just do what my grandson son has asked you to do and leave."

Sabastian was surprised; the professor spoke near perfect English. "Professor Sung. My name is Sabastian. Do you know who Maxwell Banks is?"

"I do. Why do you ask?"

"Because he is my father."

Professor Sung paused for a moment. As he stood beside his grandson, he astutely studied Sabastian. The knowledge he had of his old friend's personal history was what had caused him to take a moment and look at this individual with the utmost of skepticism. However, Professor Sung had been around long enough and knew better not to blatantly dismiss something, even if it seemed unlikely to be true. "Maxwell Banks' son disappeared without a trace, twenty-five years ago. Do you honestly expect me to believe that you are him?"

"I know that it's hard to believe, but if you would just give me a moment, I'll prove it to you." Sabastian didn't really know that many facts himself — he just hoped that what he did know was enough to convince the professor. "My father's brother's name is Sydney, my mother's name was Sylvia, her sister's name is Sonya, and her daughter's name is Sharice (he hoped that was the truth). Twenty-five years ago, my father was partially responsible for putting an evil man by the name of Antonio Marcone away in prison. A few weeks after his conviction, my mother was murdered and I, his son, was kidnapped. Almost three weeks ago, my father was heinously murdered. His body was found chained and incased in concrete inside of a steel crate that had been submerged into the Detroit River..." The last fact he had didn't solidify his case, but it was all that he had left. "...and there is an uncanny resemblance between me and my father." To prove that affirmation, he pulled out his vid-cell and showed the professor the photo he had of Maxwell Banks as a cadet.

In retrospect, Sabastian knew that none of the evidence that he had just presented to Professor Sung would be enough to convince the man that he was who he claimed to be — he after all, had simply just stated some facts that anyone could have done some research to obtain. But he did hope that it would at least be enough trivial information to be invited into the professor's home so that he could talk to him in a more personal, one on one setting.

Professor Sung took a moment and carefully reviewed Sabastian's assertions, while at the same time, mentally comparing the everlasting image he had of Maxwell Banks from years past and the photo that he had just been shown. He had to admit, the longer that he stood there staring at the young man, much of the uncertainty that he initially had, dissipated. Sabastian had never been found, nor had he ever been declared dead. Whether or not this young man was who he claimed to be, the professor knew that he simply could not dismiss what now stood only a few paces away from him. Therefore, the professor invited Sabastian to follow him onto his boat. Once they were both inside, he immediately headed to where he had a few old photographs that hung on an interior wall. He removed the only one he had of himself and Maxwell Banks from fifteen years ago, back when they had first met.

He looked at it differently than he ever had before, picking out certain visual aspects of his old friend's entire being. After a few moments of unequivocal scrutiny, and again reviewing the evidence that had been presented to him, the professor became satisfied that the wool was not being pulled over his eyes. In his heart, he now knew that this young man was indeed Maxwell's long lost son. "I apologize for being so hesitant to your claim. It's just that I really have to be careful these days. I, like your father, have made enemies that I'm one day certain, want to see me dead one day. Please, Sebastian, make yourself at home."

Effortlessly, you fly ever so free. It's a feeling like you never felt before, as the air sharply cuts over and under. Floating up higher than you ever imagined possible, yet for some reason, you're not scared. Just like a puppeteer, every one of your strings is flawlessly controlled — a perfect performance of pure bliss. Then, without just cause, it all suddenly stops. Slight confusion takes over for what was assumed, has now become a struggle to maintain awareness and direction. Undiminished, you surrender all control, believing that everything will return to normal shortly. That doesn't happen. Instead, one by one, your strings are cut — and there is nothing that you can do about it. Powerless, you hang there waiting for the inevitable. It happens. You fall helplessly into a growing void of nonexistence. Darkness quickly draws itself close. Your life; it has succumbed to an unscripted and unceremonious finale.

The room was dark except for a faint hue of light, and it smelled somewhat musty. Jerrelle was lying unconscious on an old beat up synth-leather couch, unaware that she wasn't alone. The company she had kept watch and patiently waited — there had been no rush to wake her up.

It had been about an hour in total from when she had first arrived until she started to gain consciousness. It wasn't like waking up from a nap; waking up when one has a slight concussion is somewhat more arduous to do. Slowly though, she began to gain her bearings — and slowly, the pain increased. "Ugh... What a strange dream. Where in the hell am I? And man does my fuckin' head hurt."

She reached up and touched the massive welt that was on the back of her skull. "Ouch! Damn! I'm gonna kill the son-of-a-bitch that did this!"

"Well, I see that your mouth is still as foul as ever," her company said, as they made their way closer to where Jerrelle was lying.

"Bai Lin? Is that you?" She was still having trouble focusing, so she took a couple of deep breaths and shook her head, hoping to shake loose the cobwebs — instead, what she had done caused the pain to increase. She grimaced; a lesson now learned. Keep your head still and just rest when you've been whacked on the back of it. "Where in the... hell am I?"

"You are inside the Extremist Clandestine Liberation's secret underground headquarters, sis."

"Jesus Christ! Your associates must have mistaken my head for a coconut and were craving its milk. They cracked it so hard, they could have fuckin' killed me. Why didn't they just bring me here?"

Although they had agreed to allow her sister to come to their underground headquarters, Bai Lin's superiors were not willing to trust that Jerrelle could keep a secret. In all the years of the Liberation's existence, no outside individual has been able to locate their headquarters; a long standing streak that they wanted to keep in tack — this was why they had chosen to render her sister unconscious instead of asking Jerrelle to simply shut her eyes.

Bai Lin went on over and sat down beside her half-sister; she then leaned in closer and embraced the only person in this world who mattered to her. "I'm sorry they did this to you, but they felt that it was necessary. To them, it is imperative that this place stay a secret."

"I get it. But they could have just blindfolded or anesthetized me instead of giving me a grade one concussion."

Bai Lin cracked a humorous smile, knowing that her sister would have not willingly complied if either of those options had been given. "Yeah right, Jerrelle. So, what in the hell brings you into my retched part of the world?"

"It's a long story. I don't suppose that you've got any sim-caf or some rice cakes? I could really use something in my stomach."

Bai Lin got up and left the room. She returned a few minutes later with some food for her sister. It wasn't sim-caf and rice cakes, but it was food nonetheless.

While Jerrelle was busy filling her stomach, she explained her reasons for tracking her half-sister down. When she was finished, Bai Lin surprised her by informing her that she and the liberation were well aware of whom Antonio Marcone was and that he had apparently, not too long ago, double-crossed them during a mutually agreed upon deal; a deal that would have made the E.C.L. a large sum of money. They had known that there was a good possibility the man would not fulfill his end of the agreement, but they had unintentionally placed themselves into a situation in which they were reluctantly forced to be a part of. Ultimately, this bad deal had caused the E.C.L. to lose not only the large amount of money that they had been promised, but also eight members of their organization to either death or arrest because of it.

Jerrelle's stomach was now full, but her headache was intensifying. She needed to close her eyes and rest for a while to not only let the pounding dissipate some, but allow her meal to settle. And as much as Bai Lin just wanted to stay in the room with sister, someone whom she hadn't seen in almost a year, she had a responsibility to uphold. So she left Jerrelle alone and went directly to her superiors in order to inform them of what her sister had told her and to explain what her intentions were.

Helping an outsider with a personal agenda wasn't something that the E.C.L. normally did. But with the revelation that there was a possibility that Antonio Marcone just might be in Japan, they immediately decided to put a hold on everything else that they were currently involved with and agreed that it made sense to use their city wide resources and help Bai Lin's sister out. Japan was a very large country, and the search throughout it for one man by one person would be much more difficult than trying to find that proverbial needle in the haystack.

To say that the higher ups within the E.C.L. were thrilled would be an understatement. The possibility was now there for them to collect on all of their incurred losses. Yes, they understood that it was still a long shot, but if the only thing that came out of their intended assistance was the elimination of Antonio Marcone and his associates, then that would be considered an acceptable outcome.

Although Tokyo, Japan, is the eleventh most populated city in the world, just under nine million, there were still many places of isolation left — and the majority of those places usually belonged to either royalty or the filthy rich. No matter who owned them, these massive estates were a semblance of beauty that was immersed in native trees, exotic plant life, and artistic landscapes and sculptures — an incredible display of uniqueness and individuality that could easily inspire anyone.

Having the connections he had, allowed Antonio Marcone to seclude himself and his associates in one of these places in the ward of Edogawa City. 'Ten'nō no Niwa' (Emperor's Garden), was the name of the estate, and it was courtesy of a man named Hiro Juisota; a long time business associate and fellow mob leader.

Surprisingly, no reason was there for him to believe he wasn't now safely hidden away. Therefore, Antonio felt that a reinitializing of his organizational operations from his new satellite location could begin right away. Unlike the last time he had to run things from somewhere other than his home base, where he now was, Japan, might pose a few problems that first needed to be worked out. However, Antonio felt confident that any issues they might come across would be fairly easy to deal with — like the one that had just been brought to his attention. "Where in the hell are my associates?"

"I really fuckin' hate this place," Sal bitched again. "It's way too damn prissy for me."

"Give it a rest! I'm really tired of hearing you complain. That's all you've done since we got here. You should be thankful that you are here and not locked away in jail… or even dead. Besides, how can you not like this remarkable place? I find it very harmonious."

"I hate the smell of the flowers and the smell of the wild animals." *'And I hate the smell of you too, Louie,'* Sal said to himself. He then purposely stepped on a few ants that were crawling at the foot of the flowerbed next to him. "I hate these Asians and their stupid customs. Their food sucks, their booze is awful, and no one in this entire country can even speak any good damn English."

"With a piss poor attitude like that, Sal, I can see why you have never been able to spend more than one night with the same woman. You're in one of the most beautiful countries in the world... and it has one of the more traditional and intriguing cultures of any other. You should be open to learning something new and just enjoy yourself while you are here."

"I won't be enjoying anything. I can't wait till we get out of here and go someplace tropical."

"Don't expect that to happen anytime soon."

A strong, stern voice from across the residence bellowed, "Both of you get your fat and lazy Sicilian butts in here.., now!" The resonance from that decree sent chills up both Louie's and Sal's spines. They weren't sure why Antonio was mad, but they were sure that they would be getting an ear full as soon as they both stepped inside the mansion.

He was waiting in the great room at the far end of the home; he didn't even give Louie and Sal a chance to sit down before he tore into them. And by the time he was finished ripping them both a new one, Louie and Sal felt obligated to apologize profusely for neglecting their responsibilities — even though neither one felt that they had done anything to warrant the verbal thrashing they had just received from Antonio.

"We truly are sorry, boss. It's just that we assumed we would be able to enjoy all of the fantastic beauty of this amazing country for awhile before we had to actually do any work," Sal lied.

"As of this moment, your vacations are over. The both of you have a lot of things that I need for you to do." Antonio went over to the stone fireplace at the far end of the great room and opened up the hand carved cigar box that had been resting on top of it. He removed from within it one very rare Cuban cigar, lit it, and then sat down beside the fireplace in his new favorite synth-leather recliner. He remained quiet for a few moments, enjoying immensely the first few relaxing puffs he had taken. After that had done what it was supposed to do, Antonio swiveled his chair around and faced both of his associates — he was now ready to let his men know why he had called them inside. "I had just finished talking to our friend, Hiro Juisota."

"Hiro Juisota," Sal repeated. "I thought that you never wanted anything to do with him and his flawed ideology. If I remember correctly, you said that he was nothing but a wannabe who was attempting to pass himself off as a legitimate mob boss."

"Don't put words in my mouth, Sal, as I never said that. I said that he had a long way to go before he got to the same level as I."

Those weren't the words that Sal had remembered his boss saying, but he wasn't about to argue the point, knowing the kind of mood that Antonio was currently in.

"Besides… if the two of us didn't have a mutual respect for each other, then I'm sure that Hiro would not have been so generous as to allow us to stay in such a nice place as this. Now, don't interrupt me again, Sal. You know very well that I won't hesitate one bit to ship your lazy ass back home... and I'll be sure to send it gift wrapped right to the doorstep of the Detroit Police Department." Antonio looked directly at Sal for a few seconds, making sure he understood that what he had just said to him was a promise and not an empty threat. "Now, before you went and interrupted me, I was about to tell you that Hiro had just brought something to my attention that I cannot ignore. Apparently, there is a strong rumor floating around the city that there are a few brave individuals who are inquiring about whether or not we are here. Therefore, I want the both of you to go out into the city and try to find out whether or not this is true."

"Does he have any idea who these people are?" Louie inquired.

"He doesn't. Normally, I'd just brush such a rumor aside until it became more credible. But we are not in our home city; so dismissing this possibility would be a foolish mistake. By the end of the day, I would like to at least know if there is any truth to this rumor."

Louie understood Antonio's concern; Sal just thought that this was going to be a complete waste of his day. Nevertheless, he felt it best to just keep his opinion to himself and do what was asked of him. So with Louie right behind him, he headed toward the front door. They then proceeded to leave the grounds of the estate together and straight into the city. Neither one of them wanted to be in the other's company for an entire day, so each went their separate way. However, before they left, in what would be considered a rare occurrence, they actually agreed upon something — individually, they would search two adjacent districts: Edogawa and Chiyoda. Then at the end of the day, they would both meet up at the Kōtō and Chūō District line — they hoped that by sunset, at least one of them would have been able to confirm the rumors, because neither one of them wanted to waste their forthcoming days searching the other forty-five districts of the city until someone was able to confirm the rumors.

After his associates had left, a sense of relief consumed Antonio — well, more like a sense of freedom, knowing that he would have the rest of this day to himself. So he reclined right back in his synth-leather chair, and slowly puffed away on his Cuban cigar, enjoying every pleasurable moment that remained of it. *'It's pretty pathetic that the only bit of personal enjoyment I get out of my life these days is when I am relaxing with a good cigar, a drink in my hand, and being separated from those damn idiots.'* Although he didn't want to leave his chair, a drink did sound pretty good at that moment. So he got up, walked over to the wet bar, and poured himself two fingers of Suntory's Yamazaki Single Malt Whisky. It wasn't what he normally drank, but beggars can't be choosers when they are half way around the world.

After returning to his chair, Antonio took a sip, took another puff of his cigar, closed his eyes, and then sunk deep into thought, *'Why I still have them as being my close, trusted associates, who overtly try to pass themselves off as dedicated, indispensible employees, I'll never know.'*

Jerrelle normally kept erected a rather large wall when it came to people that she didn't know or trust. But she found herself in a position where she had no other choice but to temporarily take that wall down — all because she had gone in search of her half-sister in order to ask her for help. And now, because she was deep inside the E.C.L.'s secret compound, she knew that she had to co-operate with individuals who were just as dangerous, if not more dangerous than she.

Yes, Jerrelle was Bai Lin's sister, but blood was irrelevant to those in charge of the Liberation. Just because she had come to them with information that they were pleased to know about, and had agreed to work with her so that she could accomplish the task she had undertaken, it still didn't mean that they were going to fully open up their world to her.

Twelve hours after she had arrived, she had been secluded in a room with three high-ranking members of the E.C.L.; all of them trusted associates of Orochi Bushido, the leader of the Liberation. After just over an hour of conversation and questioning, the supplied answers were acceptable and it was determined that Jerrelle was not an immediate risk to their organization. And it was also decided that all of the restrictions that they had initially placed on her could now be lifted with the understanding that if it ever came to light that she was responsible for disclosing the location of the E.C.L.'s headquarters to anyone, a place that was actually hidden in plain sight, subterraneous to the Byakko Gardens, that she would be hunted down and killed — in the most painful manner imaginable.

Even though there now was an ensuring threat in the back of her mind, Jerrelle finally felt a little more at ease with her surroundings, so she decided that she wanted to explore the beautiful, twenty acres of garden above — there wasn't much else that she could do at the moment anyway, since the E.C.L. had denied her request to leave the compound until those who were out doing the dirty work for her, had returned.

About an hour after she had gone topside...

"What the hell are you doing out here, sis?"

Jerrelle turned to her sister and replied, "I'm just admiring all of the magnificent garden landscape. There is nothing comparable to this back home in Detroit."

"You can roam through the gardens all you want some other time. Right now, we've got more important issues to take care of.

We've been able to come up with a possible lead on the whereabouts of Antonio Marcone."

Jerrelle was happy to hear that. Hopefully now, she'd be allowed to leave, as she was certain that Sabastian was going to be very worried about her well-being. She followed her sister over to a hidden doorway that was cleverly camouflaged as part of a large red oak tree. She then stepped through the door and headed down the spiral staircase inside that lead straight down into the ground and ended within the E.C.L. compound.

"Unfortunately, our sources were unable to find out just exactly where it is that Antonio Marcone is hiding out at. However, one of our people spotted an ominous appearing Italian man eating at the renowned Japanese America House."

"That's your lead?" Jerrelle questioned. "But that could be anyone. What makes you think he is tied to Antonio Marcone?"

"The restaurant's owner is our source. He said that the man charged his meal on his Master Express Gold Card and the name on the card was that of Salvadore Batiste."

"Hum?" Jerrelle paused for a moment. "Ok, but that only confirms that one of Antonio Marcone's associates is in Tokyo. It doesn't confirm that his boss is here as well. And even if he is here, we still don't have any idea as to where he is hiding."

"Be patient, Jerrelle. We have to be extremely careful and take this one step at a time. Trust us, we will find that backstabbing bastard soon enough."

Jerrelle looked at her sister's watch (the E.C.L. had confiscated her vid-cell upon her arrival). She tried to hide it, but impatience was clearly written on her face. She was supposed to have rendezvoused with Sabastian back at the hotel a long time ago — she just hoped that he didn't assume that she had abandoned him.

Bai Lin knew that her sister was itching to leave. And although definitive proof of Antonio Marcone's presence in Tokyo had yet to be found, what they did find was good enough. Therefore, Bai Lin had been given permission to finally allow her sister to leave. There was one problem though — calling a cab to the compound was strictly out of the question. Instead, she was going to have to give Jerrelle a lift to wherever it was that her sister wanted to go.

She walked across the room they were in, Bai Lin's own personal space within the Liberation's compound, to a shallow armoire-like cabinet that was built into the wall. She stopped in front of it and touched her index finger on an amulet that was mounted halfway to the top and right in the center of the door. Two seconds later, the armoire opened up, Bai Lin reached inside, and then supplied herself with some items of necessity: a gun, a short length silver chain that had tiny little barbs attached to the end, a handful of throwing knives, and a ten inch sheathed knife (her honor blade). It wasn't that she was about to head out to face an impending battle, but it was a standard rule amongst the elite members of the E.C.L. to never leave the compound unless you were fully armed because an enemy could be lurking anywhere.

After Jerrelle had gathered her few belongings, she followed Bai Lin out of her room. She then curiously said, "Um… I'm not going to be rendered unconscious again, am I?"

Right after his visit with Professor Sung had concluded, Sabastian headed back to the hotel. He didn't expect to learn what he had. Nonetheless, he was extremely appreciative at the abundance of information that had been shared. Upon reflection, Sabastian could do nothing but smile. Yes, he was never going to meet his father in person, but with everything that he had learned from the professor, he now had a pretty good idea what kind of a person Maxwell Banks had been.

Although it was still early in the evening, he was feeling exhausted: the long flight, time change, and his visit with Professor Sung; all of it had finally caught up with Sabastian — so he just decided to call it a night. The next morning, he woke up feeling fully rested and invigorated. To his surprise though, the second bed in their room was still made. That meant only one thing — Jerrelle had not returned to the hotel. She of course, was a big girl and there was no reason for Sabastian to worry — but a part of him did. Chances were, she had successfully made contact with her half-sister and had decided to catch up on everything since the last time they had seen each other. However, if their paths didn't cross sometime this day, then he was going to have an issue with his old friend for not keeping him in the loop.

Once he had his breakfast, did his morning workout, and then had a shower, he headed out to the East Nippon Village Trading Center in Edogawa. It was there that Professor Sung had set up a contact for him at a place called, 'Herb's Aphrodisiac & Tea Shack'. In addition to the aphrodisiacs and teas that were sold there, you could also have your fortune told or your palms read. The place wasn't really anything that a tourist would plan in advance to go and see, but it did appear to be a quaint little business that had a lot of interesting items inside.

The moment that Sabastian had stepped across the threshold, his senses were grabbed by all of the exotic smells of the different teas and the abundance of unique items that were for sale. Although he wasn't there to buy anything, he took a moment and curiously looked at all the merchandise in the shop. After browsing the selection of goods, he found a tea that caught his interest. When he took it up to the counter to pay for it, he realized that no one was there — that, he thought, was a bit odd. Nevertheless, he just stood there and patiently waited, as he doubted that the open business would not have someone around to tend to the place.

He couldn't read any of the signs posted behind the counter because they were all written in Japanese, but he did notice a very thick rope attached to a large silver bell hanging to the left of the counter. Upon his further assessment, the only logical conclusion he could make was that this bell and rope was in essence, the stores doorbell — so he pulled it twice.

A few moments went by before a rather short, stout man came out from behind some hanging faded drapery. Sabastian speculated that the man was somewhere between forty and forty-five years of age and appeared to be of an Asian/East Indian decent. "How can I a help you, sir?" The shop owner asked.

"I would like to buy this package of Matcha tea," Sabastian answered, as he removed the correct amount of yen from his wallet; he then handed it to the man. With his purchase now complete, and while he was placing his tea into the small satchel that he carried with him, he asked the shop owner a question. "I've come a long way to find a long lost friend of mine. I was hoping that you might be able to help me locate him."

"I see. You know that a friendly smile is the most a joyous of all things in this a world. But as you a see at this moment I am not a smiling." The shop owner then slid forward an antique looking glass bowl, which had amazing handcrafted details on the sides, and was sparingly accented in gold leaf.

Knowing that he did not have a lot of yen on him at that moment, Sabastian reached into his front pocket and pulled out one hundred union dollars and placed it into the bowl.

"Your generosity is a much too kind a, sir." The middle-aged man grinned from ear to ear as he leaned over to Sabastian and whispered to him — even though no one else was in the store that could potentially overhear what he was saying. "I a understand that your a lost friend may be over at the a 'Bin Dar Be Fo Café'. I a believe that he is talking to a some locals whom are also in the same business as a he is." The shop owner then promptly stepped away from Sabastian and disappeared back through that same faded drapery from which he had first come — the antique bowl disappeared right along with him.

In hopes that the information he had just received was legit, Sabastian left the shop and headed toward the café. As he was approaching the place of business, he noticed off in the distance what appeared to be a well-dressed, Italian looking man. Right there with him were two other well-dressed Japanese men — all three of them had just exited the same café that he was now walking toward.

From where Sabastian was, he was unable to clearly see these men, as he was still roughly a block away. So as quickly as he could, he dodged through the people that were sparsely staggered in front of him. As he was doing this, he thought, *'I need to get a better look at them.'*

That unfortunately, did not happen. By the time Sabastian had gotten close enough, they were gone. The two Japanese men had seamlessly blended into the oblivious crowd that walked throughout the village; both had quickly vanished from his sight. The Italian man, the one that Sabastian was the most interested in, had stepped into an awaiting black limousine that had been parked in the lot at the side of the café. However, as luck would have it, the vehicle was partially delayed from leaving the area due to that same crowd — that impediment was what had allowed Sabastian to get close enough to partially see the individual inside the limousine via its half-opened, back passenger window.

His first instinct was to get into the empty cab that was parked just down from the restaurant and follow the vehicle, but that kind of impetuousness could end up costing him the advantage he had. Now was not the time for his existence to become known. Sabastian just simply needed to be patient and continue gathering information. This was after all, the first mission that he was on without the security of having his military brethren to back him up.

With his lead now long gone, Sabastian went inside the Bin Dar Be Fo Café; not to ask questions, but to gather his thoughts. Once he had located himself a secluded table, he opened up his satchel and pulled out an envelope that Savanna had given to him just prior to his leaving for Tokyo. As he was about to remove the contents from it, the café's waitress came by. It was late morning and Sabastian wasn't really hungry, as he had eaten a rather hearty breakfast just before he left to go to Herb's Aphrodisiac & Tea Shack. But knowing that he was taking up a table that a normal paying customer should be sitting at, he respectfully ordered himself a cup of Chai tea. Once the waitress had left his table, he removed what was in the envelope: a few pictures, and a compiled, cliff notes file on Antonio Marcone and his known associates. Although he was aware of the history of the D.U.O., Sabastian felt that now was as good a time as any to refresh his memory so that any important detail was not missed. Also, he was unsure if he even remembered what the important players within the Detroit Underworld Organization looked like — the last thing that he wanted was to be in a situation where he failed to recognize any of them.

Just as he finished re-familiarizing himself with the first of the three men he had images of, the waitress returned with his tea. At that moment, his senses awoke; he became aware of not only the aroma of the tea, but also the beauty of the waitress' backside as she walked away. *'This is not the time to be thinking about things like that,'* he reminded himself — yet he did allow a moment of harmless admiration to appear. *'At least I know for certain that I'm not related to that waitress.'*

With that moment now out of the way, and his focus back to where it should be, Sabastian looked at the next photo in the file, then the last — he instantly recognized that person's face. *'Louie Mazotti? Well I'll be damned. It was you who I saw through the limousine's open window. Savanna's assumption appears to have been right. Antonio Marcone has indeed fled Detroit for Japan. I mean... as of yet, I don't have any definitive proof, but I am now willing to bet that the bastard is here... somewhere. Soon, very soon, the man responsible for so many terrible crimes is going to get the surprise of a lifetime.'*

Sabastian put everything back in the envelope, closed it, sat back, and then drank his tea — not only was it very relaxing, the uncertainty that had been there no longer was. For the first time since his world had been turned upside down, he felt empowered; he felt confident. Fate had apparently placed him on the path that he had been born to walk. The task for which he was handed the reins, he now felt worthy of accepting. And the organization that Antonio Marcone had built at the expense of others, Sabastian fully believed, he was going to tear down.

Upon arriving at the Hilton Hotel, the sisters immediately went straight up to Jerrelle's room. There was really no reason for Bai Lin to tag along, but she curiously wanted to find out what this guy, Sabastian, was all about. Plus, she wanted to spend some more sisterly time with Jerrelle, not knowing when another opportunity to do so would arise.

When they got up to the room, they discovered that Sabastian wasn't there, so they headed on down to the hotel's bar — he wasn't there either. Although she wasn't too worried about her old friend, Jerrelle asked the A.I. at the reception desk if he had seen him. He had, and informed her that her 'husband' had left shortly before ten a.m. She thought about calling him to make sure that everything was all right, but decided against it, as she had neglected to check in herself, and owed her friend the same courtesy he had given to her yesterday.

Deciding that it was best that they just wait around for Sabastian to return, Jerrelle and her sister headed back up to the room. She had a somewhat decent sleep the previous night at the compound, but for some reason, she felt a little bit tired. With her friend presumably out and about, the opportunity appeared to be there for her to take a quick catnap — but only if Bai Lin were to be nice enough and let her.

"So when did you get married, Jerrelle?"

"What? I didn't get married."

"The A.I. desk clerk said that your 'husband' left here shortly before ten this morning. When can I meet him?"

Jerrelle knew that her sister was only trying to push her buttons, but insinuating that Sabastian was now her husband really irked her. In no way shape or form was she even remotely attracted to him — they were too much alike personality wise, and he had always been like a protective big brother to her. "He's not my 'husband'… and I'm not his keeper. I know he left here right after I did to go and speak with a professor from the university. If he got any leads out of that conversation, then he's probably following up on them right now."

"Why don't you call him and find out." As Bai Lin was about to finally hand her sister back her confiscated vid-cell, her own micro-communicator began to flash. *'Bad timing,'* she thought. "I really hate it when this thing goes off when I don't want it to," she was after all, planning on using the opportunity at hand to keep pestering her sister about her apparent 'husband'.

After taking up a seat on the edge of one of the beds, Bai Lin unclipped the micro-communicator that was cleverly concealed as part of the emerald charm bracelet that she wore on her left wrist, and set it on the end table. She placed her right index finger on top of the communicator and it scanned her print. Once the device had confirmed who she was, it projected a coded message onto the hotel room's white wall.

Jerrelle had never seen nor heard of anything like that before, and now she wanted one. "That is so cool! Can you send messages with that also?"

"Yes! This comes in handy especially if you happen to be in a precarious situation, captured, or trapped. All you have to do is touch it, let it scan your fingerprint, and it will activate. But unlike a vid-cell, you can't have an open two-way conversation with it. Its only use is for sending either a quick verbal or written message in real time, or one that you had previously recorded or constructed. It can also encrypt your message if you feel that it needs to be secured."

"So much for texting someone like in the old days. So why are you being sent an encrypted message?"

"I don't know yet. I'll let you know once I know."

Unsure of how long this was going to take Bai Lin to complete, Jerrelle contemplated taking a quick power nap but instead, decided to take advantage of her sister's company. Yes, it was only nearing the hour of noon, but in her eyes, drinking and celebrating could take place whenever, so she promptly left the hotel room to go and get them some ice cold beers.

Her timing could not have been any better. No sooner had she turned the corner at the end of the hallway, Sabastian had exited the elevator — both were completely oblivious to the fact that they narrowly missed seeing each other. To his surprise as Sabastian entered his hotel room, there was this rather strange, but exotic looking, tattooed Asian woman, sitting on the edge of the bed, legs spread invitingly, and busy in her own little world — she appeared to be preoccupied with some sort of gadget.

For the third time since his arrival in Japan, Sabastian's mind promptly switched into 'that' mode — those animalistic impulses began to come alive. This woman had an intriguing allure about her: sexy but deadly, possessive but also protective. Yes, she'd probably rip him apart, but just like the world's tallest and fastest inverted rollercoaster, Sabastian would be willing to pay whatever the cost would be just to say that he tried it at least once.

Sensing an unfamiliar presence, Bai Lin looked right at Sabastian; her stare caused him to snap out of his unrealistic fantasy. Instinctively, he reached around behind his back to locate his father's gun. He then quickly removed it from the back of his pants, drew it, and aimed it at Jerrelle's sister. "I don't know who you are, but there better be a good reason as to why you are in my hotel room!"

Bai Lin got up off the edge of the bed and moved herself into a better defensive position. She then made sure that the sheath on her hip, which held her ten-inch, double-sided honor blade, was visible. "You'd better relax man, as I don't want to have to use this on you."

Sabastian actually got a laugh from that declaration. He looked at her and replied, "You do realize that I'm the one holding the gun? For your own sake, I think you best just keep your hands right where I can see them."

So as not to allow the tension in the room to grow, Bai Lin cautiously unclipped her sheath and set it and her honor blade onto the nightstand. It may have appeared then that Bai Lin was now unarmed, but every one of the concealed weapons that she carried would take her less than a second to unveil if it became necessary to do so — although she doubted that this situation would progress to the point where she would have to do just that. "I am willing to bet that you are Sabastian?"

"Yeah, I am," he replied. *'Once again, here is another person whom I don't know that just happens to know who I am. I'm starting to really hate this country.'* "Who are you?"

At that moment, Jerrelle came back into the room with a six-pack of beer. Just before she was about to say hello to Sabastian, she noticed that he was pointing his gun directly at her sister's head. Slowly, she went over to him, placed her right hand on top of his gun, and tried to persuade him to lower it. Sabastian didn't move his gun at all; his military instincts told him not to give up the advantage that he had. "Do you know who this pile of trash is?" Sabastian asked.

Jerrelle moved around in front and looked directly at her friend. This time, she was able to coax him into lowering his gun down to his side. Shaking her head slightly, she handed Sabastian a beer and then walked over to Bai Lin and handed her one. Keeping one beer for herself, she then placed the other three down onto the desk by the bathroom door. While she cracked hers open, she couldn't help but expel a little chuckle under her breath. "Just so you know... that insinuated pile of trash is my half-sister, Bai Lin."

"This... is your sister?" Sabastian replied, embarrassed as well as surprised. Although her skin color was lighter than Jerrelle's, and her look being unmistakably Asian, now knowing who she was, the features that each sister shared were plain as day. Once again, his mind had failed him. For some reason, he was unable to recognize the obvious — maybe it was because he just never expected for his friend to locate her sister so fast, let alone did he foresee her bringing Bai Lin back to their hotel room. "I didn't realize that you were Jerrelle's sister. Why didn't you tell me?"

"You didn't give me a chance to tell you." She cracked open her beer and then took a healthy swig. "I hope, Jerrelle, your friend here is not as mentally unstable as he appears to be."

"He's not usually this demented," she replied; as she took a healthy swig of her beer — she followed that it up with an attention-grabbing belch. "He must be experiencing that post-traumatic stress shit they always talk about that military people tend to suffer from."

Once again, Sabastian had drawn a conclusion without any sort of evidence to support it — a deadly confrontation could have resulted from his doing this. Had he used his brain first instead of reacting to the moment, this misunderstanding would have been avoided. He did not know what skills Bai Lin possessed, but it was easy for him to assume now that they were probably equal to her sister's — and quite possibly, even better than his. If he had erroneously fought her, there was a good chance that he would have lost.

Right then and there, Sabastian realized that he had to de-program himself of all of his military cerebral training. He had always been taught to assume the worst when faced with an unknown and then go on the offensive, because most of the circumstances that he would have found himself immersed in, would have more than likely been hellish, no-win types of situations.

At that moment, Sabastian had come to the conclusion that he had to approach everything with an open mind, take the necessary time he needed to assess what was going on, and then determine as much as he could about whom his opponent was before he decided what course of action to take, because the next impulsive mistake that he made, could have disastrous results. "I'm real sorry about aiming my gun at your head, Bai Lin."

"That's all right. I'll forgive you this time." Bai Lin took another healthy swig of her beer, almost finishing it off. "I'll even let that comment about me being a pile of trash, slide by. But next time, I won't hesitate to use my blade and carve you up like a thanksgiving turkey."

That was something that Sabastian did not doubt.

After cracking open another can of beer and passing it on over to Bai Lin, Jerrelle said, "Ok, now that we know where everyone stands, I'm sure we'd both like to hear whether or not you have found out anything else?"

Sabastian finally cracked open his beer and took a weak sip. He followed that by briefing the sisters on his visit yesterday with Professor Sung, and then explaining in detail everything that had happened to him this morning.

Both Jerrelle and Bai Lin smiled with this new information that Sabastian had brought to their attention. With the E.C.L. confirming that Salvadore Batiste was in Tokyo, and now with Sabastian's sighting of Louie Mazotti, it all but assured that Antonio Marcone was somewhere in the city as well. Now, the hard part was to locate the bastard before he even realizes that he is being sought after.

Once downing what remained of her second can of beer, Bai Lin too expelled a belch that, had she been entered into a contest, might have actually given her first place. She didn't excuse herself afterwards for her unladylike barrage of noise; she instead turned her attention away from the two of them and resumed decrypting her message.

With the assumption that Jerrelle's sister was going to be awhile with what she was doing, Sabastian went over to the hotel room's vid-comp system to order them a late lunch from room service. It wasn't a full functioning computer, it was primarily an information terminal that was built into the hotel room's desk and meant for either ordering food from the hotel's kitchen or the surrounding restaurants. However, it could also be used to do basic research on the city or to browse the Japanese main tour center directory to see what kind of attractions there were — but that was the limit of its capability.

After placing his order, Sabastian then realized that Jerrelle had left him alone with her sister. Though he assumed that she had gone to replenish their beer supply, he did feel a bit uneasy about being abandoned in a hotel room with a human weapon — he did after all, refer to her as being a pile of trash. And even though she said that she was going to let his accusation slide, Sabastian was still feeling a bit unsure, as he had no idea whether or not Bai Lin had that same 'bitch switch' Jerrelle had that would turn on every time a disparaging comment came her way.

By the time their food had arrived, Jerrelle had returned and Bai Lin had finished decoding her message. Judging by the way the two sisters were enjoying their reunion, Sabastian could tell that they both intended to spend the rest of the day getting drunk. And although he could hold his booze with the best of them, he decided not to have any more beer and stay sober. His character judgment had thus far been way off, so letting his food absorb what alcohol he already had in his system, seemed like the proper course of action to take — someone in their group had to stay alert in case the unexpected took place.

Once their lunch was over and the girls fourth beers were freshly cracked open, Bai Lin started to explain to everyone what aspects there were in her encrypted message that were pertaining to them, including the part stating that the Liberation's sources had learned that Tokyo's own mob boss, Hiro Juisota, had apparently loaned one of his estates to a visiting business associate — who exactly that business associate was though, the E.C.L. had not yet confirmed.

"Did you just say, Hiro Juisota?" Jerrelle inquired. She got up, beer in hand, and went over to her travel bag. She opened it up and removed what she had been given a few days earlier by Jason Hernandez. "I seem to recall seeing his name in this black book that I was able to acquire back in Detroit."

"Black book?" Sabastian repeated. "What black book?"

"Oh… I'm sorry, Sab. I completely forgot to tell you about it." As she was handing the book over to Sabastian, she informed him that she had already scanned through its pages, and although there were a lot of names and incriminating information within, she didn't really see anything that she thought would currently be of use to them.

"We're supposed to be working on this together, Jerrelle. No matter how 'irrelevant' you thought this book was, you still should have at least told me that you had it." Sabastian opened up the black book and began to curiously skim through the pages.

"You're right. And again, I'm sorry. Can we just forget about it for now and concentrate on finding out where Antonio Marcone is?"

"Ok. But I haven't any idea where we should start." Sabastian looked over at Bai Lin — this was her city, after all.

"Hum? Let's just assume that Hiro did loan out an estate to Antonio Marcone. Depending upon just how many this man owns I might be able to figure out which one he lent to him." Bai Lin then invited both Sabastian and Jerrelle to accompany her over at the hotel room's vid-comp terminal where she promptly ran a general search on garden estates. Using size as a basic criterion, she self-assuredly assumed that Hiro would not own any average to small-sized ones. After less than ten minutes of deductive reasoning, and some blind luck, she believed that she had found the most likely estate that Antonio Marcone could be staying at. Of course, both Jerrelle and Sabastian were curious as to how Bai Lin had come to this conclusion. But before either one had a chance to inquire, she promptly explained her reasoning. First, she had eliminated Hiro's own personal residence — that left four more possibilities to assess. She was then able to eliminate one of the other estates because it was located way too far away on the Island of Honshu, near Mount Fuji. Next, she was able to eliminate two more estates under the assumption that Antonio Marcone would not want to stay somewhere that was part of a regular daily organized tour route. That left only one possible location — Ten'nō no Niwa; an estate that was well isolated from the public.

"Can you take us there, Bai Lin?" Sabastian asked.

"Sure... I can take you both there. But unfortunately, that's as far as I will be allowed to go. Part of my encrypted message included orders from my superiors to stay out of the rest of this. You two have to finish this vendetta of yours on your own."

"But I thought that the Liberation also wanted a piece of Antonio Marcone because he had owed them a lot of money?"

"He did owe us quite a bit of money, sis." Bai Lin then went on to explain to everyone that while the E.C.L. was trying to locate the man, they had luckily been able to stumble across some information that led them to a rather large slush account, which Antonio had cleverly hidden in Hong Kong, China, under the same alias that he used to get to Tokyo. So instead of covering their hands in blood, they opted to simply hurt him in his pocket book. "We were able to retrieve the amount that had been owed to us, plus we took a rather healthy sum in addition to it as interest."

Jerrelle was visibly dejected. She had hoped that she would have had the chance to do some serious damage with her half-sister — it had been way too many years since the two of them had fought together. Her disappointment, caused her memory to return to the very first time they had done just that, standing side by side when they were both young teens, to help someone in need.

It had been just one week into Bai Lin's yearly visit to Detroit when they ended up seriously hurting two young gutter punks who were attempting to kidnap a young nurse that had made the mistake of taking a shortcut home from work through the area of the city known as 'The Dead Zone'. And it was that event in which they both had realized that there was a very special bond between them; a bond even more definitive than that of the DNA they shared.

"Damn! I was really looking forward to fighting alongside you again, Bai Lin. I wish you'd reconsider."

"I'm sorry, sis. I would love to, but I can't. As much as I love you, I have an obligation and a loyalty to the Liberation that I must uphold. Besides, the E.C.L. already attracts enough unwanted attention in this city as it is, so I can't risk it. I hope that you understand?"

"Personally, I am really disappointed," Jerrelle leaned forward and wrapped her arms around her half-sister, "but I do understand the position you are in. All that I can say is that you better be protecting your ass, because there will be a day where I will need you to fight by my side again."

"You know that I'll be looking forward to that day, sis." They each picked up their beers, sealed their promise with a toast, and continued on with their unabated drinking.

Sabastian left the hotel room — not because he didn't want to be around two soon-to-be inebriated and dangerous sisters, but because he wasn't about to let them wander the hallways when it came time to replenish their stock. If they were to be let loose out into the hotel in an alcohol fueled state, then something was bound to happen. For that reason, Sabastian volunteered to be their beer runner — and babysitter.

Because of the unexpected information that had come his way this morning, Antonio's mindset had gone from a feeling of assuredness to a low-level state of concern. From time to time, situations like that will undoubtedly arise and are usually nothing to worry about. Twelve hours later though, his aging heart nearly stopped right in the middle of his vid-conversation with his Chinese associate, Zhin Wi. The man was Antonio's eyes and ears for all of Asia, where he kept tabs on any and all activity from not only Hiro Juisota, but any organization or company in this part of the world that just might threaten the existence of the D.U.O., its continued growth, and any possibly future expansion.

Whenever Hiro would begin to make advances in his business, Zhin was always able to throw up an untraceable roadblock or cause the man to have a huge setback. And it was Zhin's ability to meticulously do these kinds of things that had allowed him to not only become one of Antonio's most relied on associates, but become the first non-Italian to be fully accepted into the 'family'.

Over the last six months, Zhin had been keeping close tabs on a certain financial company in his homeland whose business practices were allegedly unethical. This assumption was all the reason he needed to continually monitor their activities, so that he might be able to acquire enough damaging information on them to pass along to his boss, knowing that Antonio was notorious for conducting a hostile takeover. However, while he was monitoring that company, he made an unsettling discovery — a theft from one of Antonio's personal accounts. That particular financial company had not been directly responsible for that happening, but someone had cleverly re-routed it through them in order to make that company look guilty.

Antonio could not believe what Zhin had told him, or that someone would have the balls to steal from him. His secret slush account in Hong Kong had been hacked into and he was blindly robbed of almost three million dollars. This unbelievable news had ruined what so far, had been a near perfect day for Antonio.

He hadn't moved since he had finished his call. Stunned, he just stood there and stared blankly out through the large picture window. Under normal circumstances, it would be hard not to admire the beautiful gardens and landscape on the other side of the glass, but with the mood that his call had put him in, it was nearly impossible for Antonio to use what he was looking at as a conduit to help relax his enraging thoughts.

Time seemed to have stood still; he had no idea how long he had been aimlessly looking out the window — it wasn't until an unexpected reflection in it caught his eye that his transient suspension had been broken. At that moment, he realized that his men had returned from their assignment.

Needing a moment to gather himself, he looked at his associates and asked them to go into the great room and wait for him. After Louie and Sal had done what was asked of them, Antonio walked over to the bar that was just off to the right of the large window and poured himself a snifter of Suntory Super Deluxe XO Brandy. One sip later, he joined his men; claiming in the great room what had quickly become his favorite seat next to the fireplace. After taking another small sip of his brandy and letting his pallet enjoy its bold flavor, he looked at his associates and said, "I just received a disconcerting call from Zhin."

After hearing the details of his call, Louie became very leery about having to reveal what little he knew. His news, though circumstantial, wasn't all that bad — but it still had the potential to add just a bit more sting to his boss' freshly opened wound. Nevertheless, Louie was Antonio's right hand man, and he had an obligation to inform him of everything that he had learnt. "I do believe that our anonymous sanctuary here is no longer. Though neither Sal nor I have confirmed anything, I do think that someone is definitely trying to find us. I'm not sure if this is anything that we should be worried about just yet, but..." After taking a second to organize his thoughts, Louie continued "...I was eating lunch at the Bin Dar Be Fo Café this afternoon with Akira and Mamuru; two of Hiro's men. One of Juisota's trusted locals, a bartender at the restaurant, came out to our table and informed us that a local busybody, a middle-aged man who owns a small tea shop not too far from the restaurant, came by earlier in the day asking a few questions; questions that at the time, she thought were harmless. Anyway, when we were leaving the restaurant, I had noticed that a young man was coming down the street toward us in a rather hurried fashion. Not thinking much of it, I just got into my awaiting limousine. But as soon as it began to leave, I noticed that the young man had stopped dead in his tracks. He just stood there and stared almost as if he had recognized me."

Antonio looked directly at Louie; pausing and trying to decide whether or not this incident could be enough plausible evidence to support the rumors he had earlier asked his men to investigate. "I don't think that proves anything, Louie. But I do think that the possibility is there that someone may have recognized you. Do you have any idea who that person was?"

Louie sat there just shaking his bewildered head. "No idea at all. I only know that he wasn't Asian. I'm sorry, boss, but I just didn't get a good look at him before my ride drove away."

"Do you want me to go out, pay this busybody a visit, and see why he was asking questions at the restaurant?"

"Normally, Sal, I'd say yes. But I don't believe that he is our problem. I suspect that it will only be a matter of time before we find out for sure if we have a bigger issue to deal with or not."

Louie leaned back in his recliner and looked up at the ceiling — what had happened to him left him feeling a bit dumbfounded. "So.., what are we going to do now?"

"I don't know? But it would be stupid of us to just keep doing what we are doing and hope that we will not be found." Antonio wasn't at all happy that his self-imposed exile may no longer be undisclosed — but he was even more pissed off that someone would actually steal his hard earned money. Were these two incidents somehow tied together? That, he didn't know. But what he did know was that someone was unknowingly going to become a part of one of his games; a game that in the past, Antonio had always loved to play. Yes, it had taken him twenty-five years to proclaim his greatest victory against Maxwell Banks — but just like that one, Antonio knew that whomever his opponent would end up being, he would end up being the victor. "If someone is actually looking for me, then they have unknowingly become a participant in 'the game'. The dice, by proxy, has already been rolled... and it has come up snake eyes."

"Look how long it took you to win the last one. Are you sure that you are ready for another marathon match so soon?"

"Let me remind you, Louie, it was I who chose to purposely drag out the last game for as long as I did... and the sweet taste of victory has yet to dissipate any from my pallet. Yes, I may be quite a bit older than I was when I started that game against Maxwell, but I'm nowhere near ready to relinquish my title of 'Grand Champion'."

Both Louie and Sal looked at each other. Without saying a word, each knew that the other was not at all happy that 'it' was going to start all over again. But there was nothing that they could do about it. Antonio thoroughly enjoyed playing games. And as long as he was in charge, the two of them had to be prepared to support their boss and help him to win — at all cost.

It was early the next morning and Sabastian, Jerrelle, and Bai Lin, were near the perimeter of the estate where they had hoped Antonio Marcone was staying. The still of the dawn was so neurotic that they didn't dare move from their stationary positions for fear of drawing attention to themselves. And even though they made sure that they were camouflaged from the possibility of being spotted by one of the many micro-security cameras that surrounded the estate, they still had to be careful, as one wrong move on their part meant that there was a good chance they would be seen.

It sucked that they were essentially pinned down by technology, but there was nothing that they could do until this issue was dealt with. That was why the three of them had not come alone this morning, as somewhere on the estate grounds was Tadao Fatumi, another member of the E.C.L. Bai Lin had asked him to accompany them in order to help with the disabling of the entire security system — but until that happened; they just had to be patient.

Having to wait for anything was something that Jerrelle always had a tough time with. Today, what little tolerance she normally had, wasn't there — probably because she had woken up with a massive hangover and her sister had not, even though yesterday the two of them had drank an equal amount of alcohol. It just wasn't fair that she had to suffer alone.

Two extra-strength Tylenols, a sixty-four ounce bottle of Gatorade, and a hot bath — that was what Jerrelle wanted instead of sitting her ass on the damp ground next to an arachnid infested bush. "Could we not have found a different place to wait instead of here? I don't know about you, but I have no desire to allow all of these damn spiders that live in this shrubbery to use my body as an anchor to spin their webs from. Honestly... do I even remotely look like one of those gargoyle statues that are all along the perimeter of this estate?"

Bai Lin just sat there and shook her head in response to her sister's diatribe. "I'm sure Tadao will have the security system disabled for us in a few minutes."

Although the temptation was there for Sabastian to throw in his two-cents worth, he decided not to — just because Jerrelle was his friend, didn't mean that he was immune to her wrath. "I don't know about anyone else, but I'm starting to think that something is not quite right. I mean, it seems a lot quieter than it should be."

"You don't honestly expect Antonio Marcone to roll out the red carpet for you, do you?" Bai Lin asked.

"No... but I was hoping for at least some sort of clue as to which one of the three front buildings he is in?"

"My guess, Sabastian, would be that he is in none of them."

"What makes you think that, Jerrelle?"

"Because, if I were a low-life piece of crap that was trying to hide, I would want to be in a place that was as secluded as possible and would also give me the best possible avenue for escape if need be. I would bet that he and his men are hiding out inside the estate mansion, further back on the grounds behind that outcropping of trees and shrubbery."

Sensing that Jerrelle was contemplating jumping the gun, Bai Lin reached out and placed her hand on her shoulder. She was about to remind her sister of a moment from their past of which she knew would cause her to reflect and remember the consequences that came as a result of her impatience, when she saw her micro-communicator flashing. Bai Lin removed it from her bracelet, placed it on top of an adjacent, old and weathered tree trunk, and activated it. Her message was projected onto the stone wall that was right in front of it; the same one that surrounded the entire estate.

"Just out of curiosity, sis. Why do you remove your communicator before you read the message?"

It's a safety feature in case you are captured and your enemy becomes intrigued with it. It won't work unless it is detached."

"Ah… that would make sense," Sabastian said. "But what if your enemy sees your bracelet flashing? What do you do then?"

"Just like an old style cell phone, you can set it to lightly vibrate instead of flash so that its actual function would not be presumed by the enemy." Bai Lin returned her attention to her micro-communicator and read the message from Tadao; *'The entire security system is now disabled'*.

With that knowledge in hand, Sabastian promptly stood up and quickly surveyed the estate grounds. "I just hope there is no back-up system."

"As do I," Jerrclle said.

"Well then… there's no time like the present to deliver the surprise of a lifetime. Jerrelle… you and your sister can approach the front of the estate together and I'll take the rear. Wait for my signal and then…"

"That's not going to happen!" Bai Lin interrupted. She then promptly reminded Sabastian that she only agreed to bring them to where Antonio Marcone might be hiding out at and to help them to gain entry to the grounds — nothing more. "I've already stayed here longer than I should have."

Before they had come here this morning, he had accepted that Jerrelle's sister was not going to do any more than what she had already agreed to. Nevertheless, Sabastian didn't think that it would hurt to at least try to convince Bai Lin to stay and lend a hand. "Are you sure that you can't stick around?" Not sure why he suddenly felt the urge to stoop so low, but he went ahead anyway and played the one card in the deck that he shouldn't have — the guilt card. "You are her big sister after all. Is it not your responsibility to protect her at all times?"

Bai Lin just stood there, shaking her head. "Nope! My sister is fully capable of taking care of herself. If anyone needs some protection, I'm sure it will be you." She then looked over at Jerrelle and could see a look in her eyes that clearly said her friend was very close to getting bitch-slapped straight back to the womb for his dim-witted remark. "I really hope that you both succeed with this endeavor of yours. It's been a pleasure meeting you, Sabastian, but I really must go now. Goodbye and good luck." As Bai Lin was about to leave, Jerrelle stopped her — she then hugged her more meaningfully than she had since the day her mother died. She didn't know why she had done this, but maybe it was something to do with the fact that she had no idea when the next time would be that she'd get to see her sister.

After watching Bai Lin walk to where she intended to rendezvous with Tadao, at the far west corner of the estate's perimeter, Jerrelle turned her attention to Sabastian — promptly, she gave him a stare that contained so much condescension, he actually thought that she was contemplating claiming his soul and then handing it over to the devil himself in exchange for immunity from whatever sins she may commit during the remainder of her life. "Keep it up, and what I one day intend to do to your ex-father will pale in comparison to what I will do to you."

Sabastian just sat there and smiled. And although he was aware that Jerrelle could back up her words if she chose to act upon them, he knew that her threat against him was emptier than an archetypal politician's promise — it was, he believed, just her hangover that had caused her to overreact to his good-natured ribbing.

Just as they did when they breached Chevy's apartment, Jerrelle entered through the front first, then a few moments later, Sabastian entered via the rear. Surprisingly, they both were able to freely gain access to the mansion as neither door was locked — either Antonio Marcone wasn't expecting them, or he purposely left the place unlocked because he wanted to lure them into a trap.

Carefully, they made their way into the building and began by searching the main floor; no clear indication was there that they had found the right place — this though, wasn't enough to discourage them. Instead, they spent a few moments in conversation right outside of the entrance to the mansion's library. When they were done, it was agreed that their initial assumption was still correct and that they were not going to leave until they found what they were looking for or were able to conclude that they had wrongly speculated.

After heading up to the second floor, they each went their separate ways. With only seven large rooms in total on that level, it didn't take them long to verify the place was unoccupied, nor were they able to find any indication that someone recently had been staying in the place.

Feeling defeated, they both headed back down the stairs and stopped inside the great room. There, Sabastian took a moment to gather his thoughts. Although there was still no guarantees, he was now fairly certain that Antonio Marcone and his two associates were actually where he had first thought — hiding out in one of the smaller residences on the estate. But then he quickly dismissed that notion once he noticed something that both of them had earlier missed — a nearly empty brandy snifter sitting on an antique oak end table next to a brown synth-leather recliner. Upon a closer inspection of the snifter, Sabastian quickly determined that it had not been sitting there for too long a period of time because the alcohol residue on the inside walls had yet to become completely sticky.

Jerrelle could easily see the disappointment on her friend's face — not just because they appeared to be too late, but also because they had almost completely overlooked what just might be an important clue. No, this wasn't proof that Antonio Marcone had been here, but someone definitely had — and either that person just happened to coincidently leave right before their arrival, or their presence in Japan had already become known and their target was here and chose not to stick around.

Before they had entered the mansion, Sabastian believed that he was fully ready to confront his family's advisory. Now, he wasn't so sure. Just giving Antonio Marcone the shock of a lifetime wasn't going to turn the tables in his favor. He was the new kid in town — and the only way that he was going to succeed, was to do something unforeseen that would force the enemy into waving the white flag.

This dead end should not have been so deterring — but Sabastian's mind was filled with unbridled thoughts that just would not sort itself out. The sudden changes in his life clearly were the reason for this and undoubtedly, that was what had contributed to his sudden annoyance. He knew that he couldn't let this one instance of failure consume him — he instead, had to channel his emotions and use them in a positive way in order for him to achieve his goal. Only then, could the demons that possessed his family be exiled forever.

His instincts were now telling him that Antonio Marcone had somehow become aware that he was being sought. Thus, a supposition quickly formulated within his mind — the enemy, even though Sabastian was pretty sure that his identity had yet to be established, was now preparing to do the same thing that he had done with his father — play a game.

The thought of being a pawn in a madman's twisted form of entertainment bothered Sabastian more than it should have. No proof was there yet that this was going to occur, but his gut was telling him otherwise — and it irritated the hell out of him. Unbecoming of who he was, Sabastian let his frustrations dictate the moment. He hastily picked up the brandy snifter and threw it across the room — it bounced off the back cushion of a couch and then landed on the carpeted floor where oddly, only the stem of glass broke. Right after that, he picked up the opened book that had been sitting next to where the snifter had been, and he threw it in the opposite direction — it landed right in the middle of the unlit fireplace.

"Calm down, Sab. It's not the end of the world. We will find him. It just won't be as easy as we had hoped it would be."

"You are right, Jerrelle. I need to relax and think like my father; like a detective." Sabastian took a few moments and calmed himself down. "From this moment forward, we need to assume that Antonio Marcone believes that someone is looking for him... although I am willing to bet he has no idea that it is us."

"That, I would agree with. Nevertheless, you can be certain that the man will be ready for just about anything."

After a few more moments of pondering thought, Sabastian looked at his old friend and said, "His not being here, is either just a cautionary move on his part, or a test."

"I don't believe this is a test, Sab. But if this is, he will soon become aware of us."

Sabastian could not help but smile, as the expression that Jerrelle had on her face, said it all. No matter what came next, she was going to be ready — not just because she was more dangerous than a threatened mama bear, but because she hated to lose. Her competitive nature, along with the obliviousness Antonio had to Sabastian's existence, undoubtedly gave them the upper hand. It was an advantage they had to keep for as long as was possible, because the moment he learned the truth, Antonio's decision making would then become calculated and precise.

"I am almost willing to bet that as of right now, Antonio is actually thinking that the same person who drained his bank account is the one who is looking for him."

Jerrelle agreed. She then cracked an unexpected smile, as a scenario sprang forward in her mind to what it might be like for Antonio the moment he finally laid his eyes on Sabastian. That smile though, quickly disappeared as her eyes led her to an item of curiosity — one that she had actually been leaning up against.

Like Sabastian, she too had looked right past it. But instead of getting angry with herself, she calmly opened up the top drawer of the antique oak desk. Jerrelle then said, as she began to look through it, "So... let's just assume that Antonio Marcone is now playing a game with us. It then would make sense to me that the man had to have left some sort of clue behind for us to find."

"If he did, it's not obvious. And I would not doubt that a trap of some sort might also be left behind right along with it."

They didn't care that the estate belonged to Hiro Juisota, a man with nearly as many connections throughout the country as its Internet service has. They needed a lead; something that could at least point them in the right direction. So with a lot of caution from each, they both spent about an hour inside the estate, leaving no corner of it unchecked, hoping that they would find something significant. Unfortunately, that didn't happen.

Disappointment again encompassed Sabastian. Thankfully this time, he hadn't gotten frustrated to the point where he again needed to throw something. "You didn't find anything either, huh?"

"Just an old palm-top... but I don't think that it works. Other than that, I didn't find jack shit!"

"I'd have settled for finding a piece of toilet paper that Antonio Marcone had wiped his ass with. At least then, he would have left us his DNA, proving that he had been here. Either the man was never was, or he's a germaphobe and keeps everything hospital clean." Sabastian took a moment and tried to clear his mind. "I think we've wasted way too much time here. He then reached into his pocket and pulled out his vid-cell. "I need to make a call before we leave."

"Who the hell are you going to call?"

"I'm going to call my friend, Baylor, and see if he has any other ideas about where Antonio Marcone could have gone." Sabastian made his way over to the synth-leather recliner that was by the fireplace and sat down. But before he made his call, he had a brief flashback to a moment from his past — it gave him an idea.

With the assumption that the operating system on the palm-top that Jerrelle had found might be corrupted, he took it and connected it into the X-slot on the bottom edge of his phone — he hoped that maybe he could use his phone's operating system and network into it. He knew the system on his phone wasn't near as complex as the palm-top, but both of the items were Samsung — which meant that the palm-top more than likely used the same Android XXV platform.

However, unlike his friend, Sabastian wasn't that tech savvy. He wasn't exactly sure what he was doing, but he did remember Baylor telling him that it was possible to network the two together, so Sabastian tried by memory to repeat the steps he had once before watched his friend perform.

While he was attempting to do that, the book Sabastian had earlier thrown into the fireplace, strangely caught his eye. Thinking nothing of it, he continued on with what he was doing. After a few seconds, he was able to get his phone to recognize the palm-top — but he still wasn't sure what to do next. As he tried to search his memory for what he needed to do next, his eyes wandered back over to the book in the fireplace. There was no logical reason why this book should snag his curiosity — but it did.

He moved his gaze away from it and tried his best to put this unwanted distraction out of his mind so that he could resume with the task at hand — but he just couldn't stop glancing over at that damn book. Finally, his curiosity got the best of him, so he set his phone and the palm-top down on the end table next to where he was sitting and took a few steps closer to the fireplace. The way the book had landed from his earlier throw, had left it partially opened, exposing what appeared to be, upon a closer inspection, the deep indentation left behind of some handwritten text. Those words could be just about anything, but Sabastian felt that they had nothing to lose by taking a moment and confirming what it was that he was now looking at.

"You better hurry up with whatever it is you're doing there, Sab. Who knows if Hiro or one of his men will show up here?"

"Hold on a minute, Jerrelle. I might have found something." Recognizing immediately that nearly a third of the pages in the book had been torn out, Sabastian began to quickly skim through what was left of it — he saw nothing else. He then went over to the oak desk and opened up the top drawer. After successfully finding a pencil, he began to scribble all over the page that had the indentation. "Well I'll be... I do believe that I may have sort of found Marcone's location."

"Sort of?" Jerrelle repeated. "So tell me oh great, Sherlock. How did you come to sort of figure out where he is?"

Sabastian scrutinized the page once again, hoping to find more there than he already had. "This book seems to be some sort of a daily personal log. A good portion of the pages have been torn out, but it does appear that an imprint has been left behind on this page." Sabastian showed it to Jerrelle. "The problem is... the only thing that I can make out here is — Plan B, Air Euro, flight 46... 3 or maybe it's an 8."

Jerrelle stood there admittedly impressed. "And to think that we just spent over an hour combing over every square inch of this place in search of clues when what we had been looking for all along had been in your hand right from the start. You're so fuckin' lucky that there wasn't an already lit fire going when you threw it in the fireplace."

"Yeah, no shit. The question now is... where in Europe did they go?" Sabastian went back over to the recliner by the fireplace, sat down in it, picked up his vid-cell, disconnected it from the palm-top, and then called Baylor.

6

By the time they had returned to their hotel, Baylor had called back with the information Sabastian had requested pertaining to flights out of Japan to Europe. He used the same method as before and was not at all surprised when Tony Ignatius's name had appeared on the passenger list for flight 468 to Germany. Unfortunately for Sabastian and Jerrelle, no other last minute flights were available — this left them with no other option but to stay another night and try again the next morning.

Ten hours later, they were finally in route to Germany. While in the air, Jerrelle went over all of the files that Savanna had supplied to Sabastian. Included in them was a detailed record of Maxwell Banks' police and private detective career; a stellar one that had allowed Jerrelle to envision the probability of what her friend might one day become if he was anything like his father. In those files was also a list of all of Maxwell Banks' overseas contacts throughout the years, as well as documentation pertaining to all of Antonio Marcone's overseas assets and suspected foreign associates.

Missing something important, as trivial as it might seem to be, could possibly end up costing them more than just a simple advantage — that, Jerrelle knew, they could not let happen, as it could be the sole reason why they just might lose this fight. With that in mind, she carefully cross-referenced the list of associates in the file with the names that were in the black book she scored. All but four of the names matched up with the ones in the file — they were complete unknowns that for now, she didn't believe they had to worry about. However, Jerrelle knew that if they were to cross paths with any of those four individuals and not already knowing at least something about them, it would put her and Sabastian at a severe disadvantage. Therefore, when time permitted, some research had to be done.

While Jerrelle was busy studying, Sabastian had taken the troubleshooting instructions that Baylor had sent to him and again tried to use his vid-cell and link it into the operating system of the damaged palm-top. For more than an hour, he tried and failed. He just could not seem to access any of the programs or files on the device. It clearly was frustrating, but Sabastian wasn't deterred any.

Because of what he was able to do, it became apparent to him at that point that the palm-top's operating system wasn't what was damaged. This left him to draw the only logical conclusion that he could — the device had either a power source issue or damaged hardware. This meant that Sabastian was left with no other choice but to wait until he returned to the agency so that he could hand it over to Baylor to repair.

As soon as they landed in Berlin, Sabastian immediately left for the train station to go to Frankfurt, as he remembered reading that his father, five years earlier, had gone there because he had been asked to work on a case that involved an exchange student who had been accused of murdering his roommates. The young man's parents had asked Maxwell to find whatever helpful information he could, as they felt adamant that some key evidence was purposefully being withheld that could exonerate their son. And they had been correct, as several high-ranking police officers, with ties to a few German political figures, had been using their influence to prevent the truth from ever coming out.

Lt. Myrinna Kragtov of the German Police Force had been a big help to Sabastian's father during the case — although initially her assignment, which had actually come from one of those same high-ranking officers, was to do all that she could to prevent Maxwell from finding the needed evidence. Reluctantly, she had agreed to do what she had been assigned — but only because she did not want to rock the boat and cause a rift between her and the rest of her police brethren. However, Maxwell was able to get her to open up her eyes and see just how corrupt her superiors were. At that point, she no longer cared about her job; only what she knew was right — so she decided to help him. And by her doing so, the two of them were not only able to obtain proof of the young man's innocence, but in the process, they were able to expose all the bad seeds that were within the German Police Force.

To Sabastian, it made sense for him to try and establish contact with her before he did anything else. Jerrelle on the other hand, immediately switched planes and took a forty-five minute commuter flight to Munich so that she could try to locate an old acquaintance of hers that she had once known during the early part of her military career.

After only a few weeks into her first posting in Munich, she had met a German Military Lieutenant named Helfred Nemchieve — they had subsequently engaged in a brief relationship that did not end well. Unfortunately, with what she and Sabastian were now doing, she found herself having no other option but to revisit that part of her past. She would have preferred to never see the man again, but it was the only way that she felt she would be able to help out her friend.

During her research into Helfred's probable whereabouts, she stumbled across a surprising fact — the man had been promoted twice and now held the military rank of captain. That rank gave him certain privileges which Jerrelle knew she could exploit. He had been smitten with her, and she knew that she could tug at his heartstrings. It was cruel and cold to do such a thing, but to her, he was just a notch on her bedpost.

Her now having to walk back into his life unannounced, and being overtly kind to him so she could get what she wanted, might give off the wrong impression. Therefore, she had to make sure that he understood the door she was opening was not going to be kept open — it was going to again close once Jerrelle was able to get what she came for.

She remembered that Helfred, along with many of the military personnel who were stationed at the Luxembaum Army Base, would frequently gather in the old town district of Munich when they were not on duty. There were many places in that area where the German Military personnel liked to drink — including a place that catered not only to them, but also to the naïve university crowd. It was that place, the Neue Bavarian Hofbrauhaus, where Jerrelle was headed, as she felt pretty certain that this would still be Helfred's favorite hang out.

The first thing that came to Jerrelle's mind when she entered the bar was that it had not changed one bit since she had been here last, three years ago. It was filled with the same horny military guys that lied to every single girl they met; each one of them trying to convince the girls that this evening was actually going to be their last before they shipped out to some war torn country for a two-year tour of duty. The sad thing was, these girls were the same as well: generally young and looking for instant love, prestige, or to satisfy a bet — and each were usually willing to give up that piece of tail to get it. It was shallow, but a lot of them erroneously believed that by doing this, they were contributing to their country's freedom by sating a soldier before they 'went off to war'.

Jerrelle made her way through the compressed crowd and went straight over to the bar. Nonchalantly, she bumped an inebriated private off of his stool and staked claim to his former spot. However, she didn't even have time to order herself a beer before she spotted her target. He was real easy to locate because he was not so indiscreetly nudging all the semi-drunk bodies in his path to the side so that he could make his way across the club — his radar was locked onto something.

Helfred was six foot six inches tall and built solid as a truck. His hair was dirty blonde and cut square. He had a small scar just underneath his left ear and a tattoo on his right bicep that depicted a skeleton, dressed raggedly in military garb, and brandishing an assault rifle and a bayonet — a tattoo inspired by, though not a direct copy of, the iconic Iron Maiden mascot, Eddie.

After stopping his forward progress, Helfred leaned against a pillar — he had arrived at his target. For a few moments, he stood there astutely dissecting his prey. For Jerrelle, it was easy to see what he was planning on doing next — and it disgusted her.

After siphoning back his beer, Helfred took two steps forward in order to position himself for what would normally get any man arrested and charged — his targets had no idea that they were both about to be violated.

Discreetly, he nestled himself in between the unsuspecting young ladies — and his hands suddenly became one with them. He had succeeded; he was now feeling both of them up — the sad thing was that those slightly inebriated young girls were actually allowing Helfred to get away with what he was doing.

'These girls don't even look like they are old enough to be in this place, Jerrelle thought. *I think that I shall go over there and spoil Helfred's little patting party and rudely introduce myself.'* Jerrelle left

169

her seat at the bar and made her way over toward him, careful not to let her old acquaintance see or sense her approach. "Well... I see that the arrogant, perverted jerk in you still likes to come out and play. You fuckin' disgust me, Helfred."

Shock, perplexity, and embarrassment enveloped Helfred all at the same time. Never did he expect to see Jerrelle again — not after everything that had taken place. The pain of them having been forced apart by military policies all those years ago was something that they both at the time, had trouble accepting. Now, seeing Jerrelle again, had instantly brought back that same pain he had struggled for a very long time to deal with, as she had been the only woman that Helfred had ever admitted to himself that he had truly fallen in love with.

"Well... aren't you going to say anything, Helfred?"

"I... I never ever expected to see you again, Jerrelle."

"Yeah... me too. Can we go and talk somewhere private?"

"Sure... I guess." Helfred removed his hands from where they had been resting and placed them into his pockets. "This really wasn't what you thought it was."

"What wasn't what?" Jerrelle said, derisively.

"Those two young ladies I was just talking to. It really wasn't anything at all."

"You don't have to explain yourself to me, Helfred." Jerrelle decided in that moment that now was the perfect time to satisfy her own curiosity. She had always wanted to find out if, especially after all the time that had passed, whether or not her ex-boyfriend really had any kind of feelings for her — after all, no hint whatsoever had been there during their brief relationship. "Tell me something though... When did you find the time to learn sign language?"

"Sign language?" Helfred repeated, while looking at Jerrelle a bit dumbfounded. "I don't know sign language."

"That's funny.., because it looked to me like you were communicating quite easily with your left hand on the top band of the skirt of that blonde and your right hand around the waist of that redhead." Before Helfred could respond, Jerrelle smacked him right across the side of his head. She then shot him the dirtiest of looks before she turned and walked away.

"I've always cared about you, Jerrelle. Don't you care about me?"

That was exactly what she wanted to hear. However, she had no plans on ever revealing that she too had similar feelings for him, as she was content to just get on with her life — the last thing she needed right now was someone complicating it. "Get real, Helfred. What makes you think that I actually cared about you? It's been more than three years… and you know very well that it would not have worked out anyway. So just drop it. I didn't come here to rekindle our past relationship."

"Then… why did you come here?"

"I need your help."

What Helfred had hoped for, but honestly never thought would occur, just had. That proverbial window had opened up — albeit, only a small crack. If he didn't at least try to pry it open wider, then his one and only shot of possible true happiness would be lost forever. He knew that Jerrelle was a very tough nut to crack and that she had higher and thicker walls than a maximum security prison, but fate had just given him an opportunity to regain the most important thing in his life that he honestly believed he had lost forever. "Ok. Whatever it is, I will help you with it."

Over the next hour, Jerrelle and Helfred talked. They had a lot of catching up to do. It was hard for him, even painful at times to just sit there and listen. All that he wanted to do was wrap his arms around her, pretend that the three missing years did not happen, and make long, slow, passionate love to her. But he knew that wasn't going to happen right now. Too much time had passed. However, the damage that had been done by their respective governments, he truly believed could be repaired. It certainly wouldn't happen overnight, but he was willing to be patient and allow her to be the one to make the all-important first move. However, if she did as he expected and refused to allow her true feelings for him to come to the surface, then Helfred was prepared to completely embarrass himself and share his.

While riding in the back of the cab on his way to see Lt. Kragtov, Sabastian had time to reflect about everything that had happened up to this point. It was a complicated situation that he had keenly gotten himself into; one that he felt compelled to follow through with until the bitter end. *'I'm now beginning to understand why my father spent a good majority of his life seeking revenge against Antonio Marcone. The man appears to be very meticulous at whatever it is that he does. He may have rightfully claimed victory over my father, but I will see to it that he loses the rematch. I, on the other hand, must not make the same kind of mistakes that my father made and I must make sure that I don't fall into the same traps that the man will undoubtedly try to lead me into.'*

Upon his arrival at the downtown Berlin Police Station, a bit of nervousness oddly began to surface. This was the first time that he had to deal with the police and he was not too sure just how they would react to him and his plans — especially considering that he wasn't even a German citizen. "Excuse me, officer. I am looking for a Lt. Myrinna Kragtov."

"She hasn't been a lieutenant for almost two years now," the desk officer said. "She is now the captain."

"Oh? May I then please see Captain Kragtov?"

"No," the desk officer stated. "She's real busy right now. You'll have to come back some other day."

'Why does this have to be so difficult?' Sabastian thought. "I don't know how long I will be in the country. Are you sure there isn't any possible way that I can see her today?"

"I'm sorry, but she's very busy."

"Ok. I understand. Thanks for your time." Sabastian turned and started to walk away; giving off the impression as he did this that he had accepted the officer's denial of his request. However, after only a few short steps taken, he took a brief glance over his shoulder. As he had hoped, the desk officer had lowered his head to resume his paperwork — which meant that he no longer was paying any attention to the lobby. This was the opening that Sabastian needed, so he turned back around, moved forward as quickly as he could, jumped the half door that divided the lobby and the precinct area, and walked uninvitingly into it in search of Captain Kragtov.

The other officers in the precinct quickly rose up from behind their desks and positioned themselves as they had been trained to do. And as expected, right in front of him, two officers, with their hands resting on their side arms, resolutely approached Sabastian. He knew that they would not draw on a non-threatening individual, so he calmly waited for them to get close to him, where he then used his military training, not to defeat them, but to only partially resist their efforts at stopping him.

With his background, Sabastian believed that could have easily hurt those two officers, but that was not his plan — it was simply to cause a scene and hope that it would draw the attention of the captain. And after just a few seconds of struggling with the officers, his plan had succeeded.

Standing at the threshold of her office, Captain Kragtov said, with enough force in her voice to make everyone in the precinct feel as if they were guilty of something, "What the hell is going on out here?"

Myrinna was undoubtedly a beautiful lady who appeared to be in her early forties. She stood about five foot eight inches tall, and had wavy, shoulder length brunette hair. Her face was relatively narrow and she had a tiny, dot-like beauty mark just above her upper lip. However, her most distinctive feature was something that any man of any age would instantly be drawn to — and not just with their eyes. That being her perfectly placed and ample unenhanced breasts. For Sabastian, he was easily able to differentiate between her physical distraction and her physical presence. He had only come here to talk to her, not to admire what she had been blessed with.

In a moment of odd, ill-timed thought, Sabastian realized that 'it' didn't happen this time. Captain Kragtov was definitely a 'hot-tamale' that for some reason did nothing for him. His libido had strangely stayed dormant this time; a freak occurrence that he was thankful for at that moment. He also realized, just by looking at this woman's demeanor, that she had the capability of ripping someone a new anal cavity if they even remotely looked at her the wrong way.

Clearly recognizing her picture from his father's files, Sabastian respectfully addressed the captain. "I've come here to speak with you about something important but your officers are preventing that from happening."

"Get this guy out of here, now," Captain Kragtov ordered, "and everyone get back to work!"

"Wait!" Sabastian pleaded. "I came to talk to you about my father, Maxwell Banks."

Captain Kragtov had been in the process of shutting her office door when she paused. *'Maxwell Banks,'* she repeated to herself as she stood still and recalled a man from her past whose path she had once crossed and who had been responsible for changing her life in many different ways. Curiosity quickly consumed her, so she turned back around and walked away from her office. She then sauntered right up to Sabastian and said, "Hold on a minute! What in the hell did you just say?"

"Captain.., I'm sorry for the chaos I just caused here, but... I came all the way here to talk to you about my father's murder. My father was Maxwell Banks."

The captain remembered reading not too long ago on the International Newsnet about the murder. And although the man's murder did not affect her on an emotional level, her heart did ache for him. Because of what had happened to her, her life had been flipped upside down. Her ascension to the captaincy was directly contributed to the fallout that had occurred from the house cleaning the police department had done. However, the years that followed that scandal were filled with continual backlashes from those who knew and were close to the officers connected to the whole situation. All who had been involved, not only had lost their jobs, but also ended up in jail. It wasn't until she received the rank she now held that all of the contempt that had existed finally stopped.

Captain Kragtov took a moment and thoroughly scrutinized the young man now standing just a few feet away from her. She tried to compare the images she had brought forward in her mind of Maxwell Banks, but she still was unsure — after all, she never knew a younger version of the man. Nevertheless, her skepticism wasn't enough to dismiss Sabastian's claim so she ordered her officers to release their hold on him. "Are you really Maxwell's son?"

"Yes, I am."

Now wanting to find this out for sure, Captain Kragtov invited him to follow her into her office. Once they both had entered, she asked him to sit. After moving around to her side of the desk and then taking a seat, she again looked curiously at him — what she saw, did not give her any inkling whatsoever that he might have a hidden agenda. "So tell me.., what is your name?"

"My name is Sabastian."

The more the captain studied this stranger sitting in front of her, the more her memory became clearer. "I do have to admit, from what I remember about Maxwell Banks, you do seem to look quite a bit like him. But I am far from convinced that you are who you claim to be, as I do seem to recall him telling me that his son had disappeared without a trace a very long time ago?"

"That's correct, captain. But if you'll give me the chance, I'll explain everything to you and I'll explain why I am here." Sabastian was about to begin his incredible story when one of the officers who had initially restrained him, entered the office.

"Excuse me, captain. I apologize for this intrusion but I'm not the only one here who thinks this here stupid Yankee yahoo is just here to cause trouble and is only wasting your valuable time." The sergeant then walked up to Sabastian and grabbed his right arm from behind. "I can lock him up for trespassing or just have him removed from the building."

"Let go of this man now, sergeant, or I'll find a reason to have your impetuous ass suspended."

Obeying her order, the sergeant removed his grip on Sabastian and reluctantly left the office.

Still feeling bad about the method he had used in order to see the captain, Sabastian again apologized. After that, he spent almost an hour telling his entire story to Captain Kragtov. Once his tale was completed, Myrinna took a moment and did her best to process all of the information that she had just been given. The young man's story was incredible; maybe even too outrageous to believe. Yet, during the entire time that she had listened to the story being told not had there been any moments where she felt he was feeding her a bunch of bullshit. In the end, the only logical decision that she could make was to unconditionally accept Sabastian's words as being the truth. Unfortunately, nothing could be done to bring this man's father back, but Myrinna did have the ability to help Maxwell Banks' son achieve his goal of restoring his family honor — it was the least that she could do, considering the immense debt she felt she owed Maxwell for his taking a bullet that clearly had been meant for her.

Both Sabastian and Jerrelle had made arrangements earlier that day to meet up just after three p.m. at the Dossal Café for a late lunch. They had decided during their trip from Japan that their first day in Germany would be used to establish contact with their sources, and then gather all the information that they could before agreeing on a proper course of action, as the last thing they wanted was to make another mistake like they did in Japan. It had not been intentional, but Antonio Marcone nevertheless, had somehow learned that someone was looking for him. Now, the element of surprise was all but gone.

"Sorry I'm late again, Sab. I didn't realize that it would take me as long as it did to fly to Munich and back again."

"No problem, Jerrelle. This is Captain Myrinna Kragtov. At one time, she knew my father."

"It's very nice to meet you, captain," Jerrelle lied; as she was never one to feel comfortable around the police, let alone trust a cop.

"Likewise," Captain Kragtov replied.

"So.., did you locate your friend?"

"Yes I did, Sab. He said that he would do all that he could to help us."

"I agree that this Antonio Marcone should be found and stopped, but I think that the two of you better be careful around here. This is not like where you are from. Germany is a very old country and set in its ways. The laws here are much stricter than they are in the Union. Just try to keep as low a profile as you can, as there is no guarantee that I can impede your arrest if you do happen to draw the attention of my brethren."

"You don't have to worry about us, captain. Sabastian and I are both highly trained former military personnel. By the time we are done, no evidence will be left behind that we were ever here to begin with." Jerrelle took her eyes off of the captain momentarily, reached into her pocket, and removed her vid-cell. "Excuse me for a moment, will ya? I seem to have an incoming call." Jerrelle got up from the table and found herself a secluded part of the café. Her call only lasted long enough for Sabastian to take a couple of sips of his rather appalling sim-caf before she returned back to the table. Without sitting back down, Jerrelle folded her napkin around her untouched pita wrap, and then finished off the remainder of her equally appalling sim-caf.

"What was that call all about?"

"I've got to leave and meet my contact across town. I hate to run out on our lunch, but if I remember correctly, it's going to take me almost a half hour from here to get where I need to go. I'll catch up with you as soon as I can, Sab." Jerrelle exited the restaurant, but not before indiscreetly checking out just how endowed the captain really was. And even though Jerrelle hated the police, she couldn't ignore, and had to admit to herself, just how beautiful Myrinna was — for someone of her age.

Maybe the detective in Sabastian was finally starting to surface, because he had actually noticed that Jerrelle was mentally disrobing the captain — at that, he rolled back his eyes, almost as if to say to his old friend that he was embarrassed to even be associated with her.

"I need to go as well," Myrinna said. "I've been away from the precinct for too long. Thank you very much for the late lunch, Sabastian... I'll contact you in an hour or so and I'll let you know if we are able to find out anything that can help you locate the man responsible for your father's death."

"Thank you, captain. I'll talk to you later."

Myrinna Kragtov got up and left the restaurant, leaving Sabastian alone. As he was finishing off the remainder of his food, the waitress approached the table in order to hand Sabastian the bill. Without even looking at it, it immediately dawned on him that both Jerrelle and Myrinna had stuck him with the entire amount. Needless to say, he wasn't happy. *'Damn!'*

Germany is rich in thirteenth century, medieval history. And because Antonio is an admirer of that period, he personally requested where their new place of residence would be. Again, through his business connections, he was able to relocate to the Emperor's Coronation Hall; a building that was located within the Römerberg Square in Frankfurt. For centuries, this hall was a main tourist attraction of the city. But less than a decade ago, due to government budget cuts and a continual decline in interest by tourists themselves, the hall ended up falling into disrepair.

After being closed for nearly five years, the hall was purchased by the Kölner family, whose bloodline can be traced back to a seventeenth century family that once possessed a hereditary title. The Kölner family spent years restoring the hall, with the intent to take up residence within it, but an unforeseen family tragedy changed those plans late last year; leaving the fully restored hall currently unoccupied.

To this day, the Kölner family is considered to be one of the more respected and influential in Germany. However, they would occasionally deal with individuals such as Antonio Marcone, if and when they felt it would benefit their family business interests — a fact that is all but ignored due in most part to their family lineage, but also because they would never cross that line where the authorities would then be forced to become involved.

Antonio felt comfortable in his new surroundings, and he truly felt that he was now well hidden. Being in an isolated area last time didn't work out so well, so he decided that this time, hiding in plain sight would be the next logical thing to do — the Coronation Hall was after all, right in the heart of the city and it was actually an ideal location for Antonio to continue on with his business ventures.

He had intended when he was in Japan to contact his one-time business associate, Vladi Chemzot, who oddly enough, was now a high-ranking member of the Communist Revolutionary Assembly Party. But due to the unexpected situation that had rapidly developed while he was there, he chose to hold off his plans until he felt certain that his location was secure. Now that he was comfortable where he was at, Antonio himself, reached out and contacted his old client, as Vladi needed to know that the Detroit Underworld Organization was now fully operational and could easily handle a large shipment of merchandise without any problems — just like they used to do back in the good ol' days.

Disbelief, uncertainty, even some personal contempt was preventing Vladi from seriously listening to Antonio's sales pitch. And even though the man was personally guaranteeing that nothing would ever go wrong again, he really didn't seem all that convinced.

The man had tried everything that he could think of to entice him to do business with them again, but Antonio's words just weren't enough for him to change his already made up mind — that was until he threw him an unanticipated curveball.

He hadn't yet planned on making this new, state-of-the-art merchandise available to a client, as Antonio had only recently acquired it. But he was desperate for Vladi's business, so he let it be known that he was willing to let him be the first one to examine it. That was what had enticed him — and as soon as he heard what it was that Antonio supposedly had in his possession, a merchandise viewing was quickly agreed upon.

With that now achieved, he used one of his many German connections, a less than honorable local city official, to arrange the use of the historic St. Paul's Church. Just like the Emperor's Coronation Hall, the once prevalent place of worship had closed at the beginning of the decade due to financial difficulties and a steady decline of attending parishioners.

Although Antonio knew that nothing was a certainty, he was actually willing to allow himself to relax and enjoy where he was. The sole purpose of this pending meeting with Vladi after all, wasn't to finalize a deal, it was strictly to regain and then solidify the man's trust; a trust that he knew he needed to get back so that he could officially resume their once vital and respected trade and business agreement — and once that happened, he was going to officially open up wide the organization's trade doors, reach out to any other potential client, and strike as many deals as he could with them.

The following day...

"Feel free to take as much time as you need to examine all of this impressive hardware." Louie had in front of him two rather large-sized steamer trunks of which he freely displayed its contents for Vladi to see. He stepped back and allowed the man all the space and time that he needed to look over the merchandise.

The Serbian was a very scary, intimidating looking individual. He stood somewhere between six foot six and six foot eight and weighed close to three hundred pounds. His head was shaved and tattooed with bloodied black roses; the stems of which ran parallel down his neck into the center of his back. That artwork though, wasn't what got your attention — what did, was the nearly half-inch wide, horizontal scar he had just below his jugular. The man also sported a partially grey, thickly woven goatee, as well as a black patch over his right eye. Three of his fingers were missing their tips; two on his left hand and one on his right hand. However, those weren't his only distinguishable features, as he also had a collection of numerous other visible scars all over his body — it was obvious to anyone who wasn't blind that this man had lived a harsh and violent life.

"I'm sure that this merchandise will meet your approval, Vladi."

The Serbian meticulously scrutinized every single sample piece of hardware, while at the same time, debating within himself whether or not he should even be considering doing business with the D.U.O. again. "The problem I'm having here, Louie, is not the merchandise, as it is what Antonio said it would be. I'm just not sure if I can trust your organization, knowing the kind of track record that it has."

He thought about disputing the Serbian's words, but then thought better of it — the man after all, wasn't wrong. Every business will hit that proverbial wall at one point or another, but they will only continue on if they can figure out the proper course of action to take that they hope will lead them around it. The D.U.O. had failed miserably when it came to finding a solution to their wall. For that reason, Louie simply felt it was best not to try and sell what he represented, but instead, let the merchandise sell itself, believing that the quality of it should be enough to sway Vladi into doing business with them.

Almost an hour into the showing, he was beginning to get the feeling that the Serbian was still wrestling with the idea of agreeing to a deal. Louie had hoped that his sales skills were not going to be needed this day, but if he didn't soon interject himself, he was afraid that Vladi was going to walk away — he just could not allow that to happen, knowing that his own balls were also on the line. "As you can see, these here are the latest versions of the Smith & Wesson 22 Match Heavy Barrel M-41-C series and a 38 Master Model 52-C Series Auto. Both of these weapons fire compressed solid nitro tipped bullets. Here is the Beretta Model 76-C Laser Pistol with an eight-inch muzzle for short, accurate, and extremely quiet kills. And here is the latest Winchester 70-D Magnum Laser-sight Rifle. The beautiful thing about the Winchester is that not only will it fire conventional ammunition, but it will also fire those new programmable heat-seeking mini-missiles (It was this technology that the S.M.A.R.T. microchips were first developed for, and it was this technology that had enticed Vladi into agreeing to this showing). This though, this is my favorite one of them all; the Beretta CNML 86-B, air compressed mini scud launcher. The shells for the launcher can be loaded with whatever volatile chemical or bio-weapon you desire and has a range of about five kilometers."

After carefully scrutinizing the merchandise, Vladi turned to face Louie. He was still undecided as to what he was going to do, but he was also smart enough not to completely shut the door until his own uncertainty became satisfied. "I know it's been years, but do you remember the last conversation we had?"

"I do. You said to me that you were never going to do any kind of volume business with the D.U.O. again. And you also accused us of being an organization that was on the brink of becoming unhinged."

"I'm impressed. Even after twenty-five years, your memory has not faded away."

"It has not. And I would be a fool not to admit that we have had several unforeseen problems occur over the years that we did not handle correctly. However, the foundation of the D.U.O. is more sold than ever. Rest assured, no other issues that may arise will ever become the excuse we use for failing to provide you with whatever merchandise you would request from us. I will personally guarantee it."

"For your sake, Louie, I certainly hope so."

Vladi took a few more moments and scanned over the displayed weapons one last time. After weighing all the pros and cons, he gave Louie his answer — one that he hoped he would not regret. "Ok. I think that I will do business with your organization one more time. But just remember… if this gets fuckin' screwed up, I will have no problem placing your organization right at the top of our enemies list?"

"Don't worry, Vladi. I am well aware that we don't want to become an enemy of yours. Now.., can we get down to business?"

———————————————————⟳———————————————————

Helfred had taken the same commuter flight to Berlin as Jerrelle. But instead of accompanying her to her scheduled rendezvous, he went his own way to meet up with a military friend of his, Major Hans Burmen, whose posting was at the Brandenburg Center; a building that houses all the commanding sectors of Germany's military and its intelligence. Helfred's rank allowed him access to the office like complex, but nothing else. He did not have the proper clearance to access any of the computers or archives — that was why he needed Hans.

Once he was inside the building, that ironically sat right across the street and parallel to where the historic Brandenburg Gate is located, Helfred quickly found his old friend. And although Hans had agreed to his request without any hesitation, he unfortunately was unable to find a potential location for Antonio Marcone. He was though, able to acquire some information that Helfred hoped may be of use to Jerrelle and her friend.

He could have easily just told Jerrelle what he had found out when he called her, but he had an ulterior motive; one that he hoped would help her to at least begin removing the bricks from her wall. He had remembered Jerrelle mentioning to him an unexpected aspect about her during a night of drinking that completely shocked him. She had surprisingly opened herself up to him and had let it be known that she had a fascination with reptiles — apparently in her youth, she had owned a near full-length, five-foot pet iguana named Damien.

Hoping to trigger some good memories so that she just might open up to him again, Helfred asked her to meet him at the Exoticarium at the Berlin Zoo — a place that many rare breeds of aquatic and reptilian animals called home. Admittedly, he feared that Jerrelle was again going to disappear from his life once she got what she came for. It wasn't what Helfred wanted, but he thought that maybe if he left her with an everlasting impression; one that simply wouldn't fade away in time, then maybe one day in the future, she'd finally see the light and return to him with open arms. Yes, it was wishful thinking on his part, but he didn't care — not only was he willing to wait a very long time for Jerrelle to come to her senses, he decided that he was going to fight for her heart until the day he died.

In his mind, the Exoticarium seemed like the perfect place for that needed seed to be planted: a place that he hoped she'd feel comfortable in, a place that he thought she'd enjoy — a place where she might even let her guard down and maybe even admit that she not only cared, but had actually once been in love with him. And although Helfred honestly wasn't too sure if his tactics would inspire such a possibility into taking place, he didn't see the harm in trying.

"So what kind of information do you have for me?"

"I see it's the same old Jerrelle. Not even a hello, how are you, or what's new? No small talk, just get straight down to the business at hand."

"You know very well that I don't care about trivial formalities. Just tell me what the information is that you insisted could not be said over the phone."

He was disappointed that the Exoticarium hadn't done what he had hoped it would. Nevertheless, he had agreed to help Jerrelle out — and it was clear that was all she wanted from him. The temptation was certainly there for him to try a few underhanded tactics in order to get her to open up and forget about her 'mission' for a few minutes, but peeling away each one of her hardened layers would take a lot more time than what Helfred knew she would be willing to give him. So he instead, just let her know what his old friend at the Bradenburg Command Center had found out.

First, Helfred apologized for not being able to find out anything useful about Antonio Marcone, but then he told her Hans was able to find out that the German military police had recently been alerted to some atypical movements by the Communist Revolutionary Assembly Party which in turn, caused them to treat that as being a potential concern to their national security.

"What concern? And what does this have to do with what I asked you to do?"

"There you go again, Jerrelle. You're always in such a rush. You get too anxious for information, yet you don't let anyone finish whatever it is that they are trying to tell you. Now if you'll let me finish, you'll understand why I'm delivering this information to you in person and not over the phone."

"All right, Helfred. I'm sorry. Please continue."

"As I was saying…" Helfred then explained that the Communist Revolutionary Assembly Party had recently begun to toy with the idea of expanding its activities beyond the borders of its own grouping of countries, with Germany being the first one that they have successfully infiltrated. He then let her know that it was recently learned a few high-ranking German military personnel, whom had previously been under suspicion for other various unlawful activities, had recently been linked to having an association with a prominent member of the C.R.A.P. — that man of course, was Vladi Chemzot."

That name rang a bell, as Jerrelle thought back to Japan and the information that Sabastian's cousin had given to him that documented the criminal activity between the Serbian and Antonio Marcone. Still, she wasn't certain what this all had to do with what she wanted from Helfred.

"Germany's military intelligence has documents confirming that Vladi has on numerous occasions, imported stolen weaponry from the Ameri-Can Union's military; weapons that are smuggled via the southeastern Euro-underground network to Serbia."

"Yeah, Sabastian and I are aware of Vladi's connection to stolen weapons, but we had no idea that Germany was a hub for the transfers."

"It's not just a hub. It is the main transfer point."

This bit of new information was something that Jerrelle was certain Sabastian would appreciate learning, yet she still was uncertain as to why this was an important detail that apparently affected their mission. "What else did your friend learn?"

"He told me that recently, Vladi was spotted with those same high-ranking German military officers. And because they had been seen together, a red flag was raised. Even though no proof has yet to be found, our military police are now concerned that theft of our own military weaponry has already, or might soon begin here as well." Helfred then concluded his speculative report by informing Jerrelle that Germany's border patrol had recently confiscated some of the Ameri-Can Union's stolen weapons as it was crossing into the country.

This clearly was now something more than what it was originally supposed to be. Jerrelle had agreed to help her old friend get his revenge for his father's death, but it was clearly evolving into a situation that was necessitating the involvement of an entire country. Even though she knew that Helfred's bringing her to the Exoticarium had an ulterior motive behind it, she now fully understood why he had decided to tell her everything he did in person. From this moment forward, while they were here in Germany, she and Sabastian had to tread very lightly — the last thing they wanted to do was to get in the way or impede an investigation into criminal activity that could affect the security of an entire nation.

Helfred could sense that Jerrelle was disappointed that no real significant information had been shared with her that could help her and her friend with their mission — and he could also tell that she was beginning to second-guess her decision to volunteer her services. As long as he had known her, never before had she bailed on someone or walked away from something because it turned out to be more complicated or completely different than what she had first expected. Therefore, Helfred felt that it was his responsibility to ensure that Jerrelle stayed committed to the cause — and he hoped that with what he was going to tell her next, it would be all the incentive she needed to dispel any reservations that may now be surfacing.

After taking a moment to ensure that he didn't forget any part of the information he still had left to share with her, Helfred explained that while he was waiting for Jerrelle to arrive, he had called an old friend of his whom he hadn't seen nor spoken to in a long time, just to chat and kill some time. During their conversation, his friend had mentioned to him that a friend of his, who just happened to work for the Kölner family, had mentioned that the Emperor's Coronation Hall had finally become occupied — and not by the Kölner family. He then followed that by letting Jerrelle know that the Kölner family had been suspected in the past of conducting shady business deals with people like Antonio Marcone."

This was getting much worse by the moment. Not only did she and Sabastian have to deal with a mob organization from the Union, but also three other possible entities: the German government, a radical terrorist group bent on restoring a communist regime throughout central Europe, and an unethical, once sovereign, hereditary family. "What in the hell has Sabastian gotten himself involved in?"

"I honestly don't know?" Helfred stated. "But as his friend, it is your responsibility to assure that he is fully aware of everything that I've just told you so that no unforeseen surprises become the reason why this mission of his ends badly."

"Yeah.., but I honestly think that maybe he…"

Helfred stopped Jerrelle from finishing off her sentence, as he knew exactly what she was going to say. "I'm sure Sabastian values your opinion, but it ultimately will be his decision. This is after all, his fight. You can't force him into giving up his mission because you think that this is now turning into something bigger than what the two of you can honestly handle."

Jerrelle just stood there and listened to Helfred preach; he surprisingly knew exactly what she had been thinking.

"If he decides to carry on with his mission, then you will need to decide whether or not you continue tagging along."

"You are right." Unexpectedly, Jerrelle turned around and started to walk toward the exit of the Exoticarium — almost immediately; she blended seamlessly into a rather large, elderly tour group.

Before Helfred could even react to what she had just done, Jerrelle was gone. In hindsight, he should have first bared his soul before telling her anything. But his inability at making up his mind; his hesitancy and indecisiveness, may have just cost him what he wanted — no guarantee was there that another opportunity would ever come his way again. Dejected, but not deterred, Helfred made a declaration to himself — there was no way that he was going to let what had just taken place, be the last time he ever saw her. Jerrelle was not going to walk out of his life again. She was going to need him, and he was going to make sure of that — in fact, he was going to all but force her hand so that she had no other choice but to see for herself just how much she meant to him.

———————————— ⟳ ————————————

Never before could Sabastian ever recall feeling the way he now was — useless. Jerrelle after all, had left so that she could meet up with her contact, as he supposedly had some information for her, and Captain Kragtov had returned to her work, promising that she would use her resources and try to find a possible location as to where Antonio Marcone might be hiding. He could not have asked for more from either of them.

He honestly did not know what to do while he waited for some news. He could have called home and informed Savanna or his Uncle about what had so far happened, or he could have called his grandmother and chatted for a while, but then what? He'd feel the same way afterwards.

After a few moments of random thought, Sabastian decided that, since he didn't have a connection or a lead of his own to work with, and in lieu of the fact that he was in Germany and had some obvious time to kill, he should take that free time and go do some site seeing. So after spending a few moments browsing the public computer kiosk located just outside of his hotel, he flagged down a cab and headed to the Hackeschen Höfe area; a section of the city where it and its bordering streets contained a bit more unique and offbeat selection of places to shop, eat, drink, relax, or browse, than anywhere else in the city.

At a leisurely pace, Sabastian took his time walking the area and taking in the captivating scenery. After about an hour, he found himself a quaint, semi-crowded place called the Offenbach Café, and sat outside on its patio. Though he was generally a tea and sim-caf drinker, he decided that he wanted to sample some of Germany's world famous chocolate caramel latte — a good decision on his part, because from the moment he took his first sip, the muscles throughout his entire body instantly relaxed, almost to the point of serenity. *'Mmmmm... This is incredible,'* he thought. *'Drinking this stuff almost makes it worth the long plane ride from Japan.'*

Sabastian kept his senses locked onto his latte; his surroundings became irrelevant, as he enjoyed not only the smell of his drink, but every sip he took of his chocolate heaven. As the minutes went by, the café's patio began to get a bit busier. But that didn't matter to Sabastian, because he was having a rare moment of pleasure and relaxation.

After taking a rather healthy sip of his latte, one that nearly emptied his cup, he decided to again mess with the palm-top that Jerrelle had found. What he really should do was just wait until he returned to San Antonio and then hand it over to his friend, but Sabastian didn't think that another attempt to get it to work would hurt — and so long as he didn't try anything beyond his basic computer knowledge, chances were that no harm would come to the device. The most frustrating thing about this though, was that he now knew why he had been unable to get it to work — the reason had come to him in the midst of his latte. However, what he did not know was how to solve the problem. It was so simple — the palm-top was just not getting enough power for it to work properly. *'There has to be a way for me to look at what is on this device without me having to wait until I get back home,'* he thought.

After a few moments of staring at the device, a crazy idea came across his now relaxed mind. Sabastian turned it over, pried opened the access cover in order to expose the Lithium-Zinc fusion cells, and then immediately saw what he had suspected he would. There it was; both end terminals of one of the cells were blacker than a briquette of charcoal. This, Sabastian knew, would not have happened if the device had been plugged directly into a USB or an X-slot port on a computer. More than likely, its owner did not use a voltage convertor and they stupidly plugged the palm-top's charger directly into the wall. In Japan, the voltage in an outlet is only 100 and not 120 like in North America — and a power surge would have occurred within a few seconds and done the kind of damage that Sabastian was now looking at.

He looked around, hoping to find a small wire or something that he could use to bypass the melted connection and temporarily hot-wire the good terminals together. He knew this would work, but he also knew that the device would not last for too long. It was a risk to bypass any type of fusion cell connection, because it would quickly drain what little power was left in the remaining cells. It could also possibly overload the device, causing a cascading surge that would completely short out the entire palm-top's processor and operating system, rendering it permanently useless.

As luck would have it, Sabastian found a half-smashed Bluetooth music player, along with its discarded headphones, lying on the ground near the edge of the adjacent sidewalk garbage can. After discretely retrieving the headphones, it only took Sabastian a few seconds to harvest the length of wire he needed — he then carefully 'hot-wired' the palm-top. *'I hope I don't fuck this up.'*

Not needing to network his vid-cell into it this time, he carefully turned the palm-top over and began to comb through its contents. While he was searching through it, he called the waitress over so that he could ask her for another latte.

When she arrived, she took his order and then surprised him with an unusual request. In her heavy German accent, she said, "I see that you are sitting here alone. I normally would not do this but... would it be possible if I send another costumer over to sit with you? As you see, we are getting quite busy here this afternoon and we are running out of available seats on the patio."

"I suppose that would be all right."

"Thank you very much," the waitress said as she smiled at Sabastian. "I'll see to it that your next latte is on the house." The waitress left and Sabastian returned his attention to the contents of the palm-top. After a few seconds, he decided that he should network his vid-cell into it anyway — that way, if he were to find anything interesting, he could transfer a copy of the file to his phone, just in case the palm-top were to permanently die.

About three minutes later, the waitress returned with the customer that she intended to seat with Sabastian. "I apologize for imposing on you like this. I can't believe how busy..." as the customer began to seat himself across from Sabastian, déjà-vu overtook his mind. "...how busy it is here."

Sabastian could see that this man was a bit taken back — and it was also very obvious that this stranger was looking at him in

189

bewilderment. Being the respectful person that he was though, he simply offered a warm smile to the man and invited him to take a seat.

I'm sorry. I'm normally not this rude," apologized the stranger as he took a seat. "It's just that you look like, um… like someone I once knew a long time ago."

"No problem. The same thing has happened to a few other people not too long ago. My name is Sabastian Banks." He reached out for a friendly handshake. The stranger hesitated, but did accept. "…And your name is?"

"Oh, um… my name is Osiris Salvadore."

"I'm from the Ameri-Can Union," Sabastian said. "And where might you be from?"

"I'm from… Belgium." The stranger nervously looked down at his watch and then across the table at Sabastian. It was then that he noticed the jury-rigged palm-top — and although curiosity encompassed him, he chose not to inquire about the device. Instead, he stood back up and said, "I am sorry, I must go. I uh… thought that I'd have enough time for a coffee, but I don't. I just realized that if I don't leave now, I'm gonna be late picking up my wife. Um… it's been nice meeting you." The stranger promptly left the table and hastily exited the café.

'Hum? There was something a little weird about that man,' Sabastian said to himself. Thinking little, if nothing about his odd, brief encounter with the stranger, Sabastian returned to looking at the contents of the palm-top.

A few moments later, the waitress returned with his complimentary latte. Seeing that the customer whom she had just sent over to his table had already disappeared, Sabastian offered to pay for his latte — he didn't feel right about accepting a free beverage because he was no longer sharing his table with someone he did not know.

The waitress showed her appreciation for Sabastian's integrity, yet still she insisted that he accept the complimentary latte — she left before he could object.

Deciding that he liked the friendly hospitality of the German people, Sabastian let his waitress win the dispute this time. However, he decided that he was going to leave the cost of the item on the table along with the tip when he left.

After taking a sip of his fresh latte, he returned to browsing the palm-top. Almost immediately, he realized that the battery power was quickly diminishing, so he hastily selected all of the files on the palm-top, which wasn't many, and tried to copy them all to his vid-cell. That idea of his, didn't work out so well, because what little power had been left on the palm-top was suddenly being drained even quicker — so he promptly cancelled his transfer and shut off the palm-top before there was a chance of any irreversible damage happening to the device.

Whatever secrets the device might hold, would have to wait to be discovered. And although Sabastian was curious if there was anything on it that would be useful to him now, he decided that it was best he just wait until he got back to San Antonio and hand it over to Baylor so that he, the one with the advanced computer knowledge, could safely retrieve the contents.

7

Both Antonio and Louie spent the majority of the afternoon ironing out all of the details that were needed to carry out what they believed was going to be a flawless transfer of their goods to Vladi. Unlike past business dealings, this one had more than just merchandise at stake, as the organization's reputation was on the line, and as Vladi so bluntly pointed out to Louie, this pending deal had to go off without a hitch or there was going to be ramifications that would probably start a Hatfield verses McCoy type of feud between both organizations. That was something that Antonio most certainly did not want to happen, as the C.R.A.P. was a rather large, radical political group, and they could easily eliminate the D.U.O. with little effort — if that was what they wanted to do.

"I've just finished speaking with Casper. Although those he normally uses to move the merchandise are off the grid with the rest of our people, he does not foresee there being any issues. He will though, need at least forty-eight hours to ensure that Vladi's order gets furtively shipped to our hub here in Germany."

"Good, Louie. I honestly don't know what I'd do without you. I can always count on you to do more than a competent job. Sal on the other hand… Well, he has his moments."

"And they are few and far between. Unfortunately, you can't get someone who doesn't have a working brain to make a competent decision. The only head on Sal that works correctly is the one in his pants… and usually when it should not, as we all know."

Just then, the man they were mocking came barging in through the front door, nearly ripping off the antique door's hinges and scaring the living crap out of Antonio — if it hadn't been for the cane that he uses to help him walk; a cane that had recently become a necessary vice for him because of the developing arthritis in his right hip, he would have probably lost his balance and fallen over.

With a look of pure fear on his usually stoic face, Sal headed straight over to where his boss was standing. He then said, with the utmost of seriousness, "We best be getting our fuckin' asses out of here, NOW!"

"Why? Did you go and pick up another underage prostitute and beat up her pimp?" Louie's intentionally blunt question did exactly what he anticipated it would — it right away allowed him to get underneath his associate's skin. Whenever Sal's detest for him became apparent, what intelligence the man did have would quickly disappear and more often than not, he would end up putting his foot in his mouth. And right after that occurred, Louie would proudly claim another personal victory over his rival.

Reacting impulsively is what he normally would do, but instead, Sal just stood there inert and took a few relaxing breaths — he was not going to take the bait. Had they suddenly not a crisis on their hands, he would have simply walked right up to his associate and not thought twice about making Louie swallow all of his teeth. As satisfying as that would be though, he was certain that Antonio would have stepped in and prevented him from even coming close to throwing that punch.

After he was able to successfully separate his emotions from his desire, Sal turned his attention to his boss and told him what had just happened to him. He had been over at the Hackeschen Höfe shopping district looking at new suits. After purchasing a few and instructing the clerk to have them sent over to the Emperor's Coronation Hall, Sal then decided to take a short walking tour of the area — but he wanted to relax a bit before he began his walk, so he chose to take up a seat and relax on the patio of the Offenbach Café. He then informed Antonio that the outdoor seating area had been very crowded, so the waitress had asked him if he would be all right with having to share a table with another customer.

Sal then paused for a moment, knowing that this next part of his story would probably cast a lot of doubt from Antonio and a lot more criticism from Louie. Nevertheless, Sal prepared himself for what he knew everyone's reaction was going to be. "From the moment I sat down, I immediately felt as if I was looking at a ghost from the past. I swear to you, boss, this guy was the near spitting image of Maxwell Banks."

Antonio just rolled back his eyes in disbelief; not disbelief in the possibility of Sal's story being true, but in his mind, the absurdity of it. He generally looked at things in a pragmatic way, so he took a few steps closer to Sal, placed his arm around his shoulder and then reminded him of the vital role that he had played in arranging the death of their enemy. Which, in Antonio's eyes, could only mean one thing — Maxwell, or his 'ghost' being here in Germany, was impossible.

"I'm not stupid... and I know that it wasn't Maxwell. But when this guy spoke to me, he said that his name was Sabastian... Sabastian Banks."

Louie let out a wry snicker, as everything was there for him to use to rip Sal's questionable competency apart. "Well... I think that maybe it's time for you to start seeing a psychiatrist, as you are not yet old enough to use senility as an excuse for your ineptitude."

"Oh, fuck off!" Sal had had enough. Without thinking that any consequences would surely follow his actions, he extended both of his palms, placed them on Louie's chest, and pushed him away as hard as he could — had it not been for the over-sized chair that he had fallen into, his fellow associate's ass would have hit the wood floor, hard. "Don't you both remember when we arranged to have Maxwell's wife and son killed? Supposedly, they were both eliminated. However, there was never a dead body of that damn kid found anywhere. And in case you've forgotten, the name of Maxwell's son was Sabastian. Kind of ironic, isn't it, that the guy I met today not only has the name, Sabastian Banks, but looks just like a younger version of our enemy?"

"You know something, Sal. I always thought that you were full of crap, but now I know for sure that it's spilling right out of your mouth!"

"Why don't you shut your pie hole for once, Louie, and let me finish what I'm trying to say!"

Although Antonio didn't want to believe that there could even be a remote possibility that what Sal was telling him was true, he was smart enough to realize that the impossible could actually be what his subordinate was declaring. Maxwell's kid's body was never found. And with the knowledge that someone had been looking for them during their brief stay in Japan, Antonio could only come to one conclusion. From this moment forward, he had to keep an open mind until an explanation could be found to either corroborate Sal's declaration, or to satisfy his doubt.

At that moment, Antonio promptly instructed Louie to keep all of the comments he had left in his arsenal to himself. Whatever it was that had spooked Sal, it needed to be figured out before an unexpected surprise appeared on their doorstep and ruined everything they had planned.

Happy for once that his boss had taken his side, Sal continued. "Do you both remember what Maxwell kept saying to us about his son right before we finished him off?"

"Yes. He kept asking where his son was. But honestly, Sal, I didn't know, nor did I care what happened to his son. For all I knew, the job was completed and he was killed right along with his mother. I just used the possibility of his son still being alive as a way to add more of an incentive for the man to hate me."

"Well now, I'm sure that Maxwell's son was never killed. And I'm one hundred percent certain that the man that I spoke to today was his son. I would even put money on it that he is the one that has been trying to find us."

"So what makes you think that?"

Sal took a moment to gather his thoughts. "Well, boss, I had only spoken to him briefly, but during our conversation I noticed that he had in his possession a palm-top. I'm not one hundred percent positive, but I'm almost sure that it is the same one that I left behind in Japan."

"Say what? You left behind your palm-top in Japan! Jesus Christ, Sal!"

"I'm sorry, boss. It's just that we left there in such a hurry, and I forgot that I had left it in a nightstand drawer. But don't worry… I never left anything vital on it. I always transferred the important information to a back-up stick. And I generally only used that palm-top as my daily log or to gather information when I'm out on an assignment. Besides.., the day before we left when I tried to charge it, the damn thing shorted out on me. And I'm pretty sure that it was fried beyond repair."

"You do realize that just deleting or transferring the information does not completely remove it from the device?" Louie asked. "And a fried palm-top can still be accessed if you have any extensive level of computer knowledge. You better hope that the internal storage device got fried and not just the motherboard."

"Well... there's not much that we can do about it now. We'll have to deal with that issue another time. Right now, we have something more important to focus our attention on." Antonio wasn't prepared for anything quite as unexpected as this. The thought of Maxwell's son possibly still being alive had never really crossed his mind, let alone that he would be the one who would try to destroy him.

Antonio went over to the liquor cabinet and poured himself a healthy glass of Höhler Whiskey — he then leaned himself up against the end of the synth-leather sofa and quickly downed his drink. "Ok. Let's approach this as if Maxwell's son is indeed still alive. Do you think that he recognized you, Sal?"

"No. I don't really think so. Like I said... I had only spoken to him for less than a minute."

"Ok." Antonio reached for the bottle of Höhler and poured himself another glass. "Since you believe that he did not recognize you, then that will give us a bit of an advantage."

Personally, Louie didn't want to accept the fact that Sal had seen and spoken to Maxwell's son. However, he would be a fool to intentionally ignore that possibility based on the fact that he simply did not like his fellow associate. "So what do we do now? Does this mean that our deal with Vladi is on hold?"

"No. We are not going to change our plans. We are just going to adjust them a bit. Too much is at stake here to let this minor obstacle get in our way. We are going to go ahead with our planned transaction with Vladi, and then we will deal with this new potential threat to our organization."

Wanting to ensure that nothing did go wrong, Antonio instructed Louie and Sal to go out, try to locate this man called Sabastian, and attempt to confirm whether or not he truly was Maxwell's son. And if they did end up doing that, Antonio made sure that his associates clearly understood that they were to do nothing to the man until after their business deal with Vladi was completed.

"No problem. Whatever you want from us, you'll get. Let's get out of here, Louie, and go find this guy."

As Louie was leaving with Sal, he thought to himself. *'I'll believe he's Maxwell's son when I see him for myself. If Sal is right, then there may even be hope that what's between his ears might actually work. I'd have never thought I would ever have to admit that the man might actually be somewhat intelligent after all.'*

Just like before, both Sabastian and Jerrelle set a time and a place to meet later in the day. This time, they had decided that it would be at a quaint little restaurant located inside the lobby area of the Stallën Art Institute and Municipal Gallery. Sabastian wasn't really in the greatest of moods when he finally arrived there because the cab that he had hailed from the Offenbach Café had taken him almost clear across the city; roughly thirty blocks away from where he wanted to go. The driver spoke absolutely no English; that alone should have been enough for Sabastian to exit the cab and hail himself another one. He should have trusted his instincts, but he didn't. Instead, he sat back and took an unplanned tour of the city; a tour that finally ended at a ten foot high, ivy covered stone wall that was centered by a massive old iron front gate — the ominous structure was nearly a century old and easily, it could send a chill down your spine.

He didn't understand one word of German, so reading the historical marker on the wall next to the gate was out of the question. Nevertheless, it wasn't too hard for Sabastian to figure out that he had mistakenly been taken to the wrong place. However, it wasn't until he was able to flag down another cab, almost thirty minutes later, that he actually found out where he had been dropped off — at the Stalin Institute; a facility that housed the criminally insane.

During his ride back into the city, the English speaking cab driver; English with a heavy East Indian accent, had told him that he was a very lucky man because the majority of the city's cab drivers would not even consider stopping and picking anyone up who was loitering out in front of the Institute.

By the time Sabastian arrived at the Stallën Art Institute, he was running about thirty minutes late. He had planned to get there early enough so that he could have time to order himself a meal and for once, actually sit down and enjoy it alone and in peace. Now that his plans had been ruined and his patients left behind at the asylum (pun intended), he just sat there perturbed.

Every thirty seconds, Sabastian kept looking at the time displayed on his vid-cell, then up at the clock on the wall, then over to the entrance of the restaurant — Jerrelle was running even later than he had. *'That's it!'* Sabastian said to himself. *'I'm only going to give her two more minutes before I get up and get the hell out of here. One minute and thirty seconds...'* Sabastian finished up the last of his sim-caf while he continued to follow the hands on the wall clock. *'One minute to go and I am out of here... Thirty seconds...'* Sabastian got up out of his chair and as he was about to leave, instantly felt this shooting pain in his right elbow. Realizing then that someone was behind him, his military instincts kicked in — whoever was there was going to quickly realize that they had just made a mistake.

In the midst of pivoting in order to perform a specific tight quarters, offensive maneuver; one that would normally put him in immediate control of an unwanted situation, he got a surprise that he never could have anticipated — what he had done, had easily been countered. "Jesus Christ, Jerrelle! One of these days I'm gonna..."

"Yeah, whatever?" Jerrelle walked around to the opposite side of the table, took up a seat, and ordered herself an Old Fashioned (she decided that she was going to lay off the beer for a while; the binge drinking she had done with her sister in Japan still seemed to somewhat haunt her). While she was waiting for her drink, she proceeded to inform Sabastian about what she had learned from Helfred. Once she was done, she could see the uncertainty in her friend's eyes. She knew then that his doubt would soon overwhelm what hope he had — after all; some unexpected and unwelcomed information had just been thrown into his lap. She certainly could understand the hesitancy that would be there because of what was now known. However, she felt confident that the two of them could handle whatever obstacles they may come across — so long as they stayed cognizant of whatever potential threats may be lurking in the shadows and they made sure not to step on the wrong toes.

It was easy for Sabastian to see that his friend was itching to leave; she literally inhaled her mixed drink less than forty seconds after it had arrived. Jerrelle was the most impatient individual he knew; it was something that Sabastian felt she needed to improve on — especially now that she was 'working' with him. Besides, there was no way in hell that he was going to ask the waitress to put his filet mignon in a doggy bag — he was going to make Jerrelle sit there and watch him slowly eat every delicious ounce of it.

Halfway through Sabastian's meal, Jerrelle noticed a familiar person over his left shoulder, coming toward them from the far side of the room. She briefly thought about letting him know that company was about to join them, but she decided instead to let the surprise set up whatever unexpectedness that surely was to follow.

Though he was engrossed in his meal, his hearing had picked up on the approaching light footsteps. Who that person was, he had no clue. Only the abnormal change in the expression on Jerrelle's face clued him into the fact that it was someone that she recognized.

"To what do we owe the pleasure of this visit, captain?" Jerrelle said derisively, right as she arrived at their table.

Myrinna took up a chair between the two and then flagged down the waitress. After ordering herself a sim-tea, she proceeded to explain to Sabastian that she had obtained some pertinent information concerning Antonio Marcone — Jerrelle immediately felt as if she was purposely being ignored.

Yes, Sabastian was thankful that the captain had some information for him. But he found it a little odd that she had gone out of her way to hand deliver it to him. When he asked her why she had felt the need to find him, she explained that she didn't have a way of contacting him, as he had neglected to give her his vid-cell number. "Well... I really appreciate you doing this. But how did you know where to find me?"

"Oh, that was easy. We were the first European city to install the C-4 Network. However, unlike the first ones that had been installed over in the Union, our system only monitor's government buildings, public arenas, transportation facilities, and high risk areas of the city. We chose not to blanket our city with it because we felt that our citizen's privacy needed to be protected. Anyway, when our monitoring center became aware that a suspicious person was hanging out in front of the Stalin Institute, they had no choice but to look into it. And I was surprised to learn that the person on the video surveillance was you."

Sabastian was not at all happy that someone else knew he had been dropped off there. Unfortunately, there was nothing he could do now to keep that mistake from one day becoming a source for someone to use in a good-natured ribbing — although, he was sure that somewhere on down the road when he got older, he might actually be able to have a good laugh about what had happened.

"Naturally, I became curious as to what you were doing there, so I sent someone to find out. Just as he got there, you were leaving in a cab. He then followed you here. You know, Sabastian. As much as I agree that Antonio Marcone should be locked away in an institute, I could have told you right from the beginning that you would not have found him in that one."

"I didn't go there on purpose looking for him. The cab that I got in took me there instead of here. It cost me a lot of valuable time, and a lot of Euros."

It easily showed on the captain's face just how amused she was that a citizen of the Union had that much difficulty getting around in her city. "Anyway... what I had come here to tell you was that there is this place called The Emperor's Coronation Hall in the Romer complex at Romerberg Square that is owned by the Kölner family..."

Both Jerrelle and Sabastian simultaneously looked at each other. Without the benefit of a spoken word, they both knew what each other was thinking as they had just finished talking about that very same subject.

"Kölner family? Um... who are they?" Jerrelle decided to pick that moment to chime in with her two cents worth, pretending to be interested. "And what do they have to do with Antonio Marcone?"

Following an ample sip taken of her sim-tea, the captain looked again only at Sabastian and said, "The Kölner family is considered to be the last of the imperialists that this country has. To most of our people, they would be considered the German equivalent to royalty... but not really esteemed as such. It has been speculated that many generations ago, the Kölner family started our country's first and only version of the mob. But no one, not even the law, has ever been able to prove any of it. And even the majority of our governmental officials refuse to acknowledge that there may even be a shred of truth behind those allegations. Nevertheless, one of our officers just brought to my attention that they had seen on several occasions over the past few days, three older-looking Italian men frequenting the Emperor's Coronation Hall. And by the way, it is supposed to be unoccupied. So if I were to make an educated guess, I'd say that there is a good chance Antonio Marcone and the Kölner's are close allies."

'Oh.., just great,' Sabastian said to himself. Jerrelle had already informed him about the Kölner family and their possible association with Antonio Marcone. He was very surprised to learn that they could actually be the German Mob.

"Damn!" Jerrelle stated. Purposely, she slammed her long since empty rock glass down onto the table; her intent was to make the captain believe that she was completely shocked as well as pissed off at this so-called 'new' information. "This could cause us more of a problem than we first anticipated."

"Relax, Jerrelle," Sabastian suggested. "I don't foresee this as being that big of an issue for us. And even if it becomes one, I still have all the confidence in the world that we are going to complete our objective."

Captain Kragtov opened up an office sized envelope and removed a few photos from it — she then slid the photos to Sabastian. "These are surveillance photos that one of my officers took yesterday morning outside of the Emperor's Coronation Hall. Do you recognize anyone of the three men in these pictures?"

Sabastian picked up the first photo and he instantly recognized the person in it. "Yeah, this is without a doubt Antonio Marcone. And I... I do recognize this one as being Louie Mazotti." As Sabastian was about to look at the third photo, he accidentally dropped it. When he reached down underneath the table to pick up the photo, he paused for a moment and glanced at it in disbelief. "Holy fuckin' shit!"

"What's wrong, Sab?"

"I can't believe this has happened to me again? This picture here; it is of Salvadore Batiste." Sabastian paused for a moment, rubbing both of his hands on the sides of his face. 'Osiris Salvadore,' he thought to himself. 'I should have realized that he recognized me *when he, just like Savanna, Sydney, and Governor White, froze in disbelief.'* "You're not gonna believe this, but I was actually talking to him just before I came here."

"What? You spoke to him? Why didn't you tell me?"

"Because I…" Sabastian took a deep breath and gathered his thoughts. "…I am a brain-dead idiot, Jerrelle. I just now realized that it was him."

"Well… where did you see him?"

"I really didn't want to hang around the hotel and do nothing today while you and the captain were out gathering information, so I went to the Hackeschen Höfe shopping district because it looked like it would be a cool place to go and kill some time."

Sabastian then spent a few moments, explaining in full detail to the both of them what had occurred while he was sitting on the patio at the Offenbach Café.

"Ok. So you didn't recognize him," Myrinna acknowledged. "Do you think that he recognized you?"

After finishing off the last of his meal, Sabastian said, "Actually… now that I think about it, I'd say that he did recognize me. Or maybe it was just the likeness of my father that he recognized. That would probably explain why he seemed kind of edgy… and probably why he took off less than a minute after he had arrived at my table."

"Well, the main thing is that we now know for sure that Antonio Marcone is here in Germany. Let's just hope that your face didn't scare them all out of the country." Just then, Captain Kragtov's vid-cell rang. Surprisingly, instead of excusing herself from the table, she just turned her back to everyone and answered her call.

"I think it's time that we make our first move," Sabastian said to Jerrelle; his words, he thought, had been verbalized at a relatively inaudible level. With Captain Kragtov being preoccupied with her phone conversation, he really didn't think that she would have heard what he had said — right afterwards though, he regretted speaking before thinking. It's not that he didn't trust her, but she didn't need to become aware of what he had just suggested they do. Her help so far has been greatly appreciated, but this was his mission and he didn't wish to involve anyone else more than was absolutely necessary.

So that nothing else might be accidently overheard, Sabastian grabbed his vid-cell and quickly composed a message. He then sent it off to Jerrelle. *"Who knows how long the three of them will stay in Germany now that I'm sure I've spooked them. I don't want this opportunity to slip by without us at least gaining some significant ground."*

Jerrelle just sat there astutely and read the message, keeping a suspicious eye on Captain Kragtov at the same time. She then composed a message of her own and sent it back to Sabastian, *"I'm really not sure that an alike 'ghost' from their past is enough for Antonio Marcone to pack up again so soon and leave the country. He's not on the run; he's looking for a safe place to continue his business. Germany may be only one stop before he finds that place. I however, have a feeling he will be here a little while longer, considering that his weapons buyer is also here."*

So far, everything seems to have gone accordingly. They had a basic idea going into this what it was that they had to do to accomplish their goal. However, all of the information they have subsequently gathered has definitely forced them into making a major adjustment to their initial plans. These new issues have undoubtedly forced them into feeling some unwanted pressure — it was even making them both feel just a bit antsy. Neither of them liked the idea of having to fly by the seat of their pants, because doing so meant that the chances of a costly mistake being made were much greater. Therefore, whatever they may end up doing next, individually or together, it needed to be done logically and with caution so that neither of them would end up regretting their actions.

After Captain Kragtov had completed her vid-cell conversation, she turned back around to face both Sabastian and Jerrelle. She then proceeded to let them know that her call had been from one of her officers; the one she had asked to keep watch outside of the Emperor's Coronation Hall. Unfortunately, his report to her had contained no further useful information.

"I appreciate you having someone keep watch on our target for us. Knowing at all times where Antonio is will certainly give us an advantage when we are finally ready to deal with him."

"I told my officer to leave."

"What? Why?"

"We don't work for you, Sabastian. I only agreed to help you with what I felt we could without involving us too deeply. Proof isn't needed now that Antonio Marcone is in Germany, or that he has occupied the Emperor's Coronation Hall."

"You can't tell me that you aren't at all interested in what's going on over there?"

"I am, Sabastian. But just keeping an eye on the complex won't accomplish anything. With what we now know, my main objective is to try and figure out why the Detroit Mob has taken up residence in my city."

"He's here to conduct illegal business."

"More than likely, that is the case, Jerrelle… but we don't know that for sure."

The captain got up from her seat; her intent was to leave. But before she did, she turned to Sabastian and said, "If I discover anything of importance that I feel you need to know, I will be sure to inform you."

As Myrinna left the café, Jerrelle again just couldn't resist another indiscreet mental undressing of her. Too herself, she then wished, *'Goddamn! If only I could spend one night with my face buried in between those assets.'*

Sabastian imprudently threw a package of sugar at Jerrelle and hit her on the forehead — his friend may have thought that what she was doing wasn't noticed, but it had been. "Will you give it a rest, Jerrelle?"

"I'm sorry.., I just can't help myself." She got up from her seat and walked away from their table — she didn't tell Sabastian where she was going. A few minutes later, she returned, but instead of reclaiming her seat, she went right over to the same chair that the captain had been sitting in. As she stood right beside it, she passed her vid-cell underneath it and then did the same with the table.

"Where in the hell did you go, and what are you doing?" Sabastian gave her an odd look.

"First off, I needed to make a quick call. I now have another meeting with my contact in thirty minutes. Secondly, I have a friend who is a software guru back in Detroit who made me a custom app for my phone that allows me to sweep for bugs or explosive devices. As hot as Captain Kragtov is for a middle-aged woman, I still don't trust her."

"I'm kinda getting that same feeling myself, Jerrelle. At first, she seemed almost all too willing to help us out. Now, I'm not so sure?"

Feeling satisfied that their table was bug free; Jerrelle looked at Sabastian and apologized. She had, though unintentionally at first, neglected to inform her friend of a few minor details. And although she wasn't sure that he was going to believe her, she attempted anyway to convince Sabastian that she was in the process of informing him of those details right when Captain Kragtov had showed up. In retrospect, she was glad that she had waited until they were alone, as what she now knew, she felt, was something that the captain really didn't need to be made aware of.

She took a few extra moments and organized her thoughts before she spoke — what she had previously learned, surprisingly now seemed to be a bit clearer than it had been before she arrived at the café. Captain Kragtov's declaration that the Kölner family had possible mob ties had caused Jerrelle to change her assumption pertaining to them. She initially did not think that Germany's hierarchy family would pose any sort of threat to their mission, as Helfred had only said that in the past, they had conducted some shady business deals. Now, it had to be assumed that the Kölner family had the potential to be just as dangerous as the Detroit Underworld Organization.

Once Jerrelle had assembled and sorted through all of the information she now had, to her, there seemed to be only one possibility that made any sort of sense — the Kölner family had deliberately leaked out the information pertaining to Antonio Marcone's presence in Germany. Their reason for doing this, she hypothesized, was in hopes that one of his enemies, or maybe even the law, would step forward and eliminate the man and his associates so that the Kölner family could completely wipe clean whatever blood might still be on their hands due to the past association they had with the Detroit Underworld Organization.

Sabastian took a moment and contemplated Jerrelle's unsupported supposition. With their limited knowledge of the Kölner family's history, and the supposed unscrupulous deals they had made over the years with many suspect individuals, the possibility could not be dismissed that both factions knew each other and / or have had a working relationship of some kind in the past. "It's a good thing that you withheld your theory from me until after the captain had left, as there is no telling how she would have reacted to it."

"Well, the idea of that possibility never came to me until after the captain had left," Jerrelle admitted. "I just needed that one missing piece of information that she gave us about the Kölner family possibly being the German mob before it all seemed to fit together."

This was exactly why all information, no matter how irrelevant or improbable it may seem, needed to be divulged. At any point, what was withheld could end up being the missing link in a puzzle that may have otherwise, seemed impossible to solve. For that reason, Sabastian felt that it was necessary to let Jerrelle know one other detail about his encounter with Salvadore Batiste that he had neglected to share — his attempt to hotwire the palm-top that she had found in Japan. First, he let her know that he had attempted to power it up and then retrieve whatever files may have been left behind on it. But it soon became clear to him that his desire to learn what could be on it may have resulted in the device being damaged some more. Although he did not know for sure if his jury-rig had done just that, Sabastian felt that it was best to leave well enough alone — and that was why he had decided to ship the palm-top to San Antonio, instead of waiting until he returned, so that Baylor could fix it sooner and see if what he hoped, was indeed there.

"Ok. So now that we've shared all that we know with each other, do you think, you could share that bugs sweeping app you have on your phone, Jerrelle?"

"I suppose. When we have more free time, I'll transfer a copy to your phone."

Sabastian sat back in his chair and contemplated everything that may lie ahead of them. He really didn't like the way all of this was beginning to play out. Not only did he have to deal with one Mob, but the possible involvement was there of a second, as well as a large

206

supremacist organization — he just hoped that neither the Kölner family nor the C.R.A.P. chose to interject themselves and make what he wanted to do to Antonio Marcone and his organization, more difficult than it was already going to be.

Jerrelle got up from her seat and left for her meeting with Helfred. It was decided just before she did this that they both would rendezvous, in one hour's time, at the back of the Cathedral of St. Bartholomew. There, they would share whatever other information they may have learned and then form a solid and safe game plan. And then once that was in place, they both felt that they would be ready to begin the next phase of their mission to take down the man responsible for the death of Sabastian's father.

Twenty minutes later, Jerrelle had arrived at where she was to meet up with Helfred, a small park-like area across from the Café Ó Moré, just outside of the Zeil shopping street. As she approached the parcel of land, she noticed that her ex was already waiting for her at the far end, sitting on the edge of a picnic table, and looking across the small manmade pond directly in front of him. "Don't tell me I'm late for this meeting too?"

"Oh no," Helfred said. "You're actually on time. I've only been here for about ten minutes watching and feeding the loons, cranes, and geese."

'Hum… ok?' thought Jerrelle, a little taken back — because as much as she had thought she had known who Helfred was, she never would have guessed that he actually had a soft side and cared for something else in this world other than himself. And now that she had seen it first hand, she wondered why that part of who he apparently was had not influenced him to do what he should have done before they went their separate ways — fight for her heart. "Did you find out anything more about Antonio Marcone and that Serbian, Vladi?"

"Yes I did, but it's not much." Helfred then proceeded to inform her that he had surprisingly found out his friend Hans had a level of clearance at the Bradenburg Command Center that was actually higher than what he had first assumed. That meant the Major had access to not only all of the non-classified information that was stored on all the military databases and in the archives, but also had access to some governmental, lower-level classified documents as well.

Because of this, Hans had reached out and made contact with a Deputy in the Bundesnachrichtendienst (German Intelligence Service, BND), an individual who just happened to work closely with someone from the Kommando Strategische Aufklärung (Strategic Reconnaissance Command, KSA). That individual let Hans know that the KSA have been closely watching the recent activity involving the C.R.A.P., and they were certain that a possible transaction of some kind was going to be taking place very soon. Unfortunately, that person from the KSA could not confirm exactly what the transaction was or where it was going to occur — only that they strongly believe it was going to take place sometime tomorrow morning.

"So then... how does this second-hand information help us?"

Helfred turned his body a quarter-turn and looked Jerrelle straight into her eyes. He told her that he had taken the information he had received from her during their recent vid-cell conversation, the fact that Antonio Marcone may possibly be staying at the Emperor's Coronation Hall, and passed it along to his friend. Hans had told him that Antonio Marcone was probably unaware that the hall had at one time been used during a two-year period, shortly before its complete renovation, as the temporary German Military Command Center while the Bradenburg Command Center was being constructed. The major then made Helfred aware of the fact that the interior security network was never removed from the Emperor's Coronation Hall when the military vacated it in order to move into their new location. So Hans was able to use his clearance and had one of the techs at the Command Center, hack into the dormant system. Ever since then, they have been monitoring all of the activity that has been going on within that building. He then let Helfred know that, in his opinion, the transaction that the KSA is aware of is probably the same one that he had overheard being discussed while he and the tech were monitoring the video feed.

"Ok, that is a bit circumstantial, but..." Jerrelle relaxed a bit. Her mind immediately began to add another aspect to her already working supposition. "...with the alleged history and reputation of the Kölner family, you would think that they would have removed a security system that had previously been installed by a governmental institution. Nevertheless, that decision of theirs now seems to have worked in our favor. And I am willing to bet that after Antonio Marcone had made the inquiry about using the hall, the Kölner family purposely left the protection grid wide open and vulnerable, hoping that someone like the police or government... or us, would hack into it!"

"That is quite the assumption. However, the Kölner family does have a strong network of trusted business associates and contacts in Asia. And if it was brought to their attention that someone was in Japan looking for Antonio Marcone..." Immediately, Jerrelle assumed that it had to be someone inside the E.C.L. that tipped them off. "...and if they did want to disassociate themselves from the man, then yes, your theory is certainly plausible."

Jerrelle took a few relaxing breaths. For once, it was nice to hear someone support one of her wild theories. Antonio Marcone never had any qualms about using, then fucking people over for his own benefit. He toyed with Sabastian's father, screwed with the Extremist Clandestine Liberation, probably the Kölner Family, and more than likely, did so to countless others. If he did stab Germany's hierarchal family in the back, Jerrelle wouldn't blame them one bit for wanting to cut any ties they had to the D.U.O. In fact, she was all for them helping with their cause. But the longer she thought about this whole situation; the possibility that the Kölner family was indeed setting up Antonio Marcone, the more she began to believe that they, she and Sabastian, were going to end up becoming the pawns that did their dirty work — and then more than likely, they would be purged in the end, right along with Antonio Marcone and his two lap dogs.

Determined not to let that happen, she looked directly at Helfred and said, with the utmost of conviction, "That old bastard has no idea what's in store for him. The only ones walking away from this will be us." As soon as she had made that declaration, she noticed the same seriousness suddenly appear in Helfred that had been there the last time when he had told her that he was being forced to walk away and never see her again. At the time, she had tried to convince him to fight their government's insistence — but Helfred just wouldn't budge and support her want. She had thought in that moment he had come to the conclusion that he just did not love her. But now, in hindsight, she knew that he had done what he had to protect her life from becoming even more complicated than it had already been.

"When this thing finally goes down, Jerrelle, I am going to be there right beside you."

That statement floored her. She didn't expect it, nor could she accept it — yet deep down inside, she knew that his willingness to do something stupid like this was because of how he truly felt about her. She cared just as much for him — and that was why she wasn't about to let him do what he had just declared. "No way, Helfred! This will screw up your military career, big time. Besides.., this is going to be way too fuckin' dangerous. I don't want you to…"

"To what?" Helfred said. "Get hurt? You don't have to worry about me. I am a big boy and I can take care of myself!"

Jerrelle's emotions began to surface; emotions that she didn't want to openly expose to Helfred. Yet, she could not help it. "I just… don't want anything to happen to you."

"I'm volunteering my services." Those words of his were clearly unyielding. "Besides, the two of you can't take on the Detroit Mob, the C.R.A.P., and possibly even the Kölner family at the same time. You're gonna need some help. And whether you like it or not, I'm going to give it to you. Case closed!" He knew in that moment that he had her right where he wanted her — she could not say no. His actions alone should be enough to show her just how much she meant to him. This was the opportunity that Helfred had been waiting for — and he sure as hell was going to make the most of it. He was determined not to let Jerrelle disappear from his life again, nor was he willing to sit on the sidelines and wait for her to realize where her destiny lied. He was going to force his way into her existence, make her take down that wall, and admit to him that she too wanted him.

Jerrelle didn't wish to argue with Helfred. In fact, this insistence of his simply added more confusion to the way she was feeling at that moment. She wasn't sure why he was willing to risk his military career, or possibly even sacrificing his own life — that was until she looked deep into those dark, irresistible eyes of his. It was then that Jerrelle finally got the answer she had long been searching for. Helfred not only cared for her, but he actually loved her. That verity was what Jerrelle had long ago sought. And it was why Helfred was now willing to do anything for her — no matter what the consequences may end up being.

He wouldn't freely admit it, nor was he willing to let it show, but the past few days of unconfirmed questions and unknown variables had begun to take its toll on Antonio. He wasn't as young as he once was and the stress that had been placed upon him due to the recent unforeseen events had visibly begun to affect not just his sleep, but also his mind. He would have felt more at ease had Louie or Sal located this Sabastian guy and confirmed whether or not he was Maxwell's son — at least then, tomorrow's very important transaction with Vladi would not have a cloud of uncertainty hanging over it.

When it came to keeping his true emotions hidden, Antonio felt that he was proficient at it. Strangely though, Louie had the ability to sense whenever there was something bothering his boss. And even though he was certain that his advice and opinion could help him to sort out whatever issues were causing the grief, he knew that it was simply best that he ignore the situation and allow Antonio all the space he needed to deal with his problems — only if he were to be asked, would he then throw in his two cents worth. However, this instance seemed different than any others before; an unsettling change in Antonio could easily be seen and sensed. At first, Louie wasn't too sure what to make of it, but then his thoughts brought forth a scenario that he honestly never thought would happen.

The longer he contemplated that possibility, the evidence to support it started to become clearer. To him, it now appeared that the beginning of the end had finally arrived. It was only going to be a matter of time now before Antonio completely lost his objectiveness — and when that happened, another unhealthy obsession would begin. At that point, Louie knew that his long-time boss would then become his own worst enemy.

Unlike Antonio, Louie was a very patient man. Although he was admittedly eager to take over the reins of the D.U.O., he was more than willing to wait until the prospective events that he was sure were going to come, had. That way, when it was his turn to assume complete control of the D.U.O., no suspicions about his predecessor's demise could be placed upon him — not even Sal could then blame him for Antonio's death.

"I'm not at all happy that neither you nor Louie were able to find me any sort of confirmation yesterday regarding this Sabastian guy. You both are very lucky that he hasn't been able to locate me yet."

"Don't worry about it, boss. I doubt very much that he is aware that you are even here in Germany. As long as we are discrete with everything we do, we will be fine. I'm sure Louie and I will be able to locate this 'Sabastian' within the next few days. Just relax and let us do our jobs. You are gonna give yourself a heart attack if you don't keep your stress levels down to a manageable level."

"For once, I agree with Sal. You need to relax. You're not normally this uneasy before a transaction."

"I'm not worried about our deal tomorrow morning. My mind has been racing non-stop since yesterday, wondering if it could really be him. I mean, I can accept the fact that Maxwell's son might still be alive. But if this guy is really him, then you can bet that he is going to be just as big a pain in the ass as his father was." Antonio walked out of the Coronation Hall's rather large office and into the kitchen. He went straight to the refrigerator and saw the wine staring at him invitingly — but he thought better of it. Instead, he poured himself a glass of concentrated multi-lax V8 juice (Vegetable & Fruit mixed with a fiber laxative) — with everything that he had planned for this day, Antonio had to be on top of his game. Because of that, he decided that instead of putting alcohol into his system, he should put plenty of nutrients in it to help keep him alert — and regular.

Antonio was just about to return to the great room with his drink when his vid-cell rang. He took an ample swig of his drink, looked at his cell's display, and then detoured toward the privacy of the library once he realized whom it was that was calling him.

Both Louie and Sal gazed at each other with some uncertainty, each wondering what this call could be all about. Both were well aware that Antonio preferred never to take an important call in front of anyone, as those were the types of conversations their boss felt had to stay private. If what was learned from his call was important enough to be shared, then he would. Otherwise, Antonio generally kept everyone out of the loop, as he felt that they just did not need to know everything. Besides, the more that only he knew, and the less that he shared with others, it gave him not only an advantage over everyone, but it also gave him the right amount of leverage he needed in which to guarantee that he kept full control over his organization — and at the same time, control over those who were beneath him.

Sal was about halfway done his sandwich; the one he made for himself while waiting for his boss, when Antonio exited the library and returned to the great room. Immediately, both he and Louie could see that Antonio's disposition had changed from being stressed out, to relaxed and confident.

"Judging by the look on your face, I have to assume that call just made your day."

Antonio set down his now empty glass next to the medium brown-colored, synth-suede sofa, leaned up against the side of its arm, and said, "You're right, Louie. Today is gonna be a good one after all."

"Good," Sal stated. "I'm glad that vid-call put you in a better mood. So then, am I to assume that Louie and I are gonna go back out today and again try to find this Sabastian guy? You know, I think that I might have figured out a way for us to locate him."

"You're both staying here."

"How come?" Louie inquired.

"Because… As of right now, we no longer have to waste our time searching. I know exactly where he is at." Antonio took a moment and expunged a low laugh, as he actually found a little humor in the fact that he didn't even have to leave the Emperor's Coronation Hall to accomplish what his men could not do.

"And how in the hell did you manage to find him?" Sal asked, surprised.

Antonio opened up the cigar box that was sitting on top of the antique Victrola, took out a new Cuban cigar, and embraced the pleasurable aroma that hovered under his nose. "Due to what happened to us in Japan, I decided yesterday to make an offer to a drastically under paid individual with numerous connections throughout this city. As you know, money talks in middleclass economic urban jungles like this one."

Personally, it irked Sal that Antonio felt he had to resort to greasing someone's palm in order to get a job done. He was far from incompetent, yet the slap to his face didn't need to physically take place for it to sting more than a little. "Did this person confirm whether or not it really is Maxwell's kid that is after you?"

Antonio didn't answer his associate's question. He just sat there for a moment, lit his cigar, took a few enjoyable puffs, and basked in his sudden good fortune.

Louie wasn't at all happy that their boss was intentionally withholding something important from them — even the lesser intelligent Sal could see that he was not sharing all that he now knew, but Louie was also smart enough to know that he should not pester his boss for answers to questions that in time would be revealed when Antonio thought it was necessary for them to have that knowledge. And as much as his curiosity wanted to be satisfied, he had to accept the fact that he was going to be kept in the dark for a little while — he just hoped that Antonio's reluctance to share everything with the class would not get him killed. If Sal were to die from it however, he admittedly would not lose one minute of sleep.

"Louie.., would you mind leaving the room? I need to go over a very important assignment that I want Sal to undertake."

Without asking why, he got up from his chair, left the great room, and headed directly into the kitchen. He now knew that whatever secrets Antonio was keeping from him, were intended to be shared only with Sal. His decision to do that was reason enough for Louie, who was supposed to be Antonio's right hand man, to be entirely offended. But he also knew that Antonio did things for a reason. Being the boss of the D.U.O. for as long as he was, had not happened because he was a stupid man. It's just that there had been times when Antonio did things Louie found very hard to understand. *'One day, I will take control and make decisions that I know are logical and have a purpose. I will not make decisions based upon emotions, and I will operate this organization the way it was intended to be so that its survival won't ever be shrouded in uncertainty.'* That, was a promise to himself that Louie was adamant he was going to keep.

As previously agreed upon, Jerrelle met Sabastian behind the Cathedral of St. Bartholomew — only to his surprise, she was not sitting there alone. After being introduced to Helfred, Sabastian gratefully thanked him for all of the information that he had gone out of his way to provide.

"Jerrelle knows that I'd give my left nut for her without her having to even ask."

This was definitely not the right time for such a bonehead comment to be made. It was why Jerrelle felt that it was necessary for her to put her one-time boyfriend in his place; she did so by speaking in a low, monotone voice. "You need to shut the fuck up, Helfred, or I'll make sure that you'll have no nuts left to barter with!" Then, like a deer frozen in a set of headlights, Jerrelle sent a piercing stare at her ex; a stare that was intense enough to symbolically burn a neat little hole directly into the middle of his temple.

Easily, Sabastian could see just how unimpressed Jerrelle was with her old friend. In fact, the short exchange between the two reminded him of a married couple who had stayed together for the sake of the children and not because they loved each other — then again, maybe love was there and Jerrelle's known stone heart had continually failed to recognize it.

In that moment, all of Sabastian's common sense oddly disappeared. He then chose to have a little fun of his own and add a little more fuel to the already smoldering fire — the response he got from it was one that assured him he had struck a nerve. "By chance did someone jokingly substitute a body fluid for the cream you normally put in your morning sim-caf, Jerrelle?"

"No!" After sharply turning her head and barking out that response at her friend, she glanced back over at Helfred and continued on with what she had been doing; symbolically burning that same hole — it was as if she didn't want to stop until it went right on through to the other side of his skull. When she finally felt that her ex had gotten the message, she firmly asked him, "Does a day ever go by where your mind isn't firmly cemented in the gutter?"

Without answering her question, he just stayed quiet and stretched out a slight guilty smile on his face. He had always loved to push Jerrelle's buttons until she almost got to the point where that 'bitch switch' would turn on. He knew that it was a dangerous game for him to play, but not once had he ever lost at Russian roulette. He wasn't a thrill seeker, but the more he fired up Jerrelle, the more turned on he became — and the more of an animal she became when the two of them would have make up sex.

The opportunity was certainly there for Sabastian to dig even deeper into the suspected true relationship between his friend and hers, but he decided against it. He had not come to this meeting for that purpose; he came to hear what other information had been acquired that could help him achieve his goal and then construct a game plan.

Sabastian opened up the small brown paper bag that he had brought with him and removed a sugar-glazed donut and a medium-sized cup of herbal sim-tea. While he respectfully waited for someone to speak, he started to consume his early evening snack.

After some awkward silence had passed, Jerrelle pushed aside her immediate disdain toward Helfred's behavior, recognizing that this was not the time or the place to give him a piece of her mind — but that didn't mean she was going to forgive her ex-lover for his insensitivity. Yes, she had a hard exterior that was nearly impossible to see beyond, but she was also someone who didn't always want to be one of the boys — there were times when she wanted to receive a similar treatment that the rest of her gender would normally expect from a man — so long as it didn't involve flowers, a negligee, or perfume.

Once she was composed enough so that she would not accidently fly off the handle, Jerrelle proceeded to explain to Sabastian what the new information was that Helfred had obtained — circumstantial as it was. As she was just finishing up her report, something caught her attention and it caused her again to change her expression. They were no longer alone; she now had that same look on her face that she had the last time this person had been in their presence.

Sabastian noticed this and immediately turned his head; his assumption had been correct. "I should have known she'd find us here."

"Who are you talking about?" Helfred asked.

A few moments later, Captain Kragtov was in their presence; she promptly invited herself to join their group and took a seat on the curb."

"Um... good evening, captain," Jerrelle said — though by the tone of her voice, everyone could tell that she didn't really mean her words. "Let me guess... You used your extremely hypersensitive police nose and sniffed out the aroma of Sabastian's donut to find out exactly where we were? Well, now that you're here, feel free to indulge us social outcasts."

"Did someone piss in your cornflakes this morning?" Myrinna asked.

"No!" Jerrelle answered, stridently.

Both Sabastian and Helfred simultaneously chuckled just loud enough so that Jerrelle would take notice, which surprisingly, irritated her just as much as that earlier 'body fluid' comment had.

After enjoying a few moments of some harmless fun at their friend's expense, Sabastian addressed the captain. "So, is there anything new?"

Myrinna opened up the small bottle of chocolate almond milk that she had brought with her, and took a healthy sip. She then said, "Shortly after our last meeting, I rethought my decision. It's always better to be safe than sorry, as the last thing I want is a situation to materialize that could have easily been prevented. For that reason, I placed two officers back outside of the Emperor's Coronation Hall, with their orders being to document all activity in and around the place as well as follow anyone associated with the D.U.O. wherever they may go. Anyway, they ended up tailing Louie Mazotti and witnessed him meeting up with a high-ranking member of the Communist Revolutionary Assembly Party. And although I am not one hundred percent certain, I would bet that Antonio Marcone has struck some kind of trade agreement with that individual for some stolen weaponry."

Just as before, both Jerrelle and Sabastian simultaneously looked at each other; then they each glanced over at Helfred. It didn't take much intellect for Helfred to understand what both Jerrelle and Sabastian were thinking because they had already known that Antonio Marcone had dealt stolen weaponry to the C.R.A.P. in the past.

However, there was something about Captain Kragtov that rubbed Helfred the wrong way. Like Sabastian and Jerrelle, he too wasn't sure that she was trustworthy. "See… I'm not the only one who thought that he was dealing."

Captain Kragtov looked in the direction of Jerrelle. "Is this anabolic Neanderthal a friend of yours?"

It was that impertinent response from her that gave Helfred the insight that he was looking for as to what kind of person the captain was. Under normal everyday circumstances, he would not have thought twice about putting her in her place for that inaccurate reference, as he firmly believed that no matter what sex you were, if you're gonna dish it out, you sure as hell better be able to take it. Instead, he just straightened up his slouch, focused his eyes on the captain, and then addressed her. "I am. And my name is Helfred Nemchieve. Like you, I hold the rank of captain, but in this great country's military instead." He was going to ask Myrinna whom it was that she had to serve in order to achieve her rank, but thought better of questioning the captain's disposition. The last thing he wanted was to make an officer of the law his enemy who could then make his life miserable whenever he was on active duty.

"I see… Though I do find it odd that of all the thousands of candidates on the military's depth chart, no one was more qualified than you to receive such a respected ranking," Captain Kragtov said, derisively.

This time, Helfred really thought about taking that potshot, but decided again to bite his tongue. This wasn't his fight, after all. However, Myrinna Kragtov had just made Helfred's 'Hag Bag' list. Every woman that was on it, he compared to a condom. You should only use them once and then throw them away — even if you thought that they would still be good enough to utilize a second time.

Deciding then that she had wasted enough time on Jerrelle's friendly neighborhood caveman, Captain Kragtov turned her attention back over to Sabastian. "Anyway, as I was about to say… after that meeting took place, I had my men investigate it further and they have just confirmed that Antonio Marcone and the C.R.A.P. are scheduled to finalize their apparent agreement sometime tomorrow morning at the Old Goethe Museum."

Sabastian just sat there, astutely observing what all was transpiring. He then thought to himself, *'Well, finally the captain has brought us some information that we didn't already know. But the question I still have is… can I actually trust that the information is legitimate?'* Sabastian looked over at Jerrelle and he could sense that she was actually intrigued by this new bit of information. Yet, there were still some obvious signs that he could see which told him that his old friend felt the same way as he did.

"If my memory serves me correct.., did the Goethe Museum not catch fire last year?" Helfred inquired.

"It did. Although it's all boarded up, the place is still structurally sound." Captain Kragtov stood up. As she was brushing off the swath of dirt on her pant leg that was a result of it touching the ground during her short stay seated on the curb, she said, "That's all the information that I have, Sabastian. And definitely, this is the last time that I can help you. If I were to continue, then I would be obliged to inform my superiors of your part in all of this. This whole situation has now grown to where we, the law, have to step in and go by the book. I'm sorry, but that is just the way it has to be."

"That's ok. You've been extremely helpful."

"I believe that my personal debt to your father has now been paid. Good luck… and I hope that you succeed, Sabastian."

"Thank you for all your help, captain. It will only be a matter of time now before I pay back Antonio Marcone for all that he has done to my family." He reached out with his hand and respectfully shook Myrinna's. After she had left the premises, the three of them just sat there in silence while Sabastian finished off the remainder of his sim-tea.

"You do remember that I don't trust the captain?" Jerrelle pointed out. "And you're not really buying any of the crap that two-faced bitch has feed us, are you?"

"Since when did you come to that conclusion about her?" Sabastian asked. "I thought that there were certain aspects of the captain that you really liked?"

Jerrelle knew exactly what Sabastian was referencing and she wasn't about to let him elaborate any further. There was no way that she wanted Helfred to find out that she was also attracted to other women. "You are full of crap. There is absolutely nothing appealing about her."

"Oh, come on," Helfred said. "Even though we all know she is probably what Jerrelle just claimed, it's hard to ignore the fact that she is an extremely well endowed and attractive middle-aged woman that any self-respecting individual wouldn't mind taking for a spin at least once."

Jerrelle turned to Helfred and swiftly kicked him just below his right kneecap. This served two purposes; she was pissed — or more like jealous, that Helfred would even contemplate any kind of interest in another woman. But it also gave her the opportunity that she needed to make Helfred believe that she might actually still want him and wasn't interested in anyone else, of either sex — even though she would experiment if the right opportunity ever presented itself.

Deciding then that it was time to get serious and put an end to all of their unnecessary pettiness, Sabastian suggested that they should just focus their attention on the task at hand. Their safety was priority one, so they all agreed to look further into the information that the captain had just provided them. That meant that they had to first scope out the museum and then put together that foolproof plan they had initially intended to do.

As they left the cathedral grounds, it was decided that they would go their separate ways — the sun after all, was halfway from disappearing completely below the horizon. With darkness upon them, going straight to the Old Goethe Museum this evening would simply be a waste of their time. And although it might seem to be easier to scope out the place under the cover of darkness, not every nuance of the burned out building, inside and out, would be learned. Therefore, a fairly early start to their morning was their best option. Then, once they got there and gathered all their necessary Intel, they could begin to construct a plan. Antonio Marcone undoubtedly, would be prepared for anything — even if he had no idea that it was Sabastian who was coming for him.

8

With their combined military backgrounds, there should be no reason at all that any sort of stupid mistakes are made that could cost them. To ensure that didn't happen, and that they had the best opportunity to succeed, they arrived at the museum right around nine in the morning. Yes, they were still numerous hours away from doing what they came here to do, but it made sense that they gave themselves an ample amount of time to not only become familiar with their surroundings, but to ensure that the three of them were all on the same page.

First, Helfred stepped up and volunteered to scout the boarded up building. Though they could have done this together and covered every aspect of the place in a relatively short amount of time, it was determined that Sabastian and Jerrelle should instead, just hang back. It's not that they were worried about being spotted, but they needed to keep an eye on their immediate surroundings in case any unexpected visitors showed up — the last thing they wanted was their surprise being spoiled.

During his recon, Helfred mentally mapped out the entire perimeter of the museum. Once that was completed, he made a cautious attempt at looking in through whatever opening he found that showed him the interior. What he saw, was what he had expected — the place was empty. What he really wanted to do however was to step inside the museum and get an unobstructed view of the partially burned out structure. But he decided against it — not because he wasn't able to find an unimpeded opening to get inside, but this wasn't his mission. If he were to be discovered by someone that was connected to this day's supposed transaction, then he would be forced to take action that would undoubtedly ruin everything. The last thing that Helfred wanted was to have to face a livid Jerrelle, as the chances of him ever getting back together with her then, would essentially be infinity times zero.

Once his recon was completed, the three of them headed straight across the street to the adjacent park. There, they found themselves a place far enough inward so that they would not accidently draw any unwanted attention from a set of overly inquisitive eyes. After a moment spent assuring they were not going to be overheard or watched, Helfred gave Sabastian and Jerrelle his report, advising both of his opinion pertaining to which of the fire damaged areas around the museum he thought would be good areas to exploit. After that, he let them know that there didn't appear to be anyone currently in or around the museum, but he did believe that there recently had been.

Unlike the rest of the place, no evidence of a fire lay on the ground of the main lobby. Charred timbers, broken glass, burned up remnants of items that used to be in room, and water damage; all things that would indicate what had taken place here, was nowhere to be seen. To Helfred, that meant the room had to have been cleaned and prepped for today's believed transaction.

With his report complete and their best course of action finally agreed upon, the three of them discretely repositioned themselves in an area of the park that allowed them the best position available in order to keep a watchful eye on the museum. Helfred had suggested that they hide in plain sight, disguised as park attendants. Sabastian liked the idea; Jerrelle did not — but she was out voted and had no other choice but to wear an old dirty pair of work coveralls that had been previously worn by god knows whom. Jerrelle wasn't a germaphobe, but she had this thing about wearing something that someone else once had.

Two hours into their 'undercover mission', Sabastian was starting to get a little discouraged. He stopped stabbing garbage with the pole that was in his hand and he sat atop of the closest, weathered picnic table. He then pulled out his vid-cell and looked at his father's academy picture. After only a few moments of being reminded of what all had been taken away from him, and why he was here, he shut it off and put it back in his pocket. Those few moments spent reaching into his own soul was all that it took, as Sabastian was now determined more than ever to make Antonio Marcone, that narcissistic piece of crap, pay for what he has done to his family.

"Hey, Sab! What are you doing over there?" Jerrelle asked.

"Nothing! I'm just taking a break from stabbing trash." Sabastian then mumbled to himself, but still loud enough for the others to hear, "But soon, there will be a rotten piece of trash right in front of me that I won't hesitate to stab."

Hoping for some luck at that moment, he looked over toward the museum to see if there was some kind of movement going on — there was none. "If this is going to go down today, I really hope that it will happen soon. We've been waiting here in this park for more than two hours and quite frankly, I'm tired of being used as a pigeon's target.

Jerrelle stopped what she was doing, looked over at Sabastian, and said, "And I'm getting really fuckin' tired of re-raking up this same damn pile of leaves over and over again. In fact, I'd rather be at a bar drinking than here right now."

Before the two of them foolishly decided to go on strike and walk away, Helfred felt it was necessary that a reminder be given as to whom Sabastian and Jerrelle were supposed to be. "I always thought that a Union soldier was amongst the elite, but now it appears to me that they have no resolve, they're soft, and have no spine."

"What?" Sabastian rammed his pole into the ground, furious at the insinuation; Jerrelle simply wanted to make Helfred eat his words, as she knew that none of it was true.

"Come on. You basically let it be known that you were both thinking about throwing in the towel."

Neither could dispute that statement. They each had, in essence, complained as an unhappy child would about being where they were and having to wait.

"Listen... Captain Kragtov didn't say what time the deal was scheduled to take place; she only said that it was going to be sometime this morning. We are just over an hour away from noon, so I think that we should stay right where we are at least until then."

"Ok. We'll wait till twelve. Only then will we give up and leave this park." Sabastian unenthusiastically pulled his garbage pole out of the ground and he continued on with his near-perfect portrayal of a park attendant.

Helfred didn't have any doubts that Jerrelle's friend would last another hour as the man's extensive background all but assured that he had the necessary mental discipline to achieve any goal. He also knew that, even though his ex had received similar military training to his and Sabastian's, she had many times failed to display the one thing she needed the most right now — patience.

Yes, it certainly wasn't the smartest thing that he had ever done, but Helfred decided in that moment it was his responsibility to make sure that Jerrelle stayed with the program — so he gave her something to focus on. He should have used his better judgment and refrained from doing what he had done, as immediate regret consumed him — he had completely forgotten about her bipolar tendencies. It's not like his skills were not an even match to hers, but the 'bitch-switch' had promptly turned on and she clearly looked ready to kick his ass.

There was no way he could take it back — and there was absolutely no way that a simply apology would work. The repercussions of him turning his rake over, discretely maneuvering himself behind Jerrelle, and goosing her with the butt end of it, he feared, was going to be equal to what the consequences would be had he looked inside the burned out museum and been caught by the enemy.

Her anger was boiling over; she couldn't believe that Helfred had chosen this moment to act like a two-year old. No, she'd never intentionally hurt her ex, but she had no problem making him think that she would. And that was why she promptly pivoted around and in one motion, spun her rake over and swung it at Helfred — the butt end of her rake stopped only a few hairs away from the bridge of his nose. "Do you not remember the last time you did something stupid like that to me?" Jerrelle stood there and stared wrathfully at him; her intent was simply to give the man a few moments to remember what he had to endure the last time he had done something stupid like this — she also hoped that he understood her implied warning never to use his brain again without first weighing all of the possible consequences that could follow one of his bad decisions.

While Jerrelle was busy getting her point across to Helfred, Sabastian's eyes lit up. He finally saw what he had been waiting for — a black custom limousine was now pulling up in front of the museum. And even though the car was still some distance away, Sabastian had a strong feeling that the person, whom sat right on top of his family's enemy list, was definitely inside of it. "Hey! Look over at the museum."

The standoff between his friend and hers immediately ended. Helfred promptly dropped his rake, flipped down the long-range digital visual enhancers that had been clipped onto his sunglasses, of which his military rank had allowed him to access and borrow, and he intently scrutinized what was now in front of them.

A few moments were all that had passed when a rather diminutive looking limo driver got out and walked toward the rear of the vehicle. To the untrained eye, the Asian man looked like he could easily be snapped like a twig, but Helfred knew better than to simply judge a man by the way he looked. There was an aura about the driver that could easily be seen. No need was there to test whether or not his assumptions were correct, as he felt certain that the Asian man was a highly trained and dangerous individual.

As the two occupants of the limousine stepped into view, Helfred said, "According to those pictures you showed me earlier, I do believe I can confirm that Salvadore Batiste and Antonio Marcone have graced our presence."

"Well merry early fuckin' Christmas!" Sabastian looked over at both Jerrelle and Helfred, as anticipation began to develop inside of him. "I hope that the two of you are ready for what is surely to be a most festive and joyous occasion?" No sooner had Sabastian spoken his bit of metaphorical commentary, a large white cube van drove past the limousine and then turned right. Down the street that ran right beside the museum it went until it reached the end of the building, where it promptly turned right again, disappearing soon afterward — Sabastian could only assume at that point the van contained the weapons intended to be sold. "And I see that Santa has decided to show up as well in a big bright white sleigh and bring me yet another incredible gift. I don't know about you two, but I plan on being the Grinch that ruins Antonio Marcone's fucking Christmas."

Jerrelle looked at Sabastian, not too sure exactly what it was that was going on in her friend's mind. "Um… Sab? I think that your brain has been baking too long in the morning sun. You are really beginning to lose it. Are you sure that you are going to be all right?"

225

"Oh yeah," Sabastian assured her. "I'm quite all right. Is it not obvious that I'm really happy at this moment?"

There have been times throughout the years when Jerrelle had wondered about Sabastian and his sanity, but she usually just passed it off as being mental-pause, a man's version of menopause. This time however, she was beginning to wonder if this whole revenge thing had gone beyond just a want and has progressed to the early stages of affecting his mental stability, just like it had with his birth father.

Less than five minutes after the white van had pulled around to the back of the museum, another limousine showed up. This one was also black but it was extra long; it stopped right behind Antonio's limousine. The driver of that vehicle got out, opened up the passenger door, and a man who appeared to be of Serbian decent, stepped out of it. He then walked around to the back of the vehicle, lifted the already open trunk, and removed a briefcase. After his driver closed the trunk, the man proceeded to enter the museum, surprisingly alone.

Again, a sense of happiness and relief enveloped Sabastian. He had been so anxious to do what he had come here to do, it had slipped his mind that there was still one more person expected to be there — Vladi, a person that could have screwed everything up if they had jumped the gun and prematurely executed their plan. Sabastian was now very thankful that they had decided to wait. "So... how about we go knock on the front door and invite ourselves in for some eggnog?"

"No pun intended," Jerrelle said, "but Jesus Christ, Sab! If you don't kill the metaphorical bullshit, I'm gonna shove an actual eight foot dried-out Christmas tree up your ass... with the lights still on it."

Helfred just shook his head at all of this non-sense that he was hearing from the both of them. Then again, he had been guilty of many displays of immaturity in the past — and even guilty of it only a few moments ago. So he just let it all go in one ear and out the other. "Can you two please come back to reality? With all of the players now here, I think that we should just concentrate on doing what we came here to do."

To Sabastian's surprise, both of the limousines left the area. He was not sure why they had unexpectedly left, but the only conclusion he could come to was probably because they had been stopped in a no parking zone in front of a burned out building and didn't want to accidently attract any unwanted attention.

A few seconds later, and after determining that the coast was now clear; the three of them proceeded to the museum. Sabastian waited at the side door, a onetime emergency exit that had been haphazardly boarded up after the fire, for the 'go' signal. Jerrelle made her way to the opposite side of the museum and Helfred carefully climbed the unstable side-alley fire escape to the second floor emergency exit. Once he made it up there, he knew that he would be unable to enter through the probably locked door. His plan instead, was to reach out three feet away from the fire escape landing and attempt to enter through the broken adjacent window.

As Sabastian entered the place, he noticed that it was sparsely lit with a couple of low-powered, battery operated spotlights. That alone told him that what Helfred had presumed, was probably true — someone had already been here long before now to prep this place.

Unsure what other out of place items might possibly be there: cameras, motion sensors, a compensated group of street thugs waiting to beat their asses, or explosive charges planted throughout the place — like what had been done all those years ago which claimed the lives of those three Detroit police officers, Sabastian carefully maneuvered himself toward where the white van now sat right in the middle of what he assumed was once the main exhibition hall of the museum. But before he reached the threshold of the large room, he paused — what sounded like debris being kicked around made him hesitate before taking another step.

He removed his father's gun from the back of his jeans and cautiously surveyed the interior from where he stood. Other than the truck, the room appeared to be void of anything else. That was a good thing — all that Sabastian needed was an enemy with a laser sight locked onto his forehead as he walked.

He slowly made his way forward. Three steps later, he saw a ghostly image step out from the shadows down a ways from the front of the white van. He quickly scanned the room but was unable to find a suitable place for retreat. He knew that he would probably end up placing himself into an even worse situation than he already was in if he tried to hide, so he continued forward toward the van as quickly and quietly as he possibly could — and he hoped that the shadowy areas still within the room would help to camouflage his presence as he moved.

Up and off to his right, he then caught a glimpse of another shadowy image; it looked almost as if it was pouring itself over the second floor balcony railing. The entity, or whatever it was, hugged the wall and then slinked all the way down it to the ground. This wasn't good. One unknown, Sabastian was certain that he could handle. But two, especially in the muted ambiance of the room, made things a lot less optimistic in his mind. No longer was he confident that the burned out hall he had willingly walked into, would be just as easy for him to freely walk out of when this was over.

His S.N.A.F.U. training had prepared him for situations like this. Yet for some reason, nothing but negative scenarios ran through Sabastian's mind. He knew that he could not allow them to consume his thoughts — he had to find a way to push them all aside and allow his experience and instincts to take over.

With a decision made, he scampered as fast as he could to the back end of the white van. It wasn't cover, but at least his back was protected. He then flattened himself against the back corner of it and firmly held his weapon, ready to fire. Sabastian knew that he had to stay calm. He could not panic and draw any kind of attention to himself and he needed to use the ambiance of the room to his advantage.

For some reason though, the ability to find the necessary focus that was required, wasn't there — he just could not figure out a way to assume control of the situation. The knowledge that he was not alone had caused his mind to wander down a despondent path. He should not have allowed that to happen as easily as he had, but for the first time in his life, he had felt scared and unsure. He was alone and in an unfamiliar situation — unlike in the past when he had the comfort and security of his military brethren by his side to support and back him up.

The lack of what he was used to having, he could not use as an excuse. If he didn't quickly take control of his panicked thoughts, then Sabastian knew that he would succumb to whatever was in the room with him — he had to quickly regain his mental faculties, otherwise his quest to restore his family's honor would be over.

A low resonating sound startled him. Because he had still been unsure of what he was going to do next, it had caused him to unintentionally move from his 'hiding' spot — Sabastian had placed himself out in the open. He quickly spun to the right in order to defend himself. Now, facing the direction that the low sound had originated from, his military training finally kicked in. Surely, with both of his hands on his gun, he locked onto an unknown target. He still had no idea what it was — or if it was even human, because the dimness of the room had caused the shadowy figure to have a wraithlike appearance. And whatever that was, it was now getting closer to him. Sabastian needed to make a decision. He couldn't just stand there and wait until he was certain what he was seeing. His mind was telling him to open fire, but his instincts were telling him not to. This ghostly image was not giving him a reason to believe that he was in any immediate danger. So for that reason, Sabastian decided to break from protocol and announce his presence. However, before he had a chance to open his mouth and address this ominous figure, another unsettling noise occurred. This time, it came from right behind him.

He inadvertently took a few steps further away from the van; that ended up positioning Sabastian where he could not only keep a close eye on whatever it was that was to his left, but on what was also now to his right — but it also placed him in harm's way. This was not looking good for him. He had nowhere to run and nowhere to hide.

The situation had obviously changed. To him, it now appeared as if he was either gonna get his ass kicked, or he was about to be abducted and brought to some otherworldly dimension — neither one of those options were to his liking. "Speak up... whatever you both are!"

Just then, four overhead high-powered spotlights came on, revealing to Sabastian that those two mysterious images had been none other than Jerrelle and Helfred. "Jesus Christ! You both fuckin' scared the crap out of me."

"Scared is something that you should be," echoed an unfamiliar voice.

229

All three of them looked at each other perplexed. They all had heard that announcement, yet none of them had any idea who had said it. However, that mystery didn't stay one for long, as the owner of the voice stepped out from around the front of the van and willingly revealed himself. This already unsettling situation just went from bad to worse — not because the three of them had been joined by a fourth, but because that individual just happened to be Salvadore Osiris Batiste.

Brandishing a stalwart smile on his face, Antonio's associate approached, nonchalantly flaunting his gun — he did this only because he knew that he had strategically placed backup. "You are your father's son. And just like him, you stupidly walked right into a trap."

Sabastian did not reply. What element of surprise he had left, was now gone. The enemy clearly was aware that he was still alive and surely, they now knew that it was he who had been looking for them.

"If I had known yesterday that it was you, then I would have seriously thought about killing you where you sat at that café. However, taking someone's life in the middle of a busy public place should only be done as a last resort. I knew anyway that it wouldn't be too long before our paths crossed again."

"You're just lucky that I didn't recognize who you were because I would not have had a problem gutting you and letting the whole world see what the insides of a cold-hearted bastard looks like."

Sabastian was right. Sal was a cold-hearted bastard, and the malevolent persona that he intentionally projected proved that. In fact, there was a part of him that wanted to pull the trigger right in that moment and kill the offspring of the D.U.O.'s past preeminent enemy, but Sabastian had not come alone. If Sal were to do what his mind was telling him to, then he was all but certain that he would not be walking away from this unscathed. He needed to stick to the plan that Antonio had laid out for him and hope that everything went accordingly.

Sal took a moment and scanned over Sabastian. He just could not believe that he was essentially looking at a mirror image of his old nemesis from days gone by. "It truly is amazing how much you look like your old man. However, I did not come here today to satisfy my curiosity.., I came in order to make sure that what should have been

230

done all those years ago, finally takes place. And just like what had happened to your father the last time I saw him alive, you, nor your friends, will be walking out of here."

"You must really enjoy having Antonio's crap smeared all over your hands."

"What?"

"It's obvious to me that your boss is afraid of getting his own hands dirty. That is why he has sent you, his personal stable boy, here to kill me."

Again, the temptation was there for Sal to just pull the trigger and eliminate the offspring of the enemy — but he didn't. Sabastian was right. He always did Antonio's dirty work for him. In fact, he had lost count of just how many he had killed per Antonio's orders. Sal enjoyed killing immensely — almost as much as he enjoyed staining the sheets with a young teenage girl. Yes, the things that he relished doing would be considered amoral, but Sal had admittedly always been a bit of a strange animal.

For another brief second, Sal had thought about pulling the trigger — but two things were stopping him: they were not in the Union, and Antonio would have him gutted if he didn't get the opportunity to see firsthand his nemesis' son. Still, the ramifications that would follow if Sal chose to kill Sabastian now, almost seemed worth it. But then, after a moment of clarity, Sal clued in to what Sabastian was actually trying to do — the same thing the man's father was famous for doing.

He wasn't about to be goaded into deviating from the plan and he wasn't about to open up a window for this young, inspired, but extremely stupid man, to jump through. He was just going to do what he had been sent here to do. "You may be right. But in this instance, I freely accepted my task. Now, I would like for the three of you to slowly place your weapons onto the ground and then put your hands behind your head. That will make it much easier for us to keep an eye on you."

"Us," Jerrelle repeated. "Who are us?"

The back of the white van suddenly opened up and two people came out. The first was the same sergeant who had tried to remove Sabastian from Captain Kragtov's office when he had initially gone to see her. The second to exit the van was — well — let's just say that Sabastian was more than shocked at the unexpected presence of this individual. That person had led them all to believe that she was on their side — but it apparently was not the case. Sabastian's anger immediately began to rise.

Neither Jerrelle nor Helfred were at all surprised at the turn of events. What pissed them off more than anything was that Captain Kragtov had the cojones to show up there and personally rub salt into the wounds that she had just inflicted on them.

Myrinna walked right up to Sabastian; her weapon was drawn and aimed confidently right at him. The expression that she had on her face was one that clearly wasn't remorse — and that was all that he needed to see to know that this onetime ally of his father's, clearly had been bought.

Had she been baiting them all along and feeding them just enough information to keep her trust, Sabastian did not know? Even though the majority of the information that she had brought to them was information that they already had, he really didn't think that she might actually be a traitor. Some doubt should have appeared before now. That little voice that is supposed to be in everyone's head hadn't been there to tell him not to trust the captain. Still, his friend and her friend both had their doubts. Sabastian should have looked way beyond that first row of trees that outlined the forest, but he felt no reason to do that. Because of the relationship she had with his father, he just accepted her at face value and not noticed the clues that now obviously were plain as day. And because he hadn't, the three of them were now in a situation that looked rather bleak.

Even with a gun aimed at his head, Sabastian stepped right toward the captain; his intention was to look into her traitorous eyes and ask why, but he stopped his forward progress the moment he heard the sound of Myrinna's weapon being cocked. Nevertheless, he stood there steadfast, with his arms crossed, and looked at her in a manner that could not be misinterpreted. She owed him answers and he wasn't going to back down until he got them. "I fail to understand why you would choose to double cross us. You were supposed to have been an ally of my father's and I thought that you owed him a favor? This isn't how you repay someone."

"Sabastian... Sabastian," Myrinna said. "I really did like your father. And yes, I did owe him a favor. But I chose instead to look out for my own best interest. You see... even with being a captain, my pay still really sucks. Not to mention, there are those in the police fraternity that still harbor resentment toward me for what I did, turning my back on my brethren and helping out your father. It is why when Mr. Marcone offered me a substantial supplement to my income I just could not turn it down. In fact, the offer he made me was enough for me to retire after this, collect a partial pension, and then disappear. I doubt that you care, but the choice I made was an extremely difficult one."

Sal, the sergeant, and Captain Kragtov, stood there side by side like a Nazi firing squad with their weapons locked on their targets. The tension quickly began to rise in the room, as it certainly looked as if this wasn't going to turn out the way that Sabastian, Jerrelle, and Helfred had wanted — then again, one more unexpected surprise is all that it takes to trump another and change the momentum of the game in the other player's favor.

Before giving into the temptation that was there, Sal gave the order to take Sabastian and his two friends into custody. But just as the captain and her sergeant were about to do so, a small explosion occurred on the upper right balcony of the museum. It wasn't large enough to hurt anyone, but it wasn't meant to either.

Helfred had a decent knowledge of crude explosives. So, in case they needed a diversion of some kind at some point, he had quickly constructed a remote I.E.D. (improvised explosive device) from the chemicals and other items he had found in the maintenance shed at the park. It was why Helfred had chosen to enter the museum via the upper level window instead of through a ground floor opening — and that was why he had looked like that ghostly entity Sabastian had seen climbing over that balcony railing and descending on down to the floor.

Their needed diversion had worked. Without allowing any time for their adversaries to figure out what had just happened, they each went into fighting mode and took the offensive. Using their military training and instincts, they each attacked the opponent that had been directly in front of them. Their well placed strikes or kicks sent the three of them straight backwards: Sal landed on his ass, the captain landed face down, and the sergeant landed partway underneath the white truck.

The three of them could have continued on with the attack now that their opponents were downed, but they knew that getting out alive was their priority. So they quickly retrieved their own weapons from the ground and headed for cover. To assure that they were able to make it to where there was some, Helfred promptly unloaded his antique SIG Sauer P226 in a sporadic fashion; trying as best as he could to create enough cover fire so that the three of them could scramble and hide behind the pile of rubble and burnt out timbers that had fallen to the ground from his I.E.D. detonation.

Panic nearly broke out between the Sergeant and Captain Kragtov, as they both found it hard to locate a place to take cover. The dust and soot that was still mixed in the air from the explosion made their visibility nearly impossible — and it didn't help that the recurring gunfire that echoed inside the museum was directed at them.

They blindly fired back, hoping that they would get lucky and hit whoever was shooting at them. If anything, the aimless shots they took would be enough to allow them time to locate cover. It did, and thankfully, Captain Kragtov and her sergeant were able to safely get behind the charred front reception desk.

After a period of equally exchanged gunfire had become a bit more sporadic, Helfred took this as being a sign that their enemies' ammunition just might be running low. He had no proof of this, only his gut telling him that this stand-off was getting to a point where one bullet, one lucky shot was all that it was going to take for this situation to end the way it should not. That, he was certain of — and he was also certain Jerrelle was meant to be a part of his life and not just a memory from it. If something were to happen to her, then he essentially would die. Therefore, he had to make sure that a bullet did not find her.

So, after a few seconds where not one shot was heard, Helfred made an unmilitary-like decision. He maneuvered himself to the right a few feet and then rose up from behind his cover position. His intention was to move to a much better angle to fire his weapon from — seeing that he too was beginning to run very low on ammunition.

So he darted over to the spot that he wanted to be, quickly set up, and aimed his gun. He had a clear line of sight; nothing was in his way from putting a bullet into the side of the captain's temple, then her sergeant's — however, Helfred was unaware of what was happening directly above him at that exact same moment.

With his concentration locked onto his target, and he being only milliseconds away from pulling the trigger, a rather large piece of rubble, remnants from the I.E.D. explosion, fell from the above balcony at the same moment he went for the kill shot. He missed; the debris did not — it hit him on the back of his head.

Sabastian looked up when he heard the rubble fall. He didn't see it hit Helfred. He instead, saw Sal standing at the edge of the damaged balcony, gun drawn, and aimed at his intended target — him.

Simultaneously, both Sabastian and Sal fired at each other. If it weren't for the fact that the balcony was unstable, he would have easily had the opportunity to kill Maxwell's son because he was at the perfect vantage point to do so. But Sabastian rolled himself underneath the balcony overhang. Now, Sal's line of sight had changed — without his leaning over the edge, it would be impossible for him to see his target.

He knew that it was a risk to do what he wanted to at that moment, but it was a risk that he felt he had to take. Daringly, Sal leaned over the balcony railing and quickly fired off three wild shots. The railing immediately shifted forward a good three inches — it caused him to promptly rethink his unwise decision. He didn't want to die due to an unstable balcony collapse, so he chose to vacate his perch for more stable ground.

After a few seconds of not being shot at, Sabastian cautiously moved forward and looked up at the balcony's edge — he did not see Sal there. "Damn!" he yelled. "I think that Sal must have taken off out through the hole in the balcony wall that was created by the explosion. Cover me, Jerrelle. I'm going to go and look for him."

"What do you think you're doing, Sab? Are you fuckin' nuts?"

"Just cover me!" Sabastian ordered.

Jerrelle unloaded a few rounds toward the enemy, not knowing exactly where behind the front counter Captain Kragtov and her sergeant were hiding — she had to make sure that Sabastian would be able to escape safely. After she knew for sure that he was in the clear, she turned toward Helfred. Words could not describe what she saw. All along, she had thought that he was there by her side, firing shot for shot and lying down cover fire — it never occurred to her that she was doing it alone. "Helfred! Helfred! Are you ok? Get your ass up and get it back over here!" When he didn't respond, Jerrelle made the ill-advised decision to crawl over to him — she knew, but didn't care that she would be risking herself being shot by leaving the protection of her cover position.

The moment she had reached him, her worst fears had been realized. Helfred wasn't all right. He had a deep and wide laceration on the back of his head and a gunshot wound to his chest — Captain Kragtov had fired her gun at Helfred at the exact same moment that the large piece of rubble had struck him. "Helfred!" Jerrelle knelt down beside him and squeezed his hand. "Hold on, you bastard! Don't you fuckin' go and die on me!"

His entire upper back and shoulders were covered in a blanket of red; his face was ashen and his eyes were glossy. Jerrelle did not want to admit it, but she knew immediately that Helfred's injuries were severe. Still, she did not want to give up hope. She loved him, after all. "Helfred! Helfred! Please answer me."

He turned his head, drew what inner strength he had left, and looked into the eyes of his soul mate; the person whom he now knew would have to live the remainder of her life without him in it. "Did I… get the turncoat?"

Jerrelle loved Helfred with all of her heart. She didn't want to see him die; yet she knew that he was going to. "You certainly did you bastard. You got the fuckin' bitch."

Helfred could easily tell that she was lying, but he also knew that she would take care of business. For that reason, he accepted her answer. He felt that there was no need to dispute her claim as he could plainly see the hurt in her tear silken eyes; the hurt that he admittedly had caused by his wanting to be her hero. He felt that if he had been successful in accomplishing what he had decided to do, then Jerrelle would have finally understood; finally realized after all these years, that he was willing to do absolutely anything for her — no matter what the odds of success were.

With the few remaining moments he had left on this earth now slipping away, Helfred took solace in the fact that he had fought his last battle right beside Jerrelle — just like he had fought that first battle beside her the day they had met. "You do know, Jerrelle… that I always have… and always will…" Helfred took his last breath, his eyes froze, and he slipped into emptiness. He had done what he said he would do. He had sacrificed his life for Jerrelle, because he had truly loved her; loved her since the first day he laid eyes on her.

"Nooooooo!" Incredible rage immediately enveloped Jerrelle — the kind of anger she hadn't experienced since the day her mother had died because of a drive-by gang shooting ten years earlier. Now, the only one whom she ever admitted to herself that she had truly loved had just died in her arms. Someone was going to pay dearly for this, and she didn't care if that someone was responsible or not for Helfred's death.

The bitch-switch immediately turned on and the Tasmanian devil-like part of her came to life. Without any regard for her own well-being, she sprang up; her and Helfred's gun in each of her hands, and in the tradition of Bonnie and Clyde, she bolstered straight toward the enemy. "Both of your fuckin' sorry asses are mine!"

~ A solid game plan will only work when you don't come across a player who is more than willing to re-write the rules in order to win. When that happens, not only does your confidence come into question, you are forced to accept the fact that you may not be quite ready to play with the big boys." ~

The script of life never quite ends up the way we envision it to be. Its theme slowly progresses over time to an imminent conclusion. No matter how hard we try to command nature's way, many unforeseen occurrences seem to be the catalyst directing one's predetermined outcome.

Why me? Why did this happen? What am I doing wrong? Why can't I change it? We continue to ask ourselves questions like these over and over again throughout our lives without ever finding any logical answers. However, there is a purpose behind everything that happens to us. Most people take life's progression for granted and accept what direction it takes them in instead of making the effort to create and walk their own path, determine their own destiny, and become more than what had originally been intended for them.

Some time had passed before Sabastian returned to the museum. As he looked around, he realized that there was no going back. Their lives had forever changed — others had been lost. He saw that the sergeant was lying face up across the charred altered floor with a bullet hole through his temple. Not too far from him lay Captain Kragtov in a pool of her own blood, unceremoniously draped across the top of the counter. The closer that he walked to the place where her life had ended, Sabastian could see that the captain had numerous wounds throughout her entire body — enough wounds where it almost appeared as if she had been used as target practice. He really didn't need to draw any conclusions, as he knew what had taken place. Before he had left the museum, Sabastian was unaware that Helfred had been badly injured, but with the evidence that was clearly in front of him, it was pretty easy for him to determine what took place — Jerrelle had gotten revenge.

Sabastian walked in the direction of where they had earlier taken up refuge behind that burnt pile of timber and rubble. Immediately, he could see the emotional hell that his friend was now consumed with — she was sitting cross-legged on the floor, Helfred's body was in her lap, and she was covered in his blood. It didn't seem to matter to her that she too was bleeding from her arms and her legs. She just sat there, motionless, holding Helfred tightly in her arms, and openly weeping.

"Jerrelle... I'm so sorry." Sabastian had expected at some point that blood would be shed, but he wasn't prepared for a death that was unwarranted and senseless. "I, um... I wasn't able to catch Sal. By the time I'd gotten three blocks away from here, his trail had gotten pretty cold."

Jerrelle looked up at her friend with obvious hurt in her eyes. "I truly loved him, Sab. I've always loved him. And now I can never tell him how much. He's gone from my life forever."

"He's not gone from your life, Jerrelle. He will always be there. He will always be your strength."

Jerrelle tried her best to keep her emotions in check, especially in front of Sabastian, but this hurt her so much that she just wanted to sit there and weep forever. Yet, she also understood the precarious situation they were currently in. She knew that she could not stay where she was and continue to grieve. She needed to find her inner strength and gain back control of her emotions. Once this was all over, she would then mourn the loss of one of the few good things that had ever been a part of her life.

After a few private moments, Jerrelle was able to compose herself. She had to be strong, for that is what Helfred would have expected of her. She kissed him on the side of his face that was untouched by his blood, released her hold on him, and for a few silent moments, said a prayer. "Goodbye, my love. I will make sure that your death will not be in vain."

Sabastian touched Jerrelle on her shoulder and asked her, "Are you gonna be ok?"

"I will eventually." Her eyes then wandered over to where the bloodied captain lied dead. "You have always accepted me for who I was, Sab. It is why you became my best friend when I was in the military. And that is why I chose to fight beside you in this battle of yours. Now, this fight belongs to the both of us."

Those were words that Sabastian never expected to hear. He had only asked his friend to help him with his personal crusade to right what had wronged his family. And now, a tragedy has intertwined with his mission where a personal score now needed to be fully settled. This wasn't something that he had expected or wanted to happen, but Sabastian now felt even stronger than ever about making Antonio Marcone pay for the domino effect of crimes that are incorrigibly linked to him. "You know, Jerrelle. I don't think that we should continue to approach things the way we have been. I in fact, think that we need to take a chance and go straight to the Emperor's Coronation Hall."

"I agree. They certainly won't be expecting us."

Although he was happy that his friend was one hundred percent on board, Sabastian needed to be sure that Jerrelle was mentally able, so he looked into his friend's bloodshot eyes and said, "Just promise me that you won't do this," Sabastian pointed over to the dead captain and sergeant, "as soon as we get there. The only way that we're going to nail Antonio Marcone is by using our heads."

"You don't have to worry about me, Sab. I'm not gonna go el loco on you. But if I get the chance to kill that bastard before you do, I can guarantee you that his death will be of the extremely gruesome and painful kind."

That, Sabastian did not doubt. "Then let's get the hell out of here. And don't take this the wrong way but... you could use a bath. You really look and smell like a piece of shit."

"Well, you certainly don't smell like a fuckin' bottle of Old Spice either," Jerrelle replied.

As discretely as they could, they left the gruesome scene and made their way back to their hotel room. Sabastian could have easily blended into any crowd, but Jerrelle was covered in Helfred's blood — and unfortunately, the removal and disposal of Jerrelle's clothing would not be a wise option for them to choose because they didn't want to leave behind any evidence for the police to find that could possibly connect them to what had happened.

While Jerrelle was cleaning up back at their hotel, Sabastian was listening to the police radio that he had lifted from the dead sergeant back at the museum. According to what he had just heard, the police were currently working under the assumption that the two dead officers had been killed in a sting operation gone wrong, and they were treating the other victim, Helfred, as if he were the suspect, the one who had killed the two officers. With this, far from the truth information now at hand, Sabastian was thankful that they were currently not suspected of being involved with the deaths — but he felt bad that Helfred had been chosen to be the scapegoat.

She more than likely was going to hate him once she found out, but after weighing his options, Sabastian decided it was best that he keep that bit of information to himself and not tell Jerrelle. He knew that she was hurting badly inside, and this unfounded information would surely cause her to want to set the record straight. But now, he felt, was not a good time to get involved; now was the time to distance themselves from any association to it. They had more important things to do and he needed Jerrelle to keep her focus on the task at hand.

Twenty minutes was all that it had taken for Jerrelle to clean up and change her clothes. Her demeanor had also changed; that fire was back in her eyes and she was ready to continue with the mission — it was a look that Sabastian hadn't seen in his friend in a very long time; not since they had been on their last military assignment together in Cuba. That look right there, was all that Sabastian needed to see to realize that Jerrelle was back to her old self — at least, she was back to being as close as was possible, considering all that she had just been through. This was the take-no-prisoners Jerrelle that he remembered; the one that told him he had no worries at all because his back would be watched and protected — it was the sign that he needed to see from her telling him they would not be losing this fight.

He wasn't too thrilled to have to show his face and be the bait. Unfortunately, Antonio had no other choice but to be a part of the ruse that he had planned. It was the only way that he felt he would be able to eliminate the person who had been looking for him — the supposed son of Maxwell Banks.

To ensure his safety, Antonio had reached out to Zhin Wi and asked him to fly to Germany. It wasn't that he didn't trust Sal to keep him safe, but there were still too many unknown variables, so having Zhin and his proficiency in the martial arts, right there close by, was the assurance that Antonio needed to feel at ease with what he had to do that morning.

Zhin's job had been simple. Pose as Antonio's limo driver and be on alert. That is exactly what he had done — his awareness of the presence of three individuals who were attempting to blend in with their surroundings in the park, made the hassle of taking Zhin away from his duties in China, all worth it for him. That notification, though somewhat expected, had caused a little unusual nervousness to appear. Nevertheless, he knew he had no worries. However, at his age, Antonio felt that taking such a risk was something he no longer should have to do — and once this unwanted variable was officially dealt with, he was never going to do it again.

After he had exited the vehicle, Antonio headed straight to the back exit of the museum. There, Zhin had been waiting with the limousine for him. Once he got inside it, he was brought directly back to the Emperor's Coronation Hall where all that Antonio had to do then was wait for Sal to return with what was all but assured to be good news.

Before his Asian associate left to head back home to China, Antonio gave Zhin one more very important assignment — investigate the mysteriously missing money from his account. Although this was normally something that Louie would be asked to deal with, Antonio felt confident that Zhin had the capabilities to handle that kind of request. Besides, Antonio needed Louie for something of the utmost importance, a task that when completed, will have assured the organization's operational health and subsequent future.

As he sat behind the handcrafted, antique oak desk in the hall's library, he diligently went over all of the details for the evening's real meeting with Vladi. He could not help but crack a smile. And although no one was in the room with him to see it, it was satisfying to him to know that he not only still had it when it came to gamesmanship, but in the matter of only a few hours, the biggest deal in the history of the D.U.O. would be sealed.

As Antonio took a moment and reflected upon what he had just done, he had to admit that the sergeant's portrayal of Vladi was quite accurate and convincing. This elaborate charade had cost him a small chunk of change, but it was all worth it. Secretly, he had hoped that the sergeant would not survive the set up. That way, he would not have to pay the man the remaining money he had agreed to pay him for the job. The captain, on the other hand, was a whole different story. Antonio had instantly become smitten with her beauty — and he could see the possibility that she not only could become a future asset to his organization, but also a personal one to him. Unfortunately, though not through any fault of his own, it had been way too many years since he had tasted the wonders of a woman. Like Lenora Lexington, Captain Kragtov had a lot of admiring assets — all of which Antonio was more than willing to explore. But that was only if she too, survived.

Even though Antonio had yet to hear back any sort of word from Sal, he was feeling much more relaxed than he had in days. Still, a word of some kind would do a lot to settle the few uncertain questions that he had in his mind. "I wonder where in the hell Sal is?"

"Who knows where he is, boss?" Louie had entered the room only a few minutes earlier, carrying with him two cups of fresh sim-caf. "He probably decided to celebrate and pick up a young street skank. We all know that he loves his hookers."

Just then the door to the library opened up. Sal hobbled into the room and made his way directly over toward Antonio. "Sal! Where the hell have... What the hell happened to you?"

"I think I tore up my knee."

"How?"

"Long story but... let's just say that things didn't go as planned."

That wasn't what Antonio wanted to hear. Yet, in the back of his mind, a nominal fear had been there that something like this might happen. If this young man who was looking for them; supposedly Sabastian Banks, was actually he, then Antonio knew that it would not be fair to place the blame of this failure solely upon Sal's shoulders. However, before he could point the finger at anyone, Antonio first needed to hear the facts.

After taking a moment to warn Louie to keep his opinions to himself, he sat down in the closest chair, took a healthy sip of his fresh sim-caf, and encouraged Sal to speak.

"Everything was going to plan until an unexpected explosion occurred. In that moment, all hell broke loose. I was able to avoid the chaos and made my way to the upper balcony of the museum, as I felt that a higher position would allow me to see above the chaos below and pick off the enemy. But that didn't happen. I couldn't see shit because of all the dust and debris that was still floating around in the air from the explosion. Right after I had gone up to the balcony, I realized two things: it was very unstable and I had very little ammo left. I had basically fucked myself. Still, I wasn't about to give up so I fired off what few bullets I had left toward the enemy and then bailed out the fire escape. The exit to it though, for some reason was locked. Lucky for me, there just happened to be a hole in the wall a few feet over; a hole that I could only assume had been created by the explosion. So I climbed out through it and then made a leap for the fire escape. I was successful, but after a few seconds, part of the fire escape broke away from the building. I'm guessing that happened 'cause the metal was probably weakened, then rusted 'cause of the past fire. Anyway, I ended up plummeting to the ground. Then, the fire escape fell on top of me." Sal showed Antonio the large gash he had on his bicep from where it had slammed into his prone body. "I know that it was stupid of me to take a risk like that, but hell… I had no other choice. I'm just lucky I even got away." Sal then gingerly sat himself in the synth-suede chair across from his boss. He took a moment, gathered his thoughts, and proceeded to give Antonio the news that he knew his boss did not want to hear. Nevertheless, Sal knew that he needed to hear the truth. "I'm sorry, but… he is still alive."

Louie exhaled and condescendingly shook his head at Sal. The assignment that he had been given wasn't that difficult to complete yet somehow, his bonehead associate had found a way to royally screw it up. "Maybe it's time that you retire from this, Sal. In fact, I wouldn't be surprised if you were no longer able to wipe your own ass properly and had to pay someone to do it for you. You know.., maybe I should just put you out of our misery and put a bullet in your head… and then maybe the rest of Antonio's, and my life, would be not so full of stress."

"Listen to me you coattail riding piece of shit! If we didn't have a dire emergency on our hands, I wouldn't hesitate to invite you to try. But I can tell you right now that I did not fuck this up. We fucked this up a long time ago by not confirming that Maxwell's kid was indeed dead."

"Maxwell's wife and kid were your responsibility. You should have assured whomever you got to do the job, completed it."

"And Antonio left you in charge. Therefore, it was your responsibility, not mine, to make sure all that had to be done, was."

"Enough!" Antonio was starting to get a headache, not from just the bickering, but from the anxiety that was now beginning to grow within him. "Are you certain, Sal, this man is Maxwell's son?"

244

"Yes! Right before the explosion, he admitted to me that he was."

This confirmation wasn't what Antonio wanted. Now, he had no other option but to acknowledge not only the truth, but that the events which had just taken place seemed to have been an uncontrollable and unforeseen situation; a screw up that Sal really could not be blamed for.

Before they had gone to the museum to set their trap, Captain Kragtov had told Antonio that Sabastian was Maxwell's long lost son. Her declaration though, for some reason, hadn't been enough to convince him. However, his skepticism could no longer exist. The facts were there — even though he had yet to see the proof with his own two eyes. Nevertheless, Antonio had been placed in a position for which he had no other alternative but to go back to thinking the way he did during his younger days. From this moment forward, he had to do things the way he used to, way back when Maxwell Banks and the rest of the Detroit Police Department were continuously breathing down his neck.

"So now what?" Louie asked. "Does this mean that we are going to cancel tonight's plans and get the hell out of here while we still have our balls in tact?"

"Not yet, Louie." Antonio took a few moments to contemplate his next move. While he was doing so, he asked Sal to hobble over to the liquor cabinet and pour each one of them a stiff glass of Blackwood Whiskey. "I'm hoping that Sabastian doesn't know that we are here at the Emperor's Coronation Hall. Contact Vladi and tell him that our plans have changed. With the museum no longer being a viable option for tonight's meeting, tell him that it is going to happen here instead."

Without a reply being given, Louie left the room and went into the living area of the hall to make the call.

"So what do you want me to do, boss?" Sal asked as he continued to pour the drinks.

"I want you to go and get your knee looked at. You have two hours. I don't care what the doctor's diagnosis is. You better be able to function as close to one hundred percent as possible. Even though Louie is the one that will be conducting the official deal tonight, I still need you here and functional."

Sal pounded back his drink and hobbled out the front door to go find himself a doctor — as much as he was pissed at himself for letting down his boss again, he was more pissed for the risk he had taken that had ended up causing him to get injured as badly as he had.

It had begun to lightly rain earlier that evening. Up until then, the previous two weeks had been nothing but unseasonably warm temperatures, so the rain was a welcome soothing break — except for the dense fog that soon accompanied it. Sabastian and Jerrelle had been carefully watching the Emperor's Coronation Hall through the raindrops and fog; conditions that made it almost a perfect natural cover for them — but it also made it near impossible to see the place clearly.

Sabastian was used to having to adapt to the elements, as Mother Nature was brutal and unpredictable every single time his military unit trained up north in Alert, Nunavut, so to him, a little damp fog was just a minor nuisance. For Jerrelle, the not knowing if who they were looking for was actually inside the hall, made her patience run thin. She wanted to walk right up to the front door and introduce herself to the man who not only was responsible for Sabastian's father's death, but also was indirectly responsible for Helfred's. Yet, she knew that she couldn't do that. She had to hang back and wait for her friend to make the call. This was after all, still his mission — even though now, she no longer was just along for the ride.

Sabastian pulled out his vid-cell and checked the time; another hour had passed. He looked across the way and noticed between the city buildings that the bottom edge of the sun was now touching the horizon. Soon, it would be dark and they would not be able to see without getting closer than they already were.

After placing his vid-cell back into his pocket, Sabastian began to wonder whether or not they had 'missed the boat'. He was exhausted and a bit perturbed that their reason for being where they were seemed as though it was not going to come to fruition — it was also disheartening enough to motivate him into formally ending their watch.

Just as Sabastian was about to make that decision, a faint beam of light cut right through the still somewhat foggy early evening — it had come from a car that had just turned the corner onto the street that the hall was on. A few moments later, the vehicle pulled right up in front of it.

Even though neither one of them could clearly identify the person that was exiting the car, they were fairly certain that the individual was the real Serbian, Vladi. No proof was there that Antonio Marcone was actually in the hall, but Sabastian and Jerrelle each felt strongly that the man was already inside — this after all, was where he had been staying.

No more uncertainty encompassed either; both were now confident that what they had come here to do, would soon begin. For Sabastian, everything was about to come full circle — or so he hoped. What he did know, was that they not only were about to give his family's enemy the surprise of a lifetime, they were about to ruin something that was very important for Antonio Marcone.

There's nothing like a little poetic justice.

"Well… are you ready?"

"I'm as ready as I'll ever be, Sab. Let's go and ruin this fuckin' bastard's life."

Antonio was sitting in a burgundy synth-leather recliner in the great room of the Emperor's Coronation Hall, enjoying the last of his snifter of Blackwood Whiskey and puffing away on a Montecristo Platinum cigar that he had carefully preserved for a special occasion such as this. After a few cordial words to Vladi, Antonio sat back and let Louie conduct the business at hand.

Although the Serbian had previously inspected the merchandise, he still took some time to re-familiarize himself with the samples that were laid out in front of him. As was customary with every transaction that the man would make, there was not to be any ammunition for any of the weapons on hand — a safety precaution Vladi had insisted on after a near fatal double cross that had happened some twenty years earlier — hence the reason being for the ungodly scar just below his jugular.

The man's unorthodox terms for business also included bringing with him two small steel cases, which contained a palm-top in each one. The difference between the two was that one was unlocked and the device inside preset to make an immediate wire transfer of half of the agreed upon money. The other case was armed with a digital dead man's switch — the palm-top inside it, was also password protected. Once the ammunition and weapons were safely transferred to a specified location, Vladi would send a message to the first palm-top, letting the seller know that the merchandise had arrived as agreed upon. The message also informed the seller of not only the code that deactivated the digital dead man's switch, but it contained the password for the palm-top. Once the case was deactivated and the password entered, the remaining half of the money would be automatically transferred to complete the business transaction. If the seller were to decide that they did not fully trust Vladi, or became impatient and tried to pick or bypass the digital dead man's switch, then the case would automatically self-destruct. The palm-top in that case was connected to a silicone-based type of detonator and was wired up to multiple, slim in design, hydrogen fusion cells — they lined the entire top and bottom of the case. It was the same type of experimental cell technology that had once been tested as a possible alternative form of energy for fueling helicopters, airplanes, automobiles, and even shuttle vehicles for the N.A.S.A. deep space program. These cells however, were quickly abandoned when it was determined that they were just too unstable of an energy source to safely use.

Having this kind of volatile security within the case kept Vladi in control. At any point, he could end the deal if he felt that something just didn't feel right. He could either remotely shut down the palm-top inside the case, cancelling the pending transfer, or he could simply detonate the case — which he had done once before after he had learned that a member of the Russian Federal Secret Service had actually been posing as an arms dealer.

"I'm impressed, Louie," Vladi said. "You seem to finally have your shit together after all these years. I don't see any problem in doing business with your organization again in the future. Most people have an issue accepting my terms, but you don't. And I have to admit… this is by far the best quality merchandise that you have every offered to me."

"I'm glad that we have renewed your faith in us, Vladi. And we certainly look forward to doing this all over again real soon."

Antonio Marcone was just about to get up from his recliner and re-fill his snifter glass when a loud squealing noise pierced the early evening. It was followed immediately by an even louder crash that felt like it shook the foundation. It wasn't simply curiosity that drew his attention; it was the uncertainty of what was going on. This wasn't what he wanted right now.

Everyone seemed literally lost in the moment. They all began to move aimlessly, trying to figure out what was happening. Sal, who had been waiting in the hall's library in case he was needed, came hobbling out with a brace on his knee and his gun in hand. But before Sal could even open up his mouth and say what was on his mind, deftly shrill like noises came from the rear of the complex, followed by an orchestration of screaming and shouting.

"What the hell is going on out back?" Antonio asked. "Louie! You and Sal go and find out what the fuck is going on."

This chaotic diversion had done exactly what it was supposed to do — confuse. And it worked to perfection by drawing everyone's attention away from the front entrance of the complex just long enough so that no one had any idea that Sabastian and Jerrelle had walked uninvited through the front door.

"Well, Mr. Antonio Marcone," Sabastian said, with a smirk on his face. "It seems that every time you throw a little party, you fail to officially invite someone from my family. It's getting ridiculous that we have to constantly crash it." Both Sabastian and Jerrelle stood there unyielding, as they both pointed their guns right at Antonio and Vladi's heads.

He stood there frozen in time. He couldn't believe his own eyes. Even though he had been assured that Maxwell's son was alive, it still was a shock to him to see this 'ghost' from his past standing right in front of him. "Well, I'll be damned? Sabastian Banks. It's amazing. You are without a doubt the spitting image of your old man."

As much as he just wanted to blow away the bastard with his gun at that very moment, Sabastian stood firm and stared wrathfully into the man's eyes. "And you're the son-of-a-bitch who murdered my parents!"

Antonio confidently smiled at him. He took a few healthy puffs of his cigar, blew the smoke in the direction of his enemy's offspring, and finished off the last few drops of his whiskey. "And I see that you also are a foul mouth hothead… just like your old man was."

Not wavering at all, Sabastian held his ground. "I promise you this, you old bastard. You will, in some way shape or form, pay for what you did to me and my family."

Antonio took one more puff from his cigar as he recalled hearing a similar statement like that being declared not too long ago. Then, in an insolent type of manner, he tossed the still lit and half un-smoked Montecristo Platinum cigar onto the marble floor at the feet of Sabastian. "Do you honestly think that you and that little piece of street skank could actually stop me? Your dear old dad couldn't do it. What makes you so sure that you can?"

There it was — a derogatory insinuation about Jerrelle's disposition. She emphatically hated those, as they were what brought to life the Tasmanian devil which lived inside her — and that type of disrespect was all it usually took for her to freely pull the trigger or unleash the beast within. Some people clearly, just deserved to die.

Staying completely resolute with her aim, she cocked her gun. It was tough, but she held off from putting a bullet between Antonio's eyes. This asshole was Sabastian's enemy; not hers — but that didn't mean that she wouldn't do the deed if the man gave her enough reasons.

Sensing that Jerrelle's own brand of justice was close to being served, Sabastian reached over with his left hand and lightly placed it against her arm. He hoped she understood that he was asking her to relax and be patient. He didn't want her to make any unwarranted moves, because he assumed that even though Antonio Marcone was up there in age, he could easily capitalize on their inexperience or any stupid mistake that either one of them might make.

Antonio stood there insultingly laughing, fully believing that both Sabastian and Jerrelle were of no threat to him. "I've been playing games with people like you two my whole life. Do you really think that you rookies have what it takes to stop me? I think not. So why don't you just lower your weapons before you both get hurt."

Neither one did.

"Let me give you a little bit of advice, Sabastian. It would be in your best interest to just give up this stupid idea of wanting revenge. Run along home young man and go play in the sandbox where it is safe. Oh, and while you are at it... don't forget to take that anal sniffing dog with you."

"That's it!" Jerrelle took a deliberate step toward Antonio so that, in her mind, the man would die faster. Immediately though, Sabastian grabbed a hold of the back of her shirt. "Let go of me, Sab! This man deserves to have his manhood ripped off and fed to him for breakfast."

"Even if you were to serve that as a compliment to his pancakes, I don't think he'd enjoy that version of sausage and eggs."

"Enough! I'm giving you both thirty seconds to leave... and live. So get the hell out of here before I change my mind. Twenty-five seconds... Twenty seconds... Fifteen seconds..."

Sabastian and Jerrelle just looked at each other — it appeared almost as if they were actually contemplating doing what Antonio had suggested. But that was what they wanted him to think. They didn't chase the man halfway around the world to chicken out, turn back around, and run home with their tails tucked between their legs. They each wanted a large piece of the bastard for their own reasons.

Simultaneously, they both re-aimed their weapons; Antonio stopped counting and then paused for a moment. He slowly cracked himself a wry smile, while at the same time, letting out a modest chuckle, which progressively grew into a rather loud cackle. "I must admit that the two of you do have some balls. No smarts... but definitely some balls."

At that moment, Louie and Sal returned from investigating the ruckus that had taken place out back of the hall; each had their weapons drawn as they reentered the room.

"You see, Sabastian," Antonio pointed out. "You have absolutely no chance against me, so you may as well just give it up. By choosing not to leave, you've conceded to accept the same fate as your father." He only had to briefly look at Louie and Sal and they both knew what their instructions were. A plan had been previously devised, and now set into motion in the event that Sabastian had actually shown up.

Louie took a few confident, calculated steps to the left, and Sal followed to the right. In that moment, it became obvious to both Sabastian and Jerrelle that Antonio's associates were trying to position themselves so that they would have the advantage. Unfortunately, there wasn't much that Sabastian or Jerrelle could do to tilt the situation in their favor because the room they were in wasn't overly large. Instead, they just had to prepare themselves the best they could for either a close range shootout or a hand-to-hand confrontation.

Drawing on their military backgrounds, Sabastian slightly adjusted himself to coincide with each step that Sal was making; as did Jerrelle with every step that Louie made. The only difference was that Jerrelle decided to lower her gun. She placed it in the back of her pants, and then unsheathed the double-sided honor blade that her sister had given to her in Japan, right before she had left to come home — she freely brandished her new weapon with a confidence that Sabastian had never seen from her before.

Because Sal had not gotten the job done earlier in the day, he personally felt obligated to be the one to kill Sabastian — at least now, with Antonio seeing for himself that it was Maxwell's kid, he did not fear any repercussions. He also understood that his opponent would be a difficult challenge for him, especially now that he had an injured knee to compensate for. But he didn't care at this point. It was all about honor, and it was all about death. And if that death ended up being his, then he at least would have finally gained the respect that he had always wanted from Antonio since the first day their paths had crossed when they were teenagers.

Contrary to what he and Louie had earlier planned, Sal suddenly stopped, then took a few steps backwards; Louie immediately noticed the deviation, but instead of adjusting his position in order to stay equally opposite with his 'partner', he kept on moving into the position he was supposed to take. "What the hell are you doing?"

Sal wasn't listening. He had made up his mind and he wasn't going to wait. He had separated himself from Sabastian at a distance of about ten paces, just like the old west.

With his back now only a few feet from the wall, Sal removed the second hand gun that he had earlier tucked in the back of his pants, and promptly aimed both of his weapons at Sabastian.

"Sal! What in the hell are you doing? You're gonna get us both killed!"

"I should not have passed my obligations onto someone else. I should have just killed Maxwell's kid like I had been told to do." Sal had mumbled those chastising words to himself; he didn't realize that they had actually been spoken clear enough for everyone else in the room to hear.

As he cocked both of his guns in preparation for what he felt he had to do, glass flew in Sal's direction. Without warning, a vintage white Ford Explorer pickup truck, with battering rams across the entire front, came barreling right through the large stained glass front window of the hall.

For some reason, Salvador Batiste didn't even try to avoid the flying glass. He didn't move out of the way or shoot his guns at the oncoming truck. He just held his ground; eyes locked onto the vehicle like a deer caught in the headlights — it was as if he was welcoming what was about to happen to him.

Sabastian was not in the direct path of the oncoming truck, but he was in a position where he could still get seriously hurt. As he tried to get himself safely out of the way, he tripped over some debris on the floor; it caused him to fall and crack his unprotected head on the side of an end table.

As all of this was happening, Jerrelle dove for cover. Not because she wanted to get out of the way of the flying debris, but because Louie had opened fire. Once she was safely behind a sofa, Jerrelle removed her gun and fired back. As happy as she was with the feeling of the honor blade in her hand, she quickly realized that it was useless to her when bullets where flying in her direction.

After emptying her clip and realizing that she had not brought a spare, she peeked out around the corner of the sofa. Thankfully, the chaos had ceased. Louie and Antonio were nowhere to be found — but Vladi, Sal, and Sabastian, were all down.

A million scenarios immediately formed in Jerrelle's head; all of them were bad. That was until she heard her old friend first groan, then expel some profanity. It allowed her to exhale the breath that she hadn't realized she had been holding. Thankfully, it appeared that Sabastian was going to be all right.

They hadn't accomplished what they had come here to do. Like at the burned out museum, things quickly got out of control. However, the odds of their potential success had just increased. No longer was it three on two — things had at least, been evened up.

Sabastian started to recover from his self-inflicted injuries a few minutes after Jerrelle had helped him into a seated position. He looked around, but his surroundings seemed strangely confusing. Nevertheless, he tried to stand up — but Jerrelle's hand on his shoulder kept him grounded. She shouldn't have been able to do that so easily, but the lingering unbalanced feeling Sabastian had more than likely was the reason.

He took a moment, closed his eyes, and allowed what was ailing him to pass. During this time, he placed his left hand on the side of his head and it was then that he realized why he was feeling the way he was — there, sat a rather nasty goose egg.

Although he was still a bit groggy and unfocused, Sabastian took a deep breath and once again, attempted to stand up. This time, there was no hand on his shoulder holding him down. Instead, Jerrelle grabbed his right arm so that he did not need to struggle in order to gain his balance. Once upright, he still felt a bit unstable, but he somehow managed to keep both of his feet flat on the ground.

To Jerrelle, it was clear that Sabastian was currently in no shape to defend himself from his enemy. Not only did his glossy eyes tell her this, she too had recently suffered a whack to the back of the head and knew that a recovery from such trauma wasn't going to happen quickly. Thankfully, no one else was around, as having to protect a helpless friend, right along with her own ass, wasn't the ideal situation that she wanted to find herself in.

After determining that her friend wasn't anywhere near back to his old self, Jerrelle gently guided Sabastian into the chair that was next to the same end table that his head had made contact with. Seated, he seemed somewhat normal — though a bit more recovery time was obviously needed before they did anything that required her friend to use his brain and reflexes.

Sabastian hated being fussed over like a baby, but under the circumstances, he understood why Jerrelle was staying right by his side. He didn't doubt that he had a concussion — what he was unsure of though, was if he was hallucinating. Other than the two presumed dead bodies that he could clearly see lying about the room, no one else should be in the Emperor's Hall — but apparently, he and Jerrelle were not alone, as they had initially presumed. *'How is this possible?'* Sabastian thought, as they were in Germany. Yet, the individual that had calmly walked right up to his side was someone whom he didn't expect to see again so soon. "Sharice, um… What are you doing here?"

"Is it not obvious? The guardian angel in me has just saved your ass."

Sabastian looked at his cousin, speechless. Only after a few moments of his mind being allowed to sort itself out, did it dawn on him. "Ah… so then I can assume that it was you who made all the noise that we heard just before we entered this place. And it was you that drove that there truck through the window, wasn't it?"

"Of course it was. Who else would it have been?"

"How did you know that we were here?"

"An old friend of mine that I knew during my early childhood days when I lived here in Germany has been keeping me informed of what you two were up to." Sharice then looked over at Jerrelle and smiled. "His name is Nicoli Nemchieve, Helfred's brother."

"Brother?" Jerrelle repeated, surprised. "He never told me that he had a brother."

"He never told you for the same reasons that he never told anyone else."

"Which is what?" Jerrelle asked, curiously.

Sharice paused for a moment and thought about whether or not it would be ok for her to tell Jerrelle what she knew. After a few moments, she decided that it would be all right, because she also knew through Nicoli that his brother had just died. "Helfred never told you about his brother, because if word got out about him, it would have ruined his military career. You see, Nicoli is a high-ranking member of the European faction of the Extremist Clandestine Liberation."

Immediately, Jerrelle understood why Helfred had kept his brother a secret from her. It was the same reasons that her sister kept her own in-depth involvement with the E.C.L. a secret from her — the less that you know about the Liberation, the safer your family stayed.

"Well... thank you, Sharice, for showing up. I owe you one."

"I'm sure one day you'll save my butt and we'll be even."

"That may be quite a ways down the road, I'm afraid. The way things are going here, evening the score against Antonio Marcone might not even happen while he is still alive." Sabastian stood up, took a second to make sure that his balance had returned, then took a few careful steps through the scattered debris. As he was surveying the mess, he said, "Knowing my luck, an unknown heir will take over the reins of the D.U.O. and keep the war going strong for generations."

Like Sabastian initially had first thought while trying to shake out the cobwebs from his brain, there were indeed two dead bodies lying about the room. One was crushed between a wall and an antique oak desk that was being pinned there by the front of the truck that Sharice had driven — the other one was draped over the side of the overturned burgundy synth-leather recliner. Sabastian carefully made his way around to the far side of the wrecked truck and lifted up the head of the crushed victim, showing Jerrelle that it was Antonio's associate, Salvadore Batiste.

At the same time, Jerrelle had walked over to the other body and showed Sabastian that it was Vladi. *'Hum?'* she then thought. *'I'm not that lucky. Things were so chaotic, that the only thing I could do was to blindly unload my gun's clip.'* Jerrelle pointed to the bullet hole right through the base of Vladi's skull. "There is no way that the kill shot came from me. I couldn't aim worth a shit from where I was taking cover." Her eyes went back over to the sofa in order to reiterate her point — her position alone would not have allowed her to take such a precise shot.

Sabastian shrugged. "It wasn't me. I never got off a shot."

Feeling a bit disappointed that the Serbian Nationalist didn't die at her hands, Jerrelle said jokingly. "Well... I apparently wasted a clip for nothing."

"How so? It appears to me as if you were very conservative this time with your ammo... considering that it took you three clips to assure Captain Kragtov's death."

Instantly, Jerrelle gave Sabastian the same serious look that she did just before their friendship ended the first time. In that moment, he realized that his attempt at a friendly jab had actually been a very insensitive comment. Yes, the possibility was there that he might still be experiencing the effects of his head injury, but that was no excuse. He knew that he could not blame the lump on his skull for what he had just said. It admittedly was a poor choice of words for him to use — he should have just kept his mouth shut, knowing that Jerrelle was still very much hurting inside. Just because she had successfully pushed her emotions aside to continue on with this mission of his, didn't mean that she was completely back to being her usual self.

For a few moments, time seemed to have stopped. Neither one looked at each other. It was definitely an odd situation for both. Something like this had never happened between them before. Sabastian was at a loss. He wasn't even sure what he should do. He only knew that an apology was in order. The problem was that, sorry just didn't seem like it would be good enough. Still, those were words that his old friend deserved to hear from him.

Jerrelle did not respond to his heartfelt apology; Sabastian had no idea if it had been accepted or not — an uncomfortable silence then hung in the room. He knew that he should say something else, but refrained from doing so as he was uncertain that if he spoke again, he might actually drive an unnecessary wedge into their freshly repaired friendship.

"Where in hell did your cousin go?" Jerrelle asked, finally breaking the tension.

"I… I do not know? But I do have this strange feeling that this will not be the only time that she will show up when we need her to."

Sabastian walked back over to where he had hit his head on the end table, bent down, and retrieved his gun that had been lying on the floor. While he was doing that, Jerrelle took a quick survey of the room. Right from where she had been standing, she saw lying smashed on the ground, underneath the middle of the truck, what appeared to be a small opened and empty steel case. When she bent down to get a better look at the damaged item, she noticed another one on the ground by the front passenger-side of the vehicle, right by Sal's pinned legs.

She moved all the way around to the far side of the truck, squeezed herself between it and the adjacent wall, worked her way down the tight space to the ground, cleared away a bit of debris, and then reached underneath the smashed vehicle to retrieve the case. After being as careful as she could to avoid the pool of blood on the ground that encircled Sal's feet, she carefully extricated the item, herself, and then showed it to Sabastian.

Realizing that the case had an electronic lock on it, they both assumed that it probably had belonged to Vladi. They also agreed that it would probably take them quite a long time to try to crack it open, so they decided to hold off on attempting that until they had more time on their hands. "Well, I think that we've made enough noise for a while, don't you? I mean, five people dead; two of them being German Police Officers. I don't know about you, but I think that we had better be getting our asses out of this country. Like, real soon."

Sabastian agreed with Jerrelle, but at the same time, departing Germany without first knowing where the enemy currently was, was counterproductive. It just didn't make sense to him to leave until they knew what their next course of action should be. So after a few moments spent contemplating, Sabastian said, "Let's go over this place with a fine-tooth comb and see if we can turn up anything that might give us a clue or two as to where Antonio Marcone could possibly be or may be going to next."

Jerrelle understood why her friend wanted to stay right where they were and search the hall, but she also knew that time was not on their side. So before they started, she quickly peaked out through the smashed window; there were surprisingly, no signs of the law or any other unwelcomed guests approaching. After concluding that the coast was still clear for the moment, something immediately grabbed her curiosity. Once she realized what it was, she drew Sabastian's attention over to what she was looking at.

Immediately, he noticed lying part way under the overturned desk chair, a partially opened and partially blood soaked brown envelope. Sabastian promptly retrieved it and carefully removed its contents; trying his best not to let the blood smear over whatever information it held. After a quick scan of what was in his hands, he knew he had what he needed to locate Antonio Marcone. "Um, I think we can get out of here now because I believe that I have already found out where the bastard is headed."

"And where would that be?"

Sabastian took a moment and thoroughly re-scanned what was in his hand, making sure that he didn't misinterpret any key information. "I think Antonio Marcone has left for London, England."

"So... what makes you think that he has fled for England?" Jerrelle asked.

Sabastian handed Jerrelle a business card for the Ye Old Luxinberg Pub. "Besides the fact that there are quite a few pamphlets for restaurants and estates in here, I do remember my ex-father telling me while I was briefly stationed in England, that the Ye Old Luxinberg Pub was an establishment that was associated with the British underworld. As for the pamphlets on these estates, well it seems to fit Marcone's personal tastes — I mean, it's only speculation, but so far we have been right with our hunches."

Just then, Jerrelle's keen sense of hearing detected sirens off in the distance. She quickly ran back to the open window, and saw all the flashing lights in the night only a few blocks away. She immediately looked back at Sabastian, who himself, could also now hear the approaching sirens. So quickly, they both headed out of the hall through the back.

After carefully covering their tracks, they managed to return to their hotel. On their way there, they had agreed to take their time getting to England. They could have gone straight to the airport and possibly caught up with Antonio, seeing that he had less than a half an hour head start. Instead, it had been Jerrelle that had suggested they take a three or four day rest; not only for their own sanity, but it also might give Antonio a false sense of security. They had hoped that by letting a few days pass by that it would help to sell the assumption that they didn't make it out alive from the Emperor's Coronation Hall fiasco.

After cleaning themselves up, gathering up their things, and clearing the air concerning the awkward situation that had taken place due to Sabastian's insensitive comment, they rented a car and left Germany without anyone knowing — they hoped.

9

Their road trip ended in Paris, France; it was there that they had decided to drop off their rental car — not because they weren't able to drive all the way to the outskirts of the country and then take one of the many ferries across the English Channel, it just made sense to them to stop where they did. They weren't being paranoid or anything, but they'd much rather be at a stopover and then deal with anyone who may have chosen to follow them instead of having to do so in the midst of their journey.

After turning in their rental car, they asked their cab driver to take them to a nice bed and breakfast, because all that they wanted to do was to rest and recuperate. Again, they weren't sure if they had been followed to Paris or were actually being sought after because of the incidents they were a part of back in Germany — so for precautionary reasons, they decided to only stay one night. The next morning, they felt pretty confident that they were home free and had not been tailed, but they moved on to another bed and breakfast the following day, and then to another their last day, just to be on the safe side.

Knowing that each would probably never have another opportunity to visit Paris again in their lifetime, they used their imposed downtime to check out almost every inch of the famous city. They leisurely walked the historic streets, enjoyed some of the legendary cafés, took a few obligatory tours, and visited some wonderful sights — including spending half of their second day at the famous Eiffel Tower.

At night, they wound down with a few beers and reviewed everything that had happened to them in Japan and Germany. They both recognized that they had made some crucial mistakes in those cities — mostly due to their lack of experience. It made them realize that they had to adjust their current way of thinking, rely a lot less on instinct and impulse, and acknowledge that planning and patience was the best tactical strategy to employ.

Once they made it to England, they had hoped that they would, without much difficulty, be able to find Antonio Marcone. But in all honesty, they both knew that this was going to be an immense challenge for them. They had admittedly gotten lucky locating him as easily as they had when they were in Japan and Germany — and that was only due to the fact that they each had a personal connection of some kind in those countries that helped them. They also recognized just how extremely fortunate they had been. Antonio Marcone had the opportunity and could have easily killed them both, yet the man had chosen not to. He loved to play games. He had done so with Sabastian's father, and now it appeared as if he had decided to play the same kind of deadly game with them. And although this one had only just started a few short days ago, they were both getting pretty tired of being moved around at will on his board — yet, they both knew that they didn't really have a choice but to play along, one square at a time, and hope that the enemy made a wrong move. However, they were also aware that the longer they allowed him to continue on playing his game and controlling the board, and the longer they allowed him to make up and change the rules as the game progressed, the more likely the final outcome would be in his favor. So unless they could make a few unexpected moves of their own and tilted the game in the other direction, Antonio Marcone would surely keep his title of 'Grand Champion' at its conclusion.

By the morning of day four, they were ready to leave for England. Though no signs were there that they were being watched or followed, they took no chances. Jerrelle had used some of the money that she had won at the casino in Detroit and purchased two one-way tickets from Paris to London on the Euro Star high-speed passenger train. Two and a half hours later, they arrived in England — just before they got there, they both had agreed that they would first find a nice place to sit down and relax to a delicious healthy lunch before they did anything else.

At the train station, they hailed themselves a taxi and asked the driver to suggest to them a nice and quiet semi-upscale restaurant. Claiming that he knew the perfect place, the taxi driver took them to a vegetarian style restaurant called 'The Octopus' Garden', named as a tribute to England's most famous sons, the Beatles.

The place wasn't overly busy, but it was still nearly five minutes after they had sat at their table before a woman, who looked to be in her mid fifties and dressed in business attire, came over to them. "My name is Carol and I am the manager. I apologize for making you wait for some service, but we are a bit short staffed today. It should not be too much longer before a waitress will be over here to take care of you." The manager smiled, then left and headed toward the kitchen area.

Sabastian and Jerrelle did not have to wait too long after that before a waitress finally came to their table; she had with her two complimentary bottles of spring water and menus. "So what may I get for you to drink?"

"We actually know what we want. We've decide to try your special of the day and two pints of Oldcastle Light please," Sabastian replied.

"Sure thing, I'll be right back in a moment with your drinks." The waitress then left the table.

"You know, I'm really starting to get sick and tired of jumping from country to country trying to fuckin' nail this bastard."

"So am I." He let his eyes wander, as he scanned the restaurant; not looking for anything in particular, he just needed a moment for some reflective thought. "I'm beginning to understand why Antonio Marcone was such a thorn in my father's side. The bastard is extremely intelligent. He knows what strings to pull, when to pull them, and in what direction."

"Yes... there is definitely a method to that man's madness."

"I agree... He could have easily killed my father a long time ago, but he instead chose to lead him along a path, which then culminated with his mental suicide."

"It's obvious that the man lives on the edge of insanity."

The waitress returned with their beers and placed them on the table. She then said, "Here are your drinks. That will be nine pounds please."

"Oh?" Sabastian looked at the waitress a bit surprised. "I was hoping that since we had to wait so long for service that the restaurant was going to give us our drinks on the house."

"No, sir. I'm sorry. The liquor laws forbid us from doing that, which is why I brought you those two bottles of spring water."

'Oh... well that makes up for it,' Sabastian thought, cynically. "How come you need us to pay for these drinks instead of just adding them to the bill?"

"Since we are short staffed today, I have to be the waitress and bartender. Being that I am actually the bartender on shift, I am responsible for all of the alcohol sales. Normally the waitress would pay me separately each time they ordered drinks. I'm sorry, but that is policy here."

"Oh, ok. The smallest I've got is a twenty." Sabastian then handed the money to the waitress/bartender. While handing back his change, she looked at him with a bit of an unusual glare — he noticed this odd gesture, but really didn't think much of it.

After the waitress left their table, Jerrelle continued on with the topic at hand. "Somehow, the son-of-a-bitch is able to stay one step ahead. If we only had an idea as to how he... Sabastian?"

He wasn't intentionally ignoring his friend, but he now understood why the waitress had looked at him the way she did. Tucked in the middle of his change was a tiny folded piece of paper — a note that said.

"If you want to find who you are looking for, just leave the restaurant and go to the grey door at the end of the side alley. Knock twice, and then wait."

"I don't think the waitress will be coming back with our lunch."

"What do you mean?" Jerrelle asked.

Sabastian slipped the note over to Jerrelle, and as she read it, he took a quick survey of the restaurant — he thought it to be odd that no visible staff were there. That really didn't mean anything, already knowing that the restaurant was short staffed this day. Still, one would think that at least the manager should be manning the floor if the staff was occupied elsewhere while customers were present. However, none of that was of his concern; his anxiousness instead was urging him to go and learn what that note was all about. So Sabastian got up from his chair and began to leave the restaurant — he didn't bother to suggest that Jerrelle accompany him.

"Hey, wait a minute! What about my beer? Do you not know that it is considered to be a mortal sin to let a good beer like this go to waste?"

"Never mind, Jerrelle. Let's go."

If she could have taken it with her, she would have. Instead, she quickly downed as much of her beer as she possibly could, then promptly followed Sabastian out of the restaurant, around the corner, and down the side alley.

The smell of grease and food in the process of being cooked was dominant — it filled the long, boxed-in alley, and probably was due to the fact that three other restaurants backed onto it. Surprisingly, the alley was relatively clean and neat, unlike a typical alley, which left Sabastian optimistic that they were not heading somewhere they should not be going.

Upon finding the grey door, Jerrelle slowed to a cautious pace. "Wait a minute. Did you ever stop and think that maybe, just maybe, Antonio is already aware that we are here in England and has set us another trap?"

"Yeah. Considering his reputation, I thought about that. And this may be one, but my gut feeling says otherwise." Sabastian then did what the note told him to do. He knocked twice and waited. Almost a minute later, a corpulent looking, grey haired man with glasses, opened up the door. He stood there silent as he skeptically examined the both of them with his eyes, and then in a deep and raspy voice, invited them in. He led them down a hallway that had a slight smell to it; that of which could be similarly compared to that of a high school jock's locker. Up two short flights of darkened stairs they went, and then left down another short, dimly lit hallway. The man then paused in front of a paint-chipped red and black steel door, punched in a key code, and invited both Sabastian and Jerrelle to step inside.

To their surprise, sitting across the main living room area of the apartment in an old antique Portuguese rosewood caned settee was the manager from the restaurant — she warmly greeted Sabastian and Jerrelle and encouraged them both to make themselves at home.

"Hello, Sabastian," the woman said. "Boy, do you ever look like your father."

Once again, he had been recognized in another country. This scenario was becoming all too frequent of an occurrence and Sabastian was not feeling too comfortable with it. Throughout his whole life, no one had recognized who he really was. And now that he finally knew himself, it was happening all over the world. This woman, the manager, was someone whom he had no clue whatsoever who she was. Either she knew his father or she was working with Antonio Marcone — which if that were the case, then Jerrelle would have been right and they had willingly walked themselves into a trap.

The manager turned to her husband; the man who had escorted both Sabastian and Jerrelle up the stairs, and asked him to leave the room — she wanted to speak to both of them alone and in private. After her husband left, she put down her English tea on the brass coffee table directly in front of her and addressed the obvious elephant in the room. "You probably have no clue whatsoever who I am, do you?"

"Not at all, Ma'am. However, I am willing to bet that you know more than just my name."

"That I do." The woman then leaned forward, picked up the small bottle of lemon rum sitting on the coffee table, and put approximately a teaspoon full in her teacup. Next, she picked up her teapot and poured herself some more hot tea. After savoring the first sip, her heart began to ache; a painful part of her past that she had locked away forever had now returned. She could not help but be reminded of what had happened that terrible day in Detroit and she wasn't sure that this day would ever come — nor was she sure she ever wanted it to. But now that Sabastian Banks was here, she had no choice but to remember the day that forever changed her life.

There was a reason that this young man was now here and sitting in her living room. She could not help but allow an inward smile, for today she realized was the day that her own healing could finally begin. After all these years, that tiny little baby boy, whom she had vividly remembered at the hospital the day that he had come into this world, had returned to not only make those responsible, pay for what had happened to his family, but by proxy, give her the closure that she never thought she would ever attain.

After taking another sip of her fresh tea, she set it down on the coffee table in front of her and took that first step in the long-awaited healing process — she explained whom she was. "My name is Carol Shields." Your father and my first husband, Joshua Brampton, were once partners on the Detroit Police Force."

As quick as an idea would pop into your head, Sabastian felt relief, now understanding what was taking place. "Antonio Marcone is also responsible for your first husband's death, isn't he?"

"Yes he is."

"But how did you know who I was?" Sabastian asked, intrigued.

"Well… first off, I received a shocking, unexpected vid-call from Governor White last week. He had told me that you had miraculously turned up alive after all these years. I could not believe my ears when he told me the good news. And I knew almost immediately that if you were anything like your father, you would be determined to seek revenge against Antonio Marcone; vengeance that I honestly thought your father would have accomplished long ago."

"Unfortunately, he did not. But if it wasn't for his death, I would have never figured out who I was."

"And I would have never left the United States if my husband had not been killed. If that didn't happen, then I would have never met and married my current husband of twenty years. Things happen for a reason, which is why you are here now."

"But how did you know that I was in England? Governor White doesn't even know I'm overseas."

"He wasn't the one who told me."

It took Sabastian a moment before he realized who had told Carol. *'Sharice.'* Sabastian glanced over at Jerrelle with an 'I should have known' look on his face. "Did my cousin tell you?"

"Yes, she did," Carol answered.

"How do you know Sharice?"

"Other than your father and Governor White, your aunt Sonia would keep me in the loop when it came to any news pertaining to Antonio Marcone or your disappearance. Since your aunt's passing, Sharice has continued to keep me up to date. She called me several days ago and told me that you had been in Japan, then Germany, and just like your father had a tendency to do on occasion, you made a lot of noise there before you left."

"Noise!" Jerrelle finally saw an opportunity to throw in her two cents worth. "We did more than just make some noise. We sent a message that could not be ignored!"

"So, how did you know that we were going to show up at the restaurant?"

"I didn't, Sabastian. Once I knew that you were on this side of the globe, I informed a few friends that I have here to keep an eye out for you, hoping that you might eventually end up in London... although I must admit that I never expected you to come here so soon. Anyway, it was pure luck that you got into the cab at the train station that just happened to be driven by a regular customer of mine. As soon as he dropped you off in front of the restaurant, he called me and told me that you were here."

"Do you happen to have any information that can help us?" Jerrelle asked.

Carol's husband walked back into the room so that he could hand his wife her sciatica medication. After politely excusing himself, he left the room. With her tea in hand, she took her pills, took another sip of her tea, and then began explaining what she knew. Sabastian and Jerrelle were told that just three days ago, another one of Carol's friends had recently let her know that Antonio Marcone had been in contact with the owner of the Ye Old Luxinberg Pub; a Mr. Alfraido Fergini. She said her friend had also informed her that he had as well, seen Japanese mob boss, Hiro Juisota, at that same pub.

"We're both somewhat familiar with the name, Hiro Juisota," Sabastian stated. "Antonio Marcone had been staying at one the man's estates while he was hiding out in Japan. But we don't know anything about this Alfraido Fergini, nor do I recall my father having any information about him."

After taking another sip of her tea, Carol explained to Sabastian that the only thing she knew about Mr. Fergini was that he was a very well-known and respected man amongst the community, but who also had a lot of suspicious assets.

"I think I may know what they could be up to," Jerrelle said, as she leaned forward a few inches in her seat. She then proceeded to explain her next off-the-wall theory to both Sabastian and Carol, enlightening them with the information that she had obtained from her sister, while they were still in Japan, about a recent rumor floating around. Coincidently, there was this one rumor that Jerrelle had heard about a few weeks earlier back in Detroit about a sophisticated underground Japanese/Union network that had been slowly forming. At the time, neither she nor her sister believed that these two rumors were connected or had any plausibility to them. However, the other morning, Bai Lin had called her and told her that she had heard through her reliable sources that Hiro Juisota and Antonio Marcone had actually agreed to move forward with a new partnership and establish that underground network."

"Why didn't you tell me about this?" Sabastian asked.

"At the time, I really didn't think that it had anything to do with what we were doing. I just figured that our lone objective was to put a stop to Antonio Marcone and his madness."

"She's right, Sabastian. For what your intentions are, that information is trivial. However, it does appear as if Antonio Marcone is not just here in England to hide from you. My guess is that he is here to ask Alfraido Fergini to be part of his venture with Hiro Juisota. And if that is the case, then I would bet that they will be here a while hammering out all the details."

"If that is true, then I would also bet that they plan on using England as a central distribution hub for all of their business ventures."

"So what do you think we should do right now?" Jerrelle asked.

"Nothing," Carol answered. "Even if you think that a surprise visit will be to your advantage, you can't just go walking into the Ye Old Pub and ask questions. You'd regret your decision to do so the moment you got to the coat check. Besides, I have a few private detective friends searching for Antonio Marcone for you. You just have to be patient and wait."

That was what Sabastian didn't want to be; his drive for retribution was overwhelming his patients. But he was also smart enough to realize the necessity of waiting — and in this case, Carol Shields was right. Sabastian had to back off a bit and let her use her connections here in England to help him achieve his goal. Until then, he didn't know what to do.

After a few minutes of unnerving silence, Carol called her husband into the room. Upon his arrival, she whispered into his ear, and then he left the apartment. "My husband has gone to the restaurant to get us all some dinner. Is there anything about your father or mother that you'd like to know, Sabastian?"

"I'd like to know about my mother."

"I can certainly help you with that." Carol finished off the remainder of her tea and proceeded to explain to Sabastian everything that she remembered about her friend, Sylvia Banks; including the fact that she became his mother's first friend when she and Maxwell moved to Detroit — and within a matter of just a few weeks, they had become best friends.

By the time the hands on the clock had reached eleven in the evening, Sabastian finally felt that he had an idea of what his mother was like. And he was content with what he had learned about her, what she was like as a person, and what she was like as a mother — and he was overjoyed to know just how much his mother had truly loved him.

At midnight, Sabastian's vid-cell rang, startling him out of his semi-conscious sleep. At first, he was pissed that someone would dare call him this late — but when he saw on his vid-cell display that it was Baylor calling, he remembered that his friend didn't even know where he currently was — so his oversight had to be excused. Besides, his friend's reason for the late night call was to let him know that he had successfully repaired the nearly fried palm-top and that he was actually able to retrieve some information from it.

Though the information did not seem to be too interesting to Baylor, Sabastian was wise enough to acknowledge that what may appear to be trivial, may actually be of use one day. So he asked Baylor to copy the information that he was able to recover into a folder and transfer it to his father's computer. He also asked his friend to send a copy to his vid-cell — it wasn't an ideal platform to use, but his phone would work well enough for him to be able to study the new information.

After he received the zipped file from Baylor, Sabastian changed his mind. He decided to just leave it on his vid-cell until he had an opportunity to transfer it to a computer or a palm-top. But then he remembered seeing earlier in the day that Carol Shields had a personal computer. Anticipation quickly enveloped him — but just because she had once been a part of his early existence, didn't mean that he could use her computer without first asking.

With an expectation being the reason that he was now wide awake, Sabastian decided that he wanted a nightcap before officially calling it an evening, again. So he put his vid-cell back into his pocket and made his way into Carol's kitchen to see if she had anything that would help him relax before bed. To his surprise, Carol was still up and sitting at the kitchen table, drinking a glass of sim-milk.

Sabastian took up a seat next her, asked her if he could get a glass of sim-milk as well, and told her all about his call from Baylor. He then asked her if he could use her computer so that he could review the information. She didn't answer him right away. Instead, she got up from her chair and made Sabastian a fresh cup of real English tea with a teaspoon of lemon rum. She then brought it over to him and said, "This will do a much better job of relaxing your mind. After you're done looking over those files, you'll be ready for a good night's sleep."

"Thank you."

"You are welcome. Have fun... and I will see you in the morning."

Jerrelle had left Carol's place earlier that evening, right after she finished her dinner from the Octopus' Garden. They currently had no plans to look for Antonio, so she decided that she wanted go out and enjoy a few pints of real English brew. Just before one in the morning, Jerrelle had returned to Carol's place with a large meat-lover's pizza and a six-pack in hand.

Sabastian had been very close to going to bed — the tea had done what Carol had said it would, but the smell of the pizza instantly grabbed his attention. Disappointment, frustration, or maybe it was just the food and the availability of the cold beer that caused Sabastian to contemplate giving up his research. *'Maybe Baylor is right after all about there not being any useful information from that fried palm-top.'* That was until his eyes locked onto a name that had been logged in the last file folder — Alfraido Fergini. Sabastian called Jerrelle over to Carol's computer so that she could see what he was looking at. There was no incriminating evidence or anything like that, but they now had an address for the man; an address to his vacation home out in the country. It wasn't much, but it was enough to motivate a hunch to form in his gut.

They could have simply waited a few more days and hope that Carol's detective friends would turn up something substantial for them to follow up on, but neither wanted to do nothing for another forty-eight hours — so they unanimously decided to take the information they now had and look further into it. It wasn't a great lead, but it was something they felt they should follow up on. Now, all that they needed was some rest — but not before they ate the pizza and put at least one beer each in their stomachs. Yes, they needed their rest, but ending the night on a high note would certainly help to keep a positive vibe going come the next morning as they set out in search of clues as to where Antonio Marcone may be.

For once, it felt like they had the upper hand. Though there was still a lot of uncertainty as to what they were going to find, both had a strong feeling that their search of England for the enemy may not need to go any further. However, knowing the man like they now did, Antonio Marcone would probably error on the side of caution. His not knowing for sure if they had died in Germany would be the only reason he needed to keep his guard up until such time as he was certain that there no longer was a chance that Sabastian and Jerrelle would again show up at his door step.

On their way out the door the next morning, Sabastian turned to Carol and he pledged to her that he would not only restore the honor of his family, but he would also vindicate the senseless death of her late husband — it was a declaration that Carol was certain Sabastian would fulfill.

Just over an hour later...

Seventy kilometers from the city of London; in Brighton, was where they had gone. Patiently, some two hundred yards away from their target, they stood in an ankle-high grassy field behind a rather tall, very old and wide Pedunculate oak tree that was approximately ten feet in diameter. It had probably been home to hundreds of nature's creatures during its lifetime, but today, it served as cover for Sabastian and Jerrelle as they kept watch over Alfraido Fergini's, fully restored, colonial-style farm house.

The usually confident Jerrelle, for some reason felt a bit antsy. It might have something to do with the uneasy feeling of being out in the open as much as they were, or maybe it had something to do with her fear that this, what they were about to do, had no assurances whatsoever. Twice now, they had found themselves in a situation in which they should not have survived. Yet, they had. This probably meant that whatever luck they had was surely beginning to run out.

Sabastian didn't feel the same way, but he understood Jerrelle's weariness, considering what they both had been through and whom it was that they were dealing with. Nevertheless, he felt confident that this little excursion they were on would not produce any surprises.

Was Antonio Marcone actually inside the house? They did not know. The best case scenario for them was that he wasn't, because confronting him now was not the reason for their coming here today — it was for the sole purpose of gathering some useful information so that when the time came for this war to reach its conclusion, they put themselves in the best possible position to win.

No longer were they going to simply deal with a situation as best as they could. The game; Sabastian had no desire to play any longer than he absolutely had to — he wanted to have an ace to tuck up his sleeve. However, if the enemy was here, he had no problem calling checkmate.

Remembering her military training, Jerrelle stealthily maneuvered herself to the front of the turn of the century home; Sabastian kept a close watch of their surroundings from behind the old tree as she moved. Once she had made it to the house, she carefully peaked through all three of the windows across the front. After that, she made her way completely around the house, looking through every window she came upon. When Jerrelle had returned to where she had first started her tour around the outside of the home, there was one thing that she was almost certain of — the place was unoccupied.

She motioned for Sabastian to join her — there was no reason for them to delay any longer. Once he arrived at her side, they picked the front door lock, and entered the farmhouse. Ten minutes later, what they at least had hoped to find inside, they hadn't — there was no evidence whatsoever that Antonio Marcone was, or had ever been there, nor was there anything to support the rumor that Alfraido Fergini knew the man and was contemplating going into business with him.

Not even sure why she had done this, Jerrelle had brought with her the steel case that she had found in Germany. It's not that she didn't trust leaving it unattended back at Carol's place, but something inside of her was saying that its contents were too important to leave out of her sight. From Germany to Paris, during their four day stay in that city, to London, at Carol's place, and even on the trip to where they now were, Jerrelle had tried unsuccessfully, with every method that she could think of to figure out the code that opened it — she even had a beta test version of a code cracking app on her vid-cell that failed to find the correct combination. The app was supposed to allow her to scan any digital lock and come up with the correct code, but for some reason, it didn't work on this one. This forced Jerrelle to come to the conclusion that the case either had a transitional algorithmic security lock, or the app that she had used needed a lot more work before it did what it was supposed to do.

Not being able to open the case frustrated her. It also allowed her desire to know what was inside it to grow — she now believed that the contents had to be extremely important in order to have this kind of security protecting it. Selfishly, she hoped and prayed that it had contained a large amount of money — not because she was greedy, but because it had already cost her a good portion of the money she not so legitimately won at the New Book Cadillac Casino in order to get the necessary information that she was looking for at the time from the manager. A supplement to her income would be nice — and she didn't care that the money more than likely would be dirty.

Since she had insisted on bringing that thing with her, the idea of using the steel case as an enticing prop simply made sense to Sabastian — just in case Antonio happened to be watching them. He didn't care how his friend felt about it, as he believed that the curiosity of what was inside it was taking Jerrelle's focus away from what was important. Of course, as he had expected, his old friend vehemently objected to his want. Nevertheless, she understood his reasons and reluctantly agreed to place the case on top of the large marble desk that was oddly positioned in the center of the great room on the main floor of the home; oblivious as she did this to the fact that she had actually set it right next to a vid-cell and a small brown envelope.

Fifteen minutes later, they had completed their sweep of the rest of the house and had come to the conclusion that the place was, and had been for quite some time, vacant. "You're lucky that no one else is here, because if someone would have taken 'my' steel case, then I would have had no choice but to severely beat your ass."

Sabastian glanced over at Jerrelle with a look that anyone could not misinterpret — he knew that her threat was as empty as what he believed that steel case was. For a brief moment, he actually thought about walking over to the desk and grabbing the case, just to see what her reaction would be. But as he glanced over in its direction, something else harnessed his attention — it was the small brown envelope that was lying next to the case. "You didn't happen to notice what was lying on the desk, Jerrelle?"

"No. I'm sorry if I looked right past something that might be important."

A small part of his brain had concluded that his friend had missed what was clearly obvious because of her obsession with the steel case. He though, had been guilty in the past of missing the obvious because his mind had been somewhere else, so he wasn't about to chastise his Jerrelle for her blatant error.

Together, they walked over to the desk; to Sabastian's surprise, the envelope had his name on it — apparently, Antonio Marcone had been expecting them after all. "Well... so much for the element of surprise."

"The bastard is certainly a master at his craft. I think that we need to just accept the fact that we might never get the upper hand. I don't know how he could have known that we'd come here but... that is irrelevant. What we need to do now is to continue playing his game, but not follow his rules. We need to adapt and change those rules as we go until we finally position ourselves to take over this game of his and steal the win from underneath his nose."

"That could take a very long time."

"I know... but I am confident that he will eventually make that one crucial mistake. He's no spring chicken anymore. He's bound to screw up. We'll just have to keep being careful until then."

"Well, Sab. Until we have control of the game, I'd advise that you not pick another card. I think that it would be best that you put that envelope back down on the table and not look at its contents. Remember, curiosity did kill the cat."

Sabastian held the envelope up to the light in the ceiling, carefully scrutinizing it to see whether or not it was laced with a poisonous powder or some other toxic substance. After determining that it was probably safe for him to open it, he chose to ignore Jerrelle's warning and pulled out its contents by using a pair of tweezers that he had found in the desk drawer — he then laid the note on top of the desk, and read it out loud.

"You are just like your old man. He had an inner drive and intestinal fortitude like no other. He tried real hard, but he just didn't have that killer instinct. He failed to understand who I am, and he let his obsessions guide him to his death. Seeing that you insist on following in his footsteps, I'll give you one chance only to make the right move and survive the game."

At the bottom of the letter was written:

'Before you make your next move though, pick up the vid-cell and press preset number one'.

While Sabastian was reading the letter, Jerrelle turned and walked toward the front bay window; she thought that she had heard some kind of odd sound coming from outside. She looked off in the distance and immediately she saw that a helicopter was flying in their direction. She watched it for a moment, and then realized that the helicopter wasn't flying by — it had instead stopped its forward progress and was just hovering in the air not too far from the house.

"Jesus Christ!" Jerrelle cried. "I don't know what the hell is going on out there, but…"

"Yeah, well I do." Sabastian had done what the note had told him to do. The preset number on the phone belonged to the same person who was in that helicopter. Pleasantries did not need to be exchanged when Sabastian's call was answered, as he knew right away who was on the other end.

"Here's the deal!" Antonio was somewhat shocked, but not totally surprised at all that the young man had survived the chaos in Germany. Sabastian had earned his respect, but only because he had proven to be just as tough and determined as his father ever was — a worthy opponent. And as much as he would probably enjoy another decade or so controlling each and every move made, Antonio had decided that it was finally time to give up his passion for game playing and just end his long-standing feud with the Banks family.

Uncharacteristically of him, he decided to give Sabastian one more chance to walk away, letting him know that the clock was ticking and that he had thirty seconds to leave the house and abandon his desire for revenge. And if he did that, Antonio would be willing to allow him to go home and live out the remainder of his natural life without any fear of him unexpectedly resurfacing one day to kill him.

For not even one second did Sabastian contemplate the man's ridiculous offer. Instead, he made his way to the front window of the house, stood next to Jerrelle, and looked out at the hovering enemy.

He placed the vid-cell down on the coffee table and switched on its speaker so that Jerrelle could also hear his conversation. He then said, with as much conviction in his voice as he could, "No one in their

277

right mind should ever trust anything that you say. What I do think though, is that you actually want us to leave this house because there just happens to be something inside it that you want."

"You're very perceptive, young Mr. Banks, but it may not be what you think." After a few seconds of unnerving silence passed, Antonio continued, "Times up. I now officially withdraw my offer and I now claim ownership to what's inside that house."

"Good luck with that. You abandoned the steel case back in Germany. Therefore, I am now the rightful owner of it." Sabastian declared.

Jerrelle shot her friend an inquisitive look; uncertain if he honestly thought that the possession of the case was actually his to bargain with, when she had long since declared rights to it. She had no intention of ever giving it up — she just hoped that his words, under the circumstances, were spoken only in a figurative manner in order to see exactly what the enemy was really after.

"Tell you what. If you want it so bad, you should just come and take it from me. I'll even open the front door for you."

Antonio had not anticipated that Sabastian would have scooped up the 'insurance' case that Vladi had brought with him to their deal. But with that knowledge now at hand, it gave him an idea that seemed like a much better option than the one that he had initially come here with. "That is not what I was implying. What I actually want, is you.., because the one thing that would make my life complete would be to watch you, as I did your father, die." An evil smile then appeared on Antonio's face. He leaned forward from the back passenger seat in the helicopter and tapped his associate on his shoulder. No longer did he personally want to personally watch the agonizing demise of his enemy's offspring — he had a much more fun and creative idea.

There was no need for any instructions to be given; Louie knew exactly what Antonio wanted him to do. So he took the palm-top that he had brought with him, the same one that had been in the other steel case that Vladi had brought to their meeting, connected it to the helicopter's available 4G service, entered a few commands thereafter, and smiled at just how easy it had been for him to hack into the farmhouse's security system.

There was no way that Sabastian or Jerrelle could have predicted what had just taken place — the steel sliding security gates on all of the windows and doors promptly shut. All of the natural light that lit up the interior of the home had disappeared — as did the hope that Sabastian and Jerrelle might end up with the upper hand for once. Unfortunately, this elite security system that was designed to keep people, or the wrath of Mother Nature at bay, had now trapped them both inside the house. "Shit!" Sabastian yelled. "We're trapped like mice."

"Tell me something I don't know," Jerrelle replied, scathingly.

Sabastian took a moment and gathered his thoughts. He knew that Antonio Marcone had a specific reason for sealing them inside — and it wasn't to simply starve them to death. But at that moment, he just could not figure out what the enemy's motivation was for doing this? "Ok, I certainly never saw this one coming."

"Neither did your father when he would walk into one of my traps," Antonio pointed out — it wasn't necessary, but since the open vid-cell conversation with Sabastian had yet to be terminated, he decided to add a little derisive commentary, just to pour a little salt to what was obviously still an open wound.

"Just because I inadvertently did, does not mean that I am going to stay trapped in here."

Antonio could not help but chuckle at Sabastian's statement. Not because it came across as being a pronouncement that in all reality, could not be fulfilled, but because he knew first hand to never dismiss a declaration from someone of the Banks family lineage. "You know, Sabastian. I had the utmost confidence that I was going to triumph over your father. You however, I am uncertain about. It was why I had originally intended to lock you away in there only until the deal I was working on, became solidified. Once that took place, I would then be ready to commit my full attention to you."

"You already have my full attention. And trust me when I say, a day will come where I show up at your doorstep unannounced with a personal parting gift."

"That, I can guarantee is not going to happen, as I have now changed my initial plans... all thanks to you letting me know about that steel case of Vladi's that I purposely left behind in Germany."

"What are you talking about?"

"I am talking about a bit of déjà vu. You see, I know what was inside that case... and it's not money."

"Then what the hell is inside of it?" Jerrelle asked, curiously.

"A palm-top connected to multiple hydrogen fusion cells that line the inside shell of the case. You see, Vladi didn't trust me enough to just give me cash. And I never honestly trusted him to give me the correct password that disarmed the bomb within the case. So I chose instead to end my business relationship with the man by having Louie put a bullet through the back of his head as we were leaving the museum."

"Wait! Did you just say... there is a bomb in that case?" Jerrelle asked.

"No... I said that the case was a bomb. There are always new customers out there that will trust me enough not to booby-trap the money I am owed. Arming the case to do business with me was the last straw."

"So you killed Vladi? Why? To make it look like we did it so that the C.R.A.P. would then go after us instead of you?"

"I never thought of that possibility... but yes, that will work."

Once again, Antonio had out played him; Sabastian had to give the man props for continually staying one step ahead.

While trying to figure out what his next move was going to be, Sabastian went over to the steel case. Even though he now knew that it was a bomb, it really didn't make him nervous as he had been close to volatile objects like this before during his military service. From a few feet away, he closely examined it. Almost immediately, a million disastrous scenarios formed in his mind when he recognized something distinctive that a military friend of his, Richard Atwater, had once taught him about a digital locking mechanism that was not normally a part of one.

As cool as he could be, he walked over to Jerrelle and whispered into her ear, "There's a digital dead man's switch incorporated within the locking mechanism that would have detonated the bomb had you successfully picked the lock."

"Holy fuck!" Jerrelle stated, much louder than she had wanted to; her response was indicative of the fact that she now knew just how lucky she was that she had not blown herself and Sabastian to smithereens due to her incessant tampering of the lock — at the same time, she chastised herself for not noticing that small detail long before now. "I can't believe that I have been caring a bomb around with me and have been trying to open up that case for the past five days. I should be dead ten times over."

Over the still open connection of Sabastian's vid-cell, Antonio said, "It really doesn't matter that you have somehow survived up until now. Both you and Sabastian are going to die momentarily."

"We will see about that," Jerrelle stated.

"Over confidence is the reason that you are both now trapped inside this farmhouse. Like you both, your fates have been sealed."

"You under estimate us, old man," Sabastian declared.

"I haven't. You see, Sabastian.., unlike your father, you and your pet won't have the luxury of living another twenty-five years. If I weren't as close as I am to collecting an old age pension, then I certainly would be willing to drag out this game for almost as long as I did with Maxwell. But since I am not about to let that happen, I need to make sure that you expire before I do. So, as the famous character of Captain Kirk once said, 'it's been... fun'." At that moment, Antonio disconnected his vid-cell.

Any egotistical man, such as he admittedly was, would be an idiot not to use that steel case to his advantage — it was the perfect way, he felt, to end the existence of the Banks family forever. So with a few simple words spoken to Louie, Antonio sat back in the helicopter and waited for the end to occur.

With only a few commands entered on his palm-top, Louie was able to locate its sister device inside the case. But there was a problem. It wasn't as simple as just wirelessly linking the two devices together — Louie needed to find the specific detonation program on the other palm-top. If he had only known ahead of time that this was what Antonio had wanted him to do, then the enemy would be dead by now. Unfortunately, Louie needed some time to comb though the files to find exactly what program was needed to activate the digital 'dead man's switch'. For him, this wasn't that big of a deal. He felt confident that it was only going to take a few minutes to find the needed program — however, assuming that the enemy was just like their predecessor, there was no assurance that Sabastian and his friend would not find a way to escape their pending fate before the house they were in became a pile of toothpicks.

While Louie was doing what was asked of him, Antonio ordered his helicopter pilot to move further back, as he had no idea just how powerful that bomb was. Besides, the fireworks from the explosion, he assumed, could easily be admired from a fair distance away.

The moment that Antonio had severed their connection, Sabastian knew that it was only going to be a matter of a few minutes before their lives ended — he certainly did not want to go out this way. If it wasn't for the fact that they had walked into another trap, he could accept defeat and the consequences surrounding it. But he didn't want it to end this way. He didn't want his death to be like his father's — senseless. Frustrated, he took the vid-cell that Antonio had left for him and, just like he did with the log book in Japan, threw it — it smashed up against the steel security plating over the front window. What he had just done, served no purpose — but at least he knew that particular phone was never going to be needed again.

"Sab! With there being no accessible exit for us, I have an idea... but you are probably not going to like it." Jerrelle then walked over to the steel case; her intent was to take it off of the desk, bring it over to the front door of the farmhouse, and set it on the ground. Then, she was going to have Sabastian help her to construct a makeshift blast shield for them to hide behind — there were after all, quite a lot of well constructed, heavy, antique items of furniture inside the home that they could pile up and create a solid enough structure that could possibly save their lives.

Though they didn't know for sure if Antonio Marcone intended to somehow set off the bomb, Jerrelle's instincts were telling her that he was — her instincts were right. "Oh, shit!"

"What?"

"Well... we only have a few seconds left to live."

"How do you know?" Sabastian asked.

There was no time to waste on any more words the moment that Jerrelle saw the digital countdown clock appear on the lock on the case — she also knew that she did not have the time to do what she had wanted. Now, she had to improvise. "You grab the bomb and place it on the floor."

Sabastian looked at his friend with a blank, 'you have got to be kidding' stare.

"Just do it!" she ordered.

Sabastian hesitantly grabbed the bomb and placed it straight down on the floor in front of the desk. Jerrelle then placed herself between the bomb and the marble desk. In one fluid motion, she flipped the heavy desk behind her onto its side. Then, she pulled back the heavy Egyptian throw rug that had been underneath it, wrapped the case inside the rug, and slid the wrapped bomb across the hardwood floor toward the front entrance of the room. Next, she was about to order Sabastian to get his ass behind the marble desk, when she noticed that an old cellar door was right in front of her feet — it had become revealed once the Egyptian throw rug covering it, was removed. "Hurry up, Sab, and help me drag this fuckin' desk back further so that we can get this cellar door open!"

He did — and Jerrelle just prayed that the old door was not nailed or swelled shut.

10

A split second decision can save your life. Yet if you hesitate for even a moment to think about your best available options, you just may end up dead. In a matter of only days, the number of the near death situations that they had survived was nearing as many combined as they had each lived through during their military careers. At this rate, they soon won't have any available fingers on their hands to continue counting.

Jerrelle's idea for them to take cover down in the cellar instead of behind the over turned desk, had saved both of their lives. Without a doubt, they had gotten lucky, as the cellar was actually an old World War II bomb shelter? And although the nearly one hundred year old structure had done what it was originally constructed to do, they didn't walk away from the massive explosion unscathed. The shelter was old and hadn't been maintained — nor had it been designed to withstand a proximity detonation of hydrogen fusion cells.

The explosion had been immense. It had been big enough to not only completely obliterate the farmhouse, but it had left mammoth, crater like holes in the surrounding landscape — it almost looked as if the entire property was a haphazardly sifted through archeological dig site, littered with wood fragments, concrete, and glass. Nearly half of the five acres of farmland had bits of what was once a home, lying across it. There was even a BMW sedan lying upside down in the adjacent field — it had been passing by the property at the exact moment of the explosion and was forced off the road by the shockwave.

The marble desk that Jerrelle had kicked over had ended up being blown straight backwards, right through where the back wall of the house once was. It ended up in two equal pieces lying outside on the ground in front of an old carriage house, some fifty yards away. If Jerrelle and Sabastian had taken up shelter behind that desk, like they had initially planned, both of them would have become marble pancakes.

Within the cellar, an immense amount of fallen debris was now on top of them. As logical as it would be for Sabastian and Jerrelle to stay right where they were and wait for the emergency vehicles to arrive, rescue, and treat them, they knew that this was not an option. Neither one wanted to be grilled for answers by the authorities on what had happened — nor did they want them to dig further into the series of events that had led up to the explosion.

Though each of them was in quite a bit of pain from the injuries that they had sustained, they quickly extricated themselves from the rubble. No sooner had they done this, off in the distance, the approaching emergency vehicles could clearly be heard approaching. A minute or so was all they had before the place became a three-ring circus, so Sabastian and Jerrelle promptly headed straight to the still standing barn at the rear of the property. Once they were there, they took a moment, caught their breath, and then made their way into the two acres of woodland that was a stone's throw away from the backside of the barn.

It had taken them almost an hour to work their way through the dense cropping of trees to where they had parked their rental car on the east, gravel side road that ran alongside the outskirts of the farmland property. They then took turns driving back to Carol Shields' place.

Ten minutes into their trip, their battered bodies were finally starting to feel the effects of what they had just survived. Jerrelle seemed unfortunately, to be the one who got the worst of it. Her shoulders were bruised and stiffening up and her right lower leg was throbbing due to it having been pinned by a fallen structural beam. For Sabastian, other than a few cuts and bruises, it was his head that hurt the most — his already having the remnants of a concussion didn't help when the floor that had been above, crashed down onto them.

Because of what each had to endure, neither one of them could stay focused for too long a period. They should have probably gone straight to the hospital to get their injuries looked at, but if they had, the presence of two very injured citizens of the Union would certainly cause a red flag to be raised.

After they had arrived back at Carol's apartment, she and her husband patched up Sabastian and Jerrelle as best they could. Once that was done, and with a little encouragement from Carol;

encouragement that definitely had a motherly influence behind it, they had both decided that it would be in their best interest to just stay where they were for at least a week — rest and no stress would certainly give their accumulative injuries the necessary time each needed to fully heal. Besides, with everything that they had been through lately, it actually made sense for them to put their 'mission' on hold and take a much needed break away from their chaotic adventure. Also, by staying out of sight, it should allow them to finally get the upper hand. They both should have died in that explosion — and that was exactly what they wanted Antonio Marcone to believe. Their supposed death undoubtedly will allow the man to relax, let down his guard, and assume that he had succeeded in winning another one of his paltry games — it is what Sabastian and Jerrelle both believed will become the one crucial mistake that they need for him to make that will then allow them to ultimately succeed in their goal to make a well deserved man pay for all of his accumulative sins.

The next morning, Sabastian called Savanna and filled her in on everything that had happened to them over the past week. After having to spend the first thirty minutes of his call reassuring her that he was all right, he was then able to talk her into leaving the state and taking a last minute vacation with Sydney and Baylor. The 'vacation', he insisted, was only for precautionary reasons and Sabastian promised that they all would meet up in a week's time. The reason for his wanting them to do this was simple; Jerrelle had mentioned a possibility that he simply could not dismiss. Even though it was easy for them to assume that Antonio Marcone would now believe that they were both dead, he was the kind of person who would go out of his way to finish off the rest of Sabastian's family, just to be certain that no one else would be stupid enough to ever challenge him again.

Once it was agreed upon that everyone would meet up in one week's time at the destination of their 'vacation', Sabastian disconnected his call, took up a seat in the antique settee, and sunk into deep thought. Japan, Germany, and England; he firmly believed these three countries that Antonio Marcone had gone to had not been chosen at random. Other than it appearing as if he was just trying to avoid his being followed, his global jaunt had an underlying purpose. Yes, they had found small connections for Antonio being in each country, but

Sabastian was now certain that there was a bigger picture they were yet unable to see. He wanted to find out for sure why the man had come to England. He also wanted to know if Jerrelle and her sister's unsubstantiated theory of a sophisticated underground Japanese/Union network, that had the possibility of a European inclusion, were true. So the next morning, Sabastian asked Carol Shields to call in a few favors from her detective friends. He wanted her to ask them if they could use their position as officers of the law and see if they could help them confirm this rumor. Three days after she had appeased his request, Carol received word that the rebellious son of an apparent 'employee' of Alfraido Fergini's had been arrested on drug charges at Oxford University. Officers from Scotland Yard had conveniently found on the young man, two small packages of 'ice-cycles' — the latest variation of a methamphetamine. Once taken, this time-released pill sits in the stomach and then is gradually distributed throughout the person's bloodstream over a twenty-four hour period, allowing that person to consistently feel the effects of the drug all day long.

The illegal drugs, and the charge of possession with the intent to distribute, were enough leverage to convince the young man to co-operate. So he made a reluctant deal with police to help get them some information in exchange for leniency — as it was after all, his first offence. And it was that valuable information which ultimately confirmed that not only had Antonio Marcone and Louie Mazotti left England the morning after the explosion to return back to Detroit, but that further discussions between he, Hiro Juisota, and Alfraido Fergini about a possible working relationship, were planned.

Two days after receiving this information, both Sabastian and Jerrelle were finally feeling better. Though neither had yet to fully recover from their injuries, they both decided that it was time to return home — well, almost home. Instead of flying into San Antonio, they flew into Toronto. From there, they took a commuter flight into Windsor; a small city that was once the automotive capital of Canada and sits on the banks of the Detroit River. To this day, many people referred to it as an unofficial suburb of the Motor City or, as Steve Perry of the band Journey appositely sang in the song 'Don't Stop Believing' — South Detroit.

Just before they left England, Carol had made arrangements for them to stay at Caesar's Windsor, Hotel and Casino — but due to a rather large medical conference that just happened to be in town at that time, the only available room left was the Presidential Suite on the top floor of the west tower of the hotel. Blowing money on an expensive hotel room wasn't what Sabastian wanted to do. Unfortunately though, he really had no other choice. Thankfully, Jerrelle stepped up and, using some of her earlier gambling winnings, offered to pay for half. Besides, the location of the room overlooked the river and gave Sabastian a panoramic view of the entire city of Detroit — a real life 'postcard' for him to use as motivation to complete what was bestowed upon him.

When they arrived at their hotel, Sabastian and Jerrelle immediately went up to their room. Their plan was to spend the entire first day there resting, recovering, and doing whatever was necessary in order to mentally prepare themselves for when the time came to resume their mission. All of the time differences and jet lag that had been a part of their past few weeks had made that recovery a lot harder than it should have been for them — and knowing that Antonio Marcone was probably in his office on the top floor of the New Book Cadillac Hotel and basking in his victory, it didn't make it any easier for their exasperated thoughts to disappear — especially since they could clearly see across the river from their own hotel room window, his hotel and casino.

The following morning, Sydney, Savanna, and Baylor, had joined them at the hotel — they had spent the previous few days at the downtown Holiday Inn. Their reunion however was short, as Sabastian chose to seclude himself in one of the suite's bedrooms.

Not sure why he had done this, everyone just assumed that Sabastian still needed some more time to recuperate from his recent ordeal — but fifty minutes later, he exited the room and re-joined the group. He then walked over to the service bar, poured himself a fresh cup of English sim-tea, and added a little lemon rum — he had Carol to thank for introducing him to this.

With his tea in hand, he made his way over to the extra long, dark grey synth-suede lounge chair, sat down, and stared aimlessly at the view of Detroit's skyline through the room's window.

"So… are you going to tell us why you locked yourself in that bedroom for almost an hour?"

"I needed to make a private vid-call, Savanna. I had something very important that I needed to deal with of which I have been procrastinating over. So I figured that now seemed like as good a time as any to address it."

Everyone in the room stayed quiet. Although each of them could probably speculate as to what issue it was that Sabastian was referring to, none of them felt that they had the right to pry — as curious as each were.

"My head has been a mess ever since I found out who I was. I needed to confront someone and see if they would finally come clean. That was the only way that I felt I could start to clear up some of the mass confusion that still exists in my mind. And although I did not get everything that I had hoped for as far as clarification, I am satisfied enough with what I have learned."

In essence, everyone in the room was on the edge of their seats. Though this news that Sabastian was about to break to them was probably not going to shock the world, an assumption could be made that it was going to end up surprising everyone in the hotel room.

Sabastian took a moment, took another healthy sip of his tea, gathered his thoughts, and continued. "The hard part about all of this is… I find that I am currently in a position in which I have to swallow my pride and ask for a big favor from that person; one that I never thought they would actually agree to."

"Did they?" Savanna asked.

"Yes."

"So who are we talking about?" Baylor inquired.

"Yeah, who is it? Keeping something like that from me just might be what gets the both of us killed. Therefore, it is your obligation to make me aware of every single aspect of whatever plan it is that you are concocting in your concussed head."

It's not like he didn't want to tell Jerrelle who he was talking about or what he was thinking of doing, but Sabastian knew that if she were to learn the man's name, she would more than likely not hesitate to find a way of throwing him through the plate glass window of their hotel room — that, would be her way of assuring that her objection would be clearly understood. "It's not like you ever neglected to tell me something of importance before, Jerrelle. It's only fair that I keep you in the dark for a change. When the time is right, you will know what that call was all about and what I am thinking of doing. You'll just have to trust me."

"Trust you?" Jerrelle repeated. "Look what trusting you has done for me so far."

"Will you two stop the unnecessary dialogue?"

"I'm sorry, Uncle Sydney. It's just... I still sometimes find myself torn between my past life and who I really am. And until I have it all sorted out, I don't feel that it is necessary for me to share everything with the class.

"That's understandable. I'm still not used to you being alive." Sydney walked over to Sabastian and carefully gave him a hug, making sure that he did not aggravate any of his nephew's still healing injuries. He then picked up his fedora from the coffee table, placed it on his head, and left the room to go down to the casino. "Don't wait up for me."

Sabastian took another sip of his fresh sim-tea and looked at everyone in the room. "You are all probably gonna hate me but... we will be staying here for at least another three days."

"Why do you want to wait so long before we go after Antonio?"

Sabastian stayed quiet as he finished off the remainder of his tea. After setting his cup down onto the desk in the room he took another brief look through the room's window at the city across the river. "Two reasons, Jerrelle. First... because the both of us still need a few more days off to rest up and recover, as I want to make sure that we're both one hundred percent ready to go after that bastard. And secondly... the longer we can wait the better, as the person that I made the vid-call to, needs some time to do what I asked of them." Sabastian could easily see it in Jerrelle's eyes that she wasn't all too happy with his decision to keep her in the dark, so he walked over to her, placed his arm around her shoulder, and said, "Don't bother asking... you're just going to have to trust me with this one. When the time is right, you'll know."

The meeting that Antonio was supposed to have in England with Alfraido Fergini and Hiro Juisota, had been planned shortly after he had gotten released from jail. It was solely designed to iron out any outstanding issues that each had about a possible working agreement between them. It was a brilliant and bold idea that Antonio first contemplated a few years ago, but only recently had been negotiated by Louie on his behalf.

Unfortunately, Sabastian and his erroneous belief that he was obligated to follow in his father's footsteps, had forced Antonio to adjust his plans. It also, in an unexpected way, had given his life a new sense of purpose. After Maxwell's demise, Antonio thought that he could simply exist and go about his daily business until his time on this earth was meant to come to an end. However, he soon realized that he missed being in complete control of someone else's destiny. Was he thankful that Sabastian had showed up? No, he wasn't. But in a twisted sort of way, the presence of his enemy's son had restored who he was.

Sabastian had given him a run for his money. The young man never gave up and fought to the bitter end. In hindsight, Antonio had been lucky. He should not have dickered around; he should have just eliminated Sabastian the old fashion way — just like he had done to Vladi with a bullet to the back of the head. Thankfully, his competitive nature did not cost him more than just the death of an associate.

No longer could Antonio allow an individual with an agenda to distract him from what was important. His personal form of entertainment had on occasion, come close to ruining everything. Fortunately, it had not cost him his planned collaboration with Hiro and Alfraido — Antonio just hoped that this inconvenience did not send a message of uncertainty to his future business partners.

For nearly a week, he relished in his victory. After twenty-five eventful years, the final chapter in the epic saga of the unfortunate Banks family had finally come to an end. But in the process, Antonio had incurred a loss that he was unsure he could replace. Also, he had made the difficult decision to severe ties to a client that could have eventually made him richer than he could have ever imagined.

However, when one is in a business as risky as his, unforeseen circumstances do happen and difficult choices sometimes have to be made.

Shortly upon his return to Detroit, Antonio started working on a few minor issues that first needed to be addressed before his meeting with Hiro and Alfraido could take place. So that no loose ends were there that could potentially be the reason that his pending deal did not occur, he sent Louie out to address a situation that needed a more 'hands on' approach. The other issue, Antonio took care of himself — which ended up only being a restructuring of the management team of the first restaurant Manual Velasquez helped him to acquire, all those years ago — Old World Café & Restaurant.

Antonio was right in the middle of his vid-call with his new restaurant manager when he heard a surprising knock at his office door. "Pardon me for a moment, as it appears that I have an unwanted visitor." Antonio placed his call on hold and he walked over to the door — to his knowledge, no one else was currently supposed to be on the top floor of the hotel. Therefore, he could only assume that an apparent unauthorized individual had somehow gained access to it. *'If Sal was still here, the fool outside my door right now would most certainly regret the assumption they made that it would be alright to bother me. Right after Louie returns with his report, I definitely need to go over the organization's depth chart and determine who Sal's replacement is going to be.'*

Antonio opened up his office door and was completely shocked at who he saw standing there. Never in a million years did he expect to see this man, another ghost from his past — another person who was supposed to be dead. This one however, he was pretty sure had not come back to kill him. Nevertheless, why was Terrance Burelli now standing on the other side of the office threshold?

"Surprise! I must say, Mr. Marcone, you don't look half-bad for a stressed out old fart that should have long ago, been pushing up daisies."

"How in the hell..? You're supposed to be..? You need an access key for the elevator to get up here."

Without first bothering to respond to Antonio's inquiries, Terrance proceeded to invite himself into the man's office. Once inside, he took up a seat on the synth-leather sofa at the far side of the room. "Did you forget, Antonio, that I am a highly trained military man? No matter how difficult an obstacle may seem, I can find my way around it."

Antonio did not say a word. He knew that a man like Terrance, with an ego almost as big as his, had come here to gloat about something. What that was though, he hadn't any inkling.

"You are probably wondering why I am here? Well, it's simple. After I finished my twenty-five years of service to this great country of ours, I decided that it was time I give back. No… let me rephrase that. I have decided that it was time that I pay back this country of ours for all of the bullshit that they put me through while I was a member of its military. They sent me to hell and back multiple times throughout my career without any sort of recognition for my willingness to risk my own ass. So I can't think of a better way to show my appreciation to them than to offer my services to an organization like this one. Besides, I heard through the grapevine that you are now short one associate."

"How would you..?" Although Antonio was not in the mood at that moment to deal with Terrence's arrogance, a dose of reality struck him. He was indeed short an associate. The wheels in his brain began to turn. This unwanted and unexpected visit from his old grunt could actually work out in his favor. There were however, still a few things that Antonio had to first figure out before this presumed assumption of Terrance's would even be considered.

He went back to his office chair, sat down, and quickly finished off his vid-call. Once that was complete, he got up, walked over to his wet bar, poured two healthy glasses of Walker's Club, handed one to Terrance, and then began the interviewing process to replace Sal.

Louie had learned from some of the casino staff that their manager had mysteriously disappeared — so he took it upon himself to investigate this further. After he was able to confirm that Jason Hernandez had indeed vanished, he went right up to Antonio's office to report this news to him. As he was approaching the door, he noticed that it was left slightly ajar — he also heard a voice coming from

within that sounded vaguely familiar. This grabbed his curiosity —
but his instincts promptly leapt to the forefront and forced him not to
be hasty. He knew that no one was scheduled to meet with Antonio in
his office this day, so Louie lightly tapped on the doorjamb, pushed
open the door, and stepped across the threshold. He was ready for
anything — except what he saw. Time immediately stood still. Never
in a million years did he ever expect to see this man again.

Louie's anger began to rise — not because a ghost from the
past had reappeared, but because Sal, just like he had with Sabastian,
failed to do his assigned job and put this man six feet under. Now, this
insubordinate, military coward had returned — and was conversing as
if he and Antonio were two long lost, best friends. "What the fuck? I
thought that you were..?"

"Dead? Well, as you can see, I am not."

Louie just stood there dumbfounded."

"So how in the hell are you doing, you wrinkled old prune?"
Terrance asked.

"I vividly remember that Sal was supposed to take care of
you."

"He did take care of me. And now that he is dead, I no longer
have to keep up my end of the agreement."

Louie was not only confused, but he was getting even angrier.
He wished in that moment that Sal's body hadn't been sent to Sicily to
be buried so that he could dig the bastard up, take it to the Everglades,
and hang his carcass upside down from a tree limb so that the alligators
could feast upon it. "You've taken a big risk showing your face here,
Terrance. I suggest that you walk your fuckin' ass out of here right
now while you still have a working set of legs!"

"What's up your ugly butt, Louie? Just because you haven't
gotten any since Clinton was in power, and I don't mean Hillary,
doesn't mean that you have to take out your libidinous on your old
friend."

"And you're still full of crap, Terrance. Go back home and
retire like a good old soldier boy before I shove an I.E.D. down your
throat."

"Enough!" Before it got to the same point it always did
whenever Louie and Sal went at each other's throats, Antonio made

sure both men understood that the verbal joisting between the two had to stop. With everything that he needed to assure was in its proper place before the upcoming meeting with his overseas counterparts took place, a headache was something that he just did not need.

After a few moments of dead silence in the room, Antonio looked at his right-hand man — he was not at all happy to learn that the reason Terrance was now in his office was because Louie had not assured the man's death had occurred when it was ordered all those years ago. Nevertheless, he was glad now that the insubordination had occurred — but that didn't mean that he had any intention of letting Louie off the hook. The two of them were going to have a little talk about the consequences of passing off ones responsibility to someone else — especially when that someone else doesn't particularly like you.

Before Louie had returned from his task, small talk had been the only thing that was exchanged between Terrance and Antonio. Now, he was ready for a full explanation as to why, after all of these years, his one-time hired hand, had decided that this day was the one in which he had chosen to ask for his old job back.

Terrance began by stating that the debacle that had taken place at the Davis Brothers Warehouse had caused him to reassess his decision to become involved with the D.U.O. He had realized just how lucky he had been that day to not only escape with his life, but by his being there, he had been a part of something that could ultimately ruin the military career that he had just begun. So he decided to immediately return home to Ohio and he tried to distance himself from what he had mistakenly gotten himself involved with.

What came out of his mouth next was a tale that Antonio never expected to be told — it was a bit of a surprise to Louie as well. As usual, the cynical part of who he was was skeptical that it really was true. Still, he couldn't dismiss the man's story, as even the most elaborate tale ever told, usually contained a grain of truth.

According to Terrance, he had unintentionally betrayed his country's trust by becoming involved with a company that was suspected of being financially connected to the U.A.L. (United Arab League) — an organization that the U.B.I. (Union Bureau of Investigation) believed was a front for a terrorist network. Terrance then went on to explain that because of this connection, he had been accused of being a part of a money laundering scheme that apparently was solely responsible for financing the League. These accusations ultimately forced him into testifying against those within that company whom he knew might be associated with the U.A.L. in order to avoid any jail time.

Everything had been mere speculation. Terrance nevertheless, had no choice but to throw a multitude of people under the bus in order to save his own ass. And even after he had done this, he was not placed in the witness protection program. Instead, Terrance said that he was just given a dishonorable discharge from the military for his part and told good luck. He had no excuses for any of his decisions, past and present; he was just here looking for an opportunity — a fresh start.

Terrance took the last available swig from his glass of Walker's Club, set the glass down near the edge of Antonio's desk, and said, "I am a free agent now. I don't know if you are willing to wipe the slate clean or not, but I am offering you my services. I would truly appreciate it if you would give me a second chance."

There was some heavy opposition present on Louie's face that Antonio could easily see. He sat quiet for a moment, leaned back in his chair, and thought. Just because he needed someone to replace his second, didn't mean that he should automatically say yes to Terrance's offer. Like Sal, Louie seemed not to like the man. Unlike Sal, he had more of a brain — he also had the physical attributes to do all the necessary dirty work. Antonio had many pros and cons to sift through, but the one thing that he was glad for was that he had not readily dismissed Terrance the moment he saw him standing outside his office door. *'I guess that maybe it was a good thing after all that Louie had screwed up and Sal had allowed Terrance to live. Otherwise, I'd have to bring Zhin Wi over here to fill the position — which is something that I'd rather not do. Not because Zhin would not be capable of doing the job, but because he is just too valuable of an asset to take away from the ever growing Asian market.'*

A few seconds later, Antonio made an executive business decision. Yes, Terrance wasn't a pure blood Italian, but there was enough of it on one side of his family tree. That would have to be good enough, so he accepted the man's offer. However, he would be placed on probation until he earned the position of being Antonio's number two associate. Until then, Terrance would be relegated back to where he was when he first worked for him — a lackey.

As expected, Louie verbally objected to Antonio's decision. But Antonio made the obvious point even clearer than it already was — they needed someone that could physically handle the job. And although he hated hearing the truth, Louie had no other choice but to concede to his boss's point.

Waiting around in the hotel and doing nothing had begun to take its toll on everyone — except for Sabastian. He had encouraged them to use the downtime they had and go out and see the city — but only his uncle did. Sydney had spent some time in the casino and in the local adult clubs, took a tour of the Hiram Walker distilleries, Walkerville Brewery, as well as some of the areas magnificent vineyards and, since he was a bit of a history buff, he went to see some of the more significant historical sites in the area, including the two hundred and thirty-seven year old, Duff Baby House. Needless to say, Sabastian's uncle was now well stocked with pleasant memories, information, wine, and spirits.

Why don't you go out and see the city instead of pacing the room? You're beginning to drive me up a wall."

"Pacing helps me relax. Besides, I don't need to see this city. I have been here many times before, Sab. Remember, I do live right across the river."

"Then go down to the hotel's gym and work out or something. I'm sure there is some bottled up aggression within you that could use some release." Jerrelle didn't reply to Sabastian's suggestion — she just kept on pacing. "I promise to give you plenty of notice before it's time for us to leave."

"Going down to the gym is not a good idea. I have so much bottled up anger in me right now that I'd probably drill the first asshole that looks at me the wrong way. I just can't wait to get my hands on that bastard and pay him back for Helfred's senseless death."

"I know, Jerrelle, but we have to be patient and wait until the time is right."

"Hey, Sabastian... check this out," Baylor said as he exited one of the bedrooms. He had all but isolated himself there over the past few days so that he could use his laptop and research as much information as he could without being disturbed — and although he knew that his friend already had a plan in place, Baylor felt that any relevant information that he could dig up for Sabastian would most certainly be welcomed.

Once he had claimed a seat on the synth-suede sofa in the sitting area of the suite, Baylor set his laptop down on the adjacent coffee table — he then requested that Sabastian take up a seat next to him so that his friend could see what he had found. "Even though I thought that it was just going to be a waste of my valuable time, I kept tabs on some of the local public message boards like you had asked me to do."

"You only waste time when you already have it in your head you will be doing just that, Baylor."

Another time, Sabastian's friend would gladly debate his friend on that topic, but at this moment, what was important was what he knew his friend had been waiting to learn. "Anyway, I think that I may have found something. But be warned, you can't always believe what you read on message boards."

"Gullible I am not, bud. What did you find?"

"Well, first off... I must be having a rare bad day because I failed to hack into the New Book Cadillac Hotel and Casino's computers — they appear to have their own 'geek' monitoring all of their network activity, whose skills seem comparable to mine. Every move I made was countered. In fact, for the first time ever, I was out maneuvered and unwittingly nudged right back out where I had entered. And before I knew it, I was banished."

Sabastian only wanted to learn what Baylor had — but he also knew that he just had to let his friend be who he was; allow him to speak about whatever it was that was on his mind, and then once he felt that his issues were out in the open, he would be able to focus on what was actually important.

"When I realized that there was no way around this roadblock, I turned my attention to the task that you had asked of me and checked out the Detroit Metropolitan Entertainment message boards. I must admit, there were some fairly interesting topics and discussions posted there. Anyhow, I surprisingly found a posting about Antonio's casino that, to me, seemed easy to figure out what was being implied — although I have been known to be wrong on occasion."

"What was posted, Baylor?"

"Well… according to the user who posted the message, an executive, whose office is in that hotel, is supposed to be holding an afterhours private business meeting, two hours from now, at a restaurant called Thibault's by the River. Apparently, there will be two investors in attendance from overseas. Needless to say that it was the term 'overseas investors' that caught my eye. You did tell us after all, that Antonio Marcone had recently made contact with two of his mob counterparts while he was over there."

Jerrelle listened intently to what Baylor had been saying, though she too was skeptical. "Like Baylor said, don't believe everything that you read on those message boards. I'd bet you that the bastard isn't convinced we are dead and he is setting another one of his traps for us."

"That's quite possible," Sabastian acknowledged. "But I honestly think that he has organized a meeting with Hiro Juisota and Alfraido Fergini to finalize that underground network that you and your sister have hypothesized about."

Jerrelle could not dispute Sabastian's opinion. After a moment of thought, she said, "Do you have any idea, Baylor, who posted this message?"

"People who use message boards generally don't use their real names. This user went by the name, 'The Restitution Man'."

"The Restitution Man?" Savanna repeated. "It sounds like the guy has guilt issues."

"Do you all remember that vid-call I made when we first got together in this hotel room? The one where I neglected to tell everyone what it was all about?"

"Yeah," Jerrelle, Savanna, and Baylor, said almost simultaneously.

"Well, 'The Restitution Man' is my contact. He was someone from my past who owed me more than just a favor."

"So then, how would he know that we would be monitoring the message boards?" Baylor inquired.

Sabastian then explained his reasoning. He said he figured that even though he believed that they were no longer treading in dangerous waters, he felt that it would be best to still error on the side of caution and for his contact to send him his message that way instead of directly. "I would bet you, Baylor, that if you went back to that message board in fifteen minutes, the posting would no longer be there, nor would that user still be registered on that site."

"So then... who is this 'Restitution Man'? Jerrelle asked.

Sabastian paused. He took a look out of the room's window; the river was too far away for him to land in it. Therefore, he wasn't about to tell her who it was until they were both on the ground. "Like I said before, when the time is right, you will know."

An hour later, both Sabastian and Jerrelle left the hotel and headed over to Detroit. Shortly before they had left, Sabastian had contacted Governor White to inform him of everything that had already happened and to make him aware of what he had planned for Antonio Marcone — not hoping to get his help, but he just wanted his support.

As uneasy as Governor White felt concerning what it was that Sabastian was about to do, he knew that this time, he had to turn a blind eye, as he owed his old friend, Maxwell, at least that much. After all, Christopher knew better than anyone else the hell that his friends, fellow associates, and the citizens of Detroit have been put through because of Antonio Marcone's thirst for power. If he could, he'd be there tonight and make sure that the man got what was coming to him. However, he couldn't think of any other individual than the son of the best damn cop he had ever known, to be the one to put an end to it all.

What was a beautiful afternoon began gradually turning dark, dull, and dingy. The skyline seemed like it was coming to life and it was on a mission of utmost havoc. The east winds intensified and began ripping through the streets, creating diversionary tactics in order to distract one from their usual habits. Even without looking at Mother

Nature's continuously changing work of abstract art, you could sense that an unstoppable event was about to occur.

As with the lives of Maxwell, Sabastian, and Antonio, nature too has a way of paralleling itself; taking indirect paths, crossing others only when extraordinary forces are at work, then causing a devastating after effect that can leave much more than merely a few battle scars behind. The result of the aftermath, most often knocks the wind out of one's sails. But amongst the damage left behind, a seed will unknowingly be planted that will eventually become the foundation to a whole new beginning.

Forty-eight hours earlier, Terrance had returned to the organization. Right after he was provisionally welcomed back into the fold, Antonio had learned of the news pertaining to his casino manager's disappearance. Determining that to be a cause for concern, he asked both Terrance and Louie to use whatever resources they had and try to find out more details on the situation. A few hours later when they had returned, only Louie had something to report — and with what he had found out, he knew that Antonio was going to blow a gasket.

After learning almost nothing from those whom he had spoken with, he decided to check the hotel's surveillance footage. On the last day in which Jason Hernandez was seen, Louie noticed that the man was walking toward his office with a young woman. Something like this did not happen too often; only when a casino patron was lucky enough to win a large sum of money. Assuming this to be the case, Louie continued to watch the video in hopes that something would catch his eye — that happened only a few seconds later when he recognized the woman — it was Sabastian's female partner. This was not good news. Nevertheless, until he knew more, what he had just learned needed to stay with him, as the last thing that he wanted to do was prematurely run to his boss without first having learned all that he could. Therefore, he stayed put and scrutinized the subsequent few hours of footage in hopes that something else significant would happen. Nothing did — Sabastian's associate never left the manager's office.

With his suspicions rapidly drawing an unfounded conclusion, Louie took the next logical step. In order to find out the truth, he had to do some digging, so he went directly to the manager's office and conducted a thorough search of it — if the interior of the room had video surveillance like the rest of the hotel did, he would not have had to do this, but Antonio had insisted that all of the executive offices stay private, knowing that the business side of his empire need not be observed or hacked into by any unauthorized or curious individual.

During Louie's search, he discovered that the wall safe had been foolishly left open. It didn't prove anything, but knowing that Jason Hernandez's office had its own private exit, and knowing that Sabastian's associate had not left the office the conventional way, he had no other choice but to draw a conclusion as to what had taken place — their casino manager had been bribed for information on them; a big enough of a bribe to entice the man to stab his employer in the back.

After Louie's report was complete, Antonio sat back in his office chair and immediately reviewed the information. No hard facts had been given — but he had to agree with Louie's assessment. His manager, his long-time employee, had decided to screw him over. It was the only thing that made sense — there was no other possibility that could satisfactorily explain why Sabastian and his friend had been able to locate him as easily as they had.

There was only one option left for him to take. It was a shame that Antonio had to do this, because Jason Hernandez had given him twenty years of dedicated service — but he had no choice. He could not forgive a momentary lapse of reason from anyone, nor could he leave any loose ends that may come back to haunt him one day. The bed had been made, now his ex-manager had to lie in it.

Antonio wasn't too worried that the man was more than likely hiding out in some backwater country, as he now had Terrence in the fold, whose military training would come in handy when it came time to tracking him down. Yes, it angered him that someone, whom he had thought of as being 'family', had betrayed him — but his want to have this issue dealt with, wasn't near as important as what was already on his plate. Once this pended import/export trade agreement was reached, then the last of the loose ends could be dealt with.

As early evening approached, Antonio was still where he had been since he first found out about the betrayal — secluded in his office. This was an important day and he wanted to make sure that every detail was in place before he had his first formal meeting with his new, soon to be business partners. Until that took place though, he had sent his men back out in search of more information — it's not that he required irrefutable proof pertaining to what was believed had occurred, but knowing for sure what the truth actually was, would prevent any future regrets from appearing after an individual's ordered elimination took place.

About an hour before their scheduled departure, both Louie and Terrance had returned to the office — each surprisingly, had an update to give their boss. Louie had spoken with the hotel's head janitor, and she had apparently seen Jason Hernandez exit from the private stairwell, carrying with him the same kind of black satchel that normally would be used by the casino's security when transporting money to either the in-house vault or to the bank. He also was able to confirm that, according to the A.I. black jack dealer, who had been working the Elite Game Room on that same day, Sabastian's friend had indeed been gambling in the casino and had won a substantial amount of cash.

Once Louie was done with his update, Terrence proceeded to explain that he had reached out to one of the few military connections that he still had and trusted. One of them worked in the intelligence division of the army and used his resources to determine a possible location for Jason Hernandez. And what he had found was that, two days after he apparently quit, a man by that same name had boarded a flight out of Detroit, bound for Cuba.

He knew that bit of information alone didn't prove anything, but Terrance made sure that Antonio was aware of the fact that members of Jason's family had once tried to immigrate to the Union but were denied entry because a few of them had some legal issues that had not yet been addressed. At the conclusion of his brief report, Terrance decided to make his opinion be known, telling his new boss that he honestly believed Jason Hernandez had taken that apparent bribery money to Cuba for one reason only — to try and pay off a government official who would then allow his family to leave and emigrate to the Ameri-Can Union.

With no uncertainty now present, Antonio was content to do what he knew had to be done. And in his eyes, Jason Hernandez wasn't the only one who was going to pay. Yes, his family had nothing to do with this — but in a manner of speaking, they did. Wholeheartedly, he believed that his now ex-employee had intentionally fucked him over, strictly for the betterment of his own family. Therefore, they were all guilty by association.

With his mind now made up, he looked at his two men and said, "You both know what's at stake here today… and I don't want either of you to make any stupid mistakes. Remember, we lost Sal because of his ego and his foolishness. Mind you, I don't think anything will happen, but I need you both sharp and focused, just in case."

"I'm ready to exterminate any pest that happens to crawl my way. Just call me the Orkin Man," Terrance said confidently.

"Jesus Christ!" Louie bellowed. "If I didn't know any better, I'd swear that Sal was haunting your body."

"You two don't even get started," Antonio ordered. "It was bad enough that I had to put up with you and Sal constantly engaged in a war of words, but I'm telling you right now, Louie.., I don't want to hear any of that between you and Terrance. Now, we're out of here in about a half an hour, so why don't you both spend a few minutes and begin constructing a plan to get rid of our ex-manager and his entire family that has a zero chance of failing."

The weather had finally diminished to a tolerable level, which made the waiting game a little bit easier. Sabastian and Jerrelle were staked outside the restaurant in Jerrelle's vintage 69 Chevrolet Camero SS, at a concealed area across the street, patiently waiting for the arrival of Antonio Marcone. At ten thirty p.m., the lights, one by one, were shut off in the restaurant. Shortly thereafter, a man exited the place and proceeded to lock it up. That individual then got into his luxury S.U.V. and left at the same moment it appeared that the spring storm was beginning to end.

A cool and relaxing breeze now began to blow through the partially opened window on Sabastian's side of the car; it helped to keep him awake and focused. Time, as it usually does in a situation such as this, felt as if it was standing still. What he and Jerrelle were doing, he thought, was exactly what his father used to do — stake out a place and wait for Antonio to arrive. He actually felt a sense of purpose — he finally felt assured that this was his destiny. Tonight, he fully believed that he was going to succeed and close the book on a story that should have never been written in the first place.

Sabastian didn't feel nervous; he was completely at ease — just like he was supposed to feel. This was going to be a moment where he knew that his father would be there with him, to guide him, and to protect him — and this was going to be the very first moment in his new life where he believed that Maxwell Banks would be proud of him.

'This so feels like a trap,' Jerrelle thought. *'I still have this funny feeling that Antonio Marcone believes that we are alive and are coming after him.'*

Sensing that Jerrelle was not herself, Sabastian looked over at his friend and asked, "You ok there, Jerrelle? You seem to not be all there?"

"I'm fine, Sab. I'm just not sure I'm ready to almost die again."

"That isn't gonna happen because we finally have the upper hand. I do firmly believe that Antonio Marcone thinks that we are both dead."

"I hope you're right, because I'm really not as convinced as you are."

A set of approaching headlights drew their immediate attention toward the restaurant — they came from a long black limousine that drove up to, and parked right in front. Haste and agitation encircled them both, but they each knew that they had to remain patient and move in at the right moment. Two minutes later, a second, and then a third limousine arrived; both parking in front of the restaurant and directly in-line behind the first one.

Anticipation grew. In five minutes time, what they had come here to do, they would. And then, when all of this was over, not only would they finally be able to get on with their 'normal', everyday lives, but the city of Detroit and its citizens will have one less real thing to worry about.

11

So far, every plan that Sabastian and Jerrelle have executed has ended up being an epic failure. So this time, instead of one of them entering through the front and the other through the back, they both decided to enter the restaurant the same way. Jerrelle had actually been to this restaurant once before and remembered its layout pretty well. In fact, she already knew where the best place would be for them to enter unnoticed.

The last time she was here, she had to be creative and find a way to sneak out, because she had been accused of stealing a tip off a table that had been left by a regular customer. It had only been a seven dollar tip — and even though she knew that she was innocent, she didn't want to deal with the police because they were all too familiar with her and her past reputation for causing trouble.

When this happened, she was able to escape from the place unnoticed by going into the ladies restroom, lifting up the drop ceiling tiles, and maneuvering herself over the wall that divided both the washroom and, to her surprise, a private office that belonged to a bookie. This, she was able to confirm during the few minutes that she had spent snooping around the room before she exited through the only door that it had; a door that led out to the back alley.

It was this same alley door that Jerrelle and Sabastian were going to use to enter the restaurant — but there were two possible problems. The first being, since this door lead to a secret office, it was more than likely heavily secured. Secondly, there was a good chance that it would be wired inside for sound or motion. Neither one of them had any idea if the security system for that office was tied into the main restaurant's system, so they could only hope that when Jerrelle disabled it, the room was also no longer wired.

It took her about three minutes in total; one for the alarm and two for the numerous locks on the alley door that she had to manually pick — it would have been much easier for her if they were digital locks, but they were not. After opening the door, she spent a few cautious seconds scanning the room from the threshold for any independent security cameras or any infrared thermal alarms. A sense of relief enveloped her; they now had a way inside. The hardest part of this though was yet to come, as they now had to scale the wall, climb over it, and then lower themselves into the ladies room. Once that had been accomplished, it still didn't mean that they were home free, as the main dining area of the restaurant was fairly close to the restroom. That meant a sneak attack was not going to be possible. Their only option was to patiently wait for a window of opportunity, no matter how small that might be, and then rush into the dining area with their weapons already drawn.

Seated inside the restaurant, near the back bar area, was Antonio, Hiro, and Alfraido. No conversation was taking place; each instead was enjoying a drink and a cigar. Antonio hated to do business when he wasn't relaxed, so as per his usual routine, he took a few moments and indulged himself.

Louie was sitting alone near the front entrance of the restaurant keeping watch and Terrance was near the back bar's side entrance doing the same. For several minutes, the place stayed relatively quiet. Only after Antonio had finished off his first glass of Walker's Club, were any significant words spoken, "Ok, gentleman. I think that we've treated ourselves long enough. Let's get down to business."

"I agree," Hiro said. "But before we formalize our first business adventure together, I think that if any of us have any lingering issues that need to be resolved, then we should..." Hiro stopped mid-sentence the moment he realized that the five of them were no longer the only ones in the restaurant.

Immediately sensing that something wasn't right, both Antonio and Terrance looked in the same direction that Hiro's attention had been drawn. "What the Fuck?" Terrance stated. "What the hell are you doing here.., son?"

"I'm not your damn son," Sabastian emphatically replied. "Nor will I ever be your son, you back stabbing bastard!"

"Son?" Antonio was a bit shocked; yet not surprised at all to see that both Sabastian and Jerrelle were still alive. Then his memory took him straight back to Germany to the moment where Sal spoke his last words. *"I should not have passed off my obligations to someone else. I should have killed Maxwell's kid myself."* At that moment, it all became clear to him that it was Terrence whom Sal had passed the buck to and had sent to kill both Maxwell's wife and his son. "Am I to assume, Terrance, that instead of killing both of the targets Sal instructed you to, you decided to only complete half of the deed, then keep Maxwell's son as your own?"

"That's correct. But in hindsight, I should have killed him as well. He has been nothing but an ungrateful pain in my ass his entire life."

"Wait a minute!" A possibility that had never before crossed Sabastian's mind just did. Was what he had just heard, true? His 'father' had actually killed his mother? That would then mean Antonio and Louie were not the only ones in the room for which blame could be placed.

Terrance Burelli's confession promptly caused Sabastian's fury to rise. Without any regard whatsoever to the volatility of the present situation, he took a few purposeful steps toward his ex-father, and then stopped just close enough to get a good look at the shamefaced expression he wore. "For once in your life, don't lie to me. Did you really kill my mother and kidnap me?"

"Yes. I was young, stupid, and had allowed myself to be placed into a situation where I had to make a choice. Right after I made it and crossed the line, I realized that it was too late to do anything about it. I regret my actions every single day and I wish that it could be undone."

"You're full of shit!"

"Son, I… If I had completed what had been asked of me that day, then you would not be here and my life would have turned out completely different… and not for the better."

"Only you would make this about you." Sabastian then reached around behind his back and removed the gun that was tucked in the top band of his jeans, raised it up, and aimed it directly at his ex-father. "You know… I should just put a bullet through your head with this gun, just like you did to my mother. But I'm not as callous as you apparently are. Besides, I didn't come here for you. I came here for that bastard." Sabastian then pivoted, pointed his gun in the direction of Antonio, and aimed it directly at his forehead. "This is my father's gun; Maxwell Banks' gun… and it will be fitting that you die by it today."

Deciding not to interject with Sabastian's 'fun' just yet, Jerrelle walked over behind the bar and cracked open a beer. She then addressed both Hiro and Alfraido. "You know, Mr. Soto and Mr. Fettuccini… we don't have a problem with the two of you, so I suggest that you get your butts back into those shiny black limos you arrived in and return from whence you came."

Acknowledging that what was taking place wasn't something that they wanted to be a part of, both Hiro and Alfraido promptly got up from their seats and walked toward the restaurant's front door. As much as they each wanted to be business partners with Antonio, they weren't willing to risk themselves getting killed over an unresolved personal feud.

Once the men had left, Louie vacated his post by the front of the restaurant and walked in the direction of Sabastian. "You know… you really are just like your old man. The only difference is that you don't think about the risks that you are taking. Again, you have placed yourself and your friend into a no-win situation. Someone is gonna end up dead here tonight."

"He's right, Sabastian," Antonio affirmed. "Someone is gonna end up dead… and that someone is you. Terrance! I'm giving you one chance to redeem yourself for your past error in judgment. I want you to finish your assignment and kill your 'son' right now."

At that moment, Jerrelle promptly turned her attention to Terrance Burelli, remembering as she stared at him, just how much she despised the man. The perfect opportunity was there for her to kill the major, as well as gain that personal satisfaction that she for so long, desired. But that was not what she had tagged along for tonight. Nevertheless, if things evolved the way she believed it would, she was certain that an opportunity would present itself for her to finally get her revenge against the one person she held responsible for ruining her military career and the life she could have had because of it.

Making sure that she was prepared for anything, Jerrelle took out her gun and slowly raised it — but not high enough so that it was visible above the bar. Instead, she kept it hidden and aimed directly at the major's back. It was difficult for her, but she resisted — even though the temptation to pull the trigger at that moment was profound. Sabastian had asked her to trust him, and that was what she was going to do. And even though she wished she had some sort of clue as to what he had planned, she knew just by the look in his eyes that he had something unexpected up his sleeve.

So that she didn't succumb to her desire, Jerrelle took her finger off of the trigger — just as she had done that, a noise caught the attention of everyone in the restaurant. A few seconds later, a stranger dressed in a tattered and enigmatic hooded monk-style robe, staggered into the restaurant — that individual had entered through the unlocked, unwatched, front door from which Hiro and Alfraido had just left.

"What the fuck?" Louie immediately walked over to the stranger and did his best to encourage him to leave. However, the stranger just kept staggering further inside of the restaurant. He stopped in the middle of the room and just stood there, swaying in a drunken stupor back and forth.

"Listen buddy, you need to leave."

"Where is… *hiccup*, the bathroom?" The stranger said. "I really gotta… take a piss."

"I don't need to deal with this crap right now," Antonio stated. "Terrance.., go and help Louie throw this drunken bum back out on the street where he belongs."

"Sure thing, Mr. Marcone," Terrance proceeded over toward the uninvited guest and attempted to escort him out. The stranger struggled with both he and Louie, but somehow was able to hold his ground. Unexpectedly, and with almost no effort, the stranger suddenly threw Terrance over a table and to the ground, while at the same time, kicked Louie in his sternum — he was sent flying toward the front of the restaurant where his back slammed directly against the stanchion between the door and the window beside it.

Terrance was halfway to pulling himself back up to his feet when the stranger removed from his pocket a small mechanical device. He freely displayed it for all to see. Both Sabastian and Jerrelle immediately recognized what the object was — a sonic microburst (a device that replaced the stun grenade). From their previous military training, they both knew that it is used to cause a temporary

311

equilibrium jolt, a jolt that would cause everyone within the immediate vicinity to lose total control of their body's stability and senses.

They both knew that covering one's eyes and ears, or even finding cover, would not totally prevent the effects of the device — but they were also aware that it would at least lessen it some. They just hoped that if the stranger were to set off the sonic microburst, that they would be able to recover from the effects of it long before everyone else did, as they needed every bit of advantage that they could get.

Louie was pissed that he had easily been man handled by the drunken stranger. So much so that in his eyes, the man was simply expendable — cannon fodder. He intently drew his gun, wanting to immediately remove from the picture their unwanted guest; however, no sooner had Louie taken his aim, the drunk set off the device. This caused him, along with everyone else in the restaurant, to instantly evolve into an unwanted and uncontrollable frenzy.

With all self-control lost, Louie fired off his gun in a sporadic fashion. That in turn, triggered a chain reaction of return fire. Everyone fell to the ground, not just to avoid the wayward rounds, but because the effects of the sonic microburst had forced them to.

As he dropped to the floor, Sabastian quickly covered his ears with the palms of his hands, tightly shut his eyes, and kept his face pointed toward the ground. He had no time to look for cover, as the effects of the microburst would overtake him long before that happened — he only hoped that the protection that he had attempted to give himself would be enough to at least lessen the effects.

It took him almost three minutes after the last wayward bullet was fired before he was able to open up his eyes and remove his hands. And although he had regained the majority of his equilibrium, it still kind of felt to him as if the lasting effects of some kind of bad acid trip were present. To him, it almost felt like he was looking through a kaleidoscope of reality that was being stretched apart and then put back together incorrectly. Then again, his strange reaction to the effects of the sonic microburst could have had something to do with the lingering effects he still had from his recent concussion.

As Sabastian looked around and tried his best to assess what the situation was, he soon recognized that his preventative measures had actually helped him to recover a bit faster, as everyone else in the restaurant still seemed to be somewhat out of it. He had the advantage; but it was not going to be for long. However, before he could figure out how to use it, his still clearing eyes were drawn to something that immediate caused his emotions to become confused. There, right in front of him, was a person lying twisted underneath a table only a few feet away. He closed his eyes and tried to focus his thoughts. Was what he was seeing, real? If it was, he didn't know how he should feel. A few seconds later when he opened his eyes back up, there was no misinterpreting his initial assessment, as lying there on the ground and bleeding, was the same man who had raised him.

Sabastian had been trained by the best the Union Military had to offer — and Terrance Burelli had been one of those men responsible for that. But in that moment, he had forgotten all of it: forgotten to assess the situation, forgotten to make himself aware of his surroundings, forgotten to make sure that he was armed and prepared for any sudden surprises. All that Sabastian could focus on was one thing — the wrong thing.

Completely forgetting that the enemy was even in the room with him, Antonio Marcone had walked right up to Sabastian and then confidently placed a gun up against the right side of his temple. "I told you that I would win, Mr. Banks. And just like your father... you've lost."

Sabastian slowly dropped to his knees; his body felt somewhat limp. He didn't know what to think; he only knew that his emotions had just cost him the advantage he had — and maybe even his life. A miracle now appeared to be the only thing that was going to save him.

Randomly, he scanned his eyes around the room looking for it — it didn't seem to be there. Even Jerrelle was nowhere to be found. All that Sabastian could think of in that moment was that once again, pain was going to consume his family and his friends. But then, something pulled his thoughts away from the negative space that it had settled into and was able to get him to realize that his training hadn't completely failed him after all.

One chance was what Sabastian now knew he had to survive his predicament — and it would all come down to trust. "You actually think that I've lost? What you've failed to understand is that I now know the real reason why Terrance Burelli spared my life all those years ago."

"And what reason would that be?" Antonio asked, curiously.

"To one day make restitution to my family for the mistake that he made." At that moment, Sabastian dropped flat to the ground.

The boss of the Detroit's Underworld Organization had just lost the game because he failed to make himself aware that another player had chosen to insert himself into it. And because of his egregious error, Antonio Marcone fell backwards, dead from a bullet right between the eyes that came from Terrance Burelli's gun.

Sabastian crawled across the floor, away from the now dead body of the enemy, and over to where his 'adopted' father was. What Sabastian had set out to do, was accomplished — but it came at a high price. His true father's legacy has now been restored. Yet, there is also a relationship that won't have the chance to be fully repaired. Terrance had done exactly what he had asked of him, yet he didn't expect him to have to pay such a high price in doing so.

Sabastian knelt down beside the man who raised him and held his bloodied hand. Many emotions flooded his entire being; not one of them oddly enough, contained any sort of spite. "I'm not sure if I can ever forgive you for what you have done, but..."

"I don't deserve to be forgiven," Terrance replied. "I just wanted to try to make things right." He then paused for a moment, struggling to even breathe. "Jr., I... Sabastian... I have something to ask of you."

"Yes, of course."

Terrance looked into the eyes of 'his son'. As much as he never expected to be forgiven for what he had done, he could see that he had at least done what was necessary to start to make things right. And in that moment, he knew that 'his son' would no longer hate him for the remainder of his life. "Even though Edith, my mother, isn't your real grandmother... promise me that you'll always be there and take care of her."

"I will... I promise."

Terrance then closed his eyes, never to open them again. With all the contempt that Sabastian had recently developed for him, he was now forced to open up his heart and find a little room inside for a good man who unfortunately, chose to briefly take the wrong path.

"So your fath... Major Burelli was 'The Restitution Man', wasn't he?" Jerrelle asked.

Sabastian turned around and saw Jerrelle standing over him. Her left arm had a gash and she was bleeding from her temple. "Yes, he was. By the way... where were you when I had a gun pointed at my head?"

"I was unconscious and on the floor," she answered. "As you can see, I took a bullet in my arm and then fell to the ground because of it. And I think that on my way down, I struck my head on the draft tap... broke the damn handle off."

"You sure you didn't purposely break off the handle of the draft tap so that you could drink all that free flowing beer while you were doggin' it on the floor?"

"Hey, up yours! I was really hurt."

"And I was almost killed... again."

The drunken stranger, who was responsible for starting the chain of events, suddenly re-appeared. "You sure you two aren't married? I mean, you both already have the bickering part down perfectly." He approached them, removed his hood, glasses, and voice box, and revealed to them both that he was not a stranger after all — or even a man. He was actually Jerrelle's half-sister.

"Bai Lin! What the hell are you doing here?"

"Well... it seems as though a friend of yours Sabastian also knows a good friend of mine."

"Sharice?"

"That's right! Your cousin told my friend, Nicoli, everything that happened in Germany — and then he told me. I was actually headed to Chicago to tie up a few loose ends pertaining to a deal that the Liberation had been involved with, but I was curious, sis, if you were home yet from your revenge tour. So I took a slight detour. I first went to your place, but since I didn't see your car anywhere, I used the lo-jack that I had installed on it a few years back to find you."

"You went and lo-jacked my Camero? Why?"

"I rest my case."

"Hey, um… where's Louie?" Both Jerrelle and Sabastian hastily searched the room. They then looked at each other, baffled. Neither one of them had an answer as to where the Sicilian was. Somehow, during the mass confusion that was caused by the sonic microburst and then rounds of chaotic gunfire, he had slipped out the door. That meant, everything that they had come to this restaurant to accomplish, hadn't been.

As much as he should be, Sabastian just could not be content. Yes, the bastard that had caused his family, and the city of Detroit a lot of pain, had finally met his maker. However, one player still remained — and even though the D.U.O. may now appear to be much weaker than it has been in generations, he didn't believe that to be the case. Maybe not today, or tomorrow, or next month — but sooner or later, the beast is going to again rear its ugly head. And when that happened, Sabastian had a feeling that simply slaying it might not actually end its life.

Epilogue

With everything that Sabastian had been though, he needed a serious vacation — but he had made a promise he intended to keep. Instead of going back to San Antonio with Savanna and his uncle, he went to Ohio to see Edith Burelli, his grandmother. He knew that he had a lot of things to explain — he owed her that. But he also had a lot of fear inside of him; fear of breaking the heart of a person whom he had wholeheartedly loved and who had always been the foundation to his life.

Returning to the place where he had grown up, felt strange; like he didn't belong — yet, his whole life had evolved inside of that house. Yes, a lot has changed — nothing is ever going to be the same. However, even after everything that has happened, his heart was telling him that this would forever be his home.

As Sabastian stood just beyond the front steps, he tried his best to summon the courage that he needed before he finally walked up them. But before he could even take that first step, the front door opened. Standing there was Edith, with a warm embrace waiting for her grandson. He hesitated; he just didn't feel as if he deserved what awaited him, knowing the dreadful news that he carried.

Recognizing that Sabastian was unsure about the awkward moment, Edith made her way down the front steps and spoke to him with an honest face and an obvious broken heart. "I know what happened… my grandson. I do not blame you, and it is not your fault." She then embraced him with more love than what Sabastian thought was available in the entire world.

After a tearful reunion, they both walked inside the house. From that moment onward, he didn't feel so out of place — he had indeed, come home.

He spent a few days in Ohio before he returned to San Antonio. Upon his arrival, Sabastian headed directly to his father's agency — there was still something that he had to do; something that he had earlier refused to but knew it had to be done before he could finally close the book on his father's life and legacy.

"Good morning, Sab. How did everything go in Ohio?"

"It went a lot better than what I had initially expected, Jerrelle. Terrence.., my father, had left behind a note of finality. In that note, he confessed to everything that he had done because he had fully expected not to return. He knew that I was the innocent pawn in a game he had stupidly gotten himself involved with, and he was adamant that his mother not hold his mistakes against me. It was hard seeing my grandmother, because the pain was so obvious in her eyes. I mean, our military careers had prepared her for a scenario such as that, but it was still very difficult to see her go through it."

"I can only imagine how tough those past few days have been for you and your grandmother. I'm sorry, Sab."

Sabastian didn't respond to his longtime friend's condolences. He instead, just drifted off in thought; something that he had been doing almost for the entire thirty minutes he had been sitting there behind his father's desk.

Before Jerrelle came into the office, Sabastian had read the letter that his father had left behind for him, and had just finished looking over his will. For the first time since he had discovered who he was, his emotions were somewhat indiscernible. He wasn't really sad, angry, disappointed, or confused — he kind of felt cheated. What Sabastian had just read were the first words written by his father that were meant solely for him. They were heartfelt and full of love — and they were words that would stay with him for the rest of his life.

Not one for keeping her opinions to herself, Jerrelle decided to make her thoughts be known. "You should not be torturing yourself with your father's will so soon after what you've just been through."

"Thanks for your concern, but I'm good. The only thing that is messing with my mind right now is that we let Louie escape."

"Don't worry, Sab. We will find him. Besides, I really don't think that he is going anywhere too soon. From what little I've read and observed about him, I think he is just as, if not more driven than Antonio was. And I'm sure that you believe what I do; that he is going to try to keep the D.U.O. in business and attempt to build it up even more. When that happens, and when we catch up to him, he will undoubtedly fall even harder than his predecessor did."

"Agreed. Until then, I think that it's time I try to get on with my new life." Sabastian placed his father's will and the letter that accompanied it into a copper bowl that had been sitting on the far corner of the desk. He then picked up his father's antique Zippo that he had found in the desk drawer, and set them on fire.

Silence and smoke filled the room. There was no purpose for him to do what he just had, but in a symbolic sort of way, the burning papers would represent the ashes of the past. "It's time to move forward. I have my life to live and a destiny to fulfill. But you know… it can wait until tomorrow. I'm extremely hungry right now. Let's go and get something to eat."

"Yeah, that sounds good, Sab. I'm hungry too. In fact, I think that I can even splurge and pick up the tab this time."

"You're going to buy me dinner?" Sabastian replied a bit surprised. "That's a first. I better get Savanna to mark that down in the daily log. I mean, a day might come where I may have to look that up and confirm that this once in a lifetime event had actually taken place."

"Very funny… Ha, ha, ha. Just don't get used to my current generosity. Oh, and since I'm buying dinner, I will pick the restaurant. I actually want to finish a meal for once without being interrupted or distracted by something or someone."

"Don't bet on it, Jerrelle. People seem to recognize me wherever I go."

About the author

Steven F. Deslippe was born in Canada on September 24th, 1966. He grew up in a rural community, right next door to his Grandparents' farm, just outside of the town of Amherstburg, Ontario.

Farming wasn't of interest to him; however music was. Beginning in late 1987, and lasting for fifteen years, Steven worked as a disc jockey, playing music and emceeing weddings, parties, dance clubs, rock clubs and gentleman's clubs. It was during this time period where he discovered a passion for reading and writing — both of which he admittedly did not like, nor was very good at when he was younger.

As the years went by, both of these skills greatly improved — the result of this dedicated hard work, now forever captured in each book that he writes.

Facebook
https://www.facebook.com/Author.Steven.F.Deslippe.Official/

Goodreads
https://www.goodreads.com/author/show/16559506.Steven_F_Deslippe

Youtube
https://www.youtube.com/channel/UChXnJAOrOEv0vnWNdQWJbqQ

Amazon
https://www.amazon.ca/s/ref=nb_sb_noss_2/134-6867989-8132316?url=search-alias%3Daps&field-keywords=steven+f+deslippe

https://www.amazon.com/s/ref=nb_sb_noss?url=search-alias%3Daps&field-keywords=steven+f+deslippe

E-mail contact
sdeslippe@sympatico.ca

Fate's End

#1 – Inception

#2 – Following the Path

#3 – Staying the Course

#4 – Creating a Legacy

#5 – Unspeakable

#6 – The Game within the Game

#6.1 – Hell's Lounge ~ *Short story*

#7 – Falsely Accused

#8 – Hope (and a Dream)

#9 – Full Circle

#10 – In Debt Do We Part

#10.1 – Fate: Absolute (Hell's Lounge Pt. II) ~ *Short story*

*** Other releases ***

Strange Dreams – A compilation of three short stories

www.ingramcontent.com/pod-product-compliance
Lightning Source LLC
Chambersburg PA
CBHW020334180626
46812CB00001B/194